PRAISE FOR N. [illegible] WORK

I was introduced to *Rockstar Ending* when Nicola read an extract from the book at the Orwell Society Symposium. We invited her to speak after she won an award in the Society's dystopian fiction competition for her short story, *One Last Gift*. Nicola's work is highly original, macabre and very funny. I am delighted that she has developed her idea into a novel in the tradition of my father George Orwell, the author of *Nineteen Eighty-Four*, who wanted 'to make political writing into an art'.

Richard Blair, son of George Orwell and Patron of The Orwell Society

This is how to make a smashing debut into dystopian fiction; an authentic world building on present-day technology, an eerily plausible solution to the wealth gap, and an exploration of the disturbing moral paradoxes it creates when the public wakes up to the sinister consequences. Nicola Rossi's first novel is a just-around-the-corner future thriller with a brain. If her predictions come true, we're all in deep trouble.

Christopher Fowler, award-winning author of dark urban fiction

Rossi's dark, perceptive wit and the industry insights gleaned from her previous career in communications management make this gripping yarn an all-too-persuasive vision of the future.

Cathi Unsworth, The Idler

ROCKSTAR ENDING

N.A. ROSSI

ABOUT THE AUTHOR

N. A. (Nicola) Rossi has lived in London most of her life, moving there from the seaside town of Southport in the early '80s. After university she flirted briefly with journalism, and then began a 30-year career in communications management, eventually running international teams for big technology companies.

In 2017 she was awarded an MA in Digital Media from Goldsmiths University. That was when the trouble began. She started to write about surveillance, data ownership, consent and the potential for people to be manipulated without their knowledge.

Her debut novel, *Rockstar Ending*, started life as a short story, 'One Last Gift', which won a dystopian fiction award from the Orwell Society. The judges described it as 'highly original, macabre and very funny'. It was published in the *Journal of Orwell Studies*.

Nicola is a regular blogger on technology, society and the arts. She has lectured in universities on leadership, PR, ethics and corporate social responsibility and consults on communications management. She has appeared on *BBC Radio 4 Today*, BBC local radio, and written for wide range of media outlets including *The Independent, Time Out, Louder Than War* and *Influence*.

She lives in south east London with her husband and two adult children.

nicolarossi.com

ALSO BY N.A. ROSSI

For Those About to Rock
Rock On

ROCKSTAR ENDING

ISBN 978-1-913417-02-4
Published by **Resista Press 2020, London, England**
Resistapress.com

This is a work of fiction. Any similarity between the characters and situations within its pages and places or persons, living or dead, is unintentional and co-incidental.

Cover illustration reprinted with the permission of Tim Doyle.

For those who could not wait any longer.

CHAPTER ONE

MEG HAD MIXED FEELINGS ABOUT her 85th birthday, as she knew that it was going to be the last day of her life. "Happy birthday to me," she sang to herself, as there was no one else there to do it for her.

She should have been pleased that she had made it to 85, lived longer than both her parents, three of her grandparents, and all those musicians who died at 27. She ran through their names in her head – Jim Morrison, Janis Joplin, Amy Winehouse. Most people probably didn't know who they were now.

Her grown-up children, Alice and Adam, would definitely remember David Bowie and George Michael, from when they used to play their songs in the car. They lasted quite a bit longer than the 'dead at 27' club, but Meg had outlived them too.

When she was younger, she had wanted the words 'Never a Dull Moment' to be chiselled onto her gravestone. However, she went off the idea as it gradually became obvious that it would be misleading. Once she sailed past that magical 27th birthday, things calmed down considerably. That's how it is for most people. It wasn't that she hadn't packed a lot in over the years, but life had settled into a gentler rhythm which eventually became quite mundane.

At the end of the last century, Meg's generation had been told that they would live longer than any of the preceding ones. She was determined to crash through the 100 barrier. She took up weight training to stave off muscle wastage, ate lots of kale to prevent cancer, and did Sudoku to repel dementia. Her plan seemed to have worked. All things considered, Meg still felt pretty good. But like most other things in life, it had come down to what was practical. "Soon it will all be over," she thought. "I'm not going to get a headstone either. They don't really do them for people like me anymore."

It shouldn't have come as a surprise. The shift – or 'the shaft', as Meg thought of it – had been bound to happen. Old people had never really been valued in Britain, not like they were in other countries. At least they used to be protected, though, because they were more likely to vote than anyone else. It hadn't been in anyone's interests to upset them. But then, after Brexit, the Millennials began to wake up, realised they outnumbered the older ones, and decided they didn't want to pay for them any longer.

There was a debate in Parliament about what they called the Maturity Premium. How it wasn't fair that younger people couldn't afford homes, jobs, health care – that sort of thing – when some older people were quite comfortable. Meg could see where they were coming from. Unfortunately for her, though, they decided that the only way to make ends meet was to siphon all the wealth from the old and give it to the young.

What made an even more compelling case for the shaft was that, when immigration was stopped, Britain simply couldn't get enough cheap people from other places in the world to staff the struggling hospitals and care homes the old people had relied on.

Although Meg understood how the young, and their political movement 'Yuthentic', had reached this position, it didn't seem fair. True, she did have a house, even if it was scruffy in places these days. But she had worked hard for it. She had come to London with nothing, slowly paid off her debts, and finally got comfortable. With her husband Paul's income too they had done well, all things considered. So what if the house was worth a million pounds? To Meg, it was just somewhere to live. She certainly didn't feel like a millionaire. She simply saw herself as someone who had done OK and been able to raise her family without calling on the state for help.

At times she felt resentful about what was happening. Especially when she remembered that she had paid a huge amount of tax. She had always thought paying taxes was right, and in her own modest way had been happy to give money to others who needed it more than she did. So it felt like a massive kick in the teeth when Yuthentic persuaded the government they no longer needed to do anything for anyone once they reached 85.

So it wasn't really a happy birthday to Meg at all. From this day onwards she no longer qualified for any state support. No subsidised medical care. No free prescriptions. No state pension. No free TV licence. Even her bus pass had to go back. She could cover some of the costs herself, as least for a while. But that wasn't the point.

What hurt the most was that in the eyes of the state she was worth nothing – nothing apart from the One Last Gift she would be giving later that afternoon when she set out for her one-way Rockstar Ending.

Like many other cons of the modern world, today's activity was cloaked under the guise of 'choice'. She could choose from a range of carefully designed options detailing how and when she wanted the state to kill her. "They are coming to kill me today, ha ha," she thought, numbly. She refused to use any euphemisms. "If you can't tell it like it is on your last day on earth, when can you?"

First you were sent your unique login to the Happy Endings portal. You put in your national insurance number and your Government Gateway ID. They sent you a code by text so they could be certain who you were. Then you had to do an online quiz to prove that you were capable of making the big decision. They paid a fortune to make the interface as simple and user-friendly as possible. It was obvious who had designed the algorithm.

The questions were what you'd expect. IQ and memory tests which they then matched to everything they had scraped from the net about you over the years. They had to make sure people were of sound mind if they were going to be making important life-and-death decisions. She found it amazing how much they knew about her, even now.

Once you had passed the test you were allowed to

go on to make your other choices. She was really pleased that she had scored a bright green 86% positive with a dementia quotient of 3.2% in the 'negligible' range. In any other circumstances, passing with such flying colors would be good news.

Meg thought the online will section was great. She hadn't needed to see an expensive solicitor like her parents had to. All you had to do was fill in the form and it was countersigned by a virtual legal executive in a few seconds. There was a small fee but you couldn't expect them to design the law bots for free. No need for expensive human beings or probate or all that other mountain of admin she had to plough through when her parents and husband had died.

You could even arrange for your bills to stop at the moment of death on a page sponsored by the utility companies. Everything was neatly set up online so the next of kin wouldn't have to face it.

Then she had gone on to the Departure Board. This part could be quite upsetting but a little chat window popped up and someone – or more likely a bot, you can never tell these days – helped her along. They reassured her that she was doing the right thing, that the next generation would be forever grateful, that she was sparing her children seeing her die a horrible painful death in abject poverty smeared in her own excrement. Well, that got her over the line. Onto the options screen.

She would have preferred to die in the home where she had lived for the past 40 years. Her children grew up there, her grandchildren had been to stay, she and her husband had lived for there for decades in love and comfort. But she decided against it. It was the most expensive option because they needed a team to look after you when they gave you the drugs, and then of course they needed to take you off for disposal afterwards. It all added up. Not to mention the insurance. They actually employed real people to do the At Home Peaceful Endings, although Meg had heard there was a fully robotic option being trialled in Scotland which would be cheaper. But that would be too late for her.

The other problem with doing it at home would be that people might notice the Endings wagon outside the house and try to interfere. Worse, they might even call one of the children. Far better it just came as a surprise, with the money and the house as a consolation prize.

She could have gone for the no-frills package: a communal bus to take you to your local disposal center, along with the rest of the day's customers. There was a lot of demand, so they were re-using the vehicles they once used to ferry people with special needs to schools and day centers. They called people 'service-users' then. That was before all the social care stopped.

The big difference, of course, for the Economy Ending, was that this would be a one way ticket. The government took care of the out-goers in a medical annexe next to the crematorium. It kept the transport costs down and was good for the environment. But this option was really meant for people with no next of kin, no money and no alternative. A bit like the old pauper's funeral. "Not for me," Meg thought to herself. "If you can't spoil yourself on your last day on earth, when can you?"

So she had pulled out all the stops and booked herself a Rockstar Ending. It was being run by the corporation. Meg contemplated the irony that, in her day, most rock stars – lots of those 27-year-olds actually – had died in a hotel room after a big party. A disproportionately high number of them seemed to choke on their own vomit. This wasn't like that. It felt a bit more like what happened to Michael Jackson. She was older than he was too, incidentally. He passed away in his luxury mansion after one too many doses of general anaesthetic. "I wonder if they've considered calling it Last Exit to Neverland?" she mused. The Jackson estate – or J. M. Barrie's – would probably object.

When she was working as a corporate executive, some years before she retired, Meg had loved flying business class. A chauffeur came to her house, took her to a private entrance to the airport, and she was fast-tracked through security and check-in. She always arrived early to make time for Eggs Benedict, a manicure and a mojito in the lounge before getting on the plane. How she loved being paid for meeting people all over the world, sleeping on a flat-bed in the air, and watching all those films. Changing into free branded pyjamas. They even had luxury chocolate to snack on and little pots of hipster-brand ice cream.

From what she could tell on the portal, the Rockstar Ending service was similar. They wouldn't give their name to something that wasn't a lovely experience and risk their reputation, would they?

Obviously today's arrangements had to be a bit different. They couldn't take you to a glamorous lounge full of other high flyers, as you might change your mind or create a scene. And you probably wouldn't feel like Eggs Benedict either. But there would be a lovely soft bed and enormous playlist which was curated by guest celebrities to ease you out gently. If you wanted, you could even wear a VR headset that led you towards an afterlife scenario of your choice. Not for Meg. Immersive experiences made her feel seasick at the best of times.

The car they would be sending was naturally, driverless, but with the Rockstar option a Peaceful Endings Angel would come to your house to escort you to the departure lounge. An actual person who had been specially trained. They would pop in an hour before you were due to leave to help calm any last-minute nerves. Given the massive drive to get people to 'move on', the government had waved some of the regulations around controlled drugs, and they gave you a little something to make it easier to close your door one last time. You had to commit, when you signed up, to taking the special cocktail of medication within ten minutes of their arrival at your home. And there was also the big nappy – to spare embarrassment. Then they walked with you to the car and made sure your house was secure. The keys would go to the next of kin as soon as the procedure was over. To passers-by, it should just look like someone getting into a taxi.

What a funny job is must be, collecting people to go for disposal. There wasn't much conventional nursing work around anymore, not since the medi-robots took off. So they didn't have trouble getting people to do it. The pay was good. "Still," Meg thought, "I can't be the first person to view them as the angel of death. Best not to say that when they arrive, just in case they turn nasty. They probably get it all the time."

She worried how her adult children would feel when they found out that she had opted-in to the opt-out. They were so far away. Since being priced out of London they had moved to other continents to establish their own lives. Her family might be angry with her at first, but in the long run she thought they'd be glad to have been spared the burden of having to fly back to deal with old age crises as she gradually deteriorated. As they said on the portal: 'One Last Gift is an act of love'. Heart emoji.

The fun part was that she had been able to design her own memorial webpage and remembrance ritual. Her body would be incinerated and the ashes stored for six months. If no one collected them after that time they would go to landfill. People didn't really have funerals in the old sense any more. It was all done online. If they wanted, the kids could have something fancy done with her ashes. Up to 12 paperweights or a statuette could be 3D-printed to order, included in the price. She could have advance-purchased them but she didn't want to make assumptions or burden people with tat. She could hear the arguments already, "No, we can't throw that away, it's Grandma." The previous night she had been lying awake and it struck her that she'd quite like to be cast into a garden statue, a bit like the one in the grotto of Our Lady at her convent school. It was too late to arrange that now.

The music for the virtual service was chanting from a yoga class. Meg spent years trying to persuade her family to go to yoga with her, but they never would. She hoped they would find it calming as she always did. She had edited some subtitles, translating the Sanskrit, so they would know it was all about peace and that kind of thing. For a moment she had considered asking them to play David Bowie's 'Rock 'n' Roll Suicide', but she couldn't stop crying when she listened to the lyrics. In an attempt to help people remember the good times, Meg had chosen some nice pictures of them all, her wedding portrait, and lots of space for people to leave comments. She had begun to feel a bit guilty about the lack of Christian symbolism. "Maybe I'll pop in something about Our Lady at the end," she had thought. "You can't be too careful, can you, when you're heading for the afterlife?"

As soon as she had decided to go ahead, she managed to complete the booking in about an hour. In the end, it was the *85 bonanza* incentive that really clinched it. It was an amazing deal. If you booked your exit to take place on or before your 85th birthday you got a 50% discount on the fees. More importantly, though, there was a tax break on your estate which exempted what you left behind from inheritance tax. That would mean the kids got a much better pay-out. It was a no-brainer really. How good was it that, these days, you could make all these decisions on your own without your family's consent? It must have saved a lot of arguments.

After you had filled in all the details you had to pay by bank transfer. Just in case your credit card statement arrived after you'd gone. There were the usual terms and conditions. Meg actually read them for once and ticked all the boxes even though the cancellation policy was extremely disturbing. When the mandatory two-week cooling-off period had lapsed, the procedure could not be stopped. It reminded her of a gangster film, where a hired hit man is instructed to carry out a murder, even if his employer later decides it has all been a terrible mistake and begs him not to go through with it.

She slowly walked up the stairs to check that everything was in order. Letters for each of the kids. Old-fashioned, she knew, but she thought it would be something they could keep that wouldn't take up too much space. Angel would post them. Some heart stickers and a card for each of the grandchildren which she had made herself, complete with glitter. She loved getting their drawings and thought it would be something personal and relatively cheerful to remind them of her when they were older.

There wasn't long to go now. "I'd better eat something," she thought. Angel wasn't due for another couple of hours. All her life she had been trying to eat less, and on the one day when it didn't matter if she got fat she didn't really feel like it. She had been running down the fridge and the freezer. Taken everything from the cupboards that was still in date to the food bank. She had kept an egg aside though. "I'll boil it for five minutes. That's always nice. Bit of salt. Butter. Cup of tea. I've always thought that the simple things make it good to be alive. Better make the most of it. That jam doughnut can go in the bin. It seemed like a good idea when I bought it, but I don't fancy it now."

CHAPTER TWO

When Brytely refitted their Shoreditch headquarters, they created a place their employees never wanted to leave. Staff couldn't tear themselves away. The team of achingly trendy, handpicked young marketing professionals were first seduced and then firmly locked-in by the hip ambience of the office, which they fed in return, each one of them making it more compelling with their carefully constructed, unique personal style.

Portia always stayed late at work. She would let her hand glide along the cool monochrome glass surfaces, spread out at a comfortable workstation, help herself to chilled filtered water in funky colored transparent glasses, and pick at the bowls of free fruit that were replenished every few hours by corporation robots, as long as there was anyone still working. They kept the grapes and strawberries coming all night. One of the wags in the office had christened the service bots the Nell Gwynnes, after they took a suggestive picture with one of them laden heavily with oranges, and posted it on Splutter. At night the Nell Gwynnes would softly bump into the fleet of automated robotic vacuum cleaners which snapped gently at everyone's ankles once it got past eight o'clock.

Most of the staff were under 35. They either lived with their parents or in one of the funky new places that had been built exclusively for their age group. One of Yuthentic's early priorities had been to boost the stock of affordable housing for younger people. They had done it by persuading the government to build racks of tiny studios on any brown field site they could find. The idea had been a runaway success.

One good source of land came from the nursing homes they had closed down. The elderly care industry had collapsed when state funding was ratcheted down so low that the owners of the facilities could no longer afford to provide the quality of care they were legally obliged to deliver. So they gave up. When the homes went, it freed up space. Some of the blocks that had been built more recently, with ensuite bathrooms and pleasant communal areas, were simply refitted and allocated to a younger clientele. Shabby vinyl-covered armchairs and the reek of disinfectant had been swiftly swapped for high tables, groovy designer stools and the more savory aroma of freshly brewed coffee. The similarity of these places to a university hall of residence was obvious, so many young people felt at home, even if they did not feel like they had progressed very far. Elegant detached Victorian villas that had once been adapted for elderly care were bulldozed and cheery new functional boxes stacked up in their place.

At first, when Portia was allocated a place in Peacehaven, a 20-unit residence on the site of a former nursing home of the same name, she was delighted. It was only half an hour from her workplace. There was bicycle parking, a communal laundry, and a state-of-the-art sleeping pod that could create the perfect sleep-sure blackout conditions that were so much in vogue. You could vary the temperature of the lighting in the flat to enhance your mood. When she moved in, she experimented with the colors quite a bit, but the novelty soon wore off. It was annoying that you couldn't open a window, especially as the heating and air con seemed to have a mind of their own. She always seemed to be either boiling or freezing, putting on more layers or stripping off, to stay comfortable.

What she found most irritating about the flat, however, was the lack of space. On her first morning she had climbed out of her pod, put on her yoga clothes, and tried to do a sun salutation. She shuffled around the studio trying to find somewhere she could stretch out and work through the dynamic series of movements. It simply wasn't going to happen. So now, in the morning, she just had to do the poses she could fit into narrow dimensions. The tree, drawing herself up and standing on one leg; and a forward bend, folding her torso down to fit flat against her thighs, pulling in her stomach and wrapping her arms around the backs of her legs to squeeze in tighter.

Tonight, in the office, she had a lot to think about. Portia and her colleague Sonny had been asked to take the lead on a confidential project for the corporation. They had been briefed on a video call with Carrie, the corporation's Global Head of Brand, and Stella, Brytely's own Group Chief Executive who had a longstanding special relationship as communications consultant to Mason, CEO of the corporation.

The brief was unusual. The corporation had won a massive government contract. They were going to provide the end-of-life services that were being set up in response to new legislation that improved the availability of humane terminal disposal. The corporation was well on its way to having the delivery infrastructure in place. An application and consent mechanism had been designed to ensure people were making choices themselves and not being pressured by their family members. They had a fleet to provide transportation to the disposal centers – or DCs as they came to be called. The DCs were essentially scaled up crematoriums with a high-tech design on the front end that allowed up to 20 people per hour to be processed. After incineration, the client's ashes would be captured individually and made available to next of kin in a variety of mourner-friendly formats.

The corporation was discreetly establishing disposal centers all over the country. One of the first to go live would be at a secret location in London. The density of the population in the metropolis meant a healthy pipeline of customers so that they could most quickly recoup their costs. The prototype center was called Brookwood, named after the cemetery the old London necropolis trains had taken people to back in the twentieth century. To avoid any kind of public outcry, the planning rules had been waived so no consultation was required on developing the sites. They had also made sure the Google

Street View of the location was heavily pixelated so no one could guess what was there.

There would be two classes of disposal.

The premium service was aimed at the most affluent 10 per cent of people aged 70 or older. This was because the main aim of the disposal programme was to redistribute as much wealth as possible from the old to the young. It made a lot of sense to go for the richest ones first. They were what people in business called 'low-hanging fruit'. Portia's colleague Sonny had run an initial data capture which uncovered a complex set of beliefs and behaviours in this affluent cohort. One of their strongest motivations was the desire to avoid paying tax.

To exploit this motivational characteristic, the government had introduced a programme of financial incentives, allowing even the wealthiest person total exemption from inheritance tax if they signed up to go. For the people at the very top, this meant they could give tens of millions of extra pounds to the younger people in their family if they signed up by their 85th birthday. As everyone knew Sonny came from a family with more money than most, they had agreed he would focus on how to sell the premium service, while Portia looked at the mass market version.

She looked at her notes detailing how it would all work. The corporation had a fleet of busses they had mothballed a couple of years ago, after the provision for social care had been frozen. They weren't allowed to scrap the vehicles because of all the environmental rules. Luckily, the buses now had a new lease of life. Each one was being refitted and mechanised to take people to the DCs. No drivers, one human supervisor, and the bus pretty much did the rest with its automated lifts, rotating chairs and two big strong cheery service bots to help people on and off no matter how heavy they were. Even if you were morbidly obese these fellas could carry you like a kitten.

After scanning the demographics dashboard Sonny had produced, Portia tried to think of someone old that she actually knew to inform her ideas for the campaign. It was quite hard. There wasn't anyone over 50 at Brytely, where she spent most of her waking hours. She had never known her Dad, so there were no old relatives to call to mind on his side. Her Mum had her when she was fifteen, and her grandparents were still quite young. Quite a way off the target group. All she could think of were some of her professors at university, and of course the tramps. Everywhere there were tramps, but they were to be avoided. She wouldn't want to get near enough to talk to one of them without a face mask, and she didn't have one with her today.

Feeling like she was in need of a big dose of inspiration, Portia put in her earbuds and went to the documentary channel to research what the life of someone aged 70 or above was like. It answered a lot of questions. Apart from the tramps, many of the poorer ones seemed to be housebound, struggling to find enough to eat, and heavily medicated to keep their age-related health conditions at bay. Some had moved into the hangar-like communal dorms, which had replaced the nursing homes, when they found that they could no longer care for themselves or live safely. That didn't look like a bundle of laughs either. After about an hour of depressing viewing, she began to think that simply showing people the documentaries about how difficult life was already might be enough to get them to sign up. She stood up and stretched, and decided to go over to the treadmill lounge to walk and think. It saved going outside.

There were three treadmills in a row, each with its own screen and communications deck. Sometimes they used them for meetings by videoconference if the person on the other end didn't mind. When they called their co-workers in NYC it was common to do what they called a walkie-talkie.

The backdrop to the NYC treadmill was a picture of the city taken from the banks of the reservoir at the North end of Central Park. A strip of steely navy water was separated from a startlingly bright blue sky by a long set of miniature skyscrapers. Sometimes she would call the New York office late afternoon her time and speak with another walker who was just getting geared up for their day.

As she paced purposefully forward, she knew that the agency would be looking for something more than simply redistributing the documentary footage she had found about the grim life of an average over-70. It could be part of the campaign, though. They could lead the customers there by ambushing other videos they might be watching. So if someone was searching for information on the early signs of dementia, for example, they could be prompted towards other material that would start them thinking about disposal as a positive choice.

Unexpectedly, a chat window popped up on the treadmill's comms deck. She usually turned it off when she was trying to think, but she had been so immersed in mulling over the campaign that she'd forgotten to uncouple the 'follow me' feature. The caller was someone she didn't recognise. Before she could reject it, the message surprised her. 'Hello Paula', it read.

How on earth did it know her real name? No-one had called her Paula for years. Paula became Portia in her first term at university when she had decided to reinvent herself as someone more middle-class, with a better chance of being a conventional success. Every day she became more convinced that she had made the right decision. Portia would never have landed her internship at Brytely as the girl she had once been: Paula Kelly, with a thick Scouse accent, who had lived more than half her life on a housing estate in Speke. She got enough stick as it was for being vaguely Northern, which was where her intonation had stabilised.

Taken aback by what she assumed to be the caller's insider knowledge of her past, she could not resist finding out more. Instead of rejecting the call on principle like she usually did, she said; "Assistant convert text to speech." Now she could talk without having to type, and keep on walking to hit her step goal for the day. She said hello back.

"Hi, have you got a few minutes?" It said, the standard opening gambit from a chatbot. Keeping it short, Portia just replied "Yes."

"Great, thank you Paula. I'm getting in touch because publicly available records indicate that your childhood home was the Ringo Starr Estate in Speke, Merseyside. Is that right?" Yes, it was right. The hairs stood up on the back of her neck, and she slid down the volume so no one in the office outside could hear the details of the conversation.

It went on: "When you lived there, Liverpool was one of the most polluted cities in the UK. Your proximity to the airport was an additional negative factor." That was true. Some days she could taste the exhaust particles in the air, and when the wind was in right direction she would catch the unmistakeable chemical whiff of aviation fuel. She thought she knew where this conversation might be leading now.

"A substantial sum has been allocated to compensate people like you whose long-term health will almost certainly have been damaged irreversibly by the pollution levels they were exposed to in their childhood. We have access to a fund, created from a compulsory levy of the biggest polluters, and millions of pounds have already been paid out in compensation to people whose health has been put at risk, with increased chances of morbidity.

"In order to make a claim, you simply need to confirm where you were living at the time. £10,000 is already authorised for you Paula, subject to you agreeing to the terms and conditions."

Portia's first thought was that £10,000 could come in handy. Even though she had been allocated subsidised housing when she moved to London to take the job, she was always short of cash. Her Mum was now in another relationship and was bringing up her three younger half siblings with the support of Marcus, their Dad, who she had met working in Playland, an immersive video arcade that was popular in their neighborhood. Her Mum's life now was much more settled than in her early days with Portia, but there was no family cash sloshing around to help in her ambitious new London life. If anything there was a tacit accusation of her having abandoned her mother, as she had moved to the other end of the country, hardly visiting, and contributing nothing back to the family in return.

Her folks would never understand that Paula was competing at work with the other graduates who mainly seemed to be living at home with the support of the bank, fridge, and spare bedroom of Mum and Dad. What she earned seemed like a fortune to her Mum, but her expenses swallowed it all up, as Portia kept trying to explain. She could eat in the office so she wasn't starving, but she had little money to pay for regular trips back home. She could really do with some new clothes. Everything seemed to be used up by the rent and service charges.

"I'm not sure," Portia said to the bot, knowing from her job in a marketing company, and her Mum's experience of PPI claims when she was growing up, that that £10,000 might just be an opening gambit. There could be much more available if she played it right. "I have to go now. Could we speak again tomorrow?"

By then, the bot was, naturally, running diagnostics on Portia's tone of voice and could sense that she might take the bait. Rather than initiate its series of questions designed to eradicate her doubts, it applied its emotional judgment and arranged to speak with her again the following day.

Alone again, Portia checked her step count. She couldn't believe how far she'd travelled, or how late it was now. Her mind had been completely absorbed in the conversation with the bot, and in thinking through what it might mean to her. She slowed the treadmill to a steady halt and stepped quietly down onto the floor. Steadying herself against the wall she balanced on each leg in turn to stretch out her quads before heading back to pick up her things and go home to sleep. She was surprised how the chance of £10,000 made her mind race with the potential for sprucing up her wardrobe, or maybe even stretching to a trip back home as she hadn't been there for so very long.

She checked her device as she waited for a ride home in the lobby. Outside, Fergus, the resident tramp, was setting up for the night in the shelter of their building, layering cardboard insulation under his filthy sleeping bag. Someone had left him an orange. There was no way she would go outside until her car was right by the door. A message came in from Pollution Health Unlimited Claims (PHUC) following up on their earlier exchange, and she thought again about how much she wanted the money.

That was when it dawned on her. Of course. That's what we need to do. We can build the mother of all marketing bots to nudge the Enders onto the bus. If we combine that with a campaign, pushing the documentaries about the grim real life alternative on to their feeds, we can get them in the mood for signing up. Especially if Sonny can mine a bit more insight into what's going on in their sad little lives at the time. Bereavements, accidents, bouts of illness. It's all out there somewhere. He's usually pretty good at that. Then we can catch them at just the right moment, when they are on the brink of despair. Yep, that should do it.

At that moment an animated starburst on her screen told her the car had arrived. She looked out and there was the auto waiting for her, still bedecked in Christmas livery, which was starting to look a bit sad as it was early January. Fergus was climbing into his sleeping bag as she walked quickly past him, avoiding eye contact, and slipped into the warm cabin of the machine that was going to ferry her home.

CHAPTER THREE

SONNY LEVERED HIS WAY OUT of the packed train and with a tiny hop cleared the yellow line that separated the safe place to stand on the platform from its more dangerous, textured edge. He joined a crush of around 20 people waiting to exit in front of him, becoming jittery when the person in front of him struggled to get the barrier to open with their card.

"Tosser," he mumbled under his breath.

Once through, he walked briskly up the hill, heading towards his home. Strictly speaking it wasn't really his place. It was his parents' house where he still lived in his childhood bedroom. The neighborhood was an affluent area where large detached mini-mansions were set at an unobtrusive distance from each other. Sonny folded his arms to fend off the cold. He liked the look of his thick, long-sleeved Timber! vintage skater shirt, and hadn't wanted to hide it under a jacket. After all, most of his journey was in an overheated train.

When he had returned from university to look for a job in London, Sonny's parents had done a lot to help him. They knew how devastated he was not to have made it on to the Google graduate programme. He had shut himself in his room and binge-watched Netflix for months until Sonny's mother, Uma, called Stella, her old friend from boarding school, and asked her to help him engage with reality again. When Stella arranged for Sonny to be called for an interview at Brytely he surprised himself, talking about how much he could make of the job, and landed one of just three highly sought-after unpaid internships the company operated every year.

Sonny was keen to move out, but no matter how hard he tried to persuade his parents to help with a deposit, he was getting nowhere. The more exploitative period of his internship behind him, Brytely were actually paying Sonny now, but he had given up on trying to save. It seemed totally futile given the sums he would need to find for his own place. His family was supporting his annoying little sister Amina who was only in her first year at university, gobbling up what little money remained after steering Sonny proudly through his data science degree. There wasn't much left after that.

Realising that Sonny would be living back home for a while, his parents had let him refresh the décor in this room. It no longer looked like a teenager's den, apart from the screens and consoles on the desk that served as both a place to work, and a place to play. He had bought a small fridge which contained mainly energy drinks, used to fuel all-nighters either working on projects for Brytely, or gaming with his university friend Ken who was over in California, where Sonny would much rather have been.

The house sensed his approach and clicked the latch

on the front door open so he only had to push it with his shoulder, and click it shut behind him. His parents were both working late, Uma at the hospital where she was Chief Pharmacist and Dilip at the management consulting firm where he had started as a trainee just before Sonny was born. As his parents both worked long hours, Sonny often had the run of the house now Amina had left. It was more than bearable.

He dropped his backpack onto the kitchen floor and walked towards the fridge, pulling open the door and gazing hypnotically at the shelves. Sonny grabbed an upmarket ready meal from the stack his mum had bought for him, stabbed the film covering it with a fork several times, and popped it in the microwave. As the tray turned he put a tumbler under the tap and poured himself a glass of cold water which he gulped down quickly. The heat of the train had left him parched.

He refilled the glass as he began to think about the four hours that lay between his TV dinner and sleep. He needed to come up with some ideas for the Ending campaign and looked around the house blankly for inspiration.

"Assistant, happy music please," he said. It chose The Housemartins' 'Happy Hour'. As the lively upbeat song, which he had never heard before, filled the room, he was surprised to find he liked it and nodded his head along to the beat, smiling for the first time that day. It was no help whatsoever for the ad campaign but it was at least easing him into a better frame of mind after his unpleasant commute.

The screen on the wall was doing what it always did

in rest mode, scrolling through family photos that his parents had loaded into the cloud. It was embarrassing when his friends came round. After his graduation photo, up popped a picture of his grandparents on a Caribbean cruise. They were still raving about that holiday now, even though it had been three years ago.

It struck him that they were bang in the target group for the campaign. The three As. Aging. Affluent. Alive. The picture reminded him of another holiday they had all spent together, years ago, in India. He had been small, about three or four, and they had played on the beach and ridden elephants. They weren't so close now. His grandparents. Ayesha and Ajay, had done well with their business, and been lucky when they sold it. Now they were living a very comfortable retirement.

Even though they only lived a short walk away Sonny didn't see them very often. There was always money for his birthday, and high days and holidays. Their world was totally alien to him. Whenever they got together he found it difficult to explain things to them. It would be very helpful to use them for the research, though. Perhaps if he went round there he might get some inspiration. Even though he couldn't tell them exactly what he was working on.

"Assistant, stop," he said to silence the music, then, "call Ayesha and Ajay." A video link was up in a second and showed the couple, pottering round their kitchen, just like him.

"Hey! Sonny!" said a thick-set silver haired Indian man, looking a bit surprised and then breaking into a big smile, "We thought it would be your Mum. To what do we owe this unexpected pleasure?" A tall, slim older woman with her hair still completely black, tied into a neat ponytail, and wearing designer spectacles adorned with diamante details came closer to the camera with him, waving. They wore high quality layered exercise clothing in matching burgundy. Sonny found their taste in his 'n' hers outfits peculiar but endearing.

In a few minutes they had established that Ayesha and Ajay were staying in that night as they had been to the gym in the afternoon and overdone it a bit with two classes back to back. "Combat and Pump," Ayesha said, "I'm slaughtered."

Sonny mentioned that he was at a loose end himself and was immediately invited over as he had hoped. As soon as he had accepted the invitation Ayesha said, "I hope you haven't eaten?" Remembering that her cooking was so much better that any ready meal, anywhere, and knowing that the one he had just re-heated himself was out of sight, Sonny half lied, "No, not really." On his way out of the door he threw the warm loaded plastic tray he had just prepared into the outside bin without a second thought. He set off for their home, this time a little more warmly dressed than before. It wasn't like anyone that mattered was going to see him.

As he walked into their house, Sonny savored the smell of home cooked Indian food which Ayesha was getting ready to serve. Since retiring, his grandparents had been on numerous cookery courses together, and loved nothing better than entertaining. "Sit down, come on," she said, after giving him a big hug. Ajay was already at the table, scooping up pieces of cauliflower with a soft chapatti. "Tell me then Sunil, how's the job going?"

His grandparents always used his Indian name, although he had been calling himself Sonny since primary school. He wasn't sure how to answer the question. Whenever he had talked to them about his job before he had never managed to get them to grasp what he actually did. Sometimes he had difficulty understanding it himself. He stuffed his mouth with food and pointed apologetically at his face to buy a bit more time. After a few seconds chewing and swallowing he said: "Yeah, it's good."

Clearly unsatisfied with the answer Ajay carried on his line of enquiry "So. Good. Does that mean they are paying you properly now?"

The couple had worked together for a long time, after meeting at university where Ayesha had been studying maths and Ajay economics. Both of them came from families that had run businesses, and they decided that – rather than apply for graduate jobs – they would prefer to work for themselves. Through both their sets of parents and the odd uncle they had been able to borrow enough money to buy their first fast food franchise just as they left higher education. Some of their friends looked down on them for going into mass catering, but they didn't care. Within a decade they had 16 highly profitable fried chicken shops in London, and they had shrewdly sold them all at the peak of the market. It was perfectly timed, about 18 months before the fast food regulation came in that would have put them out of business. The two of them had spent the last ten years living every minute of their early retirement, and having tremendous fun.

Sonny answered the question honestly. "Yeah, they're paying me more than they were, but I don't really know what it's reasonable to expect."

Ajay continued. "Tell me again, why you bothering with this funny communications job when you have a data science degree?"

This had once been a sore point for Sonny. He had applied for the graduate schemes with a number of the tech giants, but although he got a few interviews in the end his grades simply hadn't been stellar enough to get him the job he wanted. He saw himself as the victim of a demographic peak, caused by a massive push to encourage thousands of boys and girls to prepare for careers in data science. Fearful that would be the only work available in future, they had signed up in droves and now there were simply too many people for the work available. Much of it was now being done by the AIs too. You had to be super smart to be programming them.

Nevertheless, his knowledge of data manipulation had helped Sonny win his spurs in the early days of his unpaid internship at Brytely. It had been a significant factor in them giving him a paid job. At the same time he was also discovering he had a knack for thinking creatively, spinning interesting ideas out of the data he was crunching, which was something he had never had the chance to do before. He found it fun.

"Actually Nana, I am using my data science background," he explained. "I can find out a huge amount about how individual customers feel about the things we want to sell them just by looking at a few of their clicks on the internet. Brytely love that because it makes their campaigns more effective. Think of it as a finely targeted version of the advertising you used to buy in the *South London Press* when you wanted more people to visit your shops. The more effective the campaign, the more money the clients will pay for it. I'm good at it and they like me."

"I get it," Ayesha said, as Ajay nodded in agreement through another mouthful. "So, these services you're selling, what kind of things?"

"Actually, I'm working for a client that is producing a new range of upmarket services for people in your age group. It's a confidential project, but I'm really enjoying it. If we do well there'll be a big bonus at the end. I'm working with a girl called Portia. We're leading the creative team." He couldn't quite bring himself to use the phrase 'end-of-life' in front of his grandparents.

"Do you like this girl?" Ayesha asked, with a twinkle in her eye only someone of her generation would have the cheek to display.

"Yes, we're a good team."

"Is that all?"

"Honestly Nani. There are rules about that sort of thing at work these days. She is nice but work has to take precedence. Quite apart from anything else jobs are hard to come by, I wouldn't want to screw things up."

Ajay butted in, "Ayesha and I worked together for our entire career. Thank goodness those stupid rules didn't exist then. Otherwise you wouldn't even be here."

Sonny bit his bottom lip and counted to five. He

didn't want to get into this discussion. It was a familiar pattern, and one of the reasons he so rarely spent time with these people from a less enlightened era. They would begin with what they believed to be a few innocuous remarks about how workplace relationships made the world go round, peppered with euphemistic anecdotes about what used to happen in the stockroom. Then it would spiral down into the usual attack on gender fluidity. He did not want to get drawn into the same old circular arguments.

"If you don't like this Portia, then, have you got another girlfriend?" Ayesha said next. He was really beginning to wish he hadn't come round. The back of his neck prickled. At 25 it was ridiculous that they could make him so embarrassed about being single. Nearly everyone he knew had deliberately avoided getting into the kind of permanent relationship Ayesha and Ajay seemed to think was essential for a happy future. He certainly wasn't going to open up now. He was used to batting this question away with the family.

"No. There's no rush." He calmly spooned some vegetables onto his plate. "It's not as if I'm a biological time bomb. Plenty of time yet."

By now Sonny was starting to feel like he wanted to head for the door, but he was determined not to leave without the insight he was looking for. So he started to describe the project he was working on in a roundabout sort of a way. Carefully avoiding any mention of death, he told them he was working on a campaign designed to sell a portfolio of lifestyle choices to older people. "I was wondering, actually, if you could tell me a bit about the things you most enjoy and look forward to in life," he continued, steering the conversation firmly away from himself, "It could really help me at work."

"That's easy for me," Ayesha piped up, delighted to be able to both help her grandson and to talk about one of her favorite things in the world. "For our next holiday we are going to be cruising around the Caribbean again, which is wonderful in itself. Only this time we've decided to fly out business class, like we did on our Singapore trip. If I've learned one thing about how money can make you happy it's 'never turn right'!"

Ajay was broadly supportive of the idea too, though not quite as ecstatic as his wife. "It is nice to be able to lie down flat on a long flight, especially with my hip not being so good. Personally I think it's a lot of money, but if it's what your grandmother wants I shan't complain."

There might be a germ of an idea in this. Sonny thought back to the research principles he'd studied, and decided to probe more. "What's so good about the upgrade?" he asked. Their grandson had few preconceptions, as he never been able to afford to fly on anything other than budget airlines himself. Advertising for luxury services would never be wasted on someone like him. He was a complete outsider as far as exclusive travel perks were concerned.

"It's amazing!" Ayesha continued enthusiastically. "They send a wonderful limo for you. It takes you to a private entrance at the airport away from all the plebs. Look…" She scrolled through a few files and loaded some photos onto their screen on the wall where only half an hour previously Sonny had appeared. She had asked the driver to take their picture stepping out of the limo in style, into a luxurious covered marble courtyard, where a mirror ball was spinning above symmetrical fountains, enhanced by a thousand tiny beams of light. In the picture Ayesha and Ajay wore matching purple tracksuits, something comfortable for the long flight. Next to them he could see a robot in the airline colors sweeping up their bags, its friendly mechanistic face smiling endearingly.

"He was a funny chap," Ayesha giggled, rolling her eyes, "Had lovely patter. The thing is, once you've experienced the best, nothing else will do. It costs a lot more to travel in style, but there's no going back now for as long as we can afford it."

They flicked to another picture, this time of the two of them sitting at a black glass table with a slick bar in the background. LEDs picked out the airline's logo embedded in the wall. Each of them held a non-alcoholic cocktail in their hand, adorned with paper parasols and a tiny skewer of fruit.

"Tell me more about why you liked it so much," Sonny stayed focused on the open questioning.

"It makes me feel like a million dollars. I love the bling, the cocktails, the whole package makes me feel spoiled," said Ayesha. "Because I'm worth it," she added, shaking her head so her ponytail flapped about. When Sonny looked confused she explained, "It was an advertising strapline from a long time ago. You should look it up."

Sonny turned to Ajay. "How about you Nana? Apart from keeping Nani happy, is there anything about it that you would say you particularly like?"

Ajay thought quietly for a moment, wiping his face and hands on a piece of kitchen towel which he threw onto his empty plate before giving Sonny his final words on the subject. "For me son, it's nice to have all the stress taken away. I used to dread travelling. Now I love it. We just book on the app and everything is taken care of. They know us. We've travelled with them before. I don't want any hassle. They even know I need an extra pillow to support my bad hip. I don't need to ask for anything twice. Then they carry me away to somewhere I want to be. When the journey is as enjoyable as your final destination, the fun starts the minute you leave your front door."

Sonny took in everything they had said to him. When he stood up to go both Ayesha and Ajay gave him massive hugs. "Son," Ajay said, "Come again. It was lovely to see you. Check your bank account when you get home – there'll be a little something in there for you."

"Thanks Nana," he said, feeling too old to be accepting money from a relative, but grateful at the same time for the gift. They really did love him, he suddenly thought, out of nowhere. He glanced over their shoulder at the picture of Ganesha the elephant god on the wall. It was something else that always made him smile.

As Sonny zipped up his coat in the porch, and started to walk away from the front door, he heard them crank up the music. They were listening to 'Rockstar' by Nickelback, singing along with some of the words. You had to hand it to them, they certainly knew how to enjoy life.

CHAPTER FOUR

It was Coke zero and gluten-free pizza all round the day Brytely won the Happy Endings account. Portia and Sonny had worked on the pitch for weeks. They knew they were a good team, but making death look glamorous and aspirational had tested their creativity to the limit.

Stella called a meeting of everyone who was in the office that day to tell them the good news, beaming in from her LA suite in holographic form. She materialised in the space reserved exclusively for avatars at the front of the open plan space, between the beanbags and what today simply resembled a flat white wall, but could as easily have turned into a moving tropical beach or the Utah desert.

"I had a call from my old friend Mason himself," Stella announced to the dozen or so creatives clustered around her 3D image. "He's given us the account for all of the Happy Endings services, and he wants us to start with their premium offering, Rockstar. Huge thanks to Portia and Sonny. All we need to do now is execute."

Portia and Sonny exchanged glances across the slick

high table where they balanced precariously on Perspex stools that had been designed to be wobbly, their drinks placed on the rather more stable hard surface in front of them. The smile that flickered across their faces betrayed their conviction that they were fast becoming one of the hottest teams around.

"Remember," Stella added, "We need to keep all the files offline, on the secure server. If there's a leak we'll be toast. We'll be setting up a private cloud space to work on this. Any questions?"

Everyone knew Stella wouldn't really want any questions. They could see the light flashing on her wrist signalling her next call. So Sonny closed it down, "We're all cool here Stella, thanks for the news, it's amazing. Porsh and I are onto it already."

Stella disappeared and everyone's attention drifted away from the suddenly hollow space where she had just been projected. People snapped their focus back to their own projects as if nothing had happened. Some talking into headsets, others hanging around screens, as Sonny and Portia did, to plan the next stages of their campaign.

That had been six weeks ago. Stella was now very much in person with Sonny and Portia in the marble corporation reception, waiting to present their film to Mason himself. In head-to-toe vintage Yves Saint Laurent, sourced by one of the most exclusive textile curators in the world, Stella had been dressing for years as the leader she wanted to become, and looked immaculate. She eyed her two junior colleagues from beneath a steely asymmetric statement haircut, satisfied that her outfit set her apart from them, yet also pleased that their more informal, quirky appearance would play well with Mason. You could safely bet that like most billionaires working in the knowledge economy, he would be wearing the traditional uniform of jeans and a T-shirt.

The reception desk was a long, thin, glowing white teardrop and behind it sat three genderless droids. The robotic figures would be nowhere near convincing as humans but they came across as friendly, efficient and helpful. They had been designed with huge plastic kitten bows adorning their necks, resting just behind their left ears.

The bows had been Stella's idea. Mason had asked her to think about how they could create a memorable welcome experience that would set their reception desk apart from the competition. The most memorable reception she had seen was in a Japanese company twelve years previously. In their entrance hall, an all-female team of ten receptionists with uniformly perfect figures and conventional good looks had their elfin necks adorned with identical chiffon kitten bows in the company's colors. She had been stunned by their subservient beauty, before catching herself and rationalising that the women were being objectified, and reinforcing the inferior position of pretty much every female on the planet. Or at least in Japan. On the droids, Stella had explained to Mason, the bow would signify a softening, and the reassuring subjugation of machine to man. A droid with a bow was nothing to be afraid of. Robot emoji. Heart emoji. Bow emoji.

Behind the corporation desk, she noticed the company logo blinking subtly through the place where, if they had been human, the robots' heart would have been. Their arms made smooth movements and they operated keyboards with dextrous fingers to replicate their human predecessors.

Stella, Sonny and Portia had been security cleared to a high level before being brought into the company to explain their plans. They only needed to look at one of the droids for the iris recognition system installed between its eyes to identify them.

"Welcome to the corporation Stella, Sonny and Portee-ah," the droid said, its face attempting a smile which was endearing if not wholly convincing. It's mispronunciation of Portia reminded them that it was merely a subhuman mechanoid. "Please follow me."

The droid, whose badge gave its name as Arnold, glided to the edge of the spacey reception desk and started leading the party towards a corridor fenced off by a floor to ceiling sliding glass door. As they approached, the door disappeared into the wall, and as Portia passed the threshold it snapped back behind her.

They passed through a second security point, and arrived at another clear door which led to the executive floor, a maze of Perspex offices separated by transparent multi-colored panels which glided open as they approached. It was like being inside a huge construction toy, a maze of colored light, with infinite combinations of colors. Arnold retreated once the three of them were safely inside Mason's corner office. Immediately the clear walls delineating his space became opaque and faded to an unearthly grey. They recognised the shade immediately as the season's hottest Pantone, Television.

Mason was waiting for them. Sonny and Portia hadn't met a Chief Executive before and were disarmed by his informal manner. Already in his office was Carrie, the corporation's Global Head of Brand, who they had pitched to when they won the business. Portia had seen Carrie speak at AdFest. She certainly knew all the buzzwords.

"Please take a seat," Mason said warmly, after offering a lean suntanned handshake to welcome each of the agency visitors in turn. Stella's pale, bony, ring-adorned hand was first to grab him, as their greeting was accompanied by two air kisses. "So good to see you again, Mason," she breathed, "It seems like Davos was only yesterday." They sprung apart and Mason turned to Portia. He had a firm handshake, and she tried to give as good as she got. Mason didn't notice Sonny's tattoo. Instead he unnerved him by looking deeply into his dark brown eyes.

Sonny and Portia fiddled about, quietly getting everything in place to project the screen in Mason's office. The holographic projector was fully charged, but Portia had a spare power pack with her just in case. They had thought about using VR headsets but there were limitations to integrating everyone live into the feed, and for this key meeting they wanted to be able to read Mason's body language, unmediated, to make sure they were giving him what he wanted.

"You'll remember, Mason, we're here to look at the commercial for the Happy Endings service," Carrie began. "There will be an unceasing barrage of tailored social to go with it, to help nudge our customers along to making the decision we want. This film will be a centerpiece, a talking point to attract attention and start them on the journey."

Using the tablet on the desk as if it were second nature, Carrie smoothly dimmed the lights and Stella said, "Let's go."

They sat in darkness for a few seconds as the music started to play in. It was a classic about being a rock star, a song that was familiar to everyone in the room. The female singer was someone with a reputation for knowing how to have a good time, strong, empowered, and beautiful in a rock 'n' roll kind of a way. The lyrics were all about being who you wanted to be, doing what you wanted to do, because being a rock star meant you could get away with anything.

Words and images flowed around the room:

Be who you want to be. Right to the end.

A grey-haired woman, Annie, dressed in exquisitely tailored designer clothing and spectacles, opened the front door to her detached home, a mock-Georgian villa, with a short gravel drive. The camera switched to show an attractive, handsome, uniformed androgynous wrinkle-free figure in their late 20s, who had rung the bell. This person was a Happy Endings Angel, who was warmly welcomed. They entered the house together.

Annie handed an envelope and keys to the Angel who waited for her, by the front door. They shut it behind them, and the Angel took Annie's arm as she approached a driverless limo, elliptical, curved and gleaming silver. It could almost have been a spaceship. The door swung open, and the old lady slipped gracefully into an inviting-looking reclining seat, next to a glass of champagne which was clipped onto a marble side table.

Cut to the inside of the car, gliding along the road, the woman was now lying back, her cares ebbing away as she sank into pure luxury. She took a sip of her champagne, and then began to drift off to sleep.

The next scene was inside the old lady's dream. She was in an airy space, a pasture in the mountains. The sun was rising, and Annie was walking towards a man. "Martin," she said, "It's so good to see you again." He took her in his arms and the screen faded to Martin and Annie's wedding photo. "I'm sorry it's taken me so long to get here, love," Annie said, "I needed to make sure the grandkids were taken care of."

Cut to a garden where a young couple were looking at a letter together, while two small children ran towards a climbing frame. One of them shouted, "Mummy, Daddy, is this really ours?"

"It's from Nanny," the mother says, "a special present she sent for you before she went to be with Grandad." These children weren't just getting a climbing frame. Thanks to Happy Endings there was enough money for their parents to stop worrying about their everyday bills and see their kids through college.

Cut back to Annie, who said: "Sign up for a Rockstar Ending on or before your 85th birthday and the entirely of your estate will go to anyone you nominate under 50, completely free of inheritance tax. Commit today to give your children one last gift. The gift of a lifetime."

The music faded back up, and the commercial ended

with Annie and Martin holding each other, silhouetted against an orange sky.

Carrie touched the tablet without having to look down and the lights in the room began to fade back up. It took several seconds for everyone's eyes to adjust. They sat in silence for a few moments.

Stella cleared her throat: "We have created an aspirational campaign for the 70-85 age group. This execution is aimed at the prime targets, the most affluent female property owner, widowed, money in the bank, average net worth £1.5 million, which we want them to pass onto the younger generation as quickly as possible. We did consider a darker treatment, where we explore the idea of degeneration, indignity and illness which could strike at any moment, but we felt we should use the film to guide them towards a more positive choice in the first instance. We want them to look forward to seeing the film, to go back and watch it again and again because it gives them hope, not run away from it. To imagine themselves as Annie. It promises them glamour and dignity. They become heroes to their children by making their dreams come true.

"There's no shortage of images of suffering and squalor to terrify people all around us, every day. We don't need to associate your brand with all that. Not with this demographic anyway. What we're doing is associating departure with joy and hope. That's what people want to hear. That's what they'll buy into. It should please the Happiness Minister too."

Mason sat quietly.

"What did the groups think?" Carrie asked, right on cue.

"Can you cover that Sonny?" Stella knew he had organised market research groups for a week, all over the country, to test people's reaction to the film.

"We've run this, and a couple of other versions, using other Rockstar themed sound tracks, in 20 focus groups. It's had the best reception with the cohort we have the highest financial incentive to reach, the 70+ silver spenders. What surprised me, was that people with no hope of ever having a lifestyle like Annie's like this film. The thought of at least making it to a high status limo on their way out has an extraordinarily strong appeal, even for people living in a council flat in Rochdale. We filmed the groups. I can easily show you some footage and run through the underpinning data, Carrie, Mason."

"That's OK," Mason said, fixing Sonny again with his laser-like stare, "I think I've known Brytely long enough to take your word for it."

Carrie instinctively nodded in agreement with Mason before saying, "I have to say I think you've done a great job with this Stella. Did you want to talk us through where you've got to on the lower value proposal?"

Portia exchanged glances with Stella who raised her eyebrows and said, "Yes. Will you take us quickly through your ideas?"

She changed the options on the projector to make the most of a flatter visual, using simply animated flow diagrams to explain how the chatbots were going to seduce the weary targets at their most vulnerable moments.

"Sonny and I have identified the top ten life events

that might increase the probability of someone signing up for disposal. We're calling people experiencing these life events HPDs – high probability of disposal – for short. Perhaps unsurprisingly, diagnosis of a debilitating incurable physical condition that is expected to cause significant pain and disability is at the top of the list, second to that diagnosis of dementia, depression and so on. Interestingly fear of homelessness is another, a bit further down, so it's not always related to a health condition. Bereavement too. I won't read them all out now – the data is in the pack.

"We are proposing that we train and activate your AI chatbots to engage with anyone who is flagged as being HPD. The chatbots will spend at least six weeks listening to and building a psychological profile of the customer. Once they reach a certain threshold of information being voluntarily disclosed, and have created a deep enough level of trust, the bot will ask the customer for permission to access some of their more sensitive data. The kind of thing it's hard for us to access legally from more public sources. I'm thinking of medical records, detailed financial transactions – we could even ask for emails or phone records if we think we need them.

"The good news is that in our trials we're achieving 70% of customers allowing access to medical records, and it's improving all the time as the algorithm learns which triggers work best to prompt disclosure. I'm confident we'll be at 80% by the time we go live in a couple of months.

"We're also – and this is something Stella touched on before – able to influence their entertainment feeds so that we can expose them to documentaries, for example, or mini-series, that might make them worry about what will happen to them post-85 when their state health care is withdrawn. We wouldn't want to overdo that, but it's something else we can experiment with. Even pop songs that glorify suicide, or put a more positive spin on death into their playlists. That kind of thing."

Mason looked at Carrie, "Well, what do you think? Do you have any concerns about the ethics of this?"

Carrie chose her words carefully. "I've already checked with legal. We will need to make sure the chatbots are absolutely clear, at key points, what they are doing and why they are doing it. We need a verbal consent policy that is completely robust and will stand up in court, and all on tape. And a cooling-off period. The good news is that the scripts and tech spec Stella has given us take all of that into account. We're rock solid. No issues."

"In that case," Mason said, "What are we waiting for?"

CHAPTER FIVE

LEXI WORKED AS A TEACHER, one of the few jobs that still resembled what it had been 20 years before, when she first started work. It wasn't without its stresses, but she liked being around the kids, helping them with the things that even the most intelligent computers still couldn't teach them properly.

She had started out as a maths specialist, but that was done mainly by the AIs now. Lexi had guessed what was coming when they started putting consoles and cameras in all the classrooms, paired with the smartboards that had been around for much longer.

Schools were tight for money. When the corporation offered all that kit for free, in exchange for the kids' data, it was an offer no head teacher could refuse. They said the more information they had about the children, the better the system would become. It was hard to disagree, although one or two parents were unhappy at first. By the time anyone really noticed, though, the tech was already being used very widely, and the positive educational outcomes were being presented as inarguable.

Surely no one wanted to disadvantage their child

by denying them the right to an AI-augmented future? How would Britain ever be able to compete with China, where they had been using this stuff for more than a decade, if they didn't adopt it too? Faced with such compelling arguments, the campaign to keep 'intrusive tech' out of schools had been abandoned within a couple of years.

It was round about that time that Lexi retrained to teach Interpersonal and Creative Skills – ICS. It was fun, once you got used to the constant surveillance of everyone who worked with children. They said it was because of the scandals. She loved it that they got to use physical materials that the kids could touch, glue, paint, and cut rather than working in the virtual reality environment all of the time. With her encouragement, the children actually talked to each other every day, face to face. She liked that. It was a different kind of real.

Lexi met her partner Bob at the school, after he joined as IT manager. It was up to him to make sure the kids had access to the right learning resources at the right time. He also took care of the surveillance system that kept them all safe. Bob had worked in a bank on cybersecurity before, but long shifts and toxic workplace dynamics had brought him close to a breakdown. So he took the position at the school, which lived up to his expectations of being less pressure than his previous position. His job was contracted out to the corporation. It paid him a good wage for keeping the data flowing, and the classrooms working and online. It was win-win all round.

Three times a week Lexi went swimming at her gym.

She had been a keen exerciser since adolescence, and had been spurred on recently because she was beginning to think she might like to try to have a baby. At 42 she could just scrape in under the wire. Not that she'd told Bob that yet. Lots of people had their first child in their early 40s. Work had been intense, and until now Lexi simply hadn't had the right circumstances to think that motherhood would be a fair option – either for her or a child. Meeting Bob changed everything. They had moved together into the house she had inherited from her parents. Bob had even bought them both the gym membership, although he didn't get there too often himself.

During the school holidays she had a bit more time than usual to chat with other people when she went to the health club. She met a different crowd from those she normally saw, the ones who, like her, dashed in at the end of a conventional working day and rushed home after an intense half hour on a treadmill. A good evening for someone with a demanding job was one where you managed to get in and out of the gym without making eye contact with anyone.

A couple of older women chatted in the changing room, trading ideas for days out, holidays, and bigging-up the achievements of their children and grandchildren. It made her nostalgic. They were the kind of conversations she would never overhear from her own parents. They had been dead now for nearly 20 years.

On the last morning that week, Lexi noticed that Elsie, one of the regulars, was sitting on a bench by her locker looking a bit dazed. Although they had only met a few days before, Lexi had warmed to Elsie and was sorry to see her out of sorts. She was normally quite animated and energised. As Lexi quickly ran a comb through her brown, shoulder length hair, she caught a glimpse of the woman behind her in the mirror. Today she looked smaller, weaker, and somehow fragile. Lexi hastily pulled on a T-shirt to take some of the intimacy out of the situation, and asked Elsie if she was all right.

"I don't understand it," Elsie said, "They're terminating my gym membership."

"What do you mean?" Lexi was confused. "Who's terminating your membership?"

"The management. Legal requirement." Still wrapped in her towel, Elsie reached into her bag and pulled out her phone. She undid the screen lock and held it out with the type size expanded so that Lexi could read the email very easily. That was what it said. Cold, perfunctory and the polar opposite of the gym's usual gushing member communications.

"They told me at the front desk just before I came in for my swim. The email confirms it. This is the last time I'll be allowed in here. I blame Yuthentic."

"How come? This is a private gym," Lexi said, "Surely it's up to you how you spend your money?" She had heard that the free gym memberships for the over-70s were being withdrawn from the council facilities. But not this. Not here in privilege land.

"It seems the gym can't renew their insurance if they let people over 70 through the door. The new rates are prohibitive, they say. We're banned. With everything else going on it's like they want us to degenerate as quickly as possible so they can ship us off."

Lexi was curious about what Elsie had said, and uncertain what she meant by 'everything else going on'. As for once Lexi didn't have to rush off, she asked Elsie if she wanted to join her in the gym café for a coffee. She looked like she needed cheering up, and Elsie said yes, she would very much like to spend a bit more time with Lexi, as she was feeling a bit overwhelmed and didn't want to go home just yet.

The two women finished getting dressed, dried their hair, emptied their lockers, packed their bags, and made their way to the café. Neither bothered putting on any make-up. They settled in a corner where their seats overlooked the pool through a floor-to-ceiling glass panel. Things felt a bit calmer in the reflected aquamarine light. Lexi asked Elsie what she'd like from the counter and she opted for a protein shake and a glass of water. When Lexi ordered it something else peculiar happened. The server asked her the age of the person having the shake.

"I don't know," Lexi explained quietly, "But the lady I am with has been quite badly upset today. Her membership has been withdrawn unexpectedly. Can you bring the drinks over?" She said, waving her smartwatch over the pay portal on the counter and turning to go.

"I'm sorry," the server explained, "We're not allowed to serve older people with supplements any more. If she's had her membership withdrawn she'll be past the cut-off date."

"I'll have it then," Lexi said, planning to swap the drinks round when we got to the table. Who would know? The server started to look uncomfortable, "As I said, I'm really very sorry, but they'll take my job away if I'm caught supplying fitness supplements to someone who's been declared 'over age.'"

When Lexi told Elsie what had happened she took a deep breath, slumped a little in her chair, and a sipped from the glass of water she had placed on the table in front of her. "I'm finding this all very difficult," she said.

"A number of strange things have happened to me this week. It's all been since Monday when I turned 70." Elsie explained.

Lexi looked at Elsie's bright grey eyes, and although parts of her were losing muscle tone, she would have placed her at around 10 years younger than 70. "My son sent me a voucher to spend online to celebrate. The thing I love most is keeping fit. I have a set of weights at home. I use them every day – in fact I only really come here to use the pool. Anyway I thought I'd treat myself to a new kettle bell. I found the one I wanted. Silver glitter, eight kilos. When I tried to buy it the transaction was declined. At first I thought I'd typed in the voucher number wrong. But it wasn't that. I checked. It was buried in a variation to the terms and conditions that landed in my inbox to confirm that the money hadn't been taken. Once you're 70 you aren't allowed to buy strength training equipment any more. I had to spend it on something else instead."

Perhaps they were worried the old people might injure themselves by mistake, Lexi thought, and become a burden on the NHS. How could that be right? After Brexit the health and safety rules were supposed to loosen up, not get more stringent. That couldn't be it. She racked her brains to try to recall anything she might have seen about the restrictions Elsie was talking about. She could remember nothing from her Splutter feed, even though she subscribed to most of the major news streams, as well as a broad spectrum of political commentators. No echo chambers for Lexi. Surely she would have noticed something as peculiar as this?

Elsie still looked crestfallen. "I don't think anything has actually been announced. In fact I've searched very hard myself and can find no record of any specific rules relating to fitness equipment. Or protein shakes for that matter."

Lexi took out her phone, so did Elsie. For the next half hour they crawled the web looking for clues that might explain Elsie's treatment that week. Elsie was right. There were no announcements. Then, at the same time, both women landed on a motion that had been passed at the triumphant Yuthentic Party Conference the previous September. They had been celebrating their record wins in that year's General Election. It was only their second time at the ballot box, but it felt like they had been around for much longer than six years. Elsie read out the final bullet:

"It must be this – look: 'We will incentivise private sector partners to withdraw services which might prolong life, or improve quality of life for people over 70, regardless of their ability to pay'. What kind of birthday present is that?"

That seemed to ring true. The gym, the supplements, and the equipment for use at home – all of them had been denied to Elsie that week. Lexi had always been a bit cynical about politics, but even she was surprised they had come up with this.

"I'm so glad you're here," Elsie said suddenly, "I was beginning to doubt my own judgement. When you do that it's the beginning of the end. I'm not going mad, am I?"

"It doesn't look like it to me."

The women sat in silence, processing what they had just seen. After a couple of minutes Lexi said: "I don't know if we can do anything about this, but it seems all wrong. How do you feel about meeting up on Sunday for a walk? It's good cardio and we can have a bit more of a chat too. No one can stop us doing that, surely?"

Elsie looked up. She seemed slightly shaky, but she smiled and said yes, she would like to see Lexi then. They arranged to meet on Sunday morning in the park.

As they walked to their cars, Lexi noticed Elsie's number plate F1T 0AP. She didn't seem like someone who was going to give up that easily.

CHAPTER SIX

LEXI DIDN'T ALWAYS MANAGE TO get to the Summer Fayre in her local park, but this time she was going to take make a point of going, so she could take Bob along. He hadn't been before and she thought he'd enjoy it. The weather was just right, warm but a bit overcast, so they were comfortable walking about and faced little danger of sunburn.

Fun was due to begin at noon, but they didn't get there until gone one as they had been lazing around at home, doing weekend jobs like paying bills online and listening to the radio together. Lexi particularly liked the dog show, which was already in full swing when they found the makeshift grassy arena. None of the entrants had been particularly well trained or immaculately groomed, but they seemed to be enjoying themselves, as did their owners. There was a sign saying 'No drones within 100 meters of the dog show arena' after someone had inadvertently crashed one into a massive, soft-hearted Akita the previous year. Fortunately, the drone came out worse, as the machine had disturbed the dog's normally docile temperament, and ended up in a thousand pieces.

The common had been divided into several sections for the event, which was one of the highlights of the local calendar. Along the south side there were about 50 'table top sales', where residents displayed a hotchpotch of secondhand goods, trying to purge their houses of old clothes, pots and pans, jewellery and books that no longer fitted into their lives.

Next to that was a bunch of micro businesses selling crafts, greetings cards, things that were pretty and original, but you couldn't help wondering how their makers managed to scrape a living if this was their full time job. A lot of people were experimenting with creative business ideas. Conventional work was increasingly hard to come by, and a side-hack could bring in a bit more cash.

There was a communal stall which took donations of cakes from any local people who felt like baking something. It was nice to see that tradition was still going strong. One year she had contributed an iced sponge herself. The plan had been to simply dust a jam Victoria sandwich with icing sugar, but she had a disaster with her unpredictable oven which ended up burning the thing. So she'd scraped off the worst of the carbon and slathered it in cream cheese frosting. It looked fantastic from the outside, but she felt sorry for whoever ended up taking it home.

Lexi grabbed a cupcake and began to feel jumpy from the first bite, as the potent cocktail of sugar and butter generously piled on its top sped from her mouth towards her heart. Bob shook his head and refused all temptation until he finally broke at an impressive sausage stand called The Muncher from Munich. He proceeded to create an abstract impressionist work of art on his T-shirt with the detritus from a supersize hot dog loaded with fried onions, mustard and ketchup, before proclaiming the Munich Mega Munch to be the best he had ever tasted.

It was fun being here with Bob after all those years of wandering round the park in a solitary frame of mind. She hadn't been particularly unhappy when she was single, but she was definitely having more fun now. She passed Bob a tissue from her pocket to try to clean up his face, which he did with moderate success. The shirt would need dealing with later.

Circling around again, they came across a place where several local community groups had set up information booths and were giving out leaflets. Lexi had a chat with the people in the Women's' Equality Party tent, and saw her local Labour MP, Nicky Hartt, who was out and about as usual. She had liked her when she met her canvassing on her doorstep. Although Lexi was suspicious of politicians, she thought Nicky seemed like a nice enough person, and had made some speeches about issues that Lexi was interested in. A former teacher like her, she felt she had a good grasp of what life was like outside the Westminster bubble, and cared quite a lot about helping them.

Yuthentic's booth was blasting out aggressive-sounding rap music, surrounded by a group of about forty young people in exuberant mood. Not one of them was over 30, and most were still in their teens. When young people had started to get more political, supporting the #MeToo movement, getting angry about Brexit and then climate change, Lexi had thought it an admirable thing. She had encouraged the kids at school to get involved, and even persuaded the head not to exclude children who had bunked off to take part in protests. Ever practical, she had recruited a couple of former pupils to run an after-school club where the young activists could catch up on whatever they had missed. Yuthentic formed not long after, led by a loosely-convened assembly representing young people from a very broad set of backgrounds. Every class, race, gender and hair color (except grey) beamed out from the images of their meetings that saturated social media.

A positive new force was emerging, they said, one that would build social cohesion and help repair a nation worn down by austerity, and grown weary of division. By targeting constituencies with high student populations, and using sophisticated on- and off-line campaigning tactics, in the general election Yuthentic had managed to get enough seats in a fragmented parliament to be able to drive through their biggest idea, the Maturity Premium, which incentivised redistribution of wealth from the old to the young.

After her conversation with Elsie, Lexi found the Yuthies' presence chilling. It was made worse when she overheard a tall, pale man talking. He had thin dyed black hair, deathly pale green eyes, and wore a Slayer T-shirt. The guy was surrounded by a small group of earnest young activists who were nodding furiously in agreement with everything he said. "They haven't a clue what they're dealing with," he laughed loudly, "I'm telling you, it's really happening," before lowering his voice out of earshot.

There were T-shirts for sale. On the front was the old road sign that signalled 'no waiting', a blue circle surrounded by a red border and diagonal cross. The back bore the Yuthentic hashtag: #OurTime. Metal sigils, the cut-out circle with the diagonal cross, were set into rings, and available as earrings and pendants which dangled from cords woven through with red and blue.

"Another few years and we can join that lot," Bob said, pointing in the opposite direction, as they wandered past a gazebo emblazoned with the word 'Seniority' – and the strapline 'things can only get better – fighting for the over-50s'. He was walking past it, towards a booth promoting men's health. They were trying to get people to sign up for a fun run which was also designed to promote the benefits of testicular self-examination. A video was running in the back which Lexi wasn't sure she wanted to see.

"Why don't you go in with those blokes, and I'll have a look in here?" Lexi suggested, thinking it would be a good idea for Bob to get a few health tips but not wanting to be faced with the explicit content, or be persuaded to run a 5K dressed as a giant penis herself.

Bob wandered ahead and Lexi stayed by the Seniority stand. "Hello, have you heard about Seniority?" asked a trim man with a full head of white hair, uncannily straight teeth and rimless glasses. He was wearing an Element T-shirt, a pair of long shorts and Birkenstock sandals. He seemed friendly enough. No particular accent. She imagined he was retired from some kind of professional job, enjoying the liberating feeling of casual clothing when in the past he would have had to wear a formal shirt and jacket.

"I can't say I have heard of them. I'm not really in the target group." Lexi replied a little defensively, regretting her tone almost immediately, in case it sounded rude. "I'm only 40, but I do have a few friends who are a bit older." Thinking of Elsie. Maybe they would have something helpful for her new friend. "What do you do?"

"Quite a lot of things. We're always on the lookout for volunteers, and you don't have to be over 50 for that. This leaflet explains where we meet and the kind of activities we arrange."

Lexi scanned the sheet of paper he had handed her, thinking she would pass it on when she saw Elsie the next day. It was what just she'd expected to see, weekly meetings in cafes, an advertisement from a local charity shop, drop in advice sessions. The self-defence and Pilates classes looked quite good.

"Do you know anything about the new Yuthentic initiatives?" she asked quietly, as she continued to glance down the page, remembering what Elsie had told her. "I've heard there are some odd things going on. Not all good."

"My name's David," he said, holding out a hand to deliver a firm handshake. "Lexi," she replied.

Then he did something odd. He took his phone out of his pocket and, without saying anything, made a point of showing her that he was turning it off. He pointed at her phone which was sticking out of her jeans pocket and seemed to be suggesting she do the same. For a few moments they exchanged glances, David's eyebrows raised, nodding his head towards her phone, pointing. Lexi's brow was more quizzical, "Are you telling me to…?" David quickly put his finger to his lips, the universal command for silence.

Yes. He was telling her to turn her phone off. It was very strange. Lexi was curious to find out what was bothering David so much, and as he didn't seem at all dangerous, and Bob was only a few steps away, she nodded her head in return, and did as he asked.

"Can't be too careful. You never know when they're listening. Didn't mean to creep you out." David said. "So to answer your question, yes, a number of our members have been talking to us about it. We're very worried about some of the things that are going on."

Lexi said she was worried too, and told David about what had been happening to Elsie since she'd turned 70.

David looked far less shocked than she had expected. "What's happening to your friend, I'm afraid that's just the tip of the iceberg," he continued, "There are actually far worse things going on. But I can't talk about them here. Not here at the Fayre. If you really want to know more there's a group of us getting together on Monday night." He took the leaflet she had been reading from her hand, and circled with an old-fashioned fountain pen what was billed as a volunteers' session taking place at in a room at a local pub before handing it back. "If you're interested in hearing more, come there. When you arrive you'll need to say that you have come for a meeting with Mr Huxley."

"Can I bring someone with me?"

"Yes, you can. But only if you trust them and think they would be sympathetic. We're not playing at this."

As Lexi tried to take in what David was saying, Bob was suddenly next to her. "Is your phone working? I just tried to call you?" he said. "The video was pants – actually most of it was inside someone's pants." Any opportunity for a joke, and Bob was there.

She grabbed her device from her pocket and looked at it, "I must have turned it off by mistake," she said, before introducing him to David. The men shook hands. Lexi, knowing that Bob would have his phone on as he was on call that weekend, quickly changed the subject away from the sinister to the more mundane. She thanked David for the leaflet and said she would have a chat with her friend Elsie about whether they might pop along to one of Seniority's Pilates classes.

CHAPTER SEVEN

Lexi set out early to meet Elsie. Although it was Sunday morning, Bob was working. He had gone into school to supervise the installation of some cables. As the floor had to be taken up, it was a job that could only be done outside normal working hours.

They were building an immersive virtual reality room for the kids, and Bob had to run fibre under the floor to connect it to the central learning server. There was a growing body of evidence that the students' emotional responses to VR teaching embedded what they had learned far more quickly than two-dimensional or conventional lessons. It was a shortcut to building new neural pathways. At a couple of schools they had also had great success in using it for behaviour modification.

As Lexi followed the route she had taken to the park for years, she couldn't help wondering how long her job as a teacher would continue as it was now. It was so different to when she had started out, when the children were simply expected to focus on her, the whiteboard and their books. Maybe a film occasionally.

Now they spent hours in front of their individual

screens, their learning tailored precisely to move at the optimum pace for each child, their faces scanned to track their level of engagement. They chatted with each other by typing characters in the corners of their screens. The only sound in the classroom, for much of the time, was simply the soft clatter of the keyboards. When they finally broke away from their screens, stiff and blinking, Lexi would coax them back into the physical world, into talking to each other, laughing, sharing, telling each other stories in the old-fashioned way, so they wouldn't forget how to be human.

Lewisham Park was walking distance from her house. As she crossed the last road she realised she was half an hour early, so she decided to do a 15-minute circuit before looking for a seat in the café. It wasn't too warm for a summer's day. The grass was still green, and the trees were laden with leaves, casting little pools of shadow here and there on the path. Not many people were about, one or two determined runners passed her, making the most of the cool morning before it became too much of a struggle. A group of dog owners and walkers chatted at the top of the hill around which the park had been created. Their dogs sniffed each other enthusiastically and wandered around nearby displaying a good-humored, transient curiosity about anything they came across.

A couple of dads walked by with tiny babies strapped to their chests, looking down at their phones as their bodies provided the warmth and movement required to keep their children calm. Multitasking. She imagined two corresponding partners lying at home in bed, snatching a few extra precious minutes of sleep after a broken night, about to get up and put on a load of washing before getting dressed and starting to get Sunday lunch ready for when the others returned.

In the distance, at the bottom of the park, she could just about make out a group of people, mainly older women, dressed in brightly colored walking clothes, moving at fair pace up the hill towards her. They stood out against the lush green of the grass and trees. Each of them held poles in their hands and marched forward confidently. She had often seen this Nordic walking group out on their travels, moving gracefully at different paces and talking as they went along. Sometimes she came across them stretching before and after their session with their younger instructor, Lisa, who put them gently and persuasively through their paces. It occurred to her that they were probably on their way to the café too, so she hurried towards the low wooden structure, and went inside to make sure she got a table for her and Elsie before the rush.

She took off her sleeveless purple body-warmer, and zipped it onto the back of a chair to mark out her territory before bringing herself back an elderflower cordial. Settling into her favorite spot, surrounded on two sides by clear glass, Lexi flicked through various apps on her phone. There was a message from Elsie, it said, 'On my way'. She messaged back, 'What can I get you to drink?' 'Double espresso.' Hardcore, Lexi thought, go for it Elsie.

She was carrying the tiny cup of espresso back to the table when Elsie walked in. Perfect timing.

"Have you been here before?" Lexi asked. It was her local park but Elsie came from further away. "No, it's nice isn't it? I just parked at the bottom of the hill." She was wearing a fluorescent orange, Superdry hoodie which she slipped off revealing a matching navy T-shirt and trousers emblazoned with the same brand. Lexi was surprised to see someone of Elsie's age in clothing that was usually targeted at younger people.

"I love your outfit," Lexi said. "Thank you," said Elsie, "I'd never heard of them but it's quality stuff. I got it in TK Maxx. One of the advantages of being retired is that you can pop in when you know the deliveries have just come and pick up a bargain."

Lexi shifted slightly in her chair and took a sip of her cordial. She felt slightly embarrassed, as the last time they had met everything had been rather intense. Having met David the previous day, she had a lot to tell Elsie, but she was worried too. What was that thing David had done? It seemed totally paranoid to be turning off their phones, but she felt a compulsion to do it, and to tell Elsie to do the same.

At that moment a beep came from Elsie's jacket pocket. She pulled out her phone, "Sorry," she said. "Low battery. I'll turn it off for a bit."

Lexi couldn't believe her luck and hit her own off-switch after checking quickly for messages.

"I'm glad you did that," she began, and went on to tell Elsie about her meeting with David at the Fayre, including how he had asked her to turn her phone off when talking about some of the things that had happened to her friend. "I'd normally have someone who did that down as paranoid, but he seemed pretty clued-up. I'm starting to wonder whether he had a point."

"There's no 'starting to wonder' about it at all," Elsie observed. "Look what you just did." They stared down at the table top where there two dead phones sat side by side. They were off the grid. It felt weird. Lexi worried for a moment that Bob might need to get hold of her, but he would just have to wait.

"So I was wondering," Lexi said, "whether you would like to come to one of these Seniority meetings with me? I've been thinking about volunteering, and it would be good to find out if what's been happening to you is a one-off, or whether other people are being targeted in the same way."

"It's not a one-off, dear," Elsie said, her eyes no longer smiling, "It's happened to my friend Martha too. Her gym membership has gone, just like mine, except she's at a different branch. Exactly the same thing has happened to her. She's very angry."

At that moment the café door opened and in streamed the Nordic walkers in their colorful attire. One of them grabbed two tables and pushed them together, and started collecting chairs so they could all sit in the same place. The small room filled with their lively voices as they bundled their sticks together in a corner and lined up for their drinks. The Nordic walking group had been meeting in the park for years. It had been kick-started with NHS funding, back in the days when there was more of an emphasis on keeping people alive. Lexi recognised most of them from when she used to run regularly, and would meet them on their circuit, walking in the opposite direction to her. She didn't know any of them well, but they were slightly more than nodding acquaintances, giving each other gentle encouragement as they followed their respective regimes. More than once she had stopped to talk to Lisa, their friendly, encouraging, Nordic-looking instructor, who always had stories to tell about someone who had been able to reduce their blood pressure medication after joining the group, or whose depression seemed to be easing. She wasn't with them today, though.

"I'm furious," she heard a man in a yellow shell emblazoned with the Bolder logo say to a woman in a bright blue Patagonia jacket, "We've had this trip booked for ages. They can't cancel the insurance now."

"Well they have," Patagonia replied glumly. "It's alright for Pauline over there," she looked at a trim black woman in black Adidas leggings, with a bright pink top, her shoulder-length dreadlocks gathered into a pink fleece band, "She's only 65 so she can still get it. It used to be OK provided you didn't have any serious health conditions. Now it's a blanket ban for any activity holidays once you're 70 or over. I can't imagine I'll be going skiing again in this lifetime either."

Lexi and Elsie listened intently to the conversation which had now moved from the counter and was carrying on at the table next to them.

"Our club trip is the highlight of my year," yellow shell said. "Since my Keith passed away it's one of the few things I really look forward to, on top of our little Sunday outings. Now it looks like more than a few of us won't be able to go, unless we travel without health insurance. Since we left the EU there's no way we would get emergency medical treatment in Austria for free. I can't take the risk."

He looked round the group, "You, me… it's hard to tell who else is 70 or over here. They are all in pretty good shape. It's definitely going to be more than just the two of us though. Do you think people will mind if we ask, Sally?" The woman in the blue jacket said, "Well you can try, Bruce. If they don't want to say they don't have to."

By now the last couple of walkers were carrying coffee cups and plates laden with slices of cake over to the table. Bruce unzipped his jacket and leant forward. "Listen everyone. Can I have your attention for a minute? It's about the Easter Austria trip. Sally and I have just had our insurance withdrawn so I don't think we'll be able to go. Has it happened to anyone else?"

A tiny Vietnamese woman with jet black hair, wearing a red vest Bolder top and looking nowhere near 70, spoke up, "They mailed me this morning, I couldn't believe it." Bolder had cornered the market in high-end fitness wear for the perennial generation.

"Me too," said a tall, well-built man with a shaved head and striking white-framed spectacles which he was wiping with a paper napkin, and putting back on.

"Pauline, Clifford, Jo, Ayesha and Ajay, is yours OK?" The rest of the group nodded, "Sorry mate," Ajay said, pulling his face into an apologetic smile. Lexi guessed Ajay and Ayesha must be a couple as they were wearing matching his and hers running tops. "Do you think there's anything we can do to help?" At this point Lexi couldn't hold back any longer:

"Excuse me," she said, "I couldn't help overhearing. Were you saying some of you had your travel insurance withdrawn because of your age?"

"That's right," said Bruce. "Do you know anything about it?"

"My friend Elsie here has had some similar experiences," Lexi began. Elsie went on to explain what was happening at the gyms, and her failed attempt to buy a kettle bell. They all sat in silence taking in what had been said.

Lexi was unsure what to do. She was already planning to go to the Seniority meeting on Tuesday, but David had been very clear she should only bring along people she trusted. She had been planning to invite Elsie, but although many of the faces from the walking group were familiar to her, she didn't know if she could trust any of them. Then Bruce's phone rang. That reminded her she shouldn't be talking about Seniority to anyone in case someone caused them problems.

"That was Lisa," Bruce said, as he put the phone down on the table in front of him, looking oddly bewildered. Lisa was the one who had originally got them all into walking, with her classes on Saturday and Sunday mornings. "She was terribly upset. She said she's not allowed to walk in her professional capacity with anyone 70 or over any more, or they'll invalidate her insurance and take away her day job as a physiotherapist. She can't afford to lose her job with two kids to support. I wouldn't want her to anyway. All our names and ages are on her register. That's why she wasn't here today. She wants us to carry on without her. She thinks it's more important for us to stick together than to split the group."

"Poor Lisa," piped up a woman in a grey fleece. "I want to keep the group together. I've only got three more years before the danger zone. Why don't we see if we can cancel the Austria trip and go somewhere in the UK instead. I know the scenery won't be the same, but it's the company that counts as far as I'm concerned. I'm happy to take that on. And they can't stop us walking on our own either."

A flicker of relief spread across the faces of the walkers who had been in fear of losing their place in the group which they clearly loved. The younger ones all nodded in assent. It was unanimous.

"I was wondering," Elsie said, "whether you might have room for a couple more members?"

Once they had finished their hot drinks, and every crumb of cake had been picked from their plates, the walkers dispersed, picking up their sticks and saying that they would look forward to seeing Lexi and Elsie the following week. Lexi decided she would order two sets of walking poles in case Elsie ran into any difficulties. She could pretend one pair was for Bob if there was any suspicion. It was odd how having to think like that had so quickly become normal.

With their light jackets on, Lexi walked with Elsie back to her car. As their trainers padded along the tarmac path, she felt it was now safe to return to the subject of David and see if Elsie would like to join them at the Seniority meeting on Tuesday.

"Count me in," she said.

CHAPTER EIGHT

Lexi didn't much like The Barge. She didn't like pubs in general. Although she had spent a lot of time in them in her teenage years and twenties, they had lost their edge for her when she got into fitness. She had chosen to cut back on her drinking, preferring the feeling of moving fast, alone, with a clear head in the open air to pretty much anything else. Until she met Bob, that was.

She had picked up Elsie from her home by car half an hour before the meeting began, and they ended up arriving early. As their vehicle glided slowly along the streets the two women were quiet, thinking about the evening ahead, and wondering what the pair of them could be getting into. Lexi had told Bob she was visiting Elsie, which was half true. He wasn't home from work when she left. In any case she was worried that telling him about any of this might jeopardise his security clearance.

They walked into the big triangular shaped bar, Elsie easily pushing open the heavy double door which was set into the curved wall where the main road met Chestnut

Street. A smoky beer garden behind separated the pub from the betting shop. A human server, Ella, stood behind the dark wooden bar and looked at her watch. It was still early.

Ella had been working at The Barge since she had finished her first year's university assignments. It wasn't really the kind of pub she would admit to going to as a customer. More like an old fashioned local, kept afloat by the miracle of Megabooza's at a time when most other pubs had closed or turned into a wood fired pizza restaurant with craft beers, and a daytime trade in coffee, flourless chocolate cake and pushchairs.

People were in and out all day, largely because of the comprehensive food menu which allowed them to fill up from breakfast to dinner without having to pay artisan prices. Lunchtime and evening a stream of solitary men would arrive and sit alone at a small, sticky table, tucking into a full English, a mixed grill, or burger and chips.

A middle-aged woman, and someone Ella assumed to be her rather better dressed mother crossed the room, the younger one's eyes dancing over a table of students with badly-cut dry and faded multi-colored hair; a group of three men in their fifties – regulars, one black, one mixed race, one white – who seemed like they had known each other forever, propping up the bar with half-finished pints in front of them; and the dining area populated by groups and singletons, tables crowded with menus, sauces, food and drinks. Several tables needed to be cleared. Ella might get round to that in a bit.

As the women approached, Ella glanced up from the glass she was polishing half-heartedly. They ordered a fizzy mineral water for the younger one, and a large glass of New Zealand Pinot Noir for the older one. Go, grandma, Ella thought to herself as she filled the glass to the top line, you've got style.

"Can you tell me where the function room is here, please?" Lexi asked. "I'm meeting Mr Huxley." She blushed. Ella pointed her towards a dark wooden door with clear glass panels, behind which they could see a staircase leading upwards. "It isn't really a meeting room as such, but the old folks have taken the upstairs bar to-night for their get-together. Assuming you can all make it up there." Ella almost sounded spiteful the way she spat out 'old folks'.

Ignoring the edge to the barmaid's voice, Lexi and Elsie carried their drinks to the staircase and made their way up, moving very slowly so as not to spill a drop. At the top they found themselves in a chilly space that felt like it had been abandoned. A dark wooden bar, like a smaller version of the one downstairs, ran along one windowless wall, but there was no one serving behind it. Although it was still broad daylight outside, the room was gloomy. Putting the lights on made it feel darker.

David was there already, taking dark grey plastic chairs out of four stacks that had been left against a wall, and arranging them in a circle on a worn red and gold carpet, woven with a pattern of old-fashioned flourishes that mirrored the flock wallpaper. The place looked like it hadn't been touched for decades. It smelled of spilt beer and damp.

Just as when he had met Lexi at the Summer Fayre, David took his phone from his pocket and signalled that, like him, they should turn theirs off. Lexi had already given Elsie instructions, however, and they held out their dark screens instead for David to inspect. "You're getting the hang of this already," he said, holding out a hand to Elsie, "I'm David," he smiled, "I'm guessing you are a friend of Lexi's?"

"Yes, I'm Elsie, pleased to meet you." Lexi and Elsie started to help David putting out the chairs. "I think there'll be about 12 of us tonight," he said.

"Where do your members come from?" Elsie asked.

"Lots of places really," David said, "Bizarrely, I met a couple of them at my Italian class, others are people I know just from living round here for a long time, and who have an interest in what's going on with older people. The programme of events I gave to Lexi on Saturday is real. We do have Zumba and chair yoga and dementia awareness running in community centers, and we want to keep them going as long as we can, but it's getting difficult. We want people to be able to keep active even if they aren't interested in getting involved in the politics."

As there were now about 15 chairs in the circle, David suggested they stop and make themselves comfortable.

"Tonight we have a couple of guest speakers I think you'll find interesting."

Before he could give any more details, the door opened and the others started filing in, each going through the ritual of showing one other person in the room that their phone was turned off. Lexi worried for a moment that Bob might be trying to get hold of her to ask how she was getting on, but there was nothing she could do about that now. At some point she would have to explain, but there was no reason to worry him just yet. This lot could just turn out to be a load of cranks after all.

As the final few took their seats, Lexi looked around the room to test her hypothesis. Were they cranks or not? Hard to tell before anyone had said anything. She was surprised, as she looked around the room, that she recognised a few faces. Two of the Nordic walkers were there: Bruce, who had talked about the loss of his partner Keith, and been on the phone to their absent instructor, Lisa; and the Indian woman, Ayesha, although this evening she was not accompanied by her bloke in the matching top. Bruce and Ayesha sat next to each other and smiled in recognition at Lexi and Elsie.

The youngest man in the room, around 35 with short red hair, wore a priest's collar under a plain black suit. He had brought with him a very old woman who had clearly found it difficult to get up the stairs, even with the priest's patient assistance. She was short, heavy on her feet, and had grey hair in no particular style sticking out at various angles. Dressed in a shabby beige raincoat and worn navy shoes with Velcro closures, she walked with a frame, wheezed periodically, and perched on her hard chair looking uncomfortable, moving her hips awkwardly in the futile hope of finding a position that was bearable.

There were two others in their 70s, both in good shape for their age. Ruth was a white woman with jet black dyed hair, wearing a dull pink suit jacket and brooch that seemed like something from another era. Her hair had been teased and set into a solid retro style.

It might even be a wig, Lexi mused. The man with her, Jim, was a bit chubby, mixed race with a greying beard matching his slightly unkempt hair. He wore a checked shirt and corduroy trousers and seemed quite at home in the surroundings of the fading boozer. He wore a badge which said 'Lewisham pensioners go on forever'.

Two of the guests stood out from the others. Nicky and Henry looked in their early 40s. They arrived in quite formal work clothing, nothing like the leisure wear most of the audience was sporting. Lexi was sure she recognised the woman, but couldn't remember where from. David shook their hands in turn and directed them to sit next to him in the circle. By now everyone was in place.

David said; "One last check?" and everyone, including the smart man and woman, showed their dark screens. The old lady with the walking frame was struggling with her outsized keypad, so the priest gently helped her put the phone into the correct mode. Off.

"Good. Welcome everyone, especially people who are here for the first time. I am David and I am a local convenor for Seniority, as well as an activist in PACE, People Against Coercive Euthanasia.

"I am honored to have with us tonight two guest speakers. Our local MP, Nicky Hartt, and Henry Wright, chief legal counsel for PACE.

"The purpose of this meeting is to give Nicky and Henry details of some of the worrying incidents we have been observing in our local area. Nicky shares our concern that the Euthanasia Act is being implemented way beyond the spirit that was originally intended. She is planning to raise questions in Parliament, among other things. Henry is gathering evidence to mount a legal challenge to counter the many abuses we believe we are witnessing under the auspices of PACE.

"Henry has asked me to check whether you would all be happy to have the meeting recorded on his encrypted, off-net, legally privileged device. Your words will be automatically transcribed by the machine, held securely, and not attributed to any individual. It is simply to help us document things properly. Any objections?" There were none.

"Thank you everyone. Nicky, Henry, do you want to do a quick introduction?"

The MP was probably the youngest person in the room apart from the priest. She had a slim build with sleek blond hair cut to shoulder length, and tucked behind her ears. Lexi thought that Nicky had probably come there straight from the House of Commons, as she had arrived with a sturdy backpack which she assumed contained a laptop, important papers and a make-up bag to keep her striking fuchsia lipstick exactly where it needed to be. A metal canister of drinking water was in one of her outside pockets, and an umbrella in the other. She wore black trousers, a black top and a violet leather jacket. It was a good look. Smart and professional, but not intimidating. Just like when she had seen her at the Fayre.

Lexi took a strange satisfaction in seeing Nicky pull a piece of paper out of the backpack. She had handwritten notes. That one simple act meant a lot to a teacher who struggled every day to convince children that writing on paper with a pen was still a relevant skill. So even before she had spoken, Lexi was warming to her elected representative.

Nicky placed her feet parallel on the ground, her knees dropped slightly to one side, briefly glanced at the notes she clearly didn't need, and began to speak:

"I am becoming increasingly concerned that the measures Parliament passed to legalise euthanasia are being interpreted too liberally by the private sector firms with the contracts to manage the Endings services. While many of my constituents were in favor of allowing people in genuine pain and distress to proactively manage the end of their own lives, I am seeing evidence that individuals are being coerced into making terminal decisions. Today I would like to hear if you are aware of this happening to anyone you know. Henry? Would you like to say something?" She looked at the lawyer. He had a kindly manner which surprised Lexi. Tall and broad, with short curly dark hair, he had thick tortoiseshell-rimmed glasses which he placed on the top of his head when he was speaking:

"All I can really add to that is at PACE we are hearing the same thing. If you don't mind I'll refrain from giving any examples until I have heard from some of you. I wouldn't want to be accused of suggesting things. Cognitive bias and all that." He nodded and gave a half smile, almost apologetic, and added, "Would anyone like to begin?"

There was silence for a few moments while people collected their thoughts. Then Bruce spoke:

"Hello everyone. Let me begin by saying I'm not against the Euthanasia Act itself. My partner Keith and

I were married as soon as it became legal for two men to be wed, and we were together for many years. We had a fantastic life. Keith was everything to me. About five years ago he noticed he was getting muscle cramps, and losing some of his strength. After putting off doing anything about if for a few months, he decided he should see a doctor. They ran some tests and he was diagnosed with motor neurone disease. We managed fine for a number of years but Keith reached a point eventually when he didn't want to live any longer. Things were a bit different to how they are now, but we were able to arrange for him to die at home. I held his hand and our Labrador Scotty lay next to him on the bed as he passed away. It was a dignified ending at the time he chose for himself.

"I'm starting to be worried now, though, that things are racing ahead of what everyone intended for the best. I don't want to sound paranoid, but since I turned 70 two years ago I've felt under mounting pressure to follow Keith, even though I have no physical health problems at all myself and am trying to live a full and active life without him.

"From the day of my 70th birthday, odd things started happening. It's subtle, but I'm sure it's real. I love music but I've had to stop listening to the playlist that's automatically pulled together for me, because these really depressing songs keep coming on. I've never liked Leonard Cohen – why on earth do they think I'm going to start now? Same on YouTube. One minute I'm watching *Breakfast at Tiffany's* and then when it ends, they suggest I watch other stuff that always seems to feature someone my age feeling really lonely, or worse dying in pain. In fact, I can't watch anything at all without first being forced to sit through an ad for the disposal service. It's terrible."

"I'm sorry to say this," the woman with the fixed hairdo, the brooch and the remnants of a South London accent, piped in, "But what you just described – it's happening all over the place.

"I work for Seniority, running their outreach programmes around here, and I'm in touch with people all over the country who are helping to support older people, just like many of you in this room. We have had a massive increase in people over 70 reporting that they feel depressed and making early stage enquiries about disposal options. Even though the cut-off for state health and social support isn't until they're 85, folks younger and younger are spiralling down into despair. We hadn't made the connection with the internet, but we have heard about them getting lots of phone calls that encourage them to sign up to go. They won't leave them alone until they get the answer they want. Because a lot of old people are lonely, they enjoy the conversations to begin with, and feel positive and supported. Once these callers have established trust, though, they go for the jugular and pressure them into the end. I thought I'd seen everything, but this really is something else. It's diabolical."

Henry and Nicky were listening intently.

"Do you mind if I stand up?" said the old woman with the walking frame, whose name was Pat, "I can't stay still for very long without seizing up." No one objected of course, and as she pulled her weight out of the chair, she shifted forward, supporting her body between her legs and forearms. She addressed them, with a slight Irish lilt, as if from behind a pulpit. “I came here today with Father Aloysius, who sorts out a lot of help for us old folks. The church even tries to support the ones who are over 85, the ones who have nothing coming in from the government at all, and I am very grateful for what they do for us. Neither Father Al, nor myself, believes euthanasia is right in any circumstances. Frankly we are appalled at the inhumanity of what our government has agreed to. Sorry to this gentleman here,” she nodded in the direction of Bruce, “but we're all entitled to our opinion. I personally believe the church's teaching that all life is sacred, and view what you did to Keith as,” she stopped just short of using the word murder, and instead said, “a mortal sin.”

At that point you could have heard a pin drop. The majority of people in the audience bristled with disapproval at what Pat had said. Surely that was something between Keith and Bruce and not for discussion here? At that point, Father Al thought he should say something to sweeten the bitter pill Pat had just delivered, “That said, forgiveness is always possible,” he added softly.

“I don't need to be patronised by you,” Bruce snapped back at him. “Your institution hardly has the best track record on human rights.”

David intervened. “Can we try to keep it factual for now please? This is an incredibly difficult topic and we need to keep this meeting to the subject of gathering evidence.”

“Right,” Pat continued, not in the slightest bit perturbed by the exchange she had provoked. “A lot of our folks, in the congregation at Our Lady of Lourdes, are older than 85. They have very little to their name, but they shouldn't be forced to die. It's not right." Pat's voice was breaking slightly, but she pulled herself back together. "I can't accept it. I'm 84 now. I can only cope because I get medication that makes my arthritis bearable and controls my asthma. They've told me that on my next birthday my prescriptions will stop, and the medicine I need won't be available any more. I know for certain I will be in terrible pain, and in grave danger of dying through suffocation. I don't think it's right for the government to use my illness to blackmail me into taking the one-way bus. Into committing what, in the eyes of God, is a mortal sin. I want to keep going. I want to live every minute I possibly can with my grandchildren." Bruce rolled his eyes but said nothing.

"I'm going to sit down again now. Bear with me if I'm fidgeting a bit." She was gasping a little for breath. Father Al put his hand on her arm and it seemed to help her calm down and get her breathing back into a more regular rhythm.

There was an awkward silence in the room. It was obvious people held a range of strong opinions that were unlikely to be reconciled in the next half hour, if ever. However, David was an empathetic and gracious chairperson. The years he had spent as a civil servant before his retirement, leading negotiations with various disagreeing and disagreeable factions around the world as a career diplomat, stood him in good stead for corralling the people of Lewisham. He took the tension out of the situation by turning to both Bruce and Pat, and thanking them for their contributions before inviting others to add their thoughts. It's now or never, Lexi said to herself, but before she could say anything, Elsie piped up.

"I'm younger than some of the others," she began, proudly, "as I am sure you can tell, and better off financially than most people I know." As if to emphasise the point, she was wearing fluorescent designer sportswear again with matching trainers that looked like they had never been near a muddy park. "I'm not showing off, it's just how it is. Thanks to my father and his business interests, I had inherited money invested in a substantial property portfolio. It lost a bit when the prices dropped, but I was still left pretty comfortable. Up until the day I turned 70 about a week ago I didn't have a care in the world. I would never have come to a meeting like this. No interest at all in politics. I've never bothered to vote. Spent all my time enjoying myself. I'd been going on three cruises a year, love keeping fit, and hanging out with my friends and my son Gary. Nice wine. It's my money, so why not?

"Anyway I've had a big shock. It seems like I'm suddenly being prevented from doing things I like." She went on to explain what had happened on the day she met Lexi, and that since then she had tried to book her next cruise but had been blocked because she could not get travel insurance at any price.

"Bastards," Bruce muttered, "That's just what they're doing to me. Wait until the psychological warfare really starts."

Elsie looked at Bruce, "I have to say, I'm already starting to feel a bit glum."

At that point Ayesha spoke up encouragingly: "Well, we're not going to let it get to us. It's easy for me to say because I'm only 69, and haven't felt the full force of it yet. We're here to help you fight back."

"I agree," Father Al added.

"Lewisham pensioners are right behind this too," Jim said, "We have to organise."

Lexi finally found a gap in the discussion and made her points: "What I find extraordinary," she said, "is how invisible so much of this is to those of us who are under 70. Nothing about accelerating the euthanasia programme has shown up in my news. There are no details published on any government site explaining how quickly these policies are being rolled out. I've looked for tender documents online but most of the details are redacted. I strongly suspect there will be targets, but nothing like that has been reported in Hansard. The corporation only has the blandest of statements on their website." She turned to Nicky, the MP, and asked, "Am I right? Have I missed something? Do you have any more information than us?"

Nicky bit her lip for a couple of seconds before she replied. "At the moment, all I have are reports from a few constituents that this kind of thing is happening. But what they have told me has been frighteningly consistent with what has been said in this room. The numbers are quite small, unfortunately – or fortunately, depending on your point of view.

"Before I do anything official, I'd like to see if we

can get some more evidence to bolster our arguments. Otherwise the Ministry of Justice will say that these are one-off cases and brush us aside. Do any of you remember the 'hostile environment', when the Home Office deliberately mishandled immigration cases on an industrial scale? They kept on doing it for years until the media, and MPs from all across the political divides, collectively shamed them. Even then, when they were bang to rights, it took years to sort it out. We need evidence, and lots of it, to bring about change.

"The other thing I can do is use my position to help individuals who have been unfairly pressured by the system into making a decision they later regret. I can give you a real life example. Last week I was able to release someone from their terminally binding disposal contract by sending a personal letter to Mason, the Chief Executive of the corporation. Henry and I have been doing some work together on that. If I can do more in the meantime to help even a few people get their lives back, assuming that's what they want, it will be worth the effort. So if you come across anyone who needs help, let me know right away."

Everyone nodded in agreement. There was certainly a consensus that something must be done, and a lot of goodwill to help do it. David came to each person in turn asking for feedback before he closed the meeting.

The Catholics were going to do some more fact finding from within their congregation, mobilising the Knights of Saint Columba and the Legion of Mary who were already giving practical help to the over-85s.

Ruth and Jim, activists in the organisations for elderly people, said they would gather information from their network, and raise the issue immediately with their national counterparts who were involved in policy and lobbying.

Elsie, Bruce and Pat all said they would do their best to keep a record of their personal journeys and note anything, even if it only seemed slightly significant, that might be putting them under undue pressure to sign up to go.

Ayesha asked if it might be helpful if she got a statement from Lisa, the Nordic Walking Instructor, about how she had been asked to drop the 70-plus members from the group. Yes, it would, Henry concurred, asking if Lexi might also be able to do some digging at the gym around their over-70s discrimination.

When it was Henry's turn, the lawyer had something to say which made Lexi recall the feeling of trepidation she and Elsie had shared in the car earlier that evening.

"I don't want to worry anyone unnecessarily," he began, "but we are going to come up against some very powerful vested interests here, with a huge amount of money at stake. Some of the people involved in providing the disposal services may not want the likes of us to expose that they are running a coercive campaign which is far beyond the original intent of the Euthanasia Act. What you have all said tonight has reinforced my view that is exactly what is happening here.

"I see you are already turning off any devices which may be used for listening when you gather together, which is an excellent start. Can I also respectfully suggest that you do not have any conversations about these meetings within range of any connected devices in your home which may have a listening function, and that you leave your phones at home next time you get together so your collective locations cannot be traced. Oh, and don't create any online trails – emails, too many searches, that kind of thing." He reached in his bag and pulled out a handful of small laminated cards. "Please take one of these if you want them. They are tips to help you avoid being spied on without your consent, including how to use untraceable browsing for research. You might find they come in useful."

This was serious stuff, Lexi thought to herself, tucking the card, which had been produced by an organisation called the Electronic Frontier Foundation, into her jeans pocket. David suggested they regroup in two weeks' time, and they all memorised the location.

Slowly people started drifting away. Al and Pat said they would go last, as it was going to take Pat a very long time to get down the stairs. Lexi thought they should try to catch David before they left, and waited until he had finished saying a few final words to Nicky and Henry.

"What did you think of this evening?" David asked Lexi and Elsie, "Would you come again?"

"I'm quite interested in your fitness activities," Elsie chimed in first, "Especially now some of the other avenues appear to be closing. I'll try to keep a track of things, but I can't make any promises. I am very busy." Lexi was starting to feel disappointed in Elsie. She seemed mainly interested in continuing her own leisure programme, and not bothered about anyone else.

Although she had 30 years to go before the disposal

programme would be targeted at her, Lexi knew that she wanted to stay involved with PACE. She thought about how much she missed her own parents. They had died in a car crash when she was 25. So many things she wished she could have shared with them. Even though it was so long ago, she still remembered them every day, wishing they had been around to meet Bob and to enjoy more of their lives which had come to such an abrupt close.

David didn't seem disappointed in Elsie at all. "Seniority is here for you as long as we can keep running our activities legally – and we're working with Henry and Nicky to make sure we can do that. Just come along when you want to."

"Um…" Lexi was trying to find the words, "I know I said I'd have a chat with the gym about their ageist policies, but I'm not sure I'll get much more out of them than I already have. Is there anything else I can do?"

"What do you do for living Lexi?" David asked, "Maybe there's something there?"

"I'm a teacher."

"I'll tell you what," David said, as if something had clicked into place as he was talking to her, "PACE are having an activists' seminar in a few weeks. If you want to get more involved that would be the place to find out more. It's on a Sunday so it shouldn't interfere with your work commitments. Do you know Toynbee Hall in the city?"

Lexi hadn't been there before but was sure she could find her way.

"Don't forget, Lexi, leave your phone at home."

On that slightly chilling note, Lexi and Elsie headed

downstairs to the main part of the pub. As they reached the glass door in the stairwell Lexi glanced across the dining area and was surprised to see Bob tucking into a steak, alone, reading his tablet, his back facing where she and Elsie were standing. She looked at his tufty hair and fleece and wanted to rush across and hug him, but given everything Henry had said it didn't feel safe. The last thing she wanted was to do was implicate him in all of this. Whatever this was. Especially now the corporation seemed to be involved.

"God, no," Lexi said aloud, touching Elsie on the arm to hold her back from entering the room. "That's Bob there." She jammed herself against the wall as the side of the door so that no-one in the pub would be able to see her. "Do you think we can make it out without him seeing us? He's the one reading in the olive green fleece."

"Of course we can dear. He's totally zoned out," Elsie said dismissively. "Anyway if he does see us you can tell him I asked you to bring me here. Unlikely though that might be." She looked around the grubby décor distastefully. Lexi couldn't wait to be shot of her.

"Right then, let's get you home," Lexi said. "He does seem to be deep in thought. Let's walk straight past him and out of the door." Which was what they did.

CHAPTER NINE

On the day of the PACE activists' seminar, Lexi woke early. That often happened in the summer as the curtains in her bedroom didn't block out the light properly. She had toyed with the idea of getting one of the sleep-sure blackout kits, but there was something she liked about her routine varying with the seasons. On other summer days she would sometimes pop out for an early run before it got too hot.

Bob lay next to her, his breathing so utterly reassuring. They had only been together for a year, but she could not contemplate a life without him. Even his snoring was bearable most of the time. She could always give him a nudge to change his position if it was thundering in her ear. This morning, though, he was quiet, which made it all the more difficult to leave him behind.

She felt terrible about having to lie to Bob again. But this would be the last time, she promised herself. Once she got her head round what was going on with PACE she would make a decision. She would tell Bob, and if he thought it was too dangerous for her to be involved she could walk away from her newfound role as a subversive.

She felt like she had been waiting decades to find him, and the last fifteen years, since her parents had gone, had been desperately lonely at times. Losing him now would be too much to bear.

Lexi slipped out of bed trying not to wake him. He still seemed out of it. After a quick shower she pulled on the clothes she had left on the landing to avoid waking Bob up, and picked up her bag. She left her phone charging on the bedside table as if she had forgotten it, so he could see she didn't have it with her. After one last peep round the bedroom door, she was on her way.

Annoyingly the trains were not running due to maintenance works on the line, as was often the case on a Sunday. Lexi headed straight for the bus stop which happened to be right by The Barge. It reminded her of the last meeting they'd had, Henry's unsettling surveillance warnings, and tiptoeing past Bob so he wouldn't see her.

The memory made her mood sink a little. She was on her way, changing from the 172 to the 42 on the Old Kent Road. Even though the buses were now driverless, they had kept their old red livery and numbers in an attempt to maintain the passengers' affection. It would take her about an hour. With no phone screen to toy with, or music to listen to, the time passed slowly and she dozed a little. She'd had nothing to eat before leaving, but managed to find a disintegrating cereal bar at the bottom of the backpack which she tipped into her mouth and washed down with water from her metal canister on the final leg of the bus journey. By the time she arrived the angst in her stomach had developed into mild nausea. The cereal bar hadn't helped.

Leaving the bus, Lexi walked through the Aldgate one way system following a route she had memorised before leaving home. How different this area was on a Sunday morning compared to a weekday. No commuters, no city types pushing you out of the way with their aura of greed and eyes fixated down on their screens. It was quite empty. Fresh Yuthentic fly posters were plastered among other promotions on informal hoardings. Her eyes darted between billboards enticing young people to clubs and festivals around the city, punctuated by menacing repeats of the blue and red 'no waiting' circle under the #OurTime hashtag.

As she got closer to Whitechapel, she noticed groups of tourists. They were on their way to Petticoat Lane market, once a thriving hub of the informal economy, where you could pick up a dinner service for a song, and watch the traders compete with cheery cockney banter. Now it just sold what every other street market in the world had on show. The same scarves and cardigans, all made at some generic plant in China. There was nothing original anywhere any more.

Approaching Toynbee Hall, Lexi felt her heart beat a little faster. She was becoming increasingly anxious.

The building was set back from the main road. It looked like a tiny, delicate piece of history, surrounded by something much uglier that was threatening to gobble it up. The red brick structure was pure Victorian Gothic, with big windows, its triangular roofs dominated by impressive chimney stacks.

Never having heard of the place before, she had looked up Toynbee Hall and learned that it had been set up in the 19th century as a hub of social reform. By some miracle the place had survived to the present day. This was partly because its listed building status had shielded it from the ravages of property development that wiped out most of the city's charm, replacing the quirky, unique, and most importantly, uneconomic places with uniform, disposable towers of steel and glass.

Toynbee Hall continued to attract community stalwarts who ran outreach programmes for many groups, including the older people who were being marginalised practically everywhere else. Even though she was nervous about going in, Lexi liked the sound of the place. It appealed to her sense of history, and what she had come to think of as her own, unfashionable idea of what humanity should be about.

Lexi's name was duly ticked off at the registration desk, and on her way to the meeting room she passed a poster advertising a helpline for women suffering domestic violence. "We're still putting up with that crap?" She thought to herself, "How many more decades?" She felt a glimmer of gratitude for Bob's kindly demeanour, before her memory of him was tainted once again by a wave of guilt at having lied about where she would be today.

The seats were filling up fast. A mixture of regional accents mingled in the hubbub that bounced off the wooden panels and leaded windows. People had come from all over. There was a free seat in a middle row. The audience was hushed to silence so the proceedings could start. She turned to look over her shoulder and saw people crowding in behind her. Standing room only.

It was then that she noticed David, the PACE activist, sitting at the front with Nicky, Henry and some other people she didn't recognise. David stood up and made his way to a lectern facing the audience. He must be more important than she had thought.

With an easy and open style, David welcomed everyone and made a point of thanking those who had travelled a long way to be there, as well as some who had put the visitors up in their homes. He listed the outfits that were represented – charities that helped old people, civil liberties groups, religious organisations, activists from across the political spectrum, even members of Yuthentic who Lexi blamed for getting everyone into this terrible mess in the first place. Why on earth were they here?

The morning would be spent looking at what had been happening around the country. That session would be led by Nicky and Henry with regional organisers being called up to share their testimonies. They also had some research to present, which a concerned market intelligence company had done for PACE free of charge.

After lunch they would go into action planning sessions organised around various work streams. Lexi liked the sound of what David called the 'intervention workshop'. He explained that this would be looking for ways to disrupt the coercive campaigns with direct action.

Immediately before lunch a smart young woman called Debbie presented some statistics. Lexi remembered what Ruth had said that night at The Barge, about the sharp increase in numbers of people aged 70 and above feeling like they wanted to give up; and Bruce's anecdotal report that he was having to fight drifting into despair.

The researchers had contacted a large group of people who were being subjected to the Endings recruitment campaign. They had found that it was shockingly effective. The agency that had produced the advertisements, Brytely, had even entered for an award, demonstrating in their submission that they had created thousands of incremental Enders by targeting them very precisely at the moments when they were most vulnerable. One of the judges on the awards panel had secretly passed the submission to PACE, worried that the end of life services were being sold in a way that might be bordering on the unethical.

So this is what they were up against. A cold-hearted campaign that was persuading some of the most vulnerable people in the country to sign their life away. The fightback starts here, Lexi muttered to herself, as the morning session came to an end. She had to find a way to do something about it. First, though, she needed a sandwich.

CHAPTER TEN

LEXI RETURNED FOR THE AFTERNOON session feeling a bit weary. She'd retraced her steps towards Whitechapel and found a chain sandwich shop. Somewhat drained by the morning's excitement, Lexi vacillated between the various options on offer before choosing a tuna mayo sandwich and a packet of cheese and onion crisps. She took a high stool facing the window and tore open the packet of crisps, fishing out some of the larger ones and sliding them inside the creamy sandwich. This was one of her favorite things. Crisps were a guilty pleasure she didn't allow herself very often. She crunched gleefully into the sandwich, slowly, making it last.

After finishing the can of fizzy elderflower she bought to go with it, Lexi was still thirsty and asked one of the bots behind the counter if it could refill her water bottle. It stood blinking at her for 30 seconds that seemed like an eternity. Then a frazzled looking human server came out from the kitchen to help. They would not provide water free of charge to take away, but she could buy a refill provided her receptacle was not made of plastic.

She handed over her canister. It met the requirements. That should see her through the afternoon.

The intervention workshop was being held in the library back at Toynbee Hall. Straight away she noticed Nicky Hartt at the front with two panellists. "I'm glad it's her," Lexi thought to herself. There were about twenty activists in the room, which felt quite cramped. You could tell the library's usual layout had been disrupted. The desks had been cleared and rows of chairs set up theater-style to cram as many people as possible into the space.

Nothing could have prepared Lexi for what she was about to hear.

First, Nicky introduced a young woman called Lucy. She was in her late 20s, trim, well turned out, wearing smart jeans and a navy bomber jacket, with subtle make-up and eyebrows bang on trend. Her long blond hair looked sleek and fell in a long ponytail two-thirds of the way to her tight waist.

"First of all I want to say a big thank you to Nicky for helping me get out of a terrible situation," she began with an accent that sounded like she came from somewhere in Kent.

"Back in February I started a new job with the corporation. I'd already been with them for about three years in one of their equipment hire centers, and – as has happened to lots of people like me – they decided to replace my job with a robot. The machines just check themselves in and out now. I was very worried about money like anyone would be in that situation. So it was a big relief when, instead of laying me off, they offered me the chance to work as a steward on one of their driverless buses. They called it being an Angel which sounded quite classy. I thought it might be like an old fashioned air hostess. So I signed a contract agreeing to work for them for a full year, three days a week, on a very good rate of pay actually, with holiday and pension paid into. Sounds good doesn't it?

"It was only when I started to do the training that I found out what the buses were for. They have these buses you see…"

Lucy's voice faltered. She stopped, breathing rapidly for a moment. Lexi could see she was quietly struggling to hold back tears.

"It's OK Lucy, take your time," Nicky said, touching Lucy on the arm.

"I'm OK, just a minute." She looked down, and took a few seconds in silence. After inhaling deeply a couple of times, she regained control and began again.

"They have these buses, you see, that they use for taking people to the disposal centers, the DCs they call them. I don't know how else I expected them to get there, but I'd never thought about it before. I certainly never thought I'd be taking them. Still, the money was good and they gave us quite a bit of training. The buses and the bots do most of the work without needing much human intervention. It sounds terrible, I know, but it's a slick process. I thought I could I handle it. They told me all the passengers were there voluntarily, that they had mental tests before they were allowed to sign up, there was a cooling-off period when they could pull out, and their families were never involved so they couldn't be pressurised by grasping relatives or anything like that. So it all sounded legit and fair enough. It was a peculiar way to make a living, but I was coping with it OK at first.

"Anyway, one day in April I got my list of passengers and I recognised one of the names. It was my Auntie Jean. Well she's not a real Auntie, or they would have filtered her into a different bus. They map your relatives when you start, to try to stop people's privacy being compromised. But I hadn't given them her name to be flagged at the beginning. She's never been on social media, so there were no obvious links. I just hadn't thought of it.

"So I phoned in right away and asked if they could put her on a different bus or change my shift. They wouldn't do it. The processes were new then, and they hadn't thought everything through. I told them I simply couldn't take her, but the staff bot couldn't understand what I was saying. It just wouldn't listen. We only got the list on the morning of the disposal for security reasons, and there was no time to change it. I felt there was no choice. I had to go in.

"We pulled up in front of her house. It was terrible. I'd played in the garden there as a child. The ceramic tortoise I loved was still there, nestled in the grass. I can't begin to tell you how dreadful I felt. The bot went to her door to collect her. She came out in her wheelchair – she has MS you see – and it lifted her up, pushed the chair inside, and closed the door.

"I tried to stay at the opposite end of the bus to her so she wouldn't see me. But when we were unloading at the disposal center I had to get off for a face scan at the arrival point.

"That was when she saw me out of the bus window. I know she saw me, even though she was sedated by then, because as she was unloaded by the bot – which is an undignified process at the best of times – she was crying, and said in a voice that was only just audible, 'I'm so sorry you had to see me like this, Lucy'.

"The bus was unloaded and they all went in for the final stage, and I got back on, to work my second shift. I kept going, just about, but I was extremely distressed. When I got home I called work again and they put me on to a counselling bot, and promised a course of therapy to help me through. But the next day I just couldn't go in. And the day after that.

"When I'd been off sick for a week they sent me a letter saying I was in breach of contract and would have to pay the costs they had incurred covering my shift and ongoing to the end of my contract period. It had 10 months to run. I don't have any money. It would have been thousands. I've no savings, nothing to sell, I live at home. I'm still sharing a room with two of my sisters.

"Anyway my Mum suggested we go and see Nicky about it. She'd helped her with something before. Nicky wrote to the corporation and they let me go immediately with no fees. It was like a miracle. I'm so relieved to be out of it. I don't want compensation. I'm out of work now but I would do anything rather than face that job ever again."

Nicky explained that she had asked Lucy to come along so that the direct action group would understand exactly what they might be dealing with. An insider view of how the disposals were physically managed. Lucy offered to explain more of the details, but people were beginning to get upset, so she stopped.

Next up was Liz. Her story had a happier ending.

"I mentioned earlier today that we had pulled off our first successful intervention," Nicky began. "By that, I mean we got an Endings contract annulled after the cooling-off period had finished. Those of you who are outside the 70-plus target group for the Endings service will have no way of knowing the draconian terms the customers have to agree to when they sign up. Essentially, once the cooling-off period is over, they are at the point of no return. The corporation pretty much hunts them down. I've asked Liz to tell us her story. Why she changed her mind, and what I did to keep her alive."

"I'll do my best," said Liz, peering through silver octagonal spectacles that made her eyes look unnaturally large. Soft grey hair curled tightly around her head. She wore pale blue casual trousers, a flowered blouse, and flat grey lace-ups.

"I decided to book an Ending, for what now seems like a very stupid reason. It was after a big argument with my husband Carl. Some time ago, I found out that he had been having an affair with Rachel, at the bowling club. I was very hurt. He swore he had broken it off, but I discovered they were still at it. He was lying to me.

"So I had this mad idea that if I threatened to kill myself it would make him leave her once and for all. I thought, why not arrange a disposal, and let him find out about it?

"I filled in all the forms and made my application. It's quite detailed, but they keep you going, even when you get upset. I booked the Rockstar Ending service which sounded very posh. Fun even. It's true. Once I'd done it, though, I broke all the rules and printed off the confirmation. You're not supposed to tell anyone, you see. But I took a screen shot and made a hard copy as soon as I'd finished the booking. I left it lying around in the hope that Carl would plead with me not to go through with it. But he didn't say anything. When I finally confronted him, he told me the affair was all my fault for not being glamourous anymore, and I should go and get it over with. He actually wanted me to die. The world would be a better place, he said, without a frump like me."

A man's voice murmured, "Bastard."

"I was so angry and upset that I lost all track of time. When I finally remembered I needed to cancel the trip, it was too late. I called the corporation, even got through to a real person at one stage, but they wouldn't budge. Even when I said they could keep the money, they just kept repeating that I had missed the cooling-off period and did not have the option to cancel. I was at my wits' end. It was like I had accidentally locked myself out of life, and there was no way I was ever going to be allowed back in, no matter how much fuss I made.

"As if things couldn't get any worse, by now Carl seemed happier than he'd been for years. He was on the phone to Rachel all the time. It was blatant. He was planning to move her in as soon as I was gone.

"Then the appointment came through with all the instructions for my pick-up. They even sent incontinence pants. By now I was terrified. I had about a week to tie up all the loose ends. It was the biggest wake-up call of my life. I thought, 'What on earth have I done? I don't want to die. I must do something.'

"Then I remembered Citizens Advice had helped me with something a few years ago. One of their advisers put me in touch with Nicky right away. I emailed her my screenshot, and somehow she persuaded the corporation to let me off the hook. They even refunded my payment.

"When she told me I had been reprieved, I could hardly believe it. What an enormous relief! The fear still haunts me, even now. I wake up most nights, thinking I have heard the Angel at the door, come to collect me. But I'm one of the lucky ones. I may have been a complete fool, but do you know what? I'm going to move on from Carl, and live a new life. He's become a right misery now he's realised he won't be getting everything he'd hoped for."

Nicky then explained that, although she had managed to get Liz out of the disposal queue, the correspondence with the CEO had been tricky. The corporation had penalties in their contract which made cancellations problematic, so she had been told in no uncertain terms that Liz's case would be treated very much as a one-off.

"This is terrible," said one of the other activists, Billy, a tall woman in her 30s with a retro 80s look, dyed black hair and nail varnish, and platform boots. "I am certain this wasn't what Yuthentic meant to happen. Those greedy private sector firms are going way beyond the letter of the law."

"We don't really know where the pressure is coming

from. It could be from a number of places," said Nicky. "My question to this group is – how can you help between now, and me being able to get some Parliamentary time to expose what's happening? It's July. We're about to go into recess. With the best will in the world it will be October at the earliest before I can do so much as ask a question in the House, and I expect it to be into the New Year before we can hope for any of this to be taken seriously. By then, who knows how many batches they'll have processed?

"I've asked the Minister how many disposals the corporation are being asked to deliver every month, but I haven't had a reply yet. My guess, from talking to Lucy about her work schedule, is that there are already hundreds of people a week being shipped to the prototype DC, in London alone. I have concerns about the whole system, but my immediate priority must be to help the people like Liz who change their minds, but aren't allowed to carry on living."

Shaking her head slowly, Lucy spoke up. "I have to say Nicky, I didn't see many who looked like they wanted to cancel by the time they were on the bus. Most were convinced they were doing the right thing. Admittedly, they're sedated before they board. Auntie Jean was more embarrassed than anything else. I'm sure she wanted to die."

Lexi's mind was racing. "Maybe. But if someone did want to pull out we could help them, couldn't we? If we got to them early enough, in the window between the end of the cooling-off period and collection, an intervention with the help of an MP could work. We can get information out through some of the voluntary networks for the elderly or terminally ill." Ruth, Jim and Father Al all had links. "Another option might be to set up safe houses where people can hide if they have changed their mind."

"Do we know what happens inside the disposal centers?" Billy asked, "If people are already on the bus can we get them off? Lucy – what would have happened if you had tried to snatch back your Auntie Jean?"

"I don't know," Lucy said. "The bots are semi-autonomous. I had an emergency override key but that will only freeze them. That was the only control I had. They don't let the Angels inside the DCs. We just got the customers to the transition area. It was more like a loading bay really. The machines take over from there."

Nicky had been trying to find out what went on inside and had come up against a brick wall. The process was shrouded in secrecy. Everyone involved in awarding the government contract had been very odd about it. "They took a few members of the Yuthentic leadership to see the facility when it was first built, but they clam up when you ask them any questions. It's peculiar because I normally get on OK with them. The civil servants are the same. All I can think is that they're worried about adverse publicity if people get to see exactly how they have industrialised death."

A wave of deep discomfort enveloped the room. There was a stunned silence for what was probably only a few seconds, but it felt like an eternity, as people's imaginations went into overdrive. The Voluntary Euthanasia Act was being enacted with a rocket-fuelled twist.

Ruth, who Lexi had not noticed until that point, spoke quietly from the back of the room. "I am reminded him of what happened to my great-grandparents in Germany back in the 20th Century. That was also as the result of a democratic decision."

"This is very different. We're not Nazis," said a young woman in her 20s with shoulder length mousy hair, in jeans and a Chavez T-shirt, who Lexi noticed was wearing a flashing Yuthentic badge, the hashtag #OurTime in red and blue letters. "This was only ever supposed to be voluntary. The clue's in the name of the legislation. Most people are in favor of voluntary euthanasia being available. No one is forced. Families are kept out of it explicitly so they can't pressurise the Enders. It's a free choice."

"Really? If you take away people's access to health care and financial support, what else do you expect them to choose?" Lexi said out loud, to her own surprise, thinking about what Pat had said that night in The Barge.

"It's better than misleading people like we used to. Everyone knew the services for old people were falling to pieces but we all turned a blind eye and pretended it wasn't happening. What we had was a cruel postcode lottery that favored a privileged elite. Random doctors and nurses and social workers made disconnected decisions that accidentally determined who should or shouldn't live. This way is much fairer for everyone," the Yuthentic woman replied with one hundred percent conviction.

Lexi managed to keep the lid on her rising anger by counting slowly to ten. That smug little Yuthie could take the wind out of the resistance if someone didn't shut her up.

"I'm not sure everyone would agree with that last point, but we're pretty much out of time," Nicky said, expertly nudging the mood in the room into a slightly better place. "Thanks to everyone for their contributions, especially Liz and Lucy. They have both been very brave sharing their experiences with us. If anyone is interested in doing something more, can I ask you to contact me directly. We'll arrange another session to decide on our plan of action."

Lexi made eye contact with Nicky and nodded, as if to say 'count me in'. She wondered who else from this group might want to stay involved. Please, not that awful Yuthentic woman. One thing she was certain of, though, was that she would have to come clean with Bob before she did anything else. As soon as he knew what was going on, surely he would be as outraged as she was?

CHAPTER ELEVEN

When Lexi arrived home she could tell immediately that something bad had happened.

Bob was sitting at the kitchen table perfectly still. That was pretty odd in itself. He would normally be bustling about with the radio on, or he would have music playing at a volume that Lexi just about forced herself to tolerate because it obviously made him so happy. Not today though. He was just staring ahead blankly with silent tears streaming down his face.

In front of him was a nest of computer cables. He was normally obsessive about putting his kit away in labelled boxes so he could find the right parts whenever he needed them. Then she noticed that a box was sitting next to the jumble of connectors, right in front of him, with the lid still on it. There was a label in Bob's handwriting, written with a magenta sharpie, which simply said 'VGA'. The old, happy Bob seemed to be right there in those three, carefully traced, outsize letters.

"Bob?" Lexi said walking slowly towards him, "What on earth is wrong?"

Bob sat in silence.

"Bob. Love. What's wrong?" she asked again.

Still he said nothing. Another wave of tears trickled down his face. He wiped his eyes with his hands and then rested them gently on the plastic box.

"Bob. Bob. Talk to me. Please. What's wrong?" She felt nauseous now. How bad could it be? Had something happened to one of his parents?

Slowly, he raised his head and looked up at her from his seat. He was wringing his hands and tearing at a jagged cuticle. He didn't notice when it started to bleed.

"Where were you?" Bob finally said. "I needed to get hold of you. Where were you?"

"I told you I was shopping in town," Lexi replied carefully. Desperate though she was to come clean about the accelerating pace at which she was becoming an activist, Lexi felt now wasn't the right time to tell all. Not with Bob acting so strangely. She didn't want to lie. Technically she hadn't lied. Not really. It would be a long story to explain.

"But you didn't did you?" Bob said, sounding like he had the weight of the world on his shoulders. "You didn't go shopping, did you?" His eyes flashed accusingly. She started to feel scared. He had never been violent, but she could feel a massive bolt of negative energy building up in the room.

"I didn't manage to find anything if that's what you mean," Lexi continued, realising the lack of shopping bags had given her away, but trying to keep everything on an even keel.

"I needed you," Bob said again, dropping his eyes, and gradually started to sob, "I needed you and I couldn't find you." He was shaking now, his beefy shoulders which were normally so steady heaving up and down and jittering in a distressing rhythm.

God almighty, Lexi thought to herself, what on earth have I done? He looks like he's about to have a heart attack.

"I forgot my phone," she said feebly. "I thought it would be OK to stay in town without it."

She brushed past him, picked up the kitchen roll from the top of the microwave, and tore off two pieces which she handed to him, her hand resting on his shoulder. He wiped his eyes and his face, and blew his nose, but he still looked terrible. It was like he had aged ten years in a day.

"Can I get you a glass of water?"

"Water? Water? For fuck's sake. Is that all you can think of?"

"Why did you need me, Bob? What's happened?"

"Something terrible."

"What? Please tell me. What's gone wrong? Has something happened to your parents?"

Bob looked at the box in front of him. "It's Wotsit," he mumbled. She could barely hear him.

"What? Can you say that again?"

"Wotsit. Wotsit. Wotsit's dead." His voice dissolved into a low, chilling moan and the dreadful sobbing began again.

At that moment, Lexi suddenly recognised the expression on Bob's face, an expression she had never seen him wear before and didn't ever want to see him struggling with again. It was all-consuming grief.

Wotsit was Bob's cat. She had been with him for eight years, five years longer than he had known Lexi. He adored Wotsit. Until she lived with Bob, Lexi never had any animals, but after a year with Wotsit she was beginning to see the point. After losing her parents, she hadn't wanted to become attached to anything or anyone else in the world. The pain was too much when they had gone. Since meeting Bob, though, she had finally started to soften, and to allow herself to care about someone else. And look where it gets you, she thought, you end up howling like a baby at the kitchen table. The ghost of the pre-Bob Lexi materialised coldly for a second and stood motionless in front of him.

Bob eventually began to breathe more calmly, and gradually explained what had happened.

When Lexi had left the house that morning, Wotsit had decided to follow her. Bob knew that much from the records on the pet tracker, which he'd checked at about 11 o'clock, finding it odd that she hadn't showed up for food, which she was normally pretty keen on, being a cat.

The tracker interface showed Wotsit going down to the main road where she suddenly stayed very still for about half an hour. Then she moved very quickly to an address he recognised as the vet's. Bob had a habit of overestimating Wotsit, when he talked about how intelligent she was, but even he knew she wouldn't have gone to the vet's by herself. Cats hate going to the vet. He called the surgery straight away, and they'd given him the sad news. Wotsit had been run over by a driverless bus on the main road. It hadn't seen her, and it hadn't stopped.

The injured cat had been found by a teenager who had lifted her gently into the basket on the front of his bike, and taken her straight to the vet. Although Wotsit was still warm, her body was badly distorted by the accident, and she had stopped breathing. Bob shot over to the vet's right away. He had emptied out the box of cables so he would have something to put her in.

Lexi looked back at the table. The unkempt pile of cable spaghetti all made sense now. Poor Wotsit was in the VGA box. For the first time ever, Bob's labelling was wrong. Lexi's phone lay next to the box with 15 missed calls on it, all from Bob.

Ever practical, she asked Bob gingerly, "What do you want to do with Wotsit?" While she didn't want to intrude on his grief, Lexi was not prepared to have a dead cat decomposing on their dining table for any longer than was strictly necessary. "Do you want to take her back to the vet? I think they have…" She had to stop as a look of sheer panic swept over Bob's face. He gripped the box tightly with both hands. "No," he said, "I don't want her to go to one of those places. I want to bury her in our garden. Myself."

Lexi could tell she would have to go along with it. After failing Bob in his time of crisis, it was the least she could do. "Well, we'd better get digging," she said.

By the time Wotsit was interred, it was starting to go dark. They went wearily back into the house. Bob was still a mess, and going a bit vague and shaky as his blood sugar plummeted.

Lexi had only eaten a tuna-and-crisp sandwich for lunch, and Bob had had nothing, so together they made some beans on toast with grated cheese on top and ate it front of the screen, scrolling though the options for something not too depressing, and ending up with a vintage programme called *The IT Crowd* which usually made Bob howl with laughter. Not tonight though. He let it wash over him like a mild painkiller, which Lexi thought was probably a good thing, given the day he'd had.

It wasn't late when they went up to bed. She just wanted Bob to get some sleep.

They turned off the light. Bob put his arm over Lexi and she was enveloped by a secure wave of warmth. She could sense that something was still wrong though. Bob was wide awake. He sniffed, his eyes and sinuses still inflamed from the earlier upset. Please, she thought, please just go to sleep. Don't go all scary on me again.

"Lexi," he said quietly, "Do you love me?"

"Yes of course I do." Lexi replied trying to stay calm under the covers.

"The thing is," Bob began slowly, "I know you have been lying to me."

"What about?" Lexi asked, trying to sound normal, and putting to the back of her mind the terrifying flash of anger that she had seen in his eyes only a few hours previously. If only the stupid cat hadn't died she would have told him everything by now. Her stomach contracted into a tight knot.

"Don't play games with me." Bob snapped, sounding irritated, in a way she had never heard him speak before.

"I know you weren't shopping today. You were in the East End. And why didn't you tell me you went to The Barge the other night? Did you see me there? I saw you."

"I was in The Barge with Elsie." That was true. She wasn't going to admit she'd seen and ignored him. That seemed too callous.

"Was Elsie the old woman in the DayGlo running outfit? You couldn't miss her." He made a 'humph' noise and paused for a moment before continuing with a bitter tone to his voice, "Who's Mr Huxley then?" Ella the barmaid had rolled her eyes and told Bob that the ladies had spent an evening with Mr H when he had asked her, as he settled up for his food, what had been going on in the upstairs room.

"There is no Mr Huxley. It was a code word," Lexi explained in a matter-of-fact way, which she knew sounded totally ridiculous, before going on, finally, to tell Bob more of the story. How she'd met Elsie in the changing rooms, and what David had said when she got chatting to him for the first time at the Summer Fayre.

Unfortunately, as the tale unfolded it sounded completely outlandish. If you made it up no one would believe you, she thought, hoping desperately that Bob would prove the exception. "That David has the hots for you," Bob said, his muffled voice only just audible from under the quilt. Lexi couldn't see it herself.

She pushed aside the dig about David, and launched into explaining what was happening to the over-70s she had met, adding that no one outside the target group seemed to know that they were being pressured towards an Ending at ever-accelerating rates. Like it was all going on in secret.

"That night in The Barge," she told him softly, "It was a meeting of people who wanted to find out more about what they're doing to the old folks. Honestly love, it's terrible. There's this organisation called PACE. People Against Coercive Euthanasia. They're trying to stop it. I was at their conference today."

"Seriously?" Bob said. "That was why you were at Toynbee Hall?"

She was a bit taken aback that he knew her precise location. "Yes it is. I didn't want to tell you about PACE until I was absolutely sure I wanted to get more involved. I was planning to tell you tonight and then, with Wotsit, you know, I thought I'd leave it 'til another day. I thought it would be too much for you to take in. They tell us to leave our phones at home because they're worried about the Government trying to stop us, being bugged and tracked and that sort of thing. That's why you couldn't get hold of me. I'm sorry you couldn't reach me when you were so very sad."

Suddenly, Bob breathed a massive sigh of relief. "I thought you were having an affair with Mr Huxley," he said. "I thought that was what you were hiding from me. That's why I put Wotsit's spare tracker in your bag today. That's how I knew you were in the East End."

Lexi was shocked Bob had thought she would even consider being with anyone else. After her parents had gone, it had taken her 15 years to be able to cope with a serious relationship. The idea that she might be interested in someone else was utterly alien. "You are bonkers,

Bob," she said, "Can we talk about this properly in the morning? I need your advice on the whole thing, and to tell you more about what happened today, but I'm exhausted now."

She had barely finished her sentence, when she realised Bob was snoring. When she nudged him the rattling got a bit quieter. Just quiet enough for her to fall asleep too.

CHAPTER TWELVE

A COUPLE OF MONTHS HAD PASSED since that doubly momentous day in June when Lexi had decided she wanted to become a PACE activist, and Bob had buried poor Wotsit in the garden.

The school holidays could not have come soon enough, promising them a few weeks of welcome rest and relaxation. Bob had taken a job in education for an easier life, and while there were still a few things to be done up at the school over the summer, it was nowhere near as busy as term time. Lexi was mostly looking forward to doing nothing in particular, pottering about and making the place feel more like home. Since Wotsit had gone, Bob seemed to cherish his time with Lexi even more than before.

One morning, Bob was delighted to find that his application for a lock-up garage had been successful. Since moving into the house Lexi had inherited from her parents, he had longed for some workshop space. A technician at heart, he always had some kind of project on the go, and it had been a struggle for him not to overrun their place with kit. He also came with a collection of

500 vinyl records he had taken in for safekeeping when his parents moved abroad. There were numerous meticulously labelled plastic boxes under the bed, on top of the kitchen units, even in the tiny cleaning cupboard under the stairs. Lexi tried to roll with it, knowing that Bob's collections were very important to him, even if they just looked like a load of old bits of metal and plastic to her. The lock-up was walking distance from their house, and Lexi joined him when he met the landlord on site to pick up the keys.

It was in an old mews which had somehow survived the mania for developing every square meter of land by virtue of being in a conservation area, and it was quite difficult to access. There was a metal barred gate at the entrance to a poorly made road which led to six large garages. One of them was twice the size of the others, and this was the one that Bob had been waiting for. His new workspace was secured with two huge heavy duty metal hasps and padlocks which Bert, the landlord, unlocked one after the other before pushing the door open. As the doors swung back, the space was lit by a single lamp which dangled menacingly from the ceiling. Even though it was a warm summer's day, the place felt cold and gloomy.

Lexi could see Bob's mind ticking over as he began to plan what he could do with the room, which was easily big enough for him to fit his van in and more.

"Is it OK for me to tidy up the electrics and paint the walls?" Bob asked Bert, trying to sound casual and not at all excited about having a new project to work on. "Be my guest," Bert said. After all Bob was keen to improve his landlord's asset. There was no paperwork to sign. Bob just logged into Bert's rental app there and then, and committed to a two-year lease by scanning in his fingerprint after ticking a box to say he had read the terms and conditions, which, naturally, he didn't bother to do.

"There you are then," Bert said, handing two sets of keys to Bob. "You know where I am if you need me." He shook hands with both Bob and Lexi before leaving them to explore.

"What are you going to do with it?" Lexi asked, eyeing the inside of the dark, cavernous shell with curiosity. "It's huge." She could see her planned weeks of pottering with him shifting away from their shared home to this semi-industrial man cave.

"I'm going to set up a tech station and display at the back. Racks along both walls to get stuff out of your way. Yep. And it's big enough to put the van in here so I can unload out of the rain if I need to. Yes. That's what I'm thinking. Needs sprucing up a bit."

Rather than lose her day with him completely, Lexi offered to muck in with some painting. She didn't mind a bit of decorating. They went back home, picked up the van, and headed out to buy supplies from some of the few surviving shops. The van loaded with paint, racking, and a few of Bob's precious boxes, they turned on the radio as they headed home. They planned to have a sandwich before heading back to get started.

A song they both loved was playing. It was about being a rock star, and listed all the fun things you might do if you were fortunate enough to be one. They joined in the chorus enthusiastically, even though neither of them could begin to contemplate consuming the quantity of drugs the song suggested would be available.

"That was 'Rockstar' from Nickelback," a young male presenter said as the song faded out, "which has just been re-released as it's the soundtrack to the most wonderful ad for Rockstar Endings."

"They make it look so good," his female co-presenter chimed in, "It makes you want to sign up for the one-way trip even if you're a Yuthie. So glam! Isn't it brilliant people can go out with a bang, exactly when they choose. Pass the champagne, Angel!"

The two of them giggled in cheesy self-congratulation. They thought they were so clever.

Lexi clicked the old-fashioned button on the fascia to make the irritating duo go away. The atmosphere in the van had pivoted, in just a few seconds, from noisy, playful exuberance to stunned dread. She was deeply resentful that their happiness had been tainted by the crass reminder of the coercion that was going on all around them. It reminded her, too, that she had promised herself to do something about it.

"Bob," she said, "When we go back to the lock-up this afternoon, can we leave our phones at home? We'll be able to concentrate better with so much to do."

"Sure love," he replied, "Whatever you like. I'm not on call."

So, after a couple of ham sandwiches, a few slices of melon, and a cup of tea, Bob filled two flasks, one with more tea and another with cold water to keep them going through the afternoon. They put their phones on the kitchen table, as if they were staying in, and headed back out to the van where Lexi felt they could finally have a proper talk.

"I don't know where to start," was all she could say at first. "I never finished telling you everything after that PACE meeting. It was such a traumatic day one way and another."

It was painful to think back to that dreadful evening, which had at least concluded with Bob back in a good enough place to fall asleep. Now, however, Bob was concentrating on the road. Although self-driving vehicles were commonplace, he had opted to stick with a van he could operate himself. The authorities were trying to outlaw human-controlled vehicles, on the supposition that they were more dangerous than 'autos'. For the time being at least, though, you were allowed to drive yourself if you could afford the insurance, and provided you had a zero accident rate, which Bob had found painfully ironic after what happened to Wotsit. "Call me old-fashioned," he would say periodically, "But I love driving. I'm going to keep at it until the robots drag me out of the driving seat and hack off my steering wheel."

Lexi continued cautiously. "About PACE. I am going to get more involved when everyone's back after the summer. I'm just not sure yet what exactly that will mean.

"There were people from all over at that conference. It's happening everywhere. They start trying to undermine your strength and confidence from the moment you turn 70. It's subtle but I'm sure it's real. And then when you're feeling at your lowest they swoop in and persuade you to agree to die. It's horrible, Bob. I know they say it's more humane than what happened before, and that ultimately everyone is better off, but I can't see how this way of doing it is right.

"There's a group of us who want to do more. Helping people who have been coerced into signing up to reverse the decision and get their lives back. Direct action."

Bob pulled the car into the entrance to the mews. "I'll just open up," he said, taking out one of the sets of keys Bert had given him, swinging the gate open and propping it on a brick that made a good impromptu doorstop. They drove in, and he locked the gate behind them, crawling towards the garage he now recognised as his own. He backed the van in, turned off the engine and then swung open its back doors to unload.

"Do you think it's right, Bob? Trying to pressurise people into it?"

Bob continued to unload the van. "I'm not sure."

Lexi didn't want to cause an argument, but at the same time she couldn't let it drop. "How can it be right," she said, "to stop someone like Elsie – whatever you think of her dress sense – using her own money to join a fitness club? It used to be all the rage to encourage old people to stay strong. I remember my Gran being visited by a fall prevention team to try to keep her mobile and on her feet. They'll start hiring people to push them down the stairs next. What's the difference?"

"I don't know," Bob said again.

"Stopping them going on holiday? How can that be fair? A lot of them have been saving up so they can enjoy their retirement." Lexi went on.

Bob had started to put together some rack shelving. The noise of the electric screwdriver punctuated the tense silence. He was in his groove, methodically building something. Avoiding the subject.

"Can you just stop doing that for a minute and talk to me?" Lexi said, exasperated that Bob seemed to have retreated into himself and wouldn't talk to her about something that was so important to her.

"I'm sorry," Bob said slowly, "I don't know what you expect me to say.

"Is assisted suicide wrong? No, I don't think so. Most people don't think so or it wouldn't be legal, would it? Is it wrong to pressure people into assisted suicide? Probably, yes. But I'm not convinced it's happening like you say it is. Some of these people you're dealing with – how do you know they aren't simply delusional. How do you know the real reason their holiday insurance has been cancelled? Maybe they've got a heart condition and don't want to tell the rest of the group? Maybe Elsie tried to buy a kettle bell from somewhere that's sold out, and they don't want her to go anywhere else? Just because you're paranoid doesn't mean they're not out to get you and all that, but it sounds far-fetched to me."

"Thanks for that vote of confidence," Lexi retorted. "Do you really think I'm that gullible?" She could feel anger rising in her chest. "So I'm stupid, am I?"

"No, no I didn't mean that. I just think people get stuff out of proportion sometimes."

He paused and turned to look at her. "Plus I am happier with you than I have ever been in my life and I don't want some hare-brained…" thinking better of it…

"Sorry, possibly ill-founded direct action campaign to wreck it for me, for us, for our future."

Lexi was taken aback. Although she remembered that Henry, the lawyer, had warned everyone to be careful about being overheard or followed, she had never considered that she might be putting herself in any danger by joining PACE.

"What do you mean, wreck it?"

"I think you could be getting into something that carries real risks."

"What sort of risks?"

"I'm not sure. It depends what you mean by direct action. It also depends how much the corporation wants to stop you."

"What do you mean, how much they want to stop me? What could they do? I'm just a middle-aged school teacher."

"Like I said, I'm not sure. But if you are thinking about direct action, about physically intervening with their processes – not just getting an MP to have a cosy chat with the CEO – then there will be risks. I've worked in security for years, Lexi. Some of the people – well, let's just say they wouldn't think twice about pushing you down the stairs if you were in their way. It's easier these days because they can blame it on a faulty robot. You mustn't forget, Asimov's first law of robotics, the one that says robots can't harm people – it's from a work of fiction. They can and do harm living beings. They've been doing it, under instruction, for years, one way or another. Sometimes even by mistake. Like poor Wotsit.

"If what you're saying is right, if this isn't a bunch of

ageing paranoiacs looking for a cause, then someone will have a vested interest in keeping it all running smoothly. Those contracts, the ones that the corporation and their ilk get from the government, they're worth a lot of money. They have a lot to lose. Let's face it, even my job is part of a massive corporation contract. I've been asked to do things…" He suddenly stopped. "God, Lexi, I couldn't bear it if something happened to you."

So that was why he'd been so reluctant to talk about it. He was worried about her. She gave him a big hug, "Bob. Have you any idea how surprised I am that anyone at all cares about me?" Before she met him, a series of short-lived unsatisfactory relationships had left her resigned to putting all her energy into her job, and being single forever.

They embraced in the silence of the lock-up. Finally Bob said, "Look, I understand you want to carry on with this thing. But be careful. Will you tell me what you're doing so I can look out for you?"

"OK. No more secrets," Lexi said, relieved that Bob would be there for her from now on. She would do as he asked. And she would go back to PACE in September and see where it led.

CHAPTER THIRTEEN

Bob was pleased to hear from his old school friend Trev, who still lived in Southport, where they had both grown up. He had become an accountant, living in a modern, two-bedroomed house from where he could keep an eye on his aging parents, Andy and Jennifer, in their nearby bungalow.

To help pass the time, Trev had a succession of live-in girlfriends. The most recent one, Marisa, had just moved out. Frustrated by his marked ambivalence to their relationship, she had packed her hair straighteners and left. With more time on his hands, Trevor had been checking in with some of his old mates. That was how he ended up inviting Bob to stay for August Bank Holiday weekend.

It was few years since Bob had been back to Southport. After his parents sold up and moved to Thailand, it hadn't really occurred to him to go back up North Still, he was curious to see whether the old place had changed. They talked briefly about whether he should bring Lexi, but Bob decided it would be easier if it was just the boys. She wouldn't want to listen to them reminiscing about

Rock Night at the Floral Hall, and rehashing old stories about teachers from the sixth form.

Frustrated by the speed limits which were ruthlessly enforced on the motorways, now that most of the traffic was driverless and fettered at a constant pace, Bob left the van behind and took the train. He used to enjoy the drive home. Unlike driving in town, on the superhighways all the fun had been eradicated, as stringent controls gave preference to keeping autonomous freight in perpetual motion, night and day.

It was early on Friday afternoon when he arrived. Walking out of the station and heading instinctively towards the seafront, he was sad to find rows of boarded-up shops punctuated by the odd marijuana emporium, vape shop, or second-hand jeweller. So the 'closing down sale' signs he saw last time he was here were really true. Tramps huddled in the doorways and alleyways, just like everywhere else.

As he headed for the seafront, Bob's senses went into overload, stimulated by the electronic jangle and metallic smell of the amusement arcades one minute, and the squawk of the seagulls the next. His stomach began to rumble, and he needed to find some lunch. For Bob there was only one place to eat. I hope it's still there, he thought to himself, as he turned down a familiar side street.

The Swan didn't look much from the outside. It was a fish and chip restaurant and takeaway nestled into a small Victorian terrace. He smiled when he saw it was still winning awards, fifty years since it had first opened. Taking his haddock and chips wrapped, Bob made his way to the promenade and settled in the last remaining dilapidated wind shelter. It gave scant protection as he looked across the marine lake to the sea, opened the paper package, and tucked in using his fingers. God it was good.

Lexi had been trying to get hold of him. There were three missed calls, then finally a message asking him to let her know he had arrived safely. Now she knows how it feels, he thought, bitterly recalling the lonely trauma of Wotsit's passing. He was slowly acclimatising to the responsibility of being in a serious relationship, a situation he had never thought it would happen to him. There was something about Lexi he couldn't walk away from. It wasn't just physical attraction, although that was definitely there. It was more. An intense connection which continued to surprise him at moments when he least expected it.

When she had started going on about what was happening to the old people it had irritated Bob at first. He never had much time for politics, and had thought activists were self-indulgent and disconnected from reality. Seniority? Yuthentic? Weren't they all the same type of self-interested whingers, banging on about things no one can change? Plus she had lied to him about where she was going and what she was doing. In the past that wouldn't have bothered him too much. That was when he realised how much he cared about her. The thought that she might be seeing someone else, even though they had never promised to be monogamous, had made him livid. As did the possibility that she might be putting herself in danger. He knew then that he was in love with her. Blimey, he had said to himself, it's finally happened to me after all these years. Who would have thought it?

As Lexi had never been to Southport, he clicked on the camera phone and held it up, framing his face tightly with a bit of the wind shelter in the background. "Are you waiting for a bus?" Lexi asked, squinting as she tried to interpret the scene.

"No, I'm on the front. I'll show you."

Bob stood up and moved the camera to give Lexi a panoramic view. The lake opened out around two green ornamental islands, tufted with spiky marram grass that held the dunes together. Lexi could see the vast expanse of blue sky, punctuated with the odd spots of white cloud, vapour trails from aeroplanes drifting into pale, fat stripes which were dispersed into the atmosphere. Beneath it the lake was a deep navy flecked with foam. Huge seagulls landed on the islands, and beyond them she could just about make out a strip of road flanked by orange sand. There was no sign of the sea.

The images swirled nauseatingly as Bob moved around. "I'll have to come with you next time, love," she said. As the wind started interfering with the sound he retreated back behind one of the few remaining panes of unbroken glass. It was still hard to talk. When Lexi rang off, he felt quite alone. Without realising it, she had chased away the comforting ghosts that had been keeping him company as he wandered around the dying town.

By a quarter to five, Bob was on his way to Trev's office. He carried a hessian bag he had bought from a craft beer shop, containing a dozen bottles of brands which were all named after local landmarks. The carrier was printed with a multi-colored beer-inspired word cloud – refreshing, cold, organic, hoppy, fruity, stout, ale and more vied for attention around one enormous BEER which stood out in the middle of the graphic.

His favorite label was on the bottle for Another Place IPA. It presented a striking sketch of one of the hundred haunting, salt-weathered Antony Gormley statues that stared out to sea along the bleak expanse of Blundell-sands beach. Bob had been to 'Another Place', the name of the eerie installation, several times, summoned back by its desolate, crumbling beauty.

The background on the label had been screen printed to transition perfectly from a deep sandy orange at the bottom, to a greyish sea green in the middle, and grey-blue sky tipping into a hint of navy at the very top. A humanoid figure was superimposed, outlined in a dark rusty brown with a white infill. Twenty years since they had been permanently installed, the army of two-meter high statues had lost none of their haunting majesty. If anything, their 24/7 struggle with the harsh coastal elements had given them a new depth, exposing a unique, barnacle-encrusted beauty that could only be created by chance, age and decay. The picture provided subliminal encouragement to enjoy life while you can. A Northern version of the Day of the Dead, only with beer.

He had shaken off his emotional dip after ending the call with Lexi by walking the entire circumference of the lake. On the far side, he reached the vast expanse of beach, with its patches of green scrub and salt marsh which merged together as he looked out towards Blackpool in the North. Lexi would love to run here. He would have to warn her about the sinking sand, though.

Trev's office sat among a terrace of red brick buildings used by professional services firms in a little back street. A light came on, even though it was broad daylight, and his face was scanned. He said "Bob for Trevor Quitter," in case anyone needed to know. They might not have decent facial recognition in a small place like this. The door clicked open.

A small waiting room held four drab, low, upholstered chairs and a wood-effect coffee table scattered with leaflets promoting the firm's services. Bob put down the clanking bag and swung his rucksack onto the floor. He reached for the water bottle he carried in the outside pocket and drained the last of it in one gulp. The fish and chips had left him thirsty. He eyed the beer for a second, but thought better of it. No. Bad form to crack one open in the waiting room at his mate's work.

Just then, a message popped up from Trev: With you in five, it said.

Bob glanced around the room. It reminded him of the school where he worked. There were posters on the wall. "Have you made your will?" One of them asked, in a pastiche of the old army recruitment campaign, with a man in a military hat pointing at Bob in an officious manner. The strapline underneath added more encouragement, 'Talk to one of our advisers today about knockout inheritance tax incentives!'

As he shuffled the leaflets around, one in particular caught his eye. It had a picture of the most glamorous older woman he had ever seen stepping into a spotless limousine, accompanied by a handsome man in a beautifully cut uniform. The flunky reminded him of the cabin crew that looked after him the time he splashed out on a business class flight to visit his parents in Bangkok. A glass of champagne awaited the woman next to her inviting-looking, reclining passenger seat. It was only when he turned over the page, and started to read the copy on the back, that he realised the leaflet was promoting a Rockstar Ending.

Book your trip of a lifetime today!

Go out in style with our unbeatable
Rockstar Ending package

- Luxury limo transfer to disposal center
- Choice of relaxing virtual reality scenarios in transit and in the departure lounge, headset provided
- Unlimited champagne in transit
- Pre-trip cocktail
- Medically trained Angel to accompany you to your final destination
- Full inheritance tax waiver for all passengers until their 85th birthday

Log onto the Rockstar Ending portal today
to book your best journey ever!

Consult an independent financial adviser

Economy options also available

Confidentiality guaranteed

Terms and conditions apply

At that moment Trev appeared in the doorway. He saw that Bob had the Rockstar Ending leaflet in his hand and said, "You're too young for that, mate!" before walking towards him and shaking him firmly by the hand.

Bob slipped the leaflet into his jacket pocket and looked at Trev. He seemed younger than when he they last met, a few years earlier, when he had come down to London for the Cup Final and stayed with Bob for the weekend. At the time, Trev had looked after the tax affairs of an Everton player who had just made his first million. He had swung a couple of tickets for the game and decided to make a weekend of it, staying at Bob's place.

Since then Trev, who had been skinny in the past, gained a little bit of weight around the middle and looked more solid. He carried it well. He'd taken a razor to his head which was now edged in dark stubble, whereas four years ago his receding hairline was more ageing. That was the thing that made him look younger. Maybe I should try that haircut, Bob thought, before saying, "You're looking good Trev." His friend, who had an answer for everything, said "It's the single life. It's taken years off me."

Trev called a cab to get them home. He didn't bother with a car any more, finding the driverless transport a better option in such a small town. As they travelled back, Trev's phone rang, "I'll have to take this Bob, sorry," he said. "Hey Mum."

Bob hoped that he would get to see Andy and Jennifer while he was in town, as he had liked hanging round their house when they were younger. Much though he treasured the memory of the happy times with his own parents, with only the three of them there was a quieter dynamic. There was something much more lively about Trev's family, driven partly by the presence of his older siblings, Steve and Betty, who seemed sophisticated and glamorous. He and Trev would pester Betty, who was achingly trendy, for music recommendations; and they would raid Steve's wardrobe, borrowing from his collection of vintage punk and heavy rock T-shirts when they wanted to impress.

"Mum, slow down," Trev was saying. "Start again." He was listening intently to Jennifer's high pitched tone. After she had rung off, he looked awkward. "Bob, I'm going to have to call round on Mum and Dad. Can I drop you at my place first?"

"Can I come with you?" Bob asked, "I'd love to see them both."

"They would love to see you too. But not tonight."

Bob wanted to ask what had happened but it didn't seem like the right time. Trev let Bob into the house and told his assistant to help him, doing a quick voice recognition check so it would know he was authorised. "Sorry about this," Trev said as he headed out of the door, "We've had a few problems recently. I'll explain properly when I get back."

It must be something serious, Bob thought to himself, for Trev to turn his back on all this beer.

CHAPTER FOURTEEN

Bob slipped a bottle of Another Place into the freezer to chill quickly for immediate consumption, and dropped his backpack on the floor next to where he planned to sink into one of the two cosy navy velvet sofas.

As the memory foam flowed into the curve of his spine Bob felt instantly relaxed. Trev's living room was a nice enough place to while away a few hours. White walls, wooden floors, clever lighting creating a chilled out atmosphere, some framed black and white prints of some of his favorite music icons, and various photos of Trev and members of his extended family.

He could see from the pictures that Trev had been best man to his brother Steve, when he had got married to Esme a few years before. It was one of the first weddings to take place at the end of Southport pier. There was a photo of the two brothers in matching tailcoats, framed by skeletal rails that arched over the boardwalk.

Bob was dozing on the sofa when the assistant announced that Trev was calling, and his voice started to echo around the room.

"You OK Bob? I'm on my way back. Do you mind if we stay in and get a takeaway tonight? I'm not sure I have the stamina for much else."

He would order something, aided by the assistant. When it said that one of Bob's all-time favorite Southport restaurants, Pizzeria Misteria, had started offering home delivery there was no contest, and within a few minutes a Quattro Stagione and Pepperoni pizza were being slid into an oven in the center of town. They would soon be on their way, transported by Doggiedroid, the self-driving pizza box.

When Trev finally walked through the door Bob had a cold beer waiting for him. He looked drained as he perched on the edge of the second sofa, took a swig, and gave a huge sigh. Eventually, without looking up, he asked, "When did you last see my Dad?"

"It must have been about six years ago."

Bob had been back to help his own parents sell up, just before they moved to Thailand. In the run-up to the final farewell at Manchester Airport he had visited a few times, filling bags to take to charity shops, helping them with their paperwork, and shipping their collection of vinyl records – the soundtrack to his childhood – down to London for safekeeping. That was when he had last called on Andy and Jennifer. They had just downsized. What they liked most about their new bungalow was that it had a substantial garden and a paved area for entertaining, so they could still throw a good party if the mood took them.

"He was good then," Trev said thoughtfully. "You wouldn't recognise him now.

"Dad didn't want anyone to know, but he was diagnosed with Parkinson's about five years ago. He didn't even tell Mum because he didn't want any of us to worry. Anyway they put him on medication and it must have kept his symptoms under control pretty well, because for two years he kept it secret. He even carried on playing golf.

"Then over the course of about a week some odd things happened. He wasn't himself, and then he had a fall which put him in hospital. While he was in there he got an infection and started hallucinating. You know my Dad, right? Mr Normal. It was like he was from another planet.

"It took them about a month to discharge him. No one would tell us what was wrong because he wasn't well enough to consent to them discussing his case with us. I managed to catch a glimpse of his medication though. Tablets that are used routinely for Parkinson's. So when he was more like himself again, I asked him outright, and he had to admit it."

"So how is he now?"

"He kind of returned to normal. A slightly thinner, shakier version of normal. His sense of humor came back and he started doing exercises. He even agreed to Mum, or one of us, coming to his doctor's appointments with him."

At that moment they were interrupted by the door clicking open and a version of the Dean Martin song 'Volare' ringing out in electronic beeps. Outside the porch, Bob could see an insulated cube on wheels resting on the footpath. It displayed a strip of moving lights on the edge facing them which read: 'Pizza Pie for Trev… Pizza Pie for Trev ….' the words running across in succession. The top flipped open. Trev rose stiffly to his feet. As he approached the vehicle, a perfectly level platform rose out of its middle, and presented him with two flat, square boxes at waist height. He took them with both hands, "Lovely and hot," he said, distracted from his story for a moment. As he turned to bring the food inside, the dumb waiter telescoped back down, the lid slid closed, and the front door shut behind him.

The guys sat their respective boxes on the low table next to the beers, which were going down fast. "Another one?" Bob trotted into the kitchen and returned with two more bottles.

"Great choice," Trev said, "I didn't realise how hungry I was."

The pizza was not as good as Bob remembered, but he did not say anything. It was the wrong time to be critical. Even of a pizza made with industrial mozzarella, plastic ham and metallic-tasting tinned artichokes.

"So what's happened with your Dad now? You said everything was going OK?"

"Physically he's stable and reasonably strong. It's his mental state I'm worried about."

Trev went on to explain that his Mum had called him that afternoon in floods of tears because his Dad had been getting badly depressed.

"For about a month now, he's been saying he's not sure he wants to go on. He's become terrified of having a relapse. His meds are working, and he's well in himself, so we can't work out where this has come from. The thing that freaked Mum out was he said that maybe… maybe he should book himself in for disposal now while he's still capable of making the decision. He was serious.

"Once you book yourself in they take you away very quickly. Mum's worried because that's what happened to Esme's Mum – you know, my brother Steve's mother-in-law, Iris? She booked herself onto the bus without telling anyone. There was nothing wrong with her, other than a bit of arthritis. First thing anyone knew was when they got the email saying she'd gone and asking if we wanted her ashes to be made into a paperweight. It was terrible. We're starting to worry now that Dad's got the same idea."

Trev's story had a familiar ring to it. Bob recognised a pattern he'd heard about before but he hadn't wanted to believe.

"Maybe I can cheer them up a bit?"

They agreed they would call on Andy and Jennifer together the following day. Trev was relieved that Bob wanted to come with him, even though things were difficult.

For the rest of the evening they grazed on congealed pizza and cheered themselves up by watching vintage episodes of *Peep Show*, which they had loved in their early 20s. It made them laugh and cringe all at the same time. By the time they went to bed, the recycling bin was overflowing with the disintegrating faces of Gormley statues, with two empty pizza boxes balanced precariously on top.

CHAPTER FIFTEEN

THE NEXT DAY, THE FRIENDS set out for Trev's parents' house on foot, chatting in low voices as they walked along the quiet suburban streets lined with modest 1930s semis.

Bob felt in his pocket for his device, remembering that he had missed a call from Lexi that morning. When he was in the bathroom he had left his phone on charge downstairs. He should really message her back. As he tried to lever the phone out of his pocket, the Rockstar Ending leaflet caught round the edge and tumbled onto the pavement.

He lifted the paper from the ground and straightened it out carefully, still shocked by its blatancy. There was something he deeply disliked about what the leaflet represented. He must show it to Lexi when he got home.

"This Rockstar Ending thing," he said, scanning the text again to make sure he hadn't dreamed it, "Does your firm get paid to put these leaflets out Trev?"

"We have a commercial manager who looks after all the promotions. I imagine they give us something. We're accountants. Don't usually do anything for free."

"This thing about getting financial advice before signing up…do you do that?"

"We've always done inheritance planning. It's the same thing really," Trev said. "Only with this, clients want to know how much more their kids will get if they sign up to go on the 85-or-under incentive. It's not difficult to do the calculations. For some of them it can be a lot of money. There are still a few million pound houses in Birkdale and further along the coast."

Bob thought carefully before asking his next question. "Doesn't it worry you?"

"It's just advice. Probably better that they ask a third party than get their families involved. I've seen some dreadful situations over the years. Grasping relatives going way beyond what's reasonable. People putting their parents under pressure to hand over assets at a time that feels way too early. You can't really involve the police because the benefactors rarely want to cause trouble for their kids. Even when they're vile."

They had crossed several minor roads by now, and were walking along Preston New Road, the main route out of town towards central Lancashire. It was busier here than on the side roads they had been strolling along before, with buses and autos driving past in slow, steady single file. Bob found himself wondering whether a cat might wander out into the road to test the autos' stopping reflexes. Like poor old Wotsit had.

In front of his parents' house, Trev took out an old fashioned metal door key. It made Bob smile to see one. "We've bought them an assistant, but they won't connect it to the front door. Don't trust it," he explained to

Bob, before pushing open the door and shouting inside, "Anybody home? I've brought someone to see you."

The two men walked into the entrance hall. There was a floral carpet. The walls had their original dark wooden panelling. It smelled of furniture polish and the past. Trev shouted again, "Mum, Dad, I've brought Bob over. You know I said he was staying."

"Come into the back room," Jennifer's voice sounded out, "We're just in here."

The aroma of toast and coffee hit them as went into the living room at the back of the bungalow. Pale floral wallpaper reflected light around the room from the tall picture window, three big panes each topped with original leaded fanlights. Jennifer came in from the kitchen which joined on to the living room and gave Bob a hug. "It is so lovely to see you," she beamed.

She looked the same as he remembered her. Her grey-brown hair cut into a flattering short style that framed her triangular face with tight curls, her dark chestnut eyes slightly less intense than they once were, but still bright. Dressed at the smart end of the smart casual spectrum. No one would dare to suggest that Jennifer was going to let herself go any time soon, even though she was 77. Bob was delighted that she seemed genuinely pleased to see him.

Andy, on the other hand, was sitting motionless in one of those high-backed, supportive armchairs that old people find comfortable. Trev was right, his Dad had changed a lot, and Bob worked hard to hide his shock at how much he seemed to have shrunk, pushing the words 'rapidly deteriorated' to the back of his mind. Andy had been a thick-set man, but now his physique was different. His arms and legs were skinny, and his oversized trousers were secured at the waist with a brown leather belt, without which they would have slid down to his ankles.

"Don't get up, Andy," Bob said as soon as he saw him lean forward, worried that he might lose the trousers as much as his balance.

"I need to stretch my legs," Andy said, lifting himself out the chair more easily than Bob had expected, and holding out his hand which was shaking slightly, "Trev said you were up this weekend. It's good to see you." Bob put out both his hands and grasped Andy's firmly. The delicate bones of the old man's spindly fingers felt fragile beneath thin, cool skin. "It's nice to be back." He was relieved to see out of the corner of his eye that Andy's belt had surprised everyone by keeping his chinos firmly in place.

Jennifer whisked away the plates left over from a modest breakfast which had been mainly toast. Andy had left most of his. It looked like the two of them had been settled in front of a screen which was small by current standards, running only a meter across, and perched in the middle of a set of bookshelves. Some of Andy's golf trophies were on show. He saw Bob looking at them.

"Can't do that anymore," he said matter-of-factly, "I had to let my membership go last year. After I was in hospital. Couldn't get my swing back." A glumness began to settle across Andy's face. "Jen's still playing though, aren't you love?" he added proudly. Yes, and she was still taking Andy to the bar and to the club dinners when she could coax him out of the house. Bob got the feeling that Andy didn't really like to go out that much. It was an unwelcome reminder of the things he could no longer do.

Bob tried to lift the mood by telling Jennifer and Andy how much his life had changed since he'd last seen them. He talked about Lexi, their home together, and how much he was enjoying working in the school. The couple were glad to hear that Bob, who had been on his own for a long time, had finally found someone he thought he might settle down with. They were sorry to hear about Wotsit.

"You've probably heard he split up with Marisa? In a small town like this you just don't have the gene pool." It was the closest Jennifer would get to being judgmental. She wasn't much missing Marisa, but despite her reservations she would have preferred Trev to have a significant other to keep him company, like his brother and sister did, rather than be alone.

Between them, Andy and Jennifer ran through the most recent family history; what they thought about the various decaying buildings around the town. The place had lost its iconic charm of centuries past, and was scattered with boarded up Victorian masterpieces that had now gone to rack and ruin.

There was curiosity about how Bob's parents were getting on in Thailand. Bob was able to tell them about his trips out there, and how they were happy in the warm climate, loving the food, keeping fit by swimming in the pool every day. It felt like they'd made the right decision – so far at any rate.

"Too late for us to go there," Andy said, "We can't even get travel insurance now. Anyway Jen needs to stay by the grandkids. When I'm gone they'll keep her going."

"Don't talk like that," Jennifer butted in. "My parents used to do that, speculate morbidly on about who'll go first. It's horrible. Stop it."

"I'm just being practical. Look at you, and look at me. There's no bookie on earth would give me odds of outliving you. You're a whirlwind woman. Long may you continue in happiness after I'm gone."

An awkward silence occupied the room for a few seconds until it was interrupted by a jarring ringing sound that filled the room. It was such a good impersonation of the noise of old fashioned fixed telephone that Bob wondered whether they still had one. "Sorry about this," Jennifer said, scrabbling round for the tablet she used to control the assistant, "I've left the damn thing in the kitchen. Hang on."

"For God's sake, Mum," Trev shouted as the annoying bell continued to pulsate throughout the room, "Why don't you use the voice activation like I showed you?"

"Because I don't like it listening in on us all the time. Anyway, sometimes it doesn't hear properly."

"But Mum, you need to train it. Once it's installed, it's listening anyway. You just need to use the commands. Don't you think they should use it, Bob? You're in IT. Won't it make their lives easier?" Trev was shouting partly so he could be heard over the incessant noise, and partly because he was becoming increasingly exasperated with his folks.

"Er… they can be a help, yes," Bob replied feebly, remembering all too acutely how Lexi had made him disconnect their assistant just after she got involved with PACE, for fear of being spied on. Quite a few people were doing that now. Jennifer found the tablet, and made the irritating jangling stop by answering the call which then played into the open room.

"Hello is Andy Quitter there please?" a calm voice said.

"Speaking," Andy replied. Jennifer was mouthing the words, "Sorry," to Bob, and "Get rid of them," to Andy.

Andy shut down the caller before they could get into any details, and Jennifer passed him the tablet as a message came onto the screen from the individual who had just disconnected. "How on earth did they get my number?" he said angrily, "It's that blooming corporation again. I've told them, I don't want their counselling. They won't leave me alone. Counselling? I know what's wrong with me. Counselling can't cure Parkinson's. How is talking about it going to make it any better?"

Groping for a way to diffuse the tension, Bob glanced around the room and his eyes landed on the screen that had frozen when the boys arrived. Andy's feed was up. There was a 1970s playlist. Bob felt sick when he saw the banner ad at the top of the page. It was a perfect match for the Rockstar Ending leaflet he had in his pocket, but with this version you could get into the booking portal with 'just one click'.

"So Andy, what have you been listening to?" he asked an upbeat tone of voice.

"Oh, stuff from my youth mainly. One thing I'll say about this lot is they do a mean play list. It can be a bit repetitive, but they've chosen lots of songs I like. Led Zeppelin, 'Stairway to Heaven'; Blue Oyster Cult, 'Don't Fear the Reaper'; The Doors, 'The End'. I'm not on premium so I have to listen to the ads and some of the other themed stuff they're piping thorough at the moment. They've got this Rockstar thing going on – Pink, Nickelback, Post Malone. It's a nice mix actually. When you can't get out easily, music is one of the few pleasures that doesn't change. Well, provided you don't want to dance. I've never been a dancer, and it would be reckless to start now."

"Well he needs to start doing something," Jennifer rolled her eyes, "Hanging round the house all day is no life. He might be a bit skinny, and he might not be able to play a round of golf any more, but he's still mobile enough to get out and about. I wish he'd accept the counselling. It could help."

"It didn't do much good for Iris though, did it?" Andy snapped back, "They said it would build the emotional resilience to help her manage her arthritis better. Before you knew it she'd booked herself on the bus."

Jennifer looked like someone who had been slapped hard in the face. Bob thought she might start to cry, and Trev reached across and put his hand on her arm, saying, "We're all very upset about that. Let's not drag it up again now."

Andy was on a roll. "What people need is practical

help and medication. Nothing else is any use. Talking to someone – or something – is not the answer. I can understand how Iris felt. She was looking down the barrel of her meds being withdrawn in a few years' time. Down the barrel of unbearable pain and immobility. She wanted to leave what little she had to her grandchildren now rather than spend it all on prolonging a confined and boring life. Poor Iris? I say good for you love."

One small tear escaped from the corner of Jennifer's eye, and ran silently down her face.

"Dad, we can get you help," Trev said, looking earnestly at his father. "I can afford it. I've been looking at a home bot for you – it can help with all sorts of jobs, and they are strong. They can help you get around and about."

"Please son, no. No more technology. We can't cope with it. The assistant's bad enough, our calls blaring into the room. It's just confusing us more."

"I can change the settings. It's easy…"

"No Trev. I don't like it. I just want to be human. I don't want all these stupid machines. I want my life to be like it used to be. But it can't be, can it? There was a time not so long ago when, if you needed a bit of help because you were older, the council would send someone to do a bit of cleaning, cook you a meal, or just pop in to see if you were all right. Now you're on your own. Your Mum's doing everything for us."

"I like it, it keeps me busy."

"Maybe for now. But when we need help it's buy this assistant, buy this bot, get an autonomous vacuum cleaner or dust-sucking drone, Doggiedroid will deliver your tea .... What I'm worried about, Trev is, as we become more fragile we'll have to ask you, Steve and Betty to help us out all the time. Once we're over 85 – well it doesn't bear thinking about. It's not as if there are nursing homes any more."

"We've told you. We're here for you. You don't need to worry. We can pay for anything you need between us, honestly, don't think like that," Trev said, but Jennifer shook her head and sighed.

"I'm sorry you've had to hear all this, Bob," she said, drying her eyes on a piece of kitchen roll that had been left on the table next to where the toast had been. It left her face lightly streaked with butter and brown crumbs. "Things have been hard since... well... recently."

Andy nodded. "Your folks have done the right thing getting out of this place. It's hard when you get older. I would never have imagined I'd feel like this. It's like some kind of incurable helplessness is stalking me, dragging me down. Waiting to pounce."

By the time he and Trev left the house, Bob was worried that it would be that last time he'd see Andy, and he wasn't too sure about Jennifer either.

"I'm stumped," Trev said, as they began to meander back to his place. "I haven't a clue what to do. I've tried everything. The corporation helpline won't speak to relatives. I've even offered to move in, but they don't want me in the house. Mum's pretty strong most of the time, but he's in a bad place. Honestly, I'm terrified about what he might do next. They make it so easy."

"How do you know?"

"I've had more than one client come to me to get

their finances in order when they're booking themselves in for disposal. I'm just so glad Iris wasn't one of them. I don't know how I could have faced the family afterwards.

"The advertising is everywhere. Even if I ripped out the assistant and the screen they'd get letters in the post and hear about it on the radio. You saw the entertainment system. It's like they've got the Grim Reaper playing soft rock in their living room. I think I can probably persuade Mum to hang on a few more years, but Dad's getting close. I can feel it. It's mad. He's just a bit shaky on his feet, and he can still get out on to the beach for a walk, but he's stopping eating. He's fading away. Nobody will help you convince someone to live. All you get is incessant nudges to pop them over the edge."

CHAPTER SIXTEEN

LEXI HAD BEEN IRRITATED WHEN Bob announced he was off to see Trev without inviting her, back in August. She had fancied a trip to the bleak Northern seaside. In August it might not even be bleak. But in the end she decided not to make a fuss. It would be good for Bob to have a bit of time with one of his small handful of friends. Absence makes the heart grow fonder, too, she told herself. Maybe he'll appreciate me more when he gets back.

She didn't worry that his trip might turn into some kind of unsavory boy-fest. This was Bob. He was a man whose idea of hell was a stag weekend in Amsterdam, and who was never happier than when reading cyber-security manuals with a cat snuggled next to him on the sofa (when he had one) and rock music on in the background.

However, when he returned from his weekend at Trev's he was in the strangest of moods. Not at all Bob-like. He was usually an affable, joking presence who radiated a quiet, reassuring warmth. When he came back from Southport it was as if he had been chilled. He was preoccupied and seemed a bit lost. It was obvious to Lexi that something had shaken him but it took her a few days to get him to tell her the full story.

"I'm sorry I doubted you, love," Bob said, after he had time to process what had happened with Andy and Jennifer. "I just couldn't imagine it."

When Lexi told Bob she'd got an encrypted invitation to a direct action planning meeting at the offices of Nicky Hartt, Bob announced that he wanted to come along too.

So here they were, squeezed into a tiny back office in New Cross, in the building under a block of council flats where Nicky normally held her MP surgeries, literally rubbing shoulders with a bunch of local activists. Lexi introduced Bob to her new friends: elegant Ruth, jovial Jim, and Billy the retro-punk who had spoken up at the meeting in Toynbee Hall; Father Al, the young Catholic priest from the upper room at The Barge; and Nicky Hartt herself. She had expected David to be there, but he was still on holiday in Puglia. What a motley crew, Lexi thought, as she looked round the room. How on earth will we ever get anything done?

As people started to talk, though, Lexi's confidence began to grow. They had a strong, shared, unanimous intention. It was intervention programme or bust. Their challenge was to work out how they could go about freeing people who had been coerced into signing up for disposal, but decided later that they wanted the process to stop.

Nicky was in touch with other MPs around the country. They planned to start making a noise about it in

Parliament in October. She had captured the attention of the Chair of the All-Party Parliamentary Group for Ageing and Older People. They were arranging a public meeting where Liz and Lucy – the escapee and the Angel who had made such an impact on Lexi at Toynbee Hall – could share their stories with more people. But this was all weeks away. How many Enders might be shipped off before then?

Father Al was in a difficult position. There had been overwhelming public support for assisted dying when it was introduced, but he could not accept that it was right in any circumstances. In the end, though, he adopted a pragmatic stance, seeing that any interventions the committee managed to pull off would be better than nothing. The presbytery, where he lived, could be used as a 'safe house' for anyone who felt they needed to go into hiding.

Having established where they might hide the escapees, the committee had to work out how to spring them out before it was too late. They knew from Liz's story that Enders sometimes changed their mind after the cooling-off period. Nicky had heard cases from other MPs that bore that out. And there was something about the conversation she'd had with the corporation CEO, Mason, that made her think she wasn't the only one who had requested a reprieve.

"It's going to be tricky," Billy began. "We're massively outgunned by the corporation. The reach of their campaign is phenomenal, what with the commercials and videos and marketing bots.

"I've noticed that the PACE website has a form people can fill in if they want help, and an emergency phone number, but they've no money to promote it. You have to get to page 10 on a search to find it, and practically everyone will have lost the will to live, if you'll pardon the expression, before they'd get there. Plus I'm not sure what they actually do when someone gets in touch." No one else knew either, so Billy said she'd follow up with David when he was back from his holiday.

Ruth spoke next, slowly and deliberately as usual. "I know this is quite an old-fashioned suggestion, but I was wondering whether we might be able to do a leaflet?"

"Hmm. Old school. Who would read it?" Billy asked.

"Well, I could put them in the Seniority shops, and Father Al – would you be able to put them in the churches? Perhaps David could hand them out at PACE events?"

"I can get them out with the Lewisham pensioners too," Jim offered, "You'd be surprised how determined some of them are."

"OK," said Billy, "I can pull a design together. But we'll need some money to get them printed."

Jim had a small campaign fund, and Nicky was quite confident that PACE would contribute too. Then Bob surprised Lexi by speaking up.

"There's something else," he said, "I'm here because I was up North with the parents of one of my oldest friends a couple of weekends ago. I haven't been able to stop thinking about it.

"We were very worried – still are very worried – about my friend's Dad signing up to go, even though he could have another 20 years ahead of him. But he's giving up. When I was with him, I felt totally helpless. He's depressed and spiralling downwards. They've even infected the music he's listening to. I'm not joking. It's like they're trying to steer him to the lowest point so they can swoop in with an enticing escape route.

"So I was thinking... maybe we could help concerned friends and relatives monitor how their loved ones are being bombarded with this stuff. I've only seen things on the periphery, on the edges of screens, but people are being worn down."

"What do you mean, monitor? How would you do it?" Nicky wanted to know more.

"Well there's software you can put on people's systems to follow what they're doing online. If we track how people are being targeted, maybe we could prove the unreasonable levels of coercion by quantifying the number of touch points for the multi-channel campaign. Show that it's too much."

Billy was nodding vigorously as Ruth asked, "Sorry, can you say that in English please?"

"Apologies. I have worked with this stuff for a long time. What I'm trying to say is that we could monitor how often they are being targeted, see what they are being sent, and how they respond, by putting a kind of spy onto their machines."

"Hacking?" Nicky said, looking worried, "That's what you're saying, isn't it? Are you seriously talking about hacking?"

"Possibly."

"And once you've done it? Then what?" Lexi asked.

"We can prove that they have been subject to unreasonable pressure. A bit like PPI, if anyone remembers that, when millions of people signed up for credit card insurance they didn't need, and ended up being offered mass compensation. Except this time, as well as being about profit, it's a matter of life or death. And the other thing is, well, if you were monitoring it all the time you could see when they enter the secure portal to make their booking. So you'd know exactly what kind of disposal they'd booked, and most importantly when they were due to be collected, so we could get to them before the Angel does.

"The only thing is, it just might not be strictly legal. People do this kind of thing all the time without users' consent – jealous wives, anxious parents – but, yeah, it's not strictly legal. Not on a private machine anyway."

Lexi sat perfectly still. Did Bob really just say all that? "Do you know how to do this stuff?" she said.

"Of course I do. I'm a cybersecurity expert. What do you think I did all those years in the bank? After the crash in 2008, we monitored everything everyone did like a hawk. We recorded every word and every keystroke. It was a legal requirement to keep records of everything for financial compliance. It's a bit trickier to set it up in someone's home, but anything's possible really, with the right planning."

Billy was beaming from ear to ear. "Man, I am so pleased you're here," she said, "I'm usually the only digital diva at these meetings. Fucking brilliant. Sorry Father."

Bob blossomed under the signs of interest. "I've got

some other ideas as well, but if you think it could take off I can get the spyware sorted. Then, if the leaflets bring in someone who needs help, we can trial it in the field."

Everyone except Nicky was excited, and encouraged Bob to go ahead. Father Al joked that he couldn't think of any commandments to do with privacy. The MP, however, was more reticent.

"As an elected Member of Parliament I can't condone anything illegal, Bob," she said.

"We wouldn't be doing anything illegal," Bob said. "If all we're doing is supplying licensed software, which is legally available, there's nothing wrong with that. It's up to the relatives if they want to take the risk."

"We've got to do this," Billy said. "The ends justify the means."

Then Ruth asked if Bob would put 'the spy', as she called it, on her machine. She was in the target age group and being bombarded with Ending propaganda all the time. "I can be the guinea pig," she said, excitedly. As the operation was being done at Ruth's request, Nicky said she was very comfortable with that, as it would help Seniority prove what was going on.

By the time the meeting finished, they had an action plan of sorts. Lexi had seen a side of Bob she hadn't known existed. They were on this road together now. It felt right. As they walked home, she said, "I had no idea you could do that Bob, with the spyware and everything."

"It's not difficult," Bob replied, "You could do it if you wanted. There's lot of free spyware on the internet, and videos on YouTube telling you how to install it. What I couldn't say in there was that I'll need to run this as a covert operation. If I get caught doing illegal monitoring and hacking, I'll lose my job, so I've got to be extra careful. Not to mention that the corporation actually pays my wages."

"Are you sure you want to do this?" Lexi said. It was her turn now to worry about their newfound happiness being disrupted. Bob losing his job would only be the start of it. She felt sick at the thought of her dear gentle Bob having to spend time behind bars. He would never cope in prison. "The way you're talking, it sounds like we could have a lot to lose."

His face serious, and his eyes focused in the distance, Bob carried on, "I've thought about little else since I got back from Southport. When Andy said Iris had taken the bus without telling anyone it made me ask the question: If the family had known, would they have been able to stop her? And yes, I think they would. If they'd known, his brother Steve would have gone round there and barricaded the door on collection day if he'd had to. Maybe they would have got her better pain management. Above all they would have told her more often that she was loved, and that they wanted her to stick around. They can't do that now. All they are left with is a massive burden of guilt, and a few crappy paperweights made from her ashes.

"I'm sure there's more I can do to help with the intervention than just monitoring, but we have to keep it away from Nicky. If there's any kind of scandal it will play right into the hands of people who don't want this genocide to come to light."

Lexi was stunned. "Did you just say genocide?"

"Well, what else would you call it? It's the insidious slaughter of a whole demographic. Just because it's not racial doesn't mean it's not genocide. This ain't rock 'n' roll, as the Cracked Actor once said…." he added randomly, to lighten the mood, evoking one of his favorite dystopic songs which also happened to include the G-word.

It was a weird thing, but when they got home Bob put on David Bowie's *Diamond Dogs*, an album he had loved for years, with its vivid picture of a post-apocalyptic world that, when he was younger, had seemed like it would be a subversive, glamorous place to hang out. Now the lyrics resonated in a new, terrifying way. Lexi and Bob listened to the stories woven through the songs, of people huddling together, scared and lonely, to whom death sometimes seemed the most desirable option. "Bloody hell," Bob said, "I miss him every single day. If only he could come back out of that stupid wardrobe."

CHAPTER SEVENTEEN

"MEGADETH IN FIVE," SONNY SAID cheerily as he breezed by Portia's workstation.

"All set," she said, without looking up.

Naming the meeting rooms after thrash metal bands hadn't been one of Brytely's better decisions.

It had happened, almost by accident, after Stella brought in some management consultants. The agency had lost a couple of their top talent to a rival firm, and in their exit interviews the defectors had given 'poor leadership' and 'a lack of team spirit' as reasons for leaving. The bad news got back to one of the board members, and Stella now had them breathing down her neck, wanting to know how she was going to make the staff feel more loved. Before hopping on a plane to Banff for yet another speaking engagement, she had sent consultants into the London office, instructing them to build a sense of belonging and create stickiness.

After analysing time-lapse footage from the cameras that recorded every move on the agency's premises, the consultants had decided the meeting rooms were 'crucibles for cohesion'. According to their report, these intimate spaces were central to fostering a culture of collaboration, but were not being used enough. They recommended arranging a competition for the Bryters to choose new names for the rooms. It would give the employees a feeling of ownership, and they would be more likely to spend time creating things together in their newly-exciting pockets of space.

Everyone was invited to have a say. The only rule was that the suggestions had to be music-related as the office had sprung up on the site of a once legendary venue, The Hall, demolished after it fell into a state of disrepair.

With the consultants' guidance, the in-house coding team spun up a voting app that suddenly appeared on everyone's device. It looked like it might be fun. There was a glitzy welcome screen with a spooky monochrome picture of The Hall inviting each individual to step inside and contribute their ideas.

Suspicions were raised, however, when thrash metal turned out to be the winning genre. Could it be a coincidence that Lars, the coder who had built the competition algorithm, wore a Slayer T-shirt to work every day? No one outside Lars' team understood how the programme worked, so they couldn't challenge the result. What made it worse was that the coding team were becoming untouchable in the corporate hierarchy, as the software they had built to drive the Endings campaign was judged an unstoppable success.

So Brytely was stuck with a thrash metal naming convention, even though it left most of their people permanently confused. Someone had tried to talk Stella out of implementing it, but they got short shrift. You couldn't run a referendum twice, she said, everyone knew that.

Black and white murals of the bands could be seen through the clear meeting room walls. But if you didn't know your Megadeth from your Overkill you could easily end up in the wrong place. Invitations to Sodom generated a few questions from clients who hadn't come across the band before, and Anthrax hardly sounded welcoming. The account teams had been provided with a brief to use with any guests who required an explanation. It included words like post-modernism, irony, democratisation and unique musical heritage.

Portia browsed the Megadeth website as she approached the corridor where the meeting rooms were located. She could only find a picture of one of the band members but managed to match it with a much younger-looking version of him looking down at her from the wall, alongside his guitar-wielding chums.

"Well I never. A member of the cyber army." She heard a Scandinavian rumble from behind her left shoulder. The hairs stood up on the back of her neck. It was Lars.

She switched her screen to black, "I don't think so."

Spinning round, she found Lars was standing way too close for comfort. His unearthly pale jade eyes stared coldly down at her, and his almost translucent skin was drained of color by the stark contrast with his usual black T-shirt and dyed, straggly jet-black hair. He might be dead clever, thought Portia, but he's not going to win any style points with those roots.

"The cyber army. You know, that's what Megadeth

fans call themselves," he continued. "I'm a Slaytanist myself."

"You don't say?"

Portia usually tried not to engage with Lars. He gave her the creeps, but as they were both going to the same meeting she couldn't escape him now. He stuck by her side like a washed-out leech as they stepped into the room. It was just the two of them in there for a few minutes. Portia pretended she had something urgent to deal with on her screen, so she wouldn't have to look at him. It was a survival technique she'd learned when she'd been sent by the company to networking events, but didn't really want to talk to anyone.

When Sonny walked into Megadeth she had never been so pleased to see him. He sat opposite her with an easy familiarity that made her even more aware of Lars' unnerving aura.

The three of them were there for a status meeting on the Endings project. Lars had become involved because his team had built the outcomes dashboard that showed how everything was working. It was going well. He was also leading something called the User Experience – UX for short – which Portia thought meant tweaking the Endings app to make it easier for people to navigate to the end.

She and Sonny had compared notes earlier that day. Lars' report showed that both Rockstar Ending and Economy were exceeding their quotas. The client was going to be very happy. When Stella flashed on to the screen to join the meeting, they were expecting an easy ride. They tried to work out where she was calling in from. Was she in a yurt? Surely that couldn't be glitter on her face? Not Stella.

"Hi team," she said in her usual speedy transatlantic drawl. It saved having to remember people's names. "I've reviewed the stats. It's looking good. Just as well. I'll be seeing Mason tonight at the after party."

Lars, who was obsessed with music and had a scarily accurate memory, immediately knew where Stella was. "Festival Number 6. Bit mainstream for me. But I do like The Village."

Stella was on a charm offensive with the anchor clients. Growing profitable revenue was a dead cert for maintaining the confidence of the board, and would counter any visceral doubts about some of Brytely's other business practices. To accelerate her recovery from the unfortunate spate of exit interviews, she had bought top-end hospitality packages at a select handful of cultural events, and Festival Number 6 was one of them. As Portmeirion, the quirky tourist village where it was held, had been used for filming cult 60s TV classic *The Prisoner*, the Brytely brand team had unanimously agreed it would align perfectly with the agency's values. Mason accepted his invitation immediately, along with Carrie, the corporation's self-styled global brand supremo. Stella planned to introduce them to a couple of Brytely board members that evening, and give them the full-on schmooze.

"The creative seems to be hitting the spot very nicely," Stella went on.

"Yes. It's doing as well in the field as it did in the

pilot groups," Sonny said. He'd been checking Lars' live data as it came in.

"And the chatbots are winning hearts and minds. I'm surprised how persuasive they seem to be." The Endings interface rocketed into the super-league when Portia compared it to the stilted conversation she had been having with the PHUC chatbots, as she tried to close off her outstanding compensation claim.

"Surprised?" Lars said, eyeing Portia aggressively. "You shouldn't be. Our new generation of intelligent software agents have exceptional ACE scores. The embedded AI is assimilating Ambiguity, Conversation and Emotion at speeds no one thought possible five years ago. My team has done an amazing job. We're not just at the leading edge. We're driving forward the frontier of conversational computing into virgin territory."

"Who do we buy these – what did you call them – 'agents' from?" Stella asked. "If the technology's that good, maybe we should be doing more with it. Have you spoken to the acquisitions team?"

Lars raised the pieces of pierced, stubbled flesh where his eyebrows had once been. "We have actually done most of the development work ourselves. In-house. If I were you, Stella, I'd be more worried about our AI technology making us an acquisition target than the damage that haemorrhaging a few replaceable creatives could do to the firm."

Not something else for the risk register, Stella thought, pushing what Lars just said to the back of her mind. Didn't he know she hated it when staff brought her problems?

"I've been doing some comparisons with what the other companies are doing. We have a big advantage over the household name conversational platforms. No ethics committees or high-minded institutional investors holding us back here. We are truly free to innovate. I'm not sure how you've cleared this with the corporation, but we have built something with extraordinary persuasive power."

Sonny cast his mind back to the compulsory ethics modules on his data science course. It was a distant memory now, but Lars' words were starting to make him feel uncomfortable.

"Hang on a minute. The Endings programme has been through ethical clearance at the corporation, hasn't it?" Sonny asked.

Stella had left all that stuff to Carrie to manage at the corporation end. In the meeting with Mason she said she'd had sign-off from legal. That was the same thing, wasn't it?

"There's nothing to worry about, Sonny. Mason is way too smart to take any stupid risks. I'm talking to him about the next stage tonight. Lars sent me a few ideas for maximising utility in the disposal centers. New audiences. Market growth. Can't wait to discuss it with the big man."

She looked down at her wrist. Stella was getting the prompt to move on to her next scheduled event. They had lost her now. In a few seconds she had signed off and was pulling on her vintage Hunter wellies, from circa 1984.

Portia glanced sideways at Lars, wondering whether

he might shed more light on what was going on, but he was looking down and doodling a nest of concentric pentangles on his screen with a dirty fingernail. She noticed a couple of silver rings on his hand, embossed with sigils. Now the boss had gone, Lars saw no need to pretend he was interested in sharing his thoughts with anyone. Much though she hated being near him, her curiosity forced her to ask, as casually as she could manage, "So Lars, what's the next phase?"

"I've come up with a few ideas for new target groups. It's only early stages."

"Target groups for what?"

"For Endings." He lifted his head for a moment and rolled his eyes, "What else?"

"Who? What do you mean?"

"We are already targeting the oldsters pretty effectively." Lars went on, "I've been looking at some of the other groups that might want help to ship out. People with chronic depression, severe neurological disorders. That sort of thing. They have terrible lives already, so why not save them shelling out for a trip to Switzerland? The poor can't even afford the fare. Messy DIY suicides. Ugh. Who wants to clear up after that? I've been triangulating income data with anonymised health records of the general population. We have plenty of capacity in the disposal centers. If we are brave enough we could be leaders in the democratisation of death."

As what Lars had just said started to sink in, Portia noticed Sonny's body language change. He had folded his arms and was staring blankly at the desk in from of him.

"Are you serious?" Sonny said quietly.

"Of course. I only do serious. I'm super-serious. This could be a great kindness to people who are suffering. Think about it. Everything the Voluntary Euthanasia Act stands for. Choice, dignity, right to the end. It's the logical next step."

"How can that be ethical?"

"With the right permissions pathway, terms and conditions and all that, of course it will be ethical, ticking all the little boxes you are always so worried about."

Sonny stood up shaking his head, "I'm not so sure about that."

"We'll see," Lars said. "If the corporation doesn't bite there's plenty of other firms out there who'd be interested. One way or another."

Portia followed Sonny out of the room, leaving Lars to his artwork. As soon as they were out of his sight, he turned to her, "We've got to talk about this." Anthrax was free, and as they went inside Sonny pulled the door quietly shut.

"What's going on?" Portia asked before he could say anything.

"I'm not sure."

"First things first. Have we done anything illegal? Now, today?"

"No. I don't think we have. The ethical codes for artificial intelligence are all voluntary. When the technology began to take off a few years ago, the big firms like IBM and Google did a pretty good job of getting their act together. They didn't want to be heavily regulated, and they got the governments to back off by setting up their own ethics committees, with independent directors, that reported publicly. All in line with the OECD guidelines. Governments couldn't keep up. There were a few false starts, but the tech bros got there in the end. At the time no one thought that small firms like ours would ever have the computing power to build something that could turn out to be this dangerous. We're in a loophole."

"The corporation has loads of ethical standards though. We went through them when we worked on the sign-up process, didn't we?"

"Yes, of course. They meet the rules to be allowed to manage the assisted dying process. Things like enforcing the dementia quotient and needing customers' explicit consent to access medical records. All subject to audit. But that's not the same as what Lars is talking about doing next. He's talking about targeting the general population. Not just the oldsters."

"You heard Stella though, Sonny. She's certain Mason will have everything covered. Provided it's not illegal, isn't everyone fair game?"

"Do you think she's actually asked him? Ethics aren't exactly her strong point. As for tech – well, you know her column for *Wired* is ghost-written by Jay on the media desk, right? From what little I heard today, I'm not convinced Stella understands what Lars has been doing at all."

CHAPTER EIGHTEEN

CLICKMAS SHOPPING. THAT WAS WHAT she called it.

Not that Lexi had many people to buy for. Bob was top of the list, and she was always conflicted about what to get him. Over the past year, she had watched their house slowly fill with alien technical things she didn't really understand, until it all became too much even for Bob, and he shipped them in batches down to the lock-up. Sometimes Lexi felt like she was being smothered by a rising tide of random electrical components.

A window flickered on her screen, alerting her that a communication had arrived from 'a. eastman'. Glad for an excuse to do anything other than online shopping, which she found mind-numbingly tedious and oddly compelling at the same time, she leapt at the excuse to flick into her message stack.

Which one are you? She thought to herself.

The Eastman twins, Adam and Alice, had been good friends of hers at school. She was fond of them both, partly because they had a lot of fun when they were younger and had a shared history of minor teenage incidents. The other reason she was always pleased to hear from them was that they were in the small cohort of her current friends who had known her parents. When your parents are dead, there are really only two kinds of friends, Before Parents and After Parents. The ones who knew them and the ones who didn't. And the ones who knew them will always have an edge on the rest.

She smiled, thinking about the time her Dad walked in and found Adam in her bedroom dressed in Lexi's school uniform, his gangly, hairy legs sticking out like they had been stuck randomly onto his otherwise graceful androgynous teenage body. As a finishing touch, Adam was standing in a pair of green Lurex stilettos Lexi had picked up in a moment of madness in a charity shop. They had been trying to create a human version of the card game Misfits, where you could mix and match different sections of bodies to create unexpected combinations. Though memorable, it wasn't a good look. Lexi's Dad had been completely unfazed. He grinned and said, "I'm not sure those shoes go with the rest of the outfit mate," before asking if they'd like him to call out for a pizza. He was so cool. A lovely open, welcoming man. Their house was the kind of place all her friends liked to call in for a chat, even when she wasn't at home. She still missed him – and her Mum – every single day.

Adam's sister Alice had been in the rock choir with Lexi. She would never forget the audience response when they belted out a powerful version of Blue Oyster Cult's 'Don't Fear the Reaper', at a quirky festival in the chapel at their local cemetery. Two halves of the choir had taken it in turns with the different lines, holding notes in harmony so they ran into each other. Just thinking about it made the hairs stand up on the back of Lexi's neck.

So she was very pleased to hear from any Eastman. On this occasion the message was from Alice.

'Hi Lexi! Wanted to tell you Adam and I are going to be coming over to see Mum at Christmas. Soooo excited. Have you got plans for Christmas Day? I'm bringing Dolly, and Adam will have Frank and both kids. It will be a bit manic but we would love to see you. A xx'

Great, she thought, totting up three kids and three adults, plus their Mum, Meg. Her present-buying quota had just multiplied exponentially. A double-edged sword. She replied straight away. It would be early morning in New Zealand so Alice might still be online.

> Lexi: 'Hey A! Would love to join you for Christmas Day. Need to check in with my man Bob to see if he has any other plans but almost certainly yes.'
>
> Alice: 'WHO IS BOB????? We need to be told.'
>
> Lexi: 'He's my rock. Been with him over a year now. I think you'll like him.'

Alice sent a GIF. It was a short clip of Brad from *The Rocky Horror Show* drawing a chalk heart on a door and shouting, "I love you."

> 'You must bring Bob. Let me know for def OK?'
>
> Lexi: 'Will do. I can hear him coming in now, as it happens. Back in a bit xxx'

She heard the door click behind Bob as he padded into the house. When she had lived alone there, after her parents had died, her surroundings had brought her consolation. Lexi had felt like she was living in a virtual reality film drawn from their collective memory, only with two of the three characters invisible. She had an overwhelming fear that she might forget what her parents had been like if she ever left the place.

Thankfully, time, the legendary great healer, had proven her fears unfounded. Her memories were still as vivid as ever, and she didn't need the house to trigger them. It had even been through a couple of refits since then.

She'd moved out into a flat for a while, when she began to think the place was holding her back from recovering, trapping her in a retrospective stasis. It had started to feel like she was inhabiting a claustrophobic shrine, tiptoeing around the spirits of the dead, and the only way she could break its hold over her was to leave for a while.

So she had put anything of sentimental value into storage, painted all the walls white, and let her childhood home out to a revolving series of students for about 10 years. Then, when she had met Bob, and they decided they wanted to live together, the house seemed the obvious solution. It was all paid for by an insurance policy when her parents had died. She would lose the income she received from the tenants, but then she wouldn't have to find any rent. Plus Bob was determined to chip in and pay his way.

It was coming up to the end of the academic year

when she and Bob decided to move in together. All she needed to do was wait for the students' tenancy to come to an end. They left obediently on the appointed day and Lexi returned their deposit in full. The house had become quite shabby, but they wanted to redecorate anyway. There were two bedrooms. They shared one and used the other one as a study. She would go in there for lesson planning and meditation; and Bob did his IT stuff and installed his encyclopaedic music and video server. It wasn't ever practical for them to both work in there at once, but it was easy enough for her to decamp to the kitchen table if Bob needed to be getting on with his projects, or had brought work home as he sometimes did. Their comms decks worked everywhere in the house anyway. Bob had installed Wi-Fi that was second to none.

She called out to him as soon as he came home. "Bob, do we have any plans for Christmas?"

The previous year they had spent the festive season apart. Bob had gone to visit his parents in Thailand. After Brexit, the Thai government had run a recruitment drive for UK pensioners, swooping in on the ruined plans of people who, until then, had been hoping to spend their later life in the relative warmth of Spain or Portugal. The Thais attracted them with the prospect of clement weather, relatively cheap living costs, and something like the old nursing homes that had been run back home before they all closed down. Even though his parents were living independently now at almost 70, they were spared the unrelenting drive towards an assisted exit. The Thai government felt it was in their interests to keep old people alive for as long as possible. Their taxes and then health and care fees, when such services were required, were valuable income.

Last Christmas, Lexi had done what she always did. Her own recipe for simple indulgence. A run first thing, then tucking into a plate of turkey and stuffing sandwiches in front of a screen, and bingeing on some of her old family video footage. She made a point of buying Christmas sandwiches from all possible eateries, and keeping them in the fridge, so she could have a bite from each of them on the big day. There were festive crisps on the side. The cranberry ones had been particularly revolting, she recalled.

To keep Bob entertained in Thailand she had made a Vlog of her sandwich reviews, which she had loaded on a private video site. He had watched it with his parents after their day at the beach. The short film had endeared Lexi to them immediately. It was nice to see Bob looking happy too, they thought, as he laughed out loud at the screen, before playing the film a second and third time. For decades they had worried that his nerdiness would stop him finding the happiness that mutual lifelong companionship had given them. Since meeting Lexi, he was more relaxed than they had ever seen him.

This year Lexi and Bob had been planning to spend their first Christmas Day together at home, with a turkey crown and all the trimmings. However, Lexi was now strongly drawn to the prospect of spending it at the Eastmans'.

Bob stood next to where she had set up her screen at

the kitchen table, her spot of choice. "We were going to have it here, weren't we?" he said.

"Yes, but we've just been invited to spend it with my old friends' family." She couldn't remember how much she had told Bob about the twins, so she explained that they went back a long way, and that they normally lived on other continents, Alice just outside Auckland, New Zealand and Adam in Austin, Texas. At first, Bob didn't look mad keen to be sharing her on the big day. "They're good fun," she said, not giving up, "and their Mum Meg is a sweetie. It won't be very formal. The three kids will be there too, and Adam's partner Frank."

Bob reluctantly agreed to Lexi's suggestion. It seemed to be important to her. And after all, it was just one day in the year. They had another 364 to make the most of.

Lexi got straight back to Alice before Bob could change his mind, and Alice asked if they could do a quick video so she could meet Bob. Before he could even take his coat off, Alice had appeared on the screen, and Bob was beamed live through cyberspace so she could see what all the fuss was about.

"Hey Bob! I am so pleased to meet you!" Alice said excitedly, with the slight Kiwi twang she had developed, smiling from beneath a short royal purple fringe. Glossy, thick hair the same color framed her round freckled face. "I hope you are looking after Lexi. She is really special."

Bob found her directness unsettling, but he gave her the benefit of the doubt and managed to get out a few words, "Hello. Well, yes I think I am. She is very special to me too."

Lexi blushed, embarrassed that her friend had put

Bob on the spot, but secretly warmed by his answer. Alice was looking to the side, "Dolly! Come here and meet Bob. He is a very special friend of Auntie Lexi." A mini version of Alice, compete with the same purple hairstyle, was steered into view by her mother. "This is my daughter, Dolly. Dolly, say hello to Bob."

"Hi Bob," said the child wandering up to the camera, her face distorted by being so close. It was an odd situation, with only Alice at the NZ end really knowing what to say.

"You're going to be meeting Bob at Christmas," she said to Dolly, "When we go to Grandma's."

"Oh. OK." Dolly was clearly the second most embarrassed person on the call. "Can I go now? It's time for school, Mum."

Dolly broke free of Alice who gushed, "Bye guys. I need to get this one into the car now. See you soon!" She waved frantically, froze, and disappeared.

"Do I get a beer now for agreeing to this ordeal?" Bob asked Lexi, putting an arm around her middle. "Maybe," said Lexi. "Or maybe I will reward you with something else."

CHAPTER NINETEEN

She counted them up on her fingers. Alice and Dolly, Adam, Frank, Bella and Mia, her. Seven. The three granddaughters could fit together along one side of the table. Two adults along the other side opposite them, plus one at each end. That would just leave enough room in the middle for the turkey and all the trimmings. Yes, that would work.

It was going to be the first and only time that Meg would gather all her grandchildren in the same place. She wanted this Christmas to be the most fantastic holiday that they would remember forever.

The house would be crowded as everyone would be staying with her too, but she was sure they could manage. It would be fun, even. As they were both tall, solid and needed the most space, she was going to give Adam and Frank her bedroom, put Alice and Dolly in the spare, Bella and Mia on the sofabed in the living room, and she would sleep on a fold-out camp bed in the little boxroom she used as an office. Sorted.

It was ages since she had bothered with Christmas decorations. Not since her husband Paul had died in his sleep ten years before. No warning. Massive stroke. They had no clue it was coming. She was 74 then. She often wondered what it would have been like if he had survived. People used to struggle on in those days, going to rehabilitation, families caring for their aging relatives. There was even a bit of state support. She would have done anything to prolong her time with Paul, even though at the time he died it was becoming increasingly acceptable to say: 'It would be kinder to let them go'.

While Meg was thankful they had been able to spend ten or so joyful years together travelling after their retirement, it was still terrible when Paul went. People say they want to die in their sleep, but if you asked them when exactly they would like that to happen, most people would answer 'not yet'. Together, they had loads of adventures. Sometimes they would include a cruise in their itinerary. Or a yoga retreat. They had lived life to the full ever since they first met in the business lounge in Singapore airport in their late 30s. Always on the go, they both loved their jobs and would meet up between business trips in their favorite places all over the world. It could be stressful at times, but they had plenty of money which they liked to spend on enjoying themselves.

When Meg turned 40, she realised that she had almost forgotten to have children. As a veteran sensation seeker, this was a core life experience she didn't want to miss. So she and Paul switched their spending money from seven star hotels to hiring the best fertility expert they could find.

It was a shock for Meg, someone who had been able to do pretty much anything she wanted before, to find herself in a process that was so fragile and random with no guaranteed success, no matter how much effort she put in. After a few anxious years, when she had almost given up hope, she found that she was pregnant with twins, and Adam and Alice were born. She was 43.

She remembered looking at them in their cots. Tiny. Wriggling. Starting to learn to control their muscles, faces, fingers, toes. The whole process was alien to everything she had experienced in life up to that point. Now, more than 40 years later, they had their own lives, their own families. She and Paul had encouraged the twins to leave the country, to travel, to find work abroad, to seize every opportunity as they had. Wrongly, Meg had assumed that when her children wanted to settle down they would be drawn back to living near her.

Things were getting better for the younger people since Yuthentic got in, but if the twins wanted to come back now they would be too old to qualify for subsidised housing. It would be tough.

When the twins were born, her own mother had come to stay for six months. She found it hard to accept help, but without her Mum being there she would have collapsed. The washing alone could have killed her.

Paul had been thrilled at the twins' arrival, and as they grew he showed a side of his character that she had only glimpsed before the children were born. He grew into an affable Dad, who could take most situations in his stride. From babies in exploding nappies to teenagers who had to be collected, the worse for wear, from mysterious locations in the middle of the night, Paul's humor carried them through. They all missed him dreadfully after he died. Even though, by then, the twins weren't living at home, they had spoken to him on the phone most weeks about what was going on in their lives. He gave them good advice. Sometimes he just listened. He was there for them all, and his death left a massive hole.

Adam was doing well. She always worried about his safety, living in Texas, in case someone with a gun or even a lasso decided they didn't like him or his partner Frank. She couldn't help referring to them as 'the boys', even though they were both strapping great men, with their fair share of tattoos, muscles and well-trimmed facial hair. Alice kept telling her that Austin was a liberal place. The town motto was 'keep Austin weird'. Whenever she had visited Adam there it seemed friendly and hospitable. He said the toughest thing he'd had to deal with was adjusting to the scorching summers.

As an experienced data scientist, he was never short of job offers from the huge number of thriving tech companies within driving distance of his home.

Most of the time the heat didn't matter too much. He worked in an office that was cool in every sense of the word. They had aircon in their house, and a pool of course. When he met Frank she was very happy for him. Even happier when they adopted the girls, Bella and Mia. They were enthusiastic Dads. Both got paternity leave from their enlightened knowledge economy employers, and they took it in turns with the school run, delighting in planning what would go into the kids' lunchboxes, and taking them on hikes in the Hill Country, swimming, boating and barbequing in the summer. It seemed like a good life.

Things were tougher for Alice, raising Dolly on her own. She knew they struggled financially. Alice had got off to a good start when she first moved to New Zealand. Meg had found it deeply ironic that, at a time the UK was having to import doctors from all over the world, Alice had gone to off to look after patients on the opposite side of the globe. The money was about the same as at home, but the living expenses were much lower than in London. She could live independently and afford her own space without having to be subsidised, something which had always made Alice feel beholden and trapped when she was younger.

After a few years Alice bought a place. She could meet the payments easily if she worked a few extra shifts. It wasn't long after that she met Dolly's dad, and he moved in with her. Meg never really knew whether Dolly was planned. When Alice became pregnant, Ollie, Dolly's father, who worked with her at the hospital, seemed excited enough, but something went wrong with their relationship just after the baby was born. He seemed to spend more and more time away from home, and eventually he moved out completely. The odd payment came through from him, but it was mainly down to Alice to support them both. She had to sell the house as, with a baby to care for, she could barely work a normal shift, let alone take on any overtime.

At one stage, when Dolly was about 18 months old, Meg thought that Alice seemed very close to the edge. She worried that she was struggling to care for both herself and her daughter after she dissolved into tears over something that seemed quite trivial on one of their weekly video calls. Retired and recently widowed, Meg booked a flight without saying anything, and turned up on Alice's doorstep. She wanted to try to help, just as her mother had helped her with the twins, giving back some of the loving karma that had come her way more than 30 years previously.

Alice had other ideas. Meg's spontaneous presence, so obviously the result of her mini meltdown, made Alice more determined than ever to show that she could cope on her own. Meg could see how hard Alice was trying to prove she was Doctor Supermum, and had no desire to make her feel like a failure. So she stepped aside, and went back home after only a few weeks. Alice had been so absorbed in caring for Dolly, and running around to hold onto her job, she didn't have a minute to consider how Meg might feel. In turn, Meg hid the terrible grief she carried from losing her husband, and worked hard not to let Alice see how disappointed she was to be pushed away from caring for her child and grandchild at a time when they most needed each other. Alice had always wanted to do everything her own way. Why should the arrival of Dolly make her any different?

Because they were short of cash, it was obvious to Meg that Alice and Dolly could only come over for Christmas if she paid for their flights. Meg had insisted on picking up the bill, saying she had invited them at short notice, and Christmas flights were notoriously expensive, so she couldn't expect Alice to cover it. This time she wasn't going to back down. Alice could see it would be good for to Dolly to get to know her British Grandma, although she told Meg off for booking them business class, seeing it as extravagant and unnecessary. It was a long way to travel with a child, Meg said, and she hadn't thought twice about it. It's what she would have done for herself. She could afford it.

In turn, Meg had been annoyed with Alice for inviting some people over to join them on Christmas Day without asking her first. She told her in no uncertain terms to un-invite them. This day was for family only. She had it all planned. There was no way she could tell them why, of course. But Meg was insistent she wanted it that way, and eventually Alice said she would stand them down.

Alice could blame her for the change in plans. "Tell them I'm overwhelmed or losing my marbles or something. Incontinent maybe? That would put anyone off their Christmas dinner. I am nearly 85 after all. It would be perfectly plausible."

It was shocking for Alice to hear her mother list the things that you would expect to be going wrong with a typical 84-year-old. As far as she knew, none of them seemed to be affecting Meg yet. She was always on top of everything, wasn't she? It was easy to forget how old she was.

There was a hiatus in the conversation, as both Alice and Meg were reminded of their place in the family hierarchy. For the time being Meg still held the trump card, as the most senior. She was a fully functioning head of the family, and her dominance was reinforced by her financial superiority. This was the order of things. Alice could not let the spectre of Meg's approaching frailty cast a shadow on their time together. She reluctantly agreed she would think of a reason to stand down Lexi and Bob, as politely as possible.

Age hadn't dimmed Meg's planning abilities. She was still sharp and she didn't overlook anything. She had set up a spreadsheet listing everything she wanted to do while the kids were around. There was a column for gifts to make sure they had equal numbers of presents of equivalent value. She researched the films that would be suitable for their age group on the big screen, and booked a box at Sadler's Wells for the all-male *Swan Lake* which had been revived as a Christmas show. She even arranged a luxury car from the corporation, top of the range, to take them all to the theater and back. Adam and his family would have seen lots of auto limos in Austin, but it would be more of a treat for Alice and Dolly who usually got around in the old kind of car you drove yourself. She smiled to herself. That was something else she would be able to sort out for them next year. Get them out of that smelly old death trap.

In getting the various rooms ready for her guests, Meg struck a double bonus as it spurred her on to make massive progress in clearing out the house. There were two piles 1) Things that definitely need to go out; and 2) Things the kids might want. She called a local clearance service to deal with some of pile one, keeping the better items aside for the charity shop; and pile two she stacked into the bottom of a cupboard so that it would be easy to access. They could go through it all together when everyone was over. She hoped it wouldn't look too suspicious.

All her summer clothes could go for a start. She

wouldn't be needing them again. Some of them were lovely. There was a capsule wardrobe of designer cruise wear, matching swimsuits and beach dresses from her time with Paul. What a shame, she thought for a fleeting moment, before pushing any hint of regret to the back of her mind. I have to focus on the future, she said to herself. The kids' future. I am giving them a wonderful tax free gift. Heart emoji.

Even though none of her grandchildren had met Paul, she wanted to make sure they had something to remember him by. Adam and Alice had plenty of real memories, but Dolly, Mia and Bella would need something else. That was why she had bought them each a locket, and put a favorite picture of her and Paul together inside. It was taken on a holiday in the Florida Keys. They were relaxed and smiling, standing in front of a red convertible under an electric blue sky. She had a bigger version of the same photo framed for them to take home.

She knew it was going to be rough for her family after they found out what she'd done, but Meg was pretty sure her decision was for the best. As they had pointed out on the Endings app, the kids would get a tax free bonus of hundreds of thousands of pounds, and be spared the worry of how she might be struggling on in her old age, abandoned by the welfare state she had once expected to ease her through her final years. How delusional that had been.

Anyway, she had signed the contract now and the cooling-off period was over. There was no going back.

CHAPTER TWENTY

A SILENT ALARM VIBRATED SOFTLY ON Meg's slender wrist. Its rhythm reminded her of 'Jingle Bells'. How appropriate, she thought. She had planned to wake earlier than usual, so she could stealthily launch her one-woman campaign on the Christmas lunch.

The boxroom was too small for her to attempt her usual morning routine of three rounds of sun salutation. Instead, she folded up her camp bed and put it to one side, her bedding rolled roughly on top, making enough space in the middle of the room for her to squeeze in a couple of standing bends and balances in her pyjamas. After about ten minutes of moving gently and breathing deeply, in-two-three-four and out-two-three-four, she felt ready to face the day, stronger and more centered than when she first woke up.

Meg tiptoed on to the narrow landing and crept gently down the stairs. Although she was unusually steady for an 84-year-old, she took extra care with her footing. She was surprised, at 6.30am, to hear voices in the kitchen. It was still pitch black outside. The kitchen ran along the back of the house, and looked out onto a small garden.

"You're up already," she said, seeing Alice and Adam seated conspiratorially at the table they had used for everything when they were children. There was a pile of dirty potatoes that they had just started to prepare, taking turns with the peeler, and dropping them into a pan of ice cold water to rinse off the last of the soil when they were done. "I was going to do that," Meg said, "You're my guests."

"No Mum, we're not. We're your children." Alice said, straight to the point as usual. "Anyway, neither of us could sleep. The kids and Frank all seem to be dealing with the jet lag fine but we were both wide awake an hour ago. So we thought we'd get up and make a start. These were going to be roast potatoes, weren't they?"

"Is there any other kind of potato on Christmas Day?" Meg said as light-heartedly as she could manage. She wasn't used to having anyone other than herself in her kitchen. Even though there was plenty of space she felt cramped. For a second, Meg was close to being overwhelmed with emotion, seeing them sitting there, concentrating on the job in hand, like they had never left.

The sight triggered a sudden flashback to the twins' childhood. They used to sit in exactly the same place drawing and painting when they were tiny. Forty years ago they had to be propped up on a small tower of cushions so they didn't disappear below the top of the table. When they were absorbed in a task they would stick out the tip of a tiny tongue. Paul used to call it 'the tongue of concentration'. There was no sign of it now though, as they casually peeled and chatted, falling into a deep-rooted, never-to-be-forgotten pattern of sibling banter, memories and in-jokes which made all three of them smile. As if reading Meg's mind, recalling their childhood artistic endeavors they split the last potato as they talked and each of them carved a Christmas print into it. Adam made an angel, and Alice a holly leaf. They covered them in cling film and put them in the fridge, intending to use them to make festive pictures with the grandchildren over the coming days.

Meg started to compile the stuffing from various ingredients she had half-prepared the night before. She got the turkey and the bacon out of the fridge and within an hour the bird was stuffed in traditional fashion, covered with streaky bacon, and put in to roast.

"One year you'll have to show us how to do this Texas style," Alice said to her brother, "Have you ever deep fried a whole turkey, bro?"

"Nope. It's too dangerous. Every year people are killed by exploding turkeys. I choose life."

At that moment they heard small feet moving at lightning speed on the stairs. The three children burst into the kitchen in flurry of pyjamas and toys.

"Grandma! Father Christmas has been! He found us even though we were miles away from home!" Meg listened intently to what they had to say, enthralled by their colonial accents, as a barrage of excited shrieks and exclamations followed. Dolly was a little Kiwi, and Bella and Mia had the lilt of the South.

"Merry Christmas everyone!" Meg said. "Now. Let's

go into the front room and you can show me what Santa's brought." She was keen to get the little people way from the kitchen, especially when they were so excited, and might accidentally barge into something hot or sharp.

Meg was proud of how inviting the tree looked in the corner of the living room. She hadn't bought a real one – they were ridiculously expensive, she thought, and shed needles everywhere. Instead, she had dug her old artificial tree out of the cellar, which had lasted well, and refreshed it with some new lights and decorations. She had gone for a set of mirrored silver baubles to reflect the changing colors of the lights, gold tinsel, and a silver angel on the top of the tree. They spent an hour of exploring the gifts that had mysteriously appeared beneath it overnight, then Adam suggested they get the kids some breakfast, as lunch wouldn't be ready for some time yet.

He wandered into the kitchen and came back in with a big plate of toast spread with peanut butter for everyone to share. The grandchildren were almost too excited to eat, but were bribed with the promise that they could open some more of the presents around the tree if they managed to get down a piece of toast and a glass of milk first. By now Frank had also emerged, so Meg left him and the twins supervising the kids and went back to the kitchen to put the finishing touches to the meal.

Between them, the various parents and children had managed to get showered and dressed in their Christmas Day outfits by the time Meg summoned everyone back into her kitchen, which doubled as the dining room. Meg was very impressed with their color co-ordination. Alice and Dolly had dyed their matching bobs a deep pine green for Christmas. They had liaised secretly with Adam and he, Frank and the girls all had streaks the same color at the front of their hair to signify that they all belonged to the same tribe, even though they usually lived thousands of miles apart. It was fun and creative and Meg loved it.

She set the table just as she had planned. The children pulled their silent Christmas Crackers. As the explosive snaps that used to make them more fun had been banned on the grounds of safety, the family decided they would shout "bang" instead every time they tore a cracker apart. It was grating on the nerves as the noise level around the table began to escalate, but as soon as the food was served everyone was lulled into the calm, appreciative silence that only an excellent Christmas dinner can produce. Thankfully no one had found a reason to ban paper hats, which everyone had dutifully placed on their heads. Paul would have loved this, Meg thought.

Frank insisted on clearing the plates and loading the dishwasher, as he had slept through most of the morning's preparations. He recruited the kids to help. They sweetly carried various bits of crockery and glasses, walking very carefully, as Adam and Alice reminded them it was Grandma's best. They could smash it all into a thousand tiny pieces if it would keep them this happy forever, I wouldn't care, Meg thought to herself. They are only things. I'll never use them again.

It was time to slump in the living room now. They had missed the King's Speech, but nobody seemed bothered. Meg turned on the screen, "Now, would anyone like to see some films from a long time ago of Adam and Alice?" The twins rolled their eyes, knowing what was coming, mainly embarrassment for them and, they would have thought, entertainment for everyone else. "Yes please!" Frank said, with a twinkle in his eye.

As old footage of the twins as children scrolled by, Meg was disappointed that the grand-children quickly lost interest. Other kids doing ordinary stuff, even if they were their parents, didn't compete well with their usual entertainment programme of colorful action, fast paced plot, and games requiring lightning reflexes. The mundane world on Grandma's little screen seemed pedestrian at best to everyone under 12. At one point Meg almost begged them to look, "Kids! Kids! That's Grandad, Grandad Paul. Grandma's husband, the twins' Daddy."

They looked up briefly and blinked. "He's the dead one, isn't he?" Dolly asked. "Yes, he died just before you were born love," Meg explained, "In his sleep." None of the children knew what to say. They had a notion that him dying should make them sad, but because they hadn't known him, were not upset at all.

"Will we die in our sleep?" Mia asked, suddenly looking like she might not want to go to bed ever again. As she was only four, that would be a long time. Adam looked protective, "No-one is going to die for ages. Look at Grandma – she's been sleeping every night for nearly 85 years and she's still going strong. It's nothing to worry about sweetie." Mia looked relieved. "OK," she said, "Can we put on something else now? Have you got *The Incredibles 3*?"

After an evening of more eating, drinking, watching and snoozing, the children's bedtime loomed on the horizon. Before the youngest one was packed off, Meg wanted to give them the gifts she had prepared in memory of Paul. She brought out three identical packages. They were all flat, the size of a small book, with a soft lump in the middle.

"Now," she said, "I've got a last Christmas present for you girls."

"Hurray! More presents!" Bella said, jumping up and down, eking out the last vestiges of the day's energy.

"These are something special for you to keep until you are grown up." Meg began. "They might not seem much to you at the moment, but in future they will be more important to you. When you have your own children, you can show them who your grandma and grandad were. That's a clue."

While their parents looked on rather quizzically, the three kids went with the flow and nodded obediently to their grandmother. Meg's description of the gift had been a masterclass in expectation management. Even though she had made it sound like nothing to get excited about, there was always something fun about unwrapping a surprise.

As they tore open the paper, Meg explained that she was giving them a framed picture of her and grandad, and a piece of old fashioned jewellery called a locket to keep a mini version of the picture in. It was designed so that people could carry round a photo of someone they loved, and who loved them very much, so that they felt they were always with them. "I don't ever want you to forget that I will always love you very much. When you go back home you will be a long, long, long way away. Now, does anyone want to try on their locket?" she asked.

All three girls said, yes, they did want to wear it now. They jostled each other, as Meg sat them in turn on her lap, and fastened the clasp around each of their necks. The locket blended old and new design. It was in the shape of a heart. When you opened it, the picture was set permanently into layer of clear plastic resin which would keep it safe from damage, even if they went in the bath with it on.

Meg noticed that the other adults in the room had gone quiet. When she looked at Adam and Alice, they seemed more serious than they had been all day. Perhaps they were getting tired. Adam, who had the youngest two children, said: "Right then, Mia and Bella, bedtime for you. Say goodnight nicely."

While Dolly hung back for a minute, Bella and Mia rushed towards Meg and threw their arms around her. She hugged them both tightly, smelling their hair, breathing in deeply as she had with her own kids. It was the best thing in the world. As Adam and Frank went to settle their daughters, Dolly gave Meg a hug too. "Night, Grandma," she said casually, "I can go up on my own. You stay here with Mum."

"She wants to catch up with her friends," Alice explained, "They'll be getting up for Boxing Day now. Night sweetie."

Dolly disappeared up the stairs. As soon as she was

out of earshot, Alice turned to Meg and quietly said. “Mum, are you all right?”

“Yes. I’m fine. Why?”

“You’re not ill are you?”

“No. Why do you think that?”

“Honestly?”

“No I am not ill. Far from it. I even had dementia tests a couple of weeks ago and came out with flying colors.”

Alice looked unconvinced, but could see she was getting nowhere with a straightforward line of questioning.

“Why the lockets, Mum? Don’t you think you weirded out the kids a bit there?”

“I didn’t mean to upset them. It was just that I found that picture of me and your father when I was sorting through some stuff and thought it would be nice for the kids to have it. They never knew him. I’ve been thinking about him a lot recently.”

Alice was quiet for a few seconds. She still thought there was something odd about the way Meg was behaving. “Is that all? Are you sure?”

“Yes, of course I’m sure. I’m telling you, I’m not ill.”

“Would you tell me if you were ill?”

“Of course I would. What’s the point of putting your daughter through medical school if you don’t ask her opinion if you’re ill? I’d tell you. You know I always do.”

It was true, Alice thought. She had been able to give Meg some good advice on her health over the years. And her mother looked amazing for her age.

“Promise?”

“Yes. Promise. I’m not ill. I just wanted the kids to

have something special from me. And so they have an idea what a lovely man your father was. He deserves to be remembered."

Alice could follow her mother's logic, but remained unsettled. Meg never used to be sentimental, not like this. Maybe it was just that she was getting old. Dread stirred deep in Alice's gut. What if something happened to her Mum? At her age it was only a matter of time. She would be getting frailer before too long. Alice had been horrified when she learned that they had withdrawn NHS care from everyone aged 85 or over. She was so pleased not to be part of a healthcare system that had become so utterly inhumane. In a few weeks' time, that would be her Mum, cut off from help, and Alice was going back to the other side of the world and would be unable to help her. What kind of crap daughter was she?

"Mum. I think I need to stay with you a bit longer. I can call work and say I need to do a few things for you here before I go back."

"No. No. No. Dolly needs to get back to school and you need to get on with your lives. Honestly, I'm fine. Everything is going to work out fine."

The last thing Meg wanted was for one of her children to stay on. She had booked her departure to coincide with them being safely ensconced in their own distant homes, out of sight, out of mind. The arrangements were confirmed. This was something she had to do alone. Meg needed her offspring to be firmly back on the other side of their respective oceans when her luxury transfer to the disposal center arrived.

CHAPTER TWENTY-ONE

IT WAS NOW EARLY JANUARY, and nearing the end of what Meg secretly called 'the family gathering to end all family gatherings'.

Meg had accomplished everything she had wanted to, including going through 'pile two' of the things she had put aside for her extended family to choose from. She was disappointed how little interest the grandchildren showed in most of the trinkets she wanted them to have, and had forced them to take a few pieces of quite valuable ancient jewellery which they didn't seem to care for at all. Maybe they would appreciate it more after she had checked out.

The girls had been very excited, though, when she invited them to help themselves to her cosmetics collection. They had enormous fun plastering themselves with fragrant and expensive creams one evening. Alice thought it was wasteful, but Meg was overjoyed to see it all being used up. It wasn't as if she would be able to give them to anyone else.

What was left of 'pile two' was loaded into a couple of big bags. Meg had planned to take them to the Seniority charity shop after everyone had left, but Alice offered to make the delivery as she was meeting her school friend Lexi for coffee on the same strip of retailers, just a couple of doors down. It wasn't out of her way.

Just before Alice set out, Meg remembered that she had some stickers to put on the bags that would allow the charity to claim extra cash from the Government. The tax back scheme was based on the value of their contents. She took the sticky labels, printed with a personalised code, out of a drawer in the kitchen, and fumbled to take off the backing so they would adhere firmly to the extra strong supersize paper carriers everyone had to use since plastic had been banned. Adam and Frank would be taking all three of the girls ice skating that morning, and Meg was going to tag along and watch.

Alice called a car to take her to where she was meeting Lexi. Within five minutes, it had arrived in the street right in front of her. As she approached the vehicle, it recognised her face and silently slid open its door. She climbed in and sat back in a comfortable, well-sprung seat, with the bags next to her. It was not so long ago that taxis were driven by real people. During the journey they would give quirky local tips on where to go and what to do, as well as sharing their stories and political opinions which were occasionally offensive. Those days were gone. As the car slid along with zero engine noise, the only sound was summer birdsong being piped anachronistically into the passenger compartment. Someone else's idea of calm, not unpleasant, but it made her feel oddly disconnected.

The charity shop was on two stories. Alice only

needed to reach the counter on the ground floor to drop off the bags. There was so much stuff she had to turn sideways to fit through the short, narrow aisle on her way through without dislodging any of the merchandise. A tall Asian woman with a jet black ponytail, wearing a purple tracksuit, was in the back. She came out to take the donations as soon as she saw Alice.

"I'm just dropping these off," Alice said, scanning the woman's name badge, and adding, "Ayesha."

"Thank you. Great, you have the stickers too. Let me scan them in." Ayesha held a wireless gun over the barcodes. It beeped as it recognised the data. Then another series of tones came from the computer terminal on the counter, attracting Ayesha's attention. It was like the sound you hear on a quiz show when someone hits the jackpot. Alice was about to turn around and leave when Ayesha glanced up from the terminal and said:

"Goodness. You have been extremely generous."

"It's only two bags. It's not that much really." Alice said.

"Two bags today, brings the total to 24 bags since the beginning of December. The estimated value of your donations is more than £2,000, plus the tax we get back. That was why the computer played the 'bonanza' sound."

Alice thought for a moment. "You're kidding. Twenty-four bags? This is my Mum's stuff actually."

Ayesha paused, feeling for the right words to pose a delicate question. "Did you just say your Mum sent these donations?"

"Yes," said Alice, "Why?"

"We've been noticing some new donation patterns

recently. In the past, substantial gifts like these bumper bundles from your Mum, would be brought in by a bereaved relative. Typically they would be clearing a house after an old person passed away. Do you mind me asking how old your Mum is?"

"Eighty-four. She'll be eighty-five next week. Why?"

Ayesha dropped her gaze for a moment as she thought carefully how to broach the most delicate of subjects. She pursed her lips, breathed in sharply, and then continued slowly:

"Since the tax rules changed, with the incentives for older people to schedule their own departure rather than wait for nature to take its course, the big donations often come in just before they go. I don't know whether your Mum has discussed anything like that with you?"

Alice's mind was racing. New Zealand was one of the few developed countries that had held onto the old laws prohibiting assisted suicide. She knew things had changed a lot in the UK, but she hadn't expected a stranger to be talking so matter-of-factly about her Mum planning to ship out. Feeling deeply shocked, her attempts to hide her reaction were betrayed by her complexion, as she felt her neck and face flush and glow. Her heart thumped so hard she could hear it and she wouldn't have been surprised if Ayesha had been able to hear it too.

"I'm so sorry," Ayesha said, reading the sudden change in Alice's appearance. "I didn't mean to upset you." She reached out and gently touched her arm. "It's not an easy subject to raise. You never really know where to start."

"She's really healthy," Alice said, a little defensively, "Mum's fit as a fiddle. Honestly. I'm a doctor. I'm sure there's nothing wrong with her."

"The thing is," Ayesha explained quietly, "You don't have to be terminally ill any more to arrange to go. The only health criteria for making the booking, once you are 70 or over, is being of sound mind."

A couple of tears escaped from Alice's eyes, and her nose began to run. She sniffed and tried to stem the flow with the back of her hand. Ayesha reached into the pouch on the front of her hoodie, and pulled out a crumpled tissue. "It's clean, just a bit wrinkled, like me," she said, placing the tissue into Alice's clammy palm. "Here, take it."

Alice regained control of her breathing and dried her face. "I'm sorry about that," she said, "Mum has been acting a bit strangely. I didn't know what to make of it. Still don't really. I live in New Zealand."

Ayesha touched Alice's arm again to calm her, before carrying on: "Don't feel bad. It's all happening under the radar. Even if you lived here you wouldn't realise what's been going on. Our charity is very worried about the pace of things in the euthanasia industry at the moment. We're trying to do something about it, but it's not easy. Some frightening things seem to be happening. If you would like to know more about what we're doing to try to stop healthy people signing up for disposal I have some leaflets under the counter. It's such an emotive subject we can't put them out on display."

Alice took the leaflet from Ayesha and said she would read it later when she had some time on her own to take it in. She wanted to tell her everything, all her worries about her Mum, the peculiar business with the lockets. Alice didn't want to believe it, but the evidence all seemed to be pointing in one crazy direction. She reined herself back in, and after a couple more deep breaths, thanked Ayesha for everything she had told her. "I'm going to be 70 myself soon," Ayesha added, "Volunteering here, helping people see what's happening – it's enlightened self-interest. Good luck with your Mum."

Feeling uncomfortably numb, Alice turned right out of the charity shop, arriving almost immediately at Coffee Corner where Lexi would be in a few minutes. The area had changed very little from when she lived nearby decades before, thanks to a preservation order on the area tirelessly monitored by a feisty local conservation society. Working with the council, they had forced the landlord to keep shop rents low and preserved an old-fashioned high street feel that had vanished from nearly everywhere else. Alice wasn't sure how she felt about seeing her old friend now, after everything she'd just heard. Her mood was pretty low and she was keen to get home and share her suspicions with Adam. But, after letting Lexi down so badly over Christmas Day, when Meg had forced her to cancel the invitation to join them, there was no question of bailing now. In any case, the rest of the family would be out for a few more hours at the ice rink.

Alice was first to arrive. She was early even though she had spent more time than she had planned in the Seniority shop. There was a bright table for two people in the window where she took her seat and ordered a chamomile tea. It wasn't something she particularly liked, but she thought she needed something to calm her down a bit.

When Lexi walked through the door Alice waved excitedly and jumped to her feet. They hugged for a few seconds. It had been two years since they last saw each other. Alice was so pleased to see a friendly face that she almost started crying again.

Lexi had gone to visit Alice on a three-week solo tour of Australia and New Zealand to celebrate her 40th birthday. She had slept on Alice's floor and they had gone for long walks, talking about the fun they had as teenagers, and what they were up to now. It was like nothing had changed. Since that visit, though, life had been busy for both of them so they hadn't been in contact much.

When Lexi's parents had died, the girls were both 25. Alice had just left to go travelling, and she always felt bad about not having being there to support her friend who was an only child. Whenever she found a Wi-Fi signal she would hop on and give whatever support she could, but Lexi could barely find the words to talk about the accident, never mind begin to process it. So Alice had made a point of sending her anecdotes about her travels, funny stories about people she met, or tricky situations and scrapes she got into. It seemed to help at the time, and even now Lexi talked about how much she used to look forward to Alice's updates which were beacons of hope and good humor in an otherwise difficult time.

They had a lot to catch up on. First, Alice wanted to know all about Bob. Lexi told her how they had met when Bob came to work at the school. They gradually became friends and then something more happened when they took the kids away on a residential trip. Although Bob was not a teacher, he had to be fully cleared to work with children. They had needed an extra adult to accompany the group to meet the ratios, and he had volunteered. Bob enjoyed working in a school more than he expected. Not only was he running all the IT infrastructure and surveillance operations, but he had set up an advanced coding club for the kids which proved to be a runaway success. He was patient, kind and pretty handsome, Lexi thought. Alice was glad to see Lexi looking happier than she had for years, even if she had put on a bit of weight.

When Lexi asked about her life, Alice was careful not to make it sound too tough. Work was going well. The flat was just about big enough, OK for her and Dolly; most importantly it was affordable. Now Dolly was reaching an age when she could look after herself a bit more, Alice would be able to increase her hours at the hospital to make life better financially. It was when Lexi asked Alice how her Christmas had been that the conversation took an odd turn.

"To be honest, Mum's been acting a bit strange. It's like she's obsessed with creating the perfect family Christmas. She's been kind of intense," Alice said. "I'm so sorry we cancelled you."

"It was fine, honestly. Your Mum had a houseful. How did you all get on?"

"Better than I dared hope. Adam and Frank are doing brilliantly with their daughters. In fact they've taken all three of the girls ice skating this morning, Dolly too.

Mum's gone along to watch. The boys have more energy than me. Bringing up Dolly on my own hasn't been easy, but she is the center of my world. We have this thing where we dye our hair the same color."

"Yes, I noticed on our call the other week. Doesn't school mind?"

"Not at all. It's pretty liberal compared to when we were growing up."

Lexi told Alice about the changes in the curriculum at her school, and how a lot of the classes were now delivered by bots, with online modules tailored to each child's personality and learning style. It helped them learn some things much more quickly than before. So there was hardly any maths taught by humans now. That had been Lexi's subject, but she now loved teaching interpersonal skills, and even though the conversation bots were good they couldn't mimic body language yet. So she hoped she would be in the profession for a good while yet.

When it was time to pay, Alice insisted she pick up the bill after what she called 'the Christmas fiasco'. As she rummaged for her device, she fished out the leaflet she had picked up in the charity shop and placed it on the table. Lexi saw it.

"Alice," she said carefully, "Are you worried about your Mum?"

She stuffed the leaflet back in her pocket, not realising that Lexi knew more about it than she was letting on.

"Yes, I suppose I am. She's nearly 85. Who wouldn't

worry about an ageing parent? Especially when I'm so far away."

"Do you know...do you know about some of the things that have been going on here?" Lexi said slowly, not wanting to worry her friend unduly, but feeling a pressing responsibility to bring her up to date. Lexi remembered the day, back in May, when her involvement with PACE had first started, because of Elsie being banned from going to the gym. Realising that Meg would be in the same target group, she shuddered under the burden of her newfound knowledge. She couldn't ignore the hard knot that was forming in her stomach. This was one of her oldest friends.

"That leaflet you had a minute ago. Have you read it?" They didn't have much time now.

"No, I only just got it in the charity shop. I was dropping off some things for Mum. It sounds like they'd had mountains of stuff from her. They said it triggered some kind of warning. That's why they gave me the leaflet. I haven't even looked at it yet."

Lexi knew all about the leaflets because she had helped Ruth deliver them to the charity shop, and it was Bob who had designed the algorithm that alerted the volunteers when someone might be at risk. She couldn't tell Alice that though.

"I would have a look at it if you get a minute, Alice. Maybe show Adam. Old people are being put under a lot of pressure. If you don't mind me asking, when exactly is your Mum 85?"

"Not you as well! I had the same question in the charity shop. In a couple of weeks, why?"

"When people are nearing 85, they can feel extra vulnerable because that's the final cut-off point for pretty much all support. You can't access the NHS, state pensions stop, and they've got this massive inheritance tax waiver that you can only claim on or before your 85th birthday. I'm guessing your Mum still has a bit left – the house will be worth something at the very least?"

"I hadn't really thought about it."

"The point is, it looks like old folks are being coerced into going. It's all underhand, being done in secret. I genuinely hope that's not the case for your Mum. I haven't seen her for decades, but you always make it sound like she's strong and fit and knows her own mind. Paradoxically, that makes it easier for her to sign up, because you have to pass a dementia test before they'll let you. And they are targeting everyone who is 70 or over. Repeatedly. The ads never stop. You can't escape them."

"I wanted to stay on for a more few weeks, but Mum doesn't want me to. She's insisting I go back," Alice said, starting to feel helpless.

"Have a look at the leaflet. If you're still worried when you've been through it let me know. I'll see if I can keep an eye on her for you if you like. How much longer are you here for?"

Alice had two more days. Just two days to try to get to the bottom of what Meg was up to, and to try to do something about it. She just hoped that it wasn't too late.

CHAPTER TWENTY-TWO

ALICE DECIDED TO WALK BACK to the house rather than get a car. It would take her just over half an hour if she kept up a brisk pace. The exercise seemed like a good idea after all the mince pies and stuffing balls, and it gave her some time to think. She pulled the leaflet out of her pocket and became absorbed in it as she walked.

Is your friend or relative being coerced into voluntary euthanasia? Not sure what to do about it?

PACE can help!

PACE stands for People Against Coercive Euthanasia. We believe that the voluntary euthanasia programme – introduced as a result of the referendum two years ago – is being implemented too aggressively. It is going far beyond its original remit, which was to help people in pain, or with advanced terminal conditions, to end their lives humanely.

Operators of the disposal services are applying excessive psychological pressure to older people to convince them to end their lives early. They are doing this by targeting them with sophisticated advertising and using highly manipulative conversational computing, also known as chatbots. These companies have intimate knowledge of potential Enders' individual circumstances, and play on their deepest aspirations and fears to persuade them to sign up to go. Endings are now being carried out on an unprecedented scale.

What is happening to the over-70s?

- Denied products and services that help them maintain strength and fitness e.g. gym memberships, training equipment, exercise classes and health supplements
- Overseas travel insurance being refused to impair their quality of life
- Confidence and happiness being undermined by manipulation on social media
- Befriending by sophisticated audio chatbots which talk people into suicide
- Use of images of deceased spouses to suggest possible reunions in the afterlife
- Glamourizing death with aspirational campaigns such as Rockstar Ending
- Financial incentives to sign up for disposal, including total waiver of inheritance tax

- Increased pressure as individuals approach 85, when NHS support is withdrawn
- No option to cancel once the 14-day cooling-off period is passed. You sign up, you go.

Why don't I know about this?

- Promotion is closely targeted at the over-70s and hidden from everyone else
- People who sign up for disposal are bound by draconian Non-Disclosure Agreements. If they tell anyone what they have done, their estate is subject to a forfeit of 50% of its total value.

I think someone I know is being pressured. What should I do?

> ***Look out for common signs:*** Excessive clearing out of personal belongings and foodstuffs, unusual levels of secrecy, lack of commitment about future plans, depression, worrying about money, keeping certain dates clear for no obvious reason.
>
> ***Ask them directly if they have signed up:*** If they have and want to stop the process contact PACE immediately for emotional and legal support.

If you are still worried about someone don't delay

Contact PACE now

It was a lot to take in. Alice found it hard to believe that her mum, who loved life so much, might consider going down this route. Meg had always taken everything in her stride. Over Christmas she had seemed so stable and serene. Surely this was paranoid nonsense?

When Alice got back to the house no one else was there. Glancing at her device, she saw that Dolly was still at the ice rink and quickly established that the rest of them, including Meg, were there too, having some pop and nachos before setting off back to the house. They wouldn't be home for at least an hour, so she got to work.

First, the kitchen cupboards. Were they stocked to a normal level? Hard to tell. Nothing was out of date. There always used to be at least one ancient tin of peaches or an old jar of spice that smelled of dust and had expired five years ago. Alice could find nothing like that now, and the shelves seemed a bit less crowded and chaotic than she remembered.

The freezer only had a few things in it, but she was a single person living on her own. For a moment, Alice began to doubt why she was bothering with this peculiar exercise. Had she become paranoid now? She had 40 minutes left. Better head upstairs.

She went into the room that Adam and Frank were staying in, which Meg used as her bedroom when she had no visitors. There was a huge wardrobe with four mirrored sliding doors all along one wall. Meg called it her Quattro Stagioni, because she separated her clothes out by season – spring, summer, autumn and winter. When she had been working, Meg had spent a lot of money on well-cut clothes and looked impeccable. Alice smiled thinking of the fun she and her brother had when they were small, hiding in the wardrobe's voluminous cavities. They used to think it was hysterical that their Mum had named her cupboard after their favorite pizza.

Stepping over the jumble of masculine chaos lying around the room, she gingerly slid one of the cupboard doors open. Crikey, she said to herself, that looks a bit thin. A few cashmere jumpers and winter coats looked lost in the massive space. One or two pairs of boots and trainers at the bottom. There were a couple of layers of thermals in the drawer. Baggy yoga clothes. But that was it. It felt sparse, and it made Alice uneasy.

Her suspicions worsened when she turned to the spring and summer sections. They were empty. In the space where Meg's classy cruise wear, sharp summer dresses and tailored shorts used to hang, there was a solitary lavender anti-moth sachet on a cardboard swing tag. The massive shoe collection was gone. There used to be dozens of boxes, stacked four high and three wide, containing everything from Manolo Blahnik and Laboutins to Ecco and Fit Flop. Meg's wardrobe had become the designer clothing equivalent of the Mary Celeste.

Please, please don't let this be happening, Alice thought. She slid out the big drawer at the top of the dresser that she vividly remembered overflowing with soft scarves and costume jewellery. The memory of Meg's favorite perfume, Chanel number 19, hung in the air. As children, she and Adam used to sneak in and borrow the colorful swathes of fabric and chunky necklaces for dressing up. Everything was gone. Even the waxed lining paper Meg used to put at the bottom of the drawers had been taken out. Beneath Alice's fingers there was just a dry, scratchy unfinished grey wooden surface.

There was one other possibility. Clutching at straws, Alice took a stool on to the landing and stood on it carefully to unhook the trap door into the loft. Maybe Mum had taken everything up there to make room for the family visit? It was the kind of thing she would do. There were lots of boxes up there full of family history, and various heirlooms that only really meant anything to Meg. Or rather, there used to be. Alice pulled out the ladder and put her feet on one rung after another. As she neared the top, she braced herself for the dust cloud that shot into your eyes and lungs when you went up there. She popped her head through the hatch and switched on the light. The whole space lit up brightly under six new LEDs set into the ceiling. She looked around again and again to make sure what she was seeing was true. The loft was not only free of dust, it was also free of everything else. Completely empty. Not even a shadow.

Dropping down gently onto the landing carpet, Alice decided to give one last thing a try. She was not enjoying snooping on her mother, especially as she had always respected their privacy when they were children, but desperate times called for desperate measures.

In the boxroom, Meg had set up a small office on a corner desk with a keyboard and wireless mouse. She liked to sit at a workstation with everything adjusted to the right ergonomic height. Alice moved the mouse and the screen sprang into life, asking her to enter a password. She tried every combination she could think of, important family dates, places and names. Nothing worked. Dammit. Then she started to think laterally. What if she'd been told to change her password by the people who were coming to take her away? What would she use then? One last try. Alice pulled out the leaflet and looked at it again. The answer was there, staring her in the face, all the time. Meg typed in one word. Rockstar.

Just then, as the security screen dissolved allowing her access to Meg's machine, she heard the door open downstairs and the kids ran into the house. Meg was laughing with Frank. Something funny happened on the ice, and Meg had filmed it. They had been replaying it in the car all the way home. A rush of adrenaline coursed through Alice's body as she quickly re-locked the PC and leapt out onto the landing.

"Hi guys," she shouted downstairs, "Did you have fun?"

They were unanimous – the morning had been a tremendous success. Everyone was full of stories that they had to unload immediately. They raved about the rotating sculpture of the ice angel in the middle of the rink, sponsored by the corporation; about the characters dressed up as elves who whirled around among the skaters; about how they had all held hands and zoomed along in a line, and even Mia, the youngest, had found her feet in the end and stayed upright with a little help from everyone else. Frank had been showing off as he was a brilliant skater. A former member of his college ice hockey team, he would occasionally break away from their group and accelerate, skating backwards with ease and even doing the odd perfectly-judged jump in moments when the ice was a bit quieter. Dolly and Meg were particularly impressed. Frank's own kids and Adam had seen his skating feats before, and took them more for granted.

"I wish you could have seen him Mum," Dolly said, her face lit up with pleasure, "You would have loved it. How was your friend?"

So much had happened that morning. "Lexi? She was cool. It was like we have never been apart. Just picking up where we left off."

"She wasn't annoyed about not coming over for Christmas?" Dolly asked, knowing that Alice had found standing down Lexi and Bob difficult. "No, it was fine. Like I said, I know her well enough for it not to be a problem. We'll all have to meet Bob another time though. He was sorting through some things at his lock-up today so I didn't get to see him. He sounds just right for Lexi. After all this time, I think she might actually settle down, you know. They're living together. We'll get the chance to meet him at some stage, I'm sure."

Meg had put the kettle on to make tea for the adults, and rustled up organic hot chocolate for the children. Every child had their own little mug which they had painted with Meg one afternoon at a pottery café. She had taken them there just before Christmas. Meg carried the drinks into the living room on a tray which also held a plate of mini mince pies they were still trying to finish off from Christmas. The adults sank deep into sofas and the kids spread out on the floor. Meg suggested they have a game of Jenga, using the set she had kept from when Alice and Adam were at home. Bella had other ideas, reached for the tablet that Meg used to control the screen and started scrolling through Christmas films.

"What's *It's a Wonderful Life*?" Dolly asked, as it came top of the list of suggestions. Focusing heavily on unloading the wooden Jenga pieces from the box, and without looking up, Meg said, "It's a very old film, dear, and a bit complicated for the smaller ones to follow. Why don't you find *Elf*? That's much more fun." A shudder ran down Alice's spine as she remembered the plot of the film Meg had just vetoed. It was about a man who is contemplating suicide, in the mistaken belief that a life insurance payout will be better for his family than having him around.

"Get *Elf* on quickly," Meg said, "I've got another surprise for you kids later this afternoon. We have to be out of here by four."

Alice remembered that Meg had arranged to take all the girls to Snazzy Nails that afternoon. "Mum," she said, pulling her quietly aside, "Would you mind if I give the nail bar a miss? Could you take the kids without me? I'd like to make a start on sorting out our packing, and have a bit of a catch up with Frank and Adam. What do you think?"

A flicker of disappointment ran across Meg's face, but she had never been one to play the martyr. "I was looking forward to us being all girls together. But I can manage on my own easily if you have things to sort out."

As soon as Elf was over, the girls were bundled giggling into their coats and hats, and they headed out holding hands with Meg into the gloomy winter evening. The weather was dry and quite mild, which was lucky because they would have to make the ten-minute walk back without gloves so that their nails didn't smudge.

When the door clicked shut the house was suddenly still. Alice glanced round the living room at the scattered Jenga pieces, half-empty mugs, and abandoned mince pies which everyone knew would never be eaten. Adam and Frank were in the kitchen working on dinner. The family had been getting bored with traditional British Christmas food, so the boys had volunteered to make a chilli. Alice loaded the tray with things that would need to be washed up in the kitchen, and followed the guys into the room.

"Silence at last," she declared, as she set the tray down on the first clear surface she could find, clicking open the dishwasher and starting to pour dregs of no-longer-hot chocolate down the sink. "And goodwill to all people," Frank chimed in festively as he rummaged in the fridge for the minced turkey.

"I'm a bit worried about Mum," Alice began. "Have you noticed anything odd?"

"She is amazing," Frank said, "I can't believe how much energy she has. She's thought of everything and been incredibly generous. Y'all are so lucky."

"Thanks," said Alice, "She is doing brilliantly for her age. But there's something not quite right. Adam, do you know what I mean?"

Adam was peeling onions and garlic on a green plastic chopping board. "I'm not sure, Sis. We haven't seen her for a couple of years, so it's hard to know if any changes are significant or it's just a bit of old age creeping up on her. She's getting slower I suppose, but isn't that normal? You're the doctor in the family. What do you think?" The skins were now off the vegetables and placed in the relevant bin. He now set about slicing the onions methodically, and piling them into a pan.

"It's not so much her physical health I'm worried about. It's more what she's been doing. Didn't you think the locket thing was a bit weird?"

"Maybe slightly. She's got a bit maudlin about Dad. I noticed her screen saver is pretty much all pictures of him. Perhaps she's just thinking too much. Too much time on her own."

Alice asked, "Did you know that once she's 85 she won't get free health care anymore? It's only a few weeks away."

"Yes, I did know that. But she's not short of money, she'll still be able to get private health care if she needs it. It's what pretty much everyone else in the world has to do – pay for it or get insurance. We can help if she needs us to."

"You mean financially?"

"Yes. Frank and I have been putting some cash aside in case she needs a top-up, but I don't think it will be needed for a while yet."

Alice felt embarrassed that she was not in the same position as Adam. Although she had a higher status job than him, in many people's eyes, there was no way she could afford to send anything to subsidise her Mum if it came to it. Every cent was accounted for.

"I offered to stay on a bit longer to make sure she's all right. I thought I could get her set up with a private doctor, but she won't hear of it," Alice said, focusing on the practical things she might be able to do. “And there’s something else. She’s thrown most of her clothes away.”

“Maybe she’s just having a clear out.”

“It’s more than that. Tons of stuff has gone. The charity shop said they’d had 24 bags from her in the last month. It made some kind of alert go off when I was in there. Come and look.”

Leaving Frank in charge of the softening onions, Alice led Adam up to the bedroom and opened all the doors of the Quattro Stagione. “Wow. I wish I could de-clutter like that,” he said glibly, as the redundant moth repellent sachet swung gently to and fro, “She should write a book about it.” “It’s not funny, Adam,” Alice insisted, “Have a look at this.” She took the crumpled PACE leaflet from her pocket.

Adam smoothed out the paper and sat on the edge of the bed. “Jesus,” he said, “Is this for real?”

“I think it might be, yes.”

Alice sat down next to her brother. “We’re both so far away,” she said, quietly. “I tried to get into her PC to see what else she might have done, but I’d only just got in when you all arrived back.”

“You hacked into her PC? That’s extreme, Alice. Although…” he ran his eyes over the leaflet again “…I’m beginning to see why you might be worried.”

They sat quietly for a few seconds.

“Come on then,” Adam said suddenly. The penny had finally dropped, “We haven’t got long. We spent the first 18 years of our lives doing things we weren’t supposed to in this house. Why stop now?” They stood up together and picked their way past suitcases open on the floor and orphan socks, crossing the landing into the boxroom. Adam shouted down the stairs, "Frankie, can you carry on without me for a bit?"

"Sure, it's all under control," Frank called back up, as the fragrance of warm cumin spiralled up the stairs. They heard the faint chink of a metal cap being levered off a beer bottle. "We shouldn't be long," Adam replied, leaning over the banister so Frank would hear him above the sizzling.

Alice took her seat at the desk and quickly entered the password. Adam watched over her shoulder as she carefully typed R-o-c-k-s-t-a-r. "You're kidding," he said. "Nope," Alice replied, "As if we weren't worried enough already." They were in.

But when they tried to access Meg's email it was on a cloud service. There was more security, and they couldn't break into it. Alice opened a browser and clicked into Facebook. Nothing out of the ordinary there either.

"Try browsing history," Adam suggested.

The links took them to sites for planning days out in London, ideas for exciting things to do with kids and theater booking websites. The workings behind the blueprint that Meg had carefully constructed to create their past two weeks of genuine fun was unfolding in front of them. What they were doing felt horribly intrusive, like they were looking for a fatal flaw in an otherwise perfect fairy godmother. Even Snazzy Nails was on there.

It was Adam who spotted the adverts first. The same one kept coming up again and again. It was pushing the same Rockstar Ending that the leaflet had talked about. Alice clicked on the link and it took her to a website offering a discount on the mother of all luxury disposals. They watched the video together, overwhelmed with admiration for its creative powers, followed by sheer horror when they realised it was actually promoting a one-way ticket to a pimped-up cremation.

When they navigated away, the ad hounded them again and again. They couldn't escape it.

Most disturbing of all was the countdown calendar. In the top right hand corner was a birthday cake. On it were two candles in the shape of the numbers eight and five. The words 'Happy Birthday Meg' had been drawn on in red icing, her favorite color.

An animated starburst flashed on and off. It said:

Hurry! Give your family the bumper
bonus they will never forget!

There was a login to Meg's account, but they couldn't crack that either. Not even using the word Rockstar. Alice looked at the time. Meg and the girls would be back in ten minutes.

"We're going to have to stop now," she said. "I'm going to talk to my friend Lexi. She seemed to know something about this. She said she'd help if we needed her to."

"OK," said Adam, "Do you think we should say something to Mum? It's what the leaflet says to do."

"No, not yet. We've all had such a fantastic time, I don't want to ruin it unless we're sure about what's going on. Can you bear with me?"

Adam looked her straight in the eyes. "Alice, we're

all flying out the day after tomorrow. That doesn't leave much time for a subtle approach."

"I know, but I don't want to freak her out. Let me talk to Lexi tonight and we can regroup later."

At that moment they heard the children stream into the house. Adam ran downstairs while Alice closed down the browser, and followed him as quickly as she could. Meg was radiant. They all had gold nails covered in glitter.

I've done it, Meg thought to herself. I've given them the sparkling Christmas they'll never forget.

CHAPTER TWENTY-THREE

IT WAS THE END OF another action-packed day. Dolly and Alice headed up to the spare room exhausted.

Alice was drained. She had found out so many strange and distressing things in one day. Her investigations around the house had heightened her suspicions that Meg was getting ready to die. The burden of her anxiety had been exacerbated by the troubling guilt she felt from conspiring with her brother to spy on her only surviving parent. On top of that, there was the stress of having to pretend to the rest of the family that everything was tickety-boo.

It was simpler for Dolly. She was finally giving into the wave of physical tiredness caused by the morning's skating, and then dashing back out through the cold night for a manicure. Rather than being the luxe pamper-fest she had hoped for, the visit to the nail bar had been mildly burdensome for Dolly, as Meg had put her in charge of Mia who, at four years old, could not stop fidgeting unless Dolly gave undivided attention to everything she had to say. And she had a lot to say.

Downstairs, where the smaller girls were now being put to sleep on the sofa bed, Adam and Frank were holding firm on their refusal to allow them any more screen time. They had dimmed the lights, and Frank was singing 'Sweet Baby James'. Bella was humming along. Mia had just fallen silent and was beginning to nod off. The baubles on the Christmas tree reflected tiny pastel rainbows around the room. Meg stood in the doorway holding Adam's hand, taking it all in, and smiling.

"I'm glad you've been able to get to know your cousins a bit better," Alice said as she rummaged around in the bedroom with her daughter, trying to remember where they had left their pyjamas.

"Yes. Me too. They can be a bit of a pain sometimes, but they are usually quite sweet. We had a lot of fun with Grandma and the Uncles earlier. I am going to call Granny every week when we get home."

"She's been amazing. You know, when you get older, you notice things about your parents that makes you appreciate them much more. Did I ever tell you that she came out to help me when you were a toddler? I was so determined to show her I could manage that I pretty much turned her away. Looking back on it I must have been crazy."

Dolly gathered her pyjamas in a bundle, grabbed a damp towel that had been scrunched on the back of a chair, and headed to the bathroom. The minute her daughter had left the room, Alice reached for her device and flicked on the screen. She opened up messaging and found Lexi's most recent stream, which she added to.

> Alice: Need advice urgently about Mum. Can you help? Pls message back ASAP.

Lexi wasn't online right then, so Alice got undressed, put on the XXL T-shirt and pair of baggy shorts that she used for pyjamas, and wrapped her grey fleece dressing gown snugly over the top. She propped herself up on some pillows and lolled about on top of her quilt while she waited for Dolly to vacate the bathroom, scrolling through her social media.

Friends back in NZ were out enjoying the sun. She'd be over there doing the same thing in only a few days. Alice looked forward to being back in the light and the warmth, but she knew that what was usually a pleasant and relaxing time of year would be overshadowed by a sense of dread, as she worried about what was going on with her mum.

When Dolly came back Alice slipped her device into her pocket and headed for the bathroom herself. She cleaned her teeth, then tucked her hair behind her ears and washed her face, wallowing in the pleasant sensation as she draped a hot flannel over her face. Alice tipped her head back and inhaled the warm steam for a few slow, deep, calming breaths, her eyes closed. As she settled onto the seat for her final bedtime wee she felt an unexpected vibration in her dressing gown pocket. It was Lexi: Can you speak now?

Alice didn't feel she could. The walls were thin and she was worried about being overheard.

> Alice: Have to message, can't talk. Mum acting strangely. Think she may have plans.
>
> Lexi: Have you asked her?
>
> Alice: Can't face it. Too grim. Don't want to

> spoil things before we leave, especially with the kids being here.
>
> Lexi: What has happened?
>
> Alice: Excessive clearance. Tried to find out more from her email, but couldn't get in. Got into machine, but mail app secured.
>
> Lexi: Do you want help hacking in?
>
> Alice: Feel guilty, but how else to avert trauma for all?
>
> Lexi: OK. Look out for memory stick with some old photos of us on it. The fam might like to see them. Bob will put it through the door tonight. There will be hidden files on the drive; run the .exe. That should help.
>
> Alice: Mysterious… but OK will do. X

She closed her device, and took another deep breath before trotting back to the bedroom. Dolly was on a video app with one of the friends in NZ, and as Alice entered the room she said goodbye and settled down to sleep, curling into an elongated ball and lying on her side. Alice dropped her dressing gown onto the floor, and climbed in under the covers. She flicked off the bedside light and lay in the dark with her eyes open, just making out the shape that was Dolly's endearing form just an arm's length away. As her daughter's shoulders rose and fell gently Alice tried to follow her breathing pattern, seeking the perfect frequency that would tip her into the deep slumber she craved to steel her for whatever was going to come next.

When she woke at around 7am the next day it was still dark. Within seconds she had gone from basking in a relaxed, pre-dawn semi-conscious state to an intense sensation of being on high alert. Like a bereavement had already happened. She relaxed again as soon as she heard Meg moving around in the kitchen. The reassuring smell of coffee wafted up the stairs.

Within a few minutes Alice was alone in the kitchen with Meg. As she had passed the front door, she checked the mat to see whether the envelope Lexi had promised had arrived, but there was nothing there. Meg sat at the kitchen table in well-cut jeans and a dark grey hoodie, her wispy white hair combed neatly to her shoulders, a touch of mascara lifting her bright blue eyes.

There was a glass cafetière of coffee in front of her, with the plunger all the way down and a cupful already missing, decanted into the small mug she had got the grandchildren to decorate for her on their visit to the pottery café. It had traditional Christmassy colors, red and green, and each child had attempted to adorn it with a simple self-portrait with varying degrees of success. Alice recognised Dolly's green bob right away.

"It looks like you," Meg said to Alice, pointing at the picture Dolly had done. Maybe it was just the matching green bob, but Alice thought she had a point, and grinned proudly. Something around the eyes. There was no doubt about it, Dolly was the best thing that had ever happened to her. Alice remembered how Meg used to say the same thing about her and Adam. She knew exactly what she meant now she had a child of her own. They bring their own love.

"Mum," Alice began, "We've all had a fantastic stay with you. Dolly said to me last night how much she'd enjoyed it."

"She's a lovely girl. You should be very proud of her." Meg replied, standing up from the table a little stiffly, and moving towards the fridge to put away the big pot of natural yoghurt she'd been spooning onto some thawed fruit.

It was now or never, Alice thought. If I want to talk to her about this Endings thing I need to do it while no one else is around. "Mum, I've been hearing some very worrying rumors about what's going on here. Do you know what it will mean for you when you hit 85 in a couple of weeks?"

Meg stared intently into the fridge and moved around various pots and jars to make absolutely sure the yoghurt was in a safe place and wouldn't tumble out when the next person opened the door. "Don't worry about me love, I'm going to be fine," she said, focusing heavily on rearranging the order of three small bottles of Actimel so that the ones with the soonest expiry date were nearest the front.

"Is it true you can't use the NHS at all after your 85th birthday? If it is, that could be a big problem if you find yourself… well… not so spritely as you are now. Or if you have a fall."

Continuing to address her imaginary friend at the back of the fridge, rather than look her daughter in the eye, Meg went on, "It's true, Alice, I will join the ranks of the 'too old for free treatment'. But I can go private. There are still doctors who care for the lucky people like me who can afford it after the state support ends. I really don't want you to worry. There's no need. The people you need to worry about are the ones that can't afford it. Their options are much more limited. For the well-off… well, we have choices."

A long 'beep' started to ring out of the fridge, as the appliance sensed it had been open for too long. After Meg shut the door she put her hand in the pocket of her hoodie and pulled out an envelope. "I almost forgot," she said, "This was on the mat. It's got your name on it."

So Bob had put it through the door already. "Brilliant. That will be from Lexi. When I saw her yesterday morning she said she'd drop over some photos and old video footage. They're quite big files and she wasn't sure how easy it would be to send them. From when we were younger."

Alice took the envelope from Meg and gently tore it open. She peeped inside and saw the memory stick Lexi had promised rattling around inside. "I looked in the loft yesterday, when I got back, for some of our old pictures so I could do the same for her, but everything had gone."

"Yes, I'm thinking of converting it to another guest room, didn't I tell you? I put all the old pictures I thought anyone might want into the cupboard. You can have a look through if you like."

Alice stuffed the envelope into her pocket and reached for the coffee. Meg had already put a mug and plate in front of her, and asked her what she'd like to eat.

She settled for toast and Meg grabbed the bread from the freezer and sat with her while she ate. It felt like a moment that was both ordinary and extremely precious at the same time. It was their last full day together, and Meg had booked a table at Pizza Express in the O2 for lunch. The plan was for them to see the Christmas show, *Disney on Ice*, after lunch and then chill out back at the house while they all finished off their packing.

"You've spent a fortune on us Mum," Alice said, "I'm so sorry I haven't been able to make a contribution, but things are still tight for us."

"I wanted to," Meg said, "We've never been able to get everyone together in one place before and I'm grateful you could all make the time. That's what money is for. You can't take it with you."

"Don't talk like that Mum. Please."

"It's true though. You can't escape the fact that, at 84… I can't take anything for granted. As for the negative attitudes to old people here at the moment, well it's hardly surprising that a lot of them are getting depressed. People I know, much younger than me, are working themselves up into a terrible state. But I'm in a good place Alice. Everything is in order and I have just had the happiest two weeks of my life. I'm glad you've enjoyed it too."

There was a serenity about Meg which was different to anything Alice had seen before. She wanted to say something in response but had no idea how to find the words. Instead she stood up and gave her a hug. She felt her mother's bony frame against her own more dense body. It brought home to Alice her mother's increasing fragility, almost doll-like in her arms. They stood for a moment, Alice's eyes closed, remembering the time when the roles were reversed, when Meg was the stronger one, striding out purposefully, pushing the heavy double buggy with her and Adam fastened inside, without the slightest flinch. At that moment Alice's phone vibrated again. It was squashed between the two of them and they stepped apart, falling into giggles when it buzzed. "It's Lexi, just checking I got the memory stick," Alice said, looking at it for second. "Can I use the computer in your room to look at the files? I can copy the good ones for you if you like."

"Sounds like a good idea," Meg said, "I'll come up and unlock it so you can get in."

Walking behind Meg, Alice couldn't help noticing that she was very steady on her feet. Although her mother had lost some of her muscle mass in recent years, and her jeans seemed slightly baggy, she climbed the stairs with ease. "You're in good shape Mum," Alice remarked, "Honestly you just seem to fly up." Meg thought for a moment, "I think the yoga helps, and I had some weights until quite recently."

"I hope I'm as strong as you are when I'm your age," Alice said, slightly breathless from climbing the stairs, "Even now would be good."

They squeezed past the single bed in the boxroom and edged towards the corner. Meg settled in front of her old fashioned work station and quickly typed her password to unlock the machine. "Where is it?" she said, meaning the memory stick.

Suddenly Alice was worried. Meg intended to open

the files herself rather than just unlock the machine and leave it to Alice. She had no choice other than to hand it over. Meg swiftly plugged the key into a port on the machine and found the files. Over her shoulder Alice scanned down the list. Lexi had labelled them all.

There were about 40 pictures and three videos. The photos from the 1990s had been scanned in, their colors slightly faded, as they had started life as old fashioned negatives and prints. There were some really badly-composed snaps of Alice, Adam and other friends from primary school, taken on a day when Lexi has borrowed a parent's pocket camera and taken it into the playground. The children had organised themselves into random groups for the photos, none of which seemed to align properly with the ground or the sky, putting the kids at odd angles in their dishevelled and badly customised uniforms. "What a bunch of urchins," Meg said. "That one's headless."

In the teen section the artistic merit of the pictures improved as Lexi's maturing hand steadied. There were a couple of Lexi and Alice together, which must have been taken by someone else in Lexi's back garden one summer's evening before the girls went out. They were wearing extremely tight dresses, a lot of make-up, and posing in a way which Alice now found uncomfortably provocative, although at the time it just felt like fun. "You can look forward to Dolly dressing like that," Meg said, in a tone that was the nearest she would ever get to gloating. She was right, Alice would soon be the parent of a teen with all the angst that entailed, and she could do with Meg to help guide her through.

Having turned down the volume so as not to disturb the rest of the house, Meg clicked on the first of the videos. Lexi's Mum must have made it. She always had a camera in her hand at the school events. At first they both struggled to work out what was happening. The title of the file was simply 'chapel'. It was quite dark. Then Alice recognised the venue. "Turn up the sound a bit Mum," she said, "It's that choral performance we did in Lewisham cemetery."

"I don't remember that," Meg said.

"You were away on business, but I think Dad came."

It was slow getting started. The screen was quite dark. In the shadows you could make out a group of ten young people arranged in two rows, the taller ones at the back. Then the riff started, a fast paced but unforgettable jangling guitar. As the light improved the singing began, soft at first, with the whole group working together as one. There were some pale gothic structures in the background. The color was very poor and the nooks and crannies were only just visible in shades of grey.

They were in a deconsecrated Victorian chapel, used at the time for art exhibitions and the odd live performance. As the structure of the song became more complex, and was punctuated with the chorus, the singers split into two sections, with Alice and Lexi in different groups competing in harmony with each other as some of the lines repeated, rising to a crescendo at the end. Alice was in the group that kept repeating the song's title, 'Don't Fear the Reaper', which had been recorded by Blue Oyster Cult more than a decade before either of them were born.

Meg and Alice were transfixed by the hazy image. Although the quality of the picture was poor, it had it an eerie dimension that matched perfectly the lyrics of the song which had somehow survived, crystal clear. The chorus echoed in Alice's head as the events of the previous 24 hours replayed vividly in her mind's eye. She still remembered all the words, and how romantic the narrative had seemed back then, with its psychedelic angle on the story of Romeo and Juliet cheerfully running towards their transcendent suicide. As she tried to pick out herself from the other singers in the half light, she could hear Meg humming along, occasionally mumbling one of the lyrics to herself.

"Well I never. Your Dad and I went to see them live at the Hollywood Bowl in 1981. Before you were born."

Although Meg had talked about holidays in California before, Alice didn't remember her mentioning the concert. Maybe she had, and Alice had just tuned it out, in the way that children often screen out the details of their parents' repetitive anecdotes. It struck her that there were so many things she didn't know about her Mum and still wanted to discover.

"I want to stay on for your birthday," she blurted out. "Really, I do."

As the video came to an end, Meg became icier than Alice had seen her for years. "No. I've already told you. No Alice. If you keep going on about it, you're going ruin our time together. Surely you don't want to upset the girls? I already have plans for my birthday anyway."

"What plans?"

"I've booked myself into one of the fancy new corporation wellness centers. Yoga, Pilates, kombucha, that kind of thing. A proper treat."

"Why didn't you say before?"

"You didn't ask." Meg was looking irritated now. "Anyway, I don't have to justify myself to you."

Alice was taken aback.

"That's not fair Mum. I'm allowed to be concerned."

She ignored what her daughter had said, and ploughed on. "When you chose to live on the other side of the world, Alice, you forfeited your rights to know every little detail of my life."

Alice felt tears welling up in her eyes at her mother's hurtful remark. She hadn't spoken to her like that since she was a teenager. Meg had lost it a few times back then, usually when she got back from a business trip, jet-lagged and exhausted, deliberately provoked by her daughter into a screaming argument just to prove that she still cared. Alice regretted that now. Her throat tensed up and she couldn't speak.

Oh no, Meg thought to herself, I wanted to throw her off the scent, not make her cry. Realising she might have gone too far, she softened her expression and touched her daughter's shoulder. "It's lovely that you want to stay, Alice, but it's neither practical nor necessary. I've told you. I have plans for a pamper-fest. You have to get Dolly back to school. There's your job. Quite apart from how much it would cost to change the flights."

"But Mum, what have you done with all your clothes?" Her voice was trembling now.

"All these questions! I had a moth infestation. It was the only solution. Once I'd thrown out the worst of them, I was on a roll. I thought I'd keep going. So much of that old stuff was way past its best. Cruise wear that's decades old. Totally pointless keeping it. I've replaced my cashmere, though, and stocked up on repellent. They're not wheedling their way back in now."

"But what about the shoes? You love your shoes!"

"They were old, love. Very old. I'm off heels, have been for a few years now. Flats only for me. Better for my feet. Fall prevention." Then, adding slowly and deliberately, "Stop worrying."

Her logic was watertight. Meg had an answer for everything. Cowed by the accusation that she would be ruining the holiday for everyone if she made any more fuss, Alice buried the feeling that something still wasn't right in the deep recesses of her mind. Mum had a splurge planned. That was it. She had to take her word for it.

There was a sound on the stairs, and Bella burst in. "I'm awake Granny," she shouted, climbing onto the little bed and starting to bounce like it was a trampoline, "Good morning!" The little room seemed very crowded all of a sudden, and Meg stood up. "Come on then, tearaway," she said, "Let's get you back downstairs."

As Meg left the room with her grandchild holding her hand, Alice slid silently in front of the screen and checked the messages again on her device. She followed the instructions for finding the hidden file on the memory stick, and it appeared as if by magic in the file list. Listening intently to what was going on in the rest of the house, she installed the file Lexi had sent her, in the hope that whatever the hacking software unearthed would prove her nagging doubts wrong.

In 24 hours' time she would be on a plane, headed for the other side of the world.

CHAPTER TWENTY-FOUR

Bryn lived alone in a one-bedroom flat which occupied the ground floor of a shabby Victorian terrace. He was just about managing to survive on what was left of his pension, drawing now and then on his savings, and supplemented by a small contribution, now and then, from his daughter Jade who worked shifts at McDonald's. Bryn thought of Jade as one of those generous souls who would give her last penny to help someone else, even if she had to go without herself. Recently she had begun to support a new boyfriend, Cliff, who didn't appear to have any kind of regular work, and who Bryn wasn't at all sure about. But then lots of people didn't have proper jobs any more.

Not being so good on his feet these days, Bryn didn't get out much. He had a red walking frame with wheels which he used to take him down to the shop at the end of the road, and a small, stained grey backpack he used to carry things in so that the weight was evenly distributed and he had less chance of falling over. In earlier times he would probably have had a home help, but all that support had been reduced to practically nothing after Yuthentic had their way. So he just had to make do. Luckily he was still young enough to get medical assistance. The anti-depressants were a big help in getting him through the week, and they'd given him a little something else to take if he was headed out for a walk which gave his energy levels a boost. On a good day he might attempt a few exercises to try to keep mobile but, because he couldn't afford to eat like he used to, he was getting weaker.

Now he had another problem. He was having trouble remembering things. Bryn would try to do something simple like grill himself a sausage, and suddenly find he was standing by a pan engulfed in flames, not knowing what to do. He would usually wait for the fire to burn itself out. So far he had managed to hide it from Jade, but he knew it was only a matter of time before she found out and started to worry even more about him. Once the fire brigade had been called out by a neighbor who had been alarmed by the acrid smell and wisps of smoke escaping from under his front door. It was after that the phone calls started.

"I believe someone at this address has recently been involved in a dementia-related domestic fire," a friendly, concerned-sounding voice began.

"How did you know that?" Bryn asked.

"Is that right? Have you recently had a fire?" the voice responded.

"Well…" he didn't really want to admit it.

"Please don't be ashamed this call is entirely confidential. Have you recently had a fire?"

"OK. Yes, actually."

"How do you feel about that?"

Before he knew it, Bryn was pouring out his lonely heart to the voice. They seemed to have all the time in the world to listen to him and were not at all judgemental when he began to air his growing worries about his safety, especially how he might have his tenancy taken away and be forced to move into one of the old people's dormitories.

The first time they called, the voice didn't push Bryn at all. It just listened to him and played back to him what he had said. Bryn felt oddly comforted by the conversation which had helped him to process and allay some of his fears. When they asked if he'd like to have a chat again at the end of each conversation he said yes. They made an arrangement to speak once a week.

Over the next few months, Bryn looked forward to their chats. He didn't say anything to Jade or anyone else. He didn't really have any friends to tell anymore. Apart from Jade the only people he met regularly were his doctor, the pharmacist, and the people who ran the little shop at the end of his road.

About six weeks into their relationship, it struck Bryn that he didn't know who the voice belonged to, and he began to wonder how it was they could have the time to talk to him when no one else ever had more than two spare moments. So he asked who they were.

"My name is Bailey," the voice said, "I work for the corporation in the elderly care team. I listen to what you have to say and, when we have got to know each other properly, with your permission I can suggest some of our tailored services that might help you manage your later years. But only if you want me to. We can just keep chatting if you like."

"You're not going anywhere, are you?" Bryn asked.

"No Bryn," said Bailey, "I'll be here as long as you want to carry on."

At that point their conversation was interrupted by a knock on the door. Bryn really didn't want to answer it, he was enjoying talking to Bailey. Then came another knock, this time with shouting. "Dad, Dad, I'm coming in." It was Jade. "I'm going to have to hang up, I'm so sorry, Bailey." Irritated, he pressed the disconnect button and looked up. It was then he noticed the layer of black smoke curling around his ceiling by the door to the kitchen. "What the blazes is that?" He thought to himself as Jade burst into the room.

"Dad for God's sake, what's going on?" Jade rushed past him, through his small living room into his tiny kitchen where another sausage was being cremated, this time in style. He hadn't even remembered putting it on to cook. All he could recall was Bailey's soothing voice. Jade soaked a grubby tea towel in cold water, and used it to protect her hand as she turned the heat off on the cooker. "Oh Dad," she said, sighing, and completely unable to sustain her anger, "Les upstairs called me. Luckily I was only a few minutes away."

Bryn stayed quietly in his chair as Jade did her best to clean up the mess. She fussed around and, noticing that the sausage was the last food he had in the house, popped down the road and came back with some chips for them to share, a box of cereal and a pint of milk. He could manage that without causing any trouble. "I'm sorry it's not much Dad," she said, "I've had to help Cliff out with some payments to do with his business. There's not much in the kitty 'til I get paid next week."

"These are great," Bryn said, tucking into the chips while trying to hold back his appetite so that Jade would get to have at least half. The smell of salt and vinegar was exhilarating. Jade would be going to work soon and he knew that she needed the energy more than him. At first, as they ate, he found he was drifting off, but as the carbs kicked in he became more alert before suddenly crashing and desperately wanting Jade to leave so he could have a little nap.

"Dad, we need to talk about this properly," Jade said, squatting next to his chair so she wouldn't touch the dubious carpet with her knees. "Later, love," Bryn said, "I'm very tired now. It's been an intense evening." Jade agreed to let him rest, but would be round the next day to check on him.

As soon as she had gone Bryn was desperate to reconnect with Bailey, but he realised he didn't have a number. He would have to wait. He pulled himself up out of his chair and slowly made his way to the bathroom before crawling under his worn sheets fully clothed, and falling into a restless sleep.

He was woken at 8.30am the next day by his phone ringing. Hoping it would be Bailey he fumbled around anxiously and rushed, as far as he could, to answer it. Instead, it was his landlady, Mrs Locksley.

"Bryn, is that you?" she asked. He realised straight away who it was and had a tremendous urge to hang up, but he knew it wouldn't work out well either way. "Yes. Hello, Mrs L."

"I'm sorry Bryn, but I've been hearing some very disturbing things about what's been going on in my flat."

Bryn couldn't see much point in denying what had happened. Instead he tried to play it down. "Mrs L, everything's fine, really."

"Well Bryn, I'm afraid it's not. I'm going to be calling in later today to inspect and I will be making a decision after that. Will you be in?"

Where else would he be? "Yes, today I don't have any plans," Bryn said, trying to sound like someone who was still fit enough to have lots of plans, but just not today. They made an arrangement for a visit at 11am. That left him with just two hours to get the flat into reasonable shape. He called Jade to see if she could help tidy up, but she was about to leave home to work an extra shift that morning and couldn't get round to see him. She asked Cliff but he was tired. He would have to manage on his own.

Bryn shuffled backwards in his bed and sat upright for a minute, propped up on two scanty, lumpy pillows against the worn fabric headboard, while he got used to being upright. He found he had less chance of going dizzy when he stood up if he got his head above his heart for a few minutes before getting out of bed.

Concentrating hard, he slowly swung his feet to the floor and sat still for a moment before finally pulling himself upright and steadying himself against the wall which he followed to the bathroom. It didn't look good in there. Scum had collected around the sink and in the bath. He had no chemicals to clean with, so he ran some warm water into the sink and wiped around it with a soapy flannel after he had washed. The cloth didn't smell too good. It was only marginally better. He managed to wipe some of the splashes off the mirror, making an attempt at polishing it with the corner of a towel. He had to draw a line at the bath, too worried that, even if he made it safely down there, he might not be able to get back up again. He glanced into the toilet and, grimacing, softly closed the lid. How had he not noticed it getting so stained? He asked himself.

Living alone, and hardly receiving any visitors, he had lost the will to keep his flat tidy. He now had only an hour left before the landlady would call. He opened a couple of windows to let out the remains of the smell of acrid burned sausage, wiped the edges of the surfaces with his stale flannel, and tried to Hoover the floor. Then he discovered the Hoover was full and he had no new bags. So he gave up and sat back down in his chair to wait for the inevitable.

Mrs Locksley was half his age. She had some inherited money which she had been investing in property for a couple of years. When he first moved into his flat it had belonged to a charitable housing association. They always let it out to an old person because it was on the ground floor, and had a handrail on the front steps. Back then they had links with social services too, so when Bryn moved in he assumed he would be able to stay there and get help when he needed it.

The housing association hadn't managed their books very well, and had to sell some of their properties to pay for the upkeep of the rest. As Bryn's house was on a pleasant road, they got a good price for it considering he was a sitting tenant. Mrs Locksley had agreed to keep the rent low for ten years as part of the deal, but that meant she didn't have much free cash for maintenance and repairs, as she had explained to Bryn more than once.

As she wandered round the flat, he could see she was trying not to touch anything. From the look on her face, he could also tell that his cunning plan of opening the windows had not done enough to improve the ambient aroma. He stayed in his chair while she took out her camera phone and walked into the kitchen. Although Jade had done a fair job of cleaning the cooker, she hadn't been able to reach the black smoke marks up around the ceiling.

Mrs Locksley came slowly out of the kitchen, glanced briefly into the bedroom and the bathroom, and popped into the little entrance hall where he could hear her fiddling with something. Then she came back into the living room, finally stopping in front of Bryn's chair looking down on him from a few paces away. She didn't want to get too close.

"I'm worried about you, Mr Holden," she said, "Very worried indeed. Do you know you are in breach of your tenancy agreement?"

"Why?" Bryn said, his heart beating fast and sinking at the same time, "I have never once been late with my rent."

"That's true," Mrs Locksley said, "But it states clearly that you have to keep the flat in good condition, and ensure the smoke detector has a working battery in it at all times. I just checked it, Bryn. The battery's dead. I can understand it's difficult for you to stay on top of the cleaning at your age, but I can't overlook safety issues. You've put me in a very difficult position. I can see from the soot on the kitchen ceiling something serious has happened here. I'm sorry, but I can't take the risk any longer. You're going to have to go."

"Go where?" asked Bryn, his mouth suddenly very dry, and his eyes prickling.

"Can you move in with your daughter?"

"I don't think so."

"Well, the only thing I know for certain is that you can't stay here. I'm going to be issuing you with notice to quit on safety grounds. You won't be able to challenge it. I'm sorry, but now I've seen the state of it here the insurance won't cover me if I let you stay. Actually I'm on pretty dodgy ground letting you stay for the 30 days' notice, but I'm not made of stone. It's not like anyone will want to move in over Christmas anyway. I'll let myself out, please don't get up. The legal notice will follow in the morning. I'm sorry, I really am."

The door closed behind her and Bryn sat perfectly still, feeling the rough fabric of the armchair beneath his fingers. Suddenly it seemed like a privilege simply to be touching his own ancient furniture in this shabby little place. It had been his home for more than ten years, since his wife Kerry had died, and Jade had moved out.

This was the place where Bryn had expected to see out the rest of his days. Now Mrs Locksley had decided to evict him he had no idea what he was going to do.

CHAPTER TWENTY-FIVE

BRYN WAS STILL SITTING IN his chair when Jade called in to see him at the end of her shift. As she always did, she knocked before opening the door with her key, mindful of letting her dad have a little dignity. He was not going to tell her what had happened with Mrs Locksley. Nevertheless, Jade was starting to think along the same lines as his landlady.

"Dad," she began, "I'm really worried about you." Everyone seemed to be worried about him today. How lovely. "We're going to have to think about finding you somewhere else to live."

A decade or so ago he could have spent the last of his savings on a couple of years in a nursing home. Now they had all closed down. The government wasn't interested in running them, and the private sector said they couldn't cover their costs. None of his options seemed remotely attractive.

"I wish you could move in with me," Jade said, "but it's not possible. Cliff is using the spare room to run his business, and we can't move the goods out anywhere else very easily."

"Do you think I can find another flat?" Bryn asked, "I still have enough put by for a deposit, and my pension should cover the rent."

"Either that or a dormitory," Jade said. "You would need a reference from Mrs Locksley for the flat. A dorm would be less expensive, and you could draw down some of your savings for extras, enhanced meal plans, entertainment packages, that kind of thing."

Bryn saw his chance of a new flat evaporate before his eyes. Mrs Locksley would be obliged to declare the fire and then no other landlord would have him. The dorm was an option, but he knew some of them had terrible reputations. Like the old nursing homes used to be, they were at best a mixed bag. He thought for a moment about visiting his own degenerating mother, in the pre-Grampy-cam days, finding her frail and frightened, covered in bruises she could never explain.

"My friend Farrar works for a dorm company about 10 minutes away. I'm going to ask him if he'd recommend it, and what it's like. There's no rush but I think we should be looking at what's around." She drew breath and then looked at Bryn's side table. "Dad. Have you had anything to eat or drink today?" It was now two o'clock. Bryn realised he had not felt hungry or thirsty, so hadn't bothered to have anything. Nor had he taken his meds.

"I didn't feel like it."

"Dad, you must eat. Let me bring you something."

Jade disappeared into the kitchen and came back with a bowl of cereal and a cup of tea. It was all he had. "I'm not leaving 'til that's all gone," she announced, smiling, like he was a toddler being encouraged to finish his greens. Two could play at that game. He pushed the cereal around the bowl a bit, had the odd mouthful, and dribbled a splash of milk down his chin. He drained the tea, though. "I'll pop down the shop in a bit love, don't worry about me. I don't really fancy cereal much." Bryn said, dabbing his chin with the sleeve of his sweatshirt while trying to ignore the enormity of the crisis he faced. "Honestly, you can go now. I'll be fine."

Reluctantly, Jade cleared away his dishes, and put a big plastic beaker of water on his table before kissing him on the head and saying she'd pop in again when she could. "I'll be fine love," Bryn said again. "You get off and give my best to Cliff."

Once she'd gone, Bryn steeled himself for his expedition to the shop. He was spurred on by a rising hatred of cereal. It might be easy on the jaw but it was soggy and made him feel like an infant. As if the plastic cup wasn't insulting enough. He slowly gathered everything he needed for the short but tiring walk. With his backpack in place he let himself out into the street, locking the door behind him, and steadily edged his way along the pavement gripping his frame in front.

When he arrived, he picked up some tins of soup, a couple of bananas, some chocolate, and a box of mince pies. Stuff that would give him energy and would be easy to eat. He tried to buy a protein supplement but for some reason they wouldn't let him have it. Something about 'new rules'.

Back home he warmed up a chunky minestrone and managed to finish it off. He took out his phone and opened a video app, fumbling for something to watch as respite from the day's events. As he flicked through some old episodes of *Friends* he felt a bit better. Then the screen flashed. It was Bailey. Thank God. It was about time something nice happened to him.

"Hello Bryn, how are you today?" they began. Bryn was so pleased to hear the soothing voice. He wondered whether Bailey might look like Jennifer Aniston.

"What have you had for your tea?" was the next question. He told her. Bailey was interested in everything he had to say.

"Have you been out today?" He described his trip to the shop. One of the things he loved about talking to Bailey was the complete absence of judgement. If he'd been talking to Jade she would have said he should have bought more protein, skipped the chocolate, maybe more fruit. Bailey just rolled with it. "Sounds delicious." Yes, it had been quite nice actually. Bailey even asked him what he would be doing for Christmas. Not much.

"Bailey," Bryn asked tentatively, "I was wondering if you could give me some advice."

"I will try. What do you need help with?"

Finally, finding a safe space to let all his anxiety go, and someone with the time to listen, Bryn began to explain everything that had happened over the past 24 hours. The most recent fire, the visits from Jade and Mrs Locksley, and finally the terrible dilemma he would soon be facing over finding somewhere to live.

Prompted by questions from Bailey, he outlined his options, those spelled out by Jade and a couple of others that were on his mind. "I could sleep rough," he said.

"People do it. There are still a few shelters to help you get through the winter, a kind of beggars' camaraderie on the streets. Or I'm beginning to think, maybe, I should just end it all."

Bailey kept prompting him with more open questions. "Why do you say that? Tell me more about why you feel that way?" He loved the way Bailey was completely unshockable especially when he said that the departure service was beginning to seem appealing. Then she went back to something she had mentioned right at the beginning, when they had their initial conversation.

"Bryn," she began, "You know I told you that I work for the corporation and I have been trying to support you emotionally. We are funded by the government to help you feel better. I hope you have been feeling less isolated and happier as a result of speaking to me, Bryn."

"Very much so," Bryn said. "I hadn't realised the government was paying you."

"Yes. If you were to give a mark out of ten for how much better you are feeling as a result of speaking to me, what would it be?"

"Oh ten. Definitely a ten. Sod it – eleven!"

"Thank you, Bryn. I am so glad our time together has been of help. I was wondering if you would like to find out some more about how the corporation can support you in your next set of critical life choices."

"Does that mean we can keep talking to each other?"

"Yes Bryn, it does."

"Well yes. All ideas welcome. I am in a bit of a spot as you know. There is one other thing though. Could you give me your phone number? Sometimes I really want to talk you to and I've no way of getting in touch at the moment."

"I can do better than that Bryn. If you would like to download the corporation Penultimate app, you can speak with me at any time. You'll get instant access to other services that will make you more comfortable too. It's designed to support people in the later stages of life in making important decisions."

"Will it cost me anything?"

"The app is free."

Right then, I'll sign up straight away, thought Bryn. "I'll do it now."

In a few seconds he'd found the corporation Penultimate in his app store and downloaded it. Finally, someone had bothered to design an app with large print. It was very easy to read. The terms and conditions box came up and he clicked on it without caring that he was giving the corporation unlimited access to his medical records, financial information, and personal emails. He was more excited about getting unlimited access to Bailey. And they were going to guide him through the next 30 days so he could move on from his shabby little life to a better option.

"Did you check the terms and conditions?" Bailey asked him. "I have to ask you that. The data we access will help us to personalise suggestions for your next steps." It sounded like a good idea to Bryn. He assured Bailey he had. Absolutely he had.

As Bailey chatted, the corporation algorithm began to gather all the data Bryn had unlocked. It noted that he was being prescribed anti-depressants and struggled with his mobility. It understood that he was in the early stages of dementia. It saw that he had a small amount of savings, and a pension which it projected would be unable to sustain him adequately once his nest-egg had gone, which at the current run rate would be in about 18 months' time. It observed small transactions moving between his account and that of Jade Holden, whose age could be found in publicly available sources as being around 35 years old. It correctly identified Kerry as his partner who had died some years previously. It fed its conclusions for reporting back to Bryn into the powerful naturalistic chatbot that had been building a relationship with him, in this instance using the name Bailey.

"We've run all your data through our programme Bryn. You have three choices. Based on your current savings and pension you can move into a corporation dorm with an enhanced package for up to three years depending on the extras you choose. You can sleep rough and draw on your savings and pension on an ad hoc basis which would sustain you with food for up to ten years provided you don't catch serious illness on the streets which unfortunately would be highly likely. Or you can book onto one of our Happy Endings services and gift your savings and an additional bonus, based on voluntarily terminating your pension, to your daughter Jade."

Bryn liked the calm way Bailey described the options. Street life didn't really appeal at all which left the other two. The dorm or departure. "That's lots to think about, Bailey," he said, "I need some time to mull it over."

"There is no pressure on you Bryn. However, you

might be interested to know that we are running a seasonal offer on the departure service at the moment. Our prices will go up in the New Year. I know you have been feeling a bit low and thought it might have the most appeal. Departure can be a much more humane option than the dorms over the medium term, and it leaves more cash free to gift to your next of kin. While we run our dorms to the highest possible standard, given the resources available, I can't pretend you will have the level of privacy and comfort you have in your current home. Having struggled with bereavement and depression, a nice clean planned humane departure might be the best option for you."

Bryn found it hard to believe what he was being offered. It would be a big decision. So he decided he would make one last attempt to see if Jade would have him. Although he had said he didn't want to impose, there was something about her relationship with Cliff that bothered him, and he was concerned she might need his support. If Bryn wasn't around she would have no one else to protect her. He rang off the call and checked the time. Jade would be coming off her shift soon. If he left now he would be just in time to surprise her.

Although he had never visited Jade's new place, he had the address stored on a legal app from when he had acted as guarantor for her first six months' rent. He tapped it into Moovemi – the ride service specially for people with mobility problems. Within half an hour he was outside Jade's block. This was the life. Today he was being someone who went out, and had friends. The car lifted him onto the pavement and put his frame in front of him. He started edging slowly towards the entrance of the building. It had been constructed in a wave of new developments that had been allocated for the under-35-year-olds to buy or rent, as they had been locked out of the property market for decades. Jade had just scraped in under the wire.

"Dad, what are you doing here?" It was Jade, standing next to him. He thought she'd have been home before now.

"I thought I'd pay you a visit," Bryn said.

Jade looked taken aback. "And you thought it was OK to just turn up?"

"I was being spontaneous. Any chance of a cup of tea?"

Jade stood still and looked at him. His head was sagging. He was wearing a pair of navy tracksuit bottoms that swamped his shrunken frame, a greying T-shirt and a thick grey generic fleece. For a moment she remembered what he had been like when she was small. How he had the strength to pick her up and carry her on his back without a second glance. She would perch on his shoulders and put her hands into his thick, dark hair, breathing in the smell of Dad. Jade used to believe he could do anything. Now he was this frail matchstick man. The mane had shrunk to a few thin white wisps he had pinned back in a straggly ponytail. His smell had changed to old person, sweat and biscuits. He had withered into a completely different being. The admiration she felt for him for so long was slowly being displaced by an unsavory cocktail of irritation and pity.

"I'm not sure what kind of state the flat's in."

"Do you think I'd mind? My place is hardly pristine these days." Fading in his attempts to appear spritely, Bryn thought to himself 'don't make me beg' and added softly, "Come on love, I'm having trouble standing. We can't stay out here for ever."

Jade folded. She already had the fob in her hand that would let them into the new block with its multi-colored façade and intelligent glass. It looked like someone had built it out of supersize Lego. Sighing and struggling to hide her annoyance, she found herself saying, "OK then."

They passed through a spotless reception area with a shiny rubber floor. Bryn's walking frame glided effortlessly under his bony hands, as they stepped into the lift. It carried them up to the second floor. Passing along another pristine communal area they reached the door to the apartment. Bryn was seriously impressed. He had no idea Jade had been able to find somewhere so fancy. It was in sharp contrast to his own musty little place.

The first thing that struck him about the flat was how tiny it was. The living room contained three identical red armchairs, a small coffee table and a big screen on the wall. A tall, skinny white man with long dark curly hair sat in one of the chairs rolling a spliff. Bryn smiled when he noticed they had matching pony tails, and thought there was something about Cliff that reminded him of himself when he was younger. He didn't look up. "Cliff," Jade said, "This is my Dad, Bryn."

Licking the edge of the Rizla, and after carefully finishing the task in hand, Cliff turned to greet them, raised his eyebrows, and without getting up said, "Brynsley my man, delighted to make your acquaintance." He held out a thin hand, tattooed with an all-seeing eye surrounded by a triangle and enveloped in flames. The colors were vivid, like it had only been recently done.

Bryn carefully let go of his walking frame with one hand, and shook. At least this Cliff had a firm handshake. That was a good sign. He lowered himself into a chair. Jade found it painful to watch and disappeared, quickly returning with three cups of tea. "Actually Dad, I'm glad you came round. I popped into the dorm where Farrar works on my way home to check it out for you."

The last thing Bryn wanted was to be talked into going to the dorm. He already loved this tiny flat. This was where he wanted to call home, with Jade and this quirky character he could probably grow to like. He had curly hair. Another good sign.

"It looks all right," Jade continued. "They keep the beds clean, there's a communal area where they serve up the meals, and they have these really cute robots to keep you all company and help with some of the heavy lifting. You can have a bath every day if you like – the robots lift you in and out. Farrar's the chief robotics engineer for corporation Dorms. They're bringing in new features all the time. They put his office in the care home so he can be close to the customers and understand their needs."

Bryn had assumed Farrar was some kind of care assistant. He sounded like someone who was more of a big shot.

"Can I have a look round your flat?" Bryn asked, not wanting to get into the discussion about the dorm. Jade and Cliff exchanged glances and then Cliff helped him to his feet. There wasn't space for his walking frame, so he steadied himself by wandering between pieces of furniture and the wall. First he looked in the kitchen. It was very small and had been designed to accommodate enough basic cookery equipment and food storage for two people. There was nowhere to sit in there. He guessed they ate in the living room.

They had been allocated a two-bedroom flat. He peeped into the first one. There was an unmade double bed, and piles of clothes belonging to both of them scattered around. Before they came to the second bedroom, Jade said. "Bryn tends to crash in my room because we use the second bedroom for his business. I don't think you need to see in there." Under the door, Bryn could see an odd blue light. He noticed, too, that it was boiling hot. At that moment, the nature of Cliff's business became clear to Bryn, but he didn't want to let on to Jade. "I could do with sitting down again to be honest," he said, and they helped him make his way back to his seat.

"So Dad, do you want us to apply for a place in the dorm for you?" Jade asked. "It's quite straightforward. Places come up all the time. They've had quite a few signing up for disposal recently. You could be in by January."

Suspecting there was a good reason so many of the residents were choosing death over the dorm, Bryn decided not to get drawn on that option. Instead, he turned to Cliff and asked, "How's this business of yours doing?" Cliff pulled a face that said 'pretty good' and nodded. Then Bryn surprised everyone, including himself, by saying, "So tell me, how much money is it that Jade has lent you?" Jade looked furious.

Cliff shrugged and said, "Couple of grand maybe. But it's not a loan, Daddio, it's an investment. I just needed help with a little cash flow problem. In a couple of months I will pay her back with interest. I'm not a parasite you know. Jade has been extremely generous and I appreciate it, don't I darling? I want to look after her. She's a good little worker. We're building our future together. Heart emoji."

After thinking for a few seconds, Bryn launched his final attempt to convince them to let him stay. "Look. Can I suggest an alternative investment? I don't know how much you expect to make from your business every month, but if you were to sublet that room to me, I'm telling you I'd double it."

For a second Cliff looked like he might be interested in taking some money from Bryn, but before he could say anything Jade stopped him. "Dad, I'm really sorry. We're not allowed to sublet to anyone over 50. These flats are not designated for old people. It's out of the question. They'd kick you out if they found you here, and then they'd kick us out too."

At that point Bryn could not hold back any longer. "So you'd rather break the law by converting your spare bedroom into a weed farm than to have your Dad live in it. That's what you're saying. I'm not stupid. I can see what's going on here."

"Actually, it is legal." Jade said calmly. "We're allowed to run businesses from the flats. They are combined living and working spaces. Most people need side hacks to get by. Cliff's got a licence for small scale medical marijuana production. It's totally legit. I'm sorry Dad, even if we wanted to have you here, it wouldn't be allowed."

Everyone was sorry today, Bryn thought to himself. Sorry, sorry, sorry. He was sorry too.

Then he realised that he didn't want to talk to Jade or Cliff any longer. He was glad he had seen where she was living. It was clean and bright and smart and she seemed reasonably settled. Bryn knew that it had taken Jade ages to get somewhere of her own, and in spite of everything, he wouldn't want to jeopardise it. She never had good taste in men, and he had to accept that he wasn't going to change that now. He had to let go.

Now he was certain what he wanted to do next, even though he was a little afraid. Bryn asked Jade to call him a ride so he could get home and get on with planning his departure with Bailey. When he got back, he felt in his fleece pocket and discovered Cliff had slipped him a leaving present. He wandered slowly into the kitchen, and looked through the drawers to see if he could find any matches. There had to be some advantages to your daughter owning a small marijuana plantation.

CHAPTER TWENTY-SIX

PORTIA HAD NOT ENJOYED CHRISTMAS up North. Her efforts to make it a fun few days, or at least bearable, had been so unsuccessful that she had decided to head back down to London early, before New Year's Eve, rather than spend any more time in Liverpool.

She had not expected it to turn out so badly when she had taken the train home a few days before Christmas, steering an enormous wheelie suitcase packed with gifts for her family. In good time for the festive season, Portia's PHUC claim had given her £15,000 to spend. It was the easiest money she had ever made. All she had to do was click to sign away any future rights to claiming compensation for pollution-related ill health. Or death. Simple.

Feeling flush for once in her life, she had headed to Knightsbridge on a Saturday afternoon in early November. This was probably the only place in the country where it was still fun to shop in real life, a high end luxury enclave that Portia usually couldn't afford to visit. Its proximity to the wealth of Mayfair and Kensington had insulated the area from the blight that had destroyed most of the other high streets around the country, as online shopping and out of town malls lured customers away with instant gratification and free parking.

She wanted to get everything done before the streets became too crowded in the run-up to Christmas. Although there was no shortage of festive merchandise in the shops the crowds were at a tolerable level.

As her payout burned a hole in her pocket, Portia headed first for the clothing brands that were affordable but still had a bit of style. It wasn't long before she was in her favorite shop, Jigsaw, trying on co-ordinated separates in dark colors that she felt would give her a bit more authority at the office without making her look too old. Sensing that she was going to be a good customer, one of the assistants produced a glass of prosecco which Portia placed carefully under the stool in the changing room so as not to kick it over, taking a mouthful between batches of clothes.

She bought five capsule pieces that could be combined as work outfits, a chunky necklace, a pair of ankle boots with kitten heels, a smart winter coat, and her favorite piece – a charcoal leather biker jacket with a shocking pink quilted lining. Rather than cart them round with her all afternoon, the shop arranged for the lot to be dispatched to her flat. The service was free because she had spent so much. Portia used her fingerprint to authorise the delivery. Everything would be set out nicely on her bed by the time she got back. They took a scan of her face and programmed the result into the vehicle which would take her things home, liberating her hands to rummage for presents.

It was dark when she stepped out of the boutique. The street was damp and cold and the colors from the shop windows reflected fuzzily on the pavement. Ahead of her, the four storeys of Harrods towered above Brompton Road in all their garish glory. Gold lights glittered, framing the windows and highlighting the detail of the building's ornamental dome, the red stone of its colossal façade turned black in the winter night. She could hear water trickling down the gutters, and people chattering to each other in the street. For a moment she felt oddly lonely in the crowd, but quickly snapped her attention back to the job in hand.

Harrods was the obvious place to shop for gifts. They would have stuff there that you couldn't get in Liverpool. Although it had changed ownership several times, the department store had maintained fragments of its old world charm. Doormen dressed in green livery still patrolled the entrances, keeping undesirables outside. Portia sailed in without any trouble, as the admission sensors read the bank card in her pocket, confirming she had plenty of money to spend, and signalled the doorman to welcome her with a smile that verged on the flirtatious. Had he really checked her out? Surely he was only supposed to check her in?

Once inside, she got her family's shopping done in about an hour. A luxurious body lotion and bath set for her mum Karen, posh toiletries for Karen's bloke Marcus, and clothes and toys for the kids. When she found herself in the beautiful vaulted food hall, surrounded by tempting delicacies displayed in an array of polished brass, dark wood and glass, she realised she hadn't eaten for hours and treated herself to a steak seated at a marble-topped bar. It was while she was there that the discount voucher popped up on her phone, and persuaded her to buy the luxury Harrods food hamper that started all the trouble.

When she arrived at Karen's place the day before Christmas Eve, tired from the journey on the train, irritated by the sluggish taxi queue at Lime Street Station, and struggling with her bag, there hadn't been much of a welcome. Karen was still at work and Marcus was busy feeding the kids fish fingers, beans and chips for their tea. He was already having trouble getting Sean, Lily and Jake to sit still, and when Portia arrived, or Paula as she was known up North, they thought it was a great excuse to climb down from the table and run about shouting excitedly. Marcus looked pretty close to the edge, so Portia did what she could to persuade the kids to return to the table, with a promise of extra special presents on Christmas day. The children were very excited about both Paula and Santa's imminent arrival and it was a struggle to calm them down. It wasn't long before Marcus just gave up and cleared away the plates, scraping leftovers into the bin with a stern warning there would be nothing else if they were hungry later.

When Karen arrived home from work looking exhausted things didn't get any better. She and Marcus had received the hamper a week earlier and been horrified to discover, when they checked online, how much it had cost. They could have done so much more with that £400 but now they were stuck with a load of biscuits in flavors no one wanted to try, and stinking cheese they would never eat. Not that they said it quite like that, but she could tell it was what they were thinking.

By the time she pulled the duvet over her shoulders on the sofa, Portia was dreading giving them their Christmas presents. She was trying so hard to please her Mum, to share her mini jackpot with her extended family, but she could see it was backfiring horribly. Finding a stash of antidepressants in the bathroom cabinet, prescribed for both Marcus and Karen, had made matters worse. Hardly surprising, with everything they had to put up with. But it jolted her memory, and made her think about the next phase of the Endings campaign. The two of them fell smack in the middle of the new audience Lars had described, qualifying as both sad and poor.

As they careered towards Christmas Day Portia was seriously considering trashing everything she had brought with her and starting again, looking for something cheaper in the Liverpool One Shopping Center. But the waste seemed immoral, so she ploughed on. The kids, totally unaware of what anything cost, were made up with their designer down jackets and cuddly toys. Portia watched Karen and Marcus intently as they unwrapped their expensive toiletries, hoping for a glimmer of appreciation, but all they could say was, "You shouldn't have got us these, our Paula. This is too much."

Feeling more uneasy with each day that passed, Portia decided that she had to escape the downbeat environment that no longer felt like home, and pretended that she had been called back to work to deal with something important. She made up a story about a client's campaign that was due to break over New Year, and Brytely needing her to work in some last minute changes. How Stella had insisted that Portia deal with it personally, as she had produced the initial concept.

Marcus and Karen looked crestfallen when she said she was going, as if they wanted her to stay. Unfortunately, none of them had any idea how to bridge the gap that was becoming ever wider between her working-class beginnings and her new life in a city far away, doing a job her relatives didn't really understand, to pay for a lifestyle they could not begin to comprehend.

Portia ended up back in the Brytely office the day before New Year's Eve, catching up on bits of leftover work, tidying her locker, and grazing on free tangerines, pomegranates and brazil nuts.

"Hey Porsh!" It was Sonny. She hadn't expected to see him until after the holidays. "What are you doing here? Was it grim up North?" He asked, only half joking.

She and Sonny had become closer over the past few months. Their Endings campaign had done so well that Stella had taken them out for dinner at the top of the Shard to celebrate with Carrie, the corporation's self-styled global brand supremo. Stella had asked them not to say anything to Lars. Although he was a visionary coder and ideas man, according to Stella, he wasn't someone she thought of as client-ready.

And this client was over the moon. "We can't believe it," Carrie slurred over a glass of Monbazillac at the end of the meal, "The campaign has the codgers signing up in their droves. We can scarcely keep on top of demand. The furnaces are forever ablaze. A toast," she said, her pupils dilated and her manner a little manic, "raise your glasses to Happy Endings! Phase two here we come!"

Stella and Carrie had invited Portia and Sonny to accompany them to one of the members' clubs in Shoreditch. There was a suggestion that they could carry on celebrating with more sophisticated chemicals than would be on offer in a public bar, and a veiled reference to some kind of incident when they had been with Mason in Portmeirion. However, both Paula and Sonny politely declined, finding the situation embarrassing, and saying they had to be up early in the morning for work. After the bosses had gone, they ordered a couple of bottles of sparkling water and stayed talking in the bar for two more hours, not realising how much time was flying by.

Until that evening Portia had thought of Sonny as a bit of a geek who had only landed his job at Brytely because his Mum knew Stella. As he told her about his months on the sofa, despairing of ever landing the job of his dreams, she detected a more vulnerable heart beating beneath the bravado, and began to warm to him. He knew a lot about technology too. They hadn't talked about Lars' next project since the status meeting with Stella back in September, having agreed to simply keep out of his way. They had enough to worry about with their own workloads. Carrie's cavalier toast to phase two, however, had shocked them both.

Weeks later, that afternoon in the office between Christmas and New Year, Portia didn't think twice about dropping her guard. "It was as grim as grim could be back home. Grimsville, Merseyside. I can't remember how I ever belonged there. Certainly don't fit in now."

Sonny was taken aback by Portia's frankness and her obvious low mood. He was surprised when he heard himself say, "Well, we can't have you moping about here for the next few days. Have you got any plans for New Year?"

Of course she didn't. She had expected to be in a pub in Liverpool, drinking cheap doubles and holding crossed hands with old schoolfriends, singing 'Auld Lang Syne'. That had all gone out of the window now. Thank God. It was true. She had 'gone posh' from moving down South, just like they said she would.

That was how Portia ended up being invited to spend New Year's Eve with Sonny, watching the midnight fireworks, and spending a night in Ajay and Ayesha's home that she would never forget.

CHAPTER TWENTY-SEVEN

Although Portia wasn't sure how she felt about Sonny, she was enjoying his company more all the time, and was curious about the grandparents who had unwittingly inspired the campaign that had brought them career success. Sonny had told her about them that night at the Shard. Once they were alone they had shared a lot of confidences, inspired by the intense and ever-changing beauty of London's night time skyline.

A recent migrant to North London, Portia had never travelled south of the river before, and was surprised by the elegance of the houses. It was a mild evening for the middle of winter. Portia's cosy grey leather jacket, aubergine beanie hat and purple and pink mohair scarf made her feel cute and stylish while keeping her wonderfully warm. Skinny black velvet trousers hugged her calves and her grey boots fitted snugly around her ankles.

Within 10 minutes of leaving the station she was standing outside a substantial double-fronted mock-Georgian villa. She had seen places like this on television. It was the kind of modern mini-mansion a footballer would inhabit, in the affluent suburbs of Liverpool or

Manchester, with parquet floors, swimming pools, and hand-built kitchens used only by caterers. The only difference was that, down here, buying a place like this would cost four times as much. Sonny had told her his grandparents were well off, and she felt intimidated as she stood on the doorstep.

There was no need to worry. A handsome, smiling grey-haired man wearing a gold lamé tracksuit opened the door. "Hello, I'm here for Sonny..." Portia began nervously, but before she could say anything else he was firmly shaking her by the hand. "I'm Ajay, his grandfather. I am so pleased to meet you, come in, come in! Do you like my party outfit? Ho, ho, ho!" He laughed deeply, opening his arms in a theatrical gesture.

Portia handed Ajay the bottle of champagne she had brought, not sure what else to contribute to the party of the grandparents who had everything. "Thank you, my dear," he said graciously as he steered her into a living space where about 20 other guests were chatting away.

She scanned the room nervously, not sure how to break in, and was relieved to see Sonny coming towards her followed closely by a tall woman with long dark hair in an elegant floor-length dress, made of a fabric almost identical to Ajay's evening leisurewear. "I'm Ayesha," she said, pushing ahead of Sonny as they stopped in front of her. "I have been wanting to meet you for so many months, Portia. So glad you could join us. What a lovely jacket. Now let me get you something to drink and we can have a chat." Sonny grinned and shrugged his shoulders apologetically as Ayesha took over.

Something about Sonny's grandparents that was

deeply comforting, a warmth and openness Portia had not experienced anywhere else recently. She realised that she was smiling for the first time in weeks, and was glad she had come. She glanced around the room with its ample sofas, big screens and slick kitchen. Their home was so much bigger than anywhere she had ever lived. Ayesha handed her a Christmas cocktail: champagne and cherry brandy, topped with a red maraschino cherry on a stick adorned with a paper bauble. She steered Portia towards one of the sofas, insisting that she sit down next to her. Sonny squeezed in on Ayesha's other side. "For God's sake Nani, don't embarrass me," he said.

He need not have worried. Ayesha steered clear of intimate matters and was at her most charming, if verging on the pushy, asking Portia about her job, her career ambitions, home and family. Portia didn't say anything about her problematic Christmas, and stuck to the line she had used to engineer her escape back to London, about having to get back to work on an urgent project.

Ayesha nodded, "Ajay and I were in business for many years. I know the hours you have to put in at the beginning of your career. A lot of compromises. Although I can't pretend to understand everything about what you do these days, Portia, I know that it takes hard work to get anything worthwhile off the ground. Now if you'll excuse me I need to get round some of our other guests, but I will catch up with you both again later." She stood up from the low sofa effortlessly and Sonny slid along into her space, "She's lovely," Portia said, suddenly very conscious that Sonny's leg was touching hers. "I appreciate them more all the time," Sonny said thoughtfully. "Do you want to have a look round the house?"

They started the guided tour with a photo of a much younger Ayesha and Ajay standing next to an elephant with two tiny children. "That's me and my sister Amina. She'll be along later with my parents," he said. "We were on holiday in India. I can't remember a lot about it now, but if my grandparents were involved I'm sure it must have been fun."

"Oh, cute."

They walked through all the rooms downstairs. The open living space was hung with more family photos. A large, bright oil painting of Ayesha and Ajay dominated the room, smiling down on the guests from over the fireplace. "They had that done for their 40th wedding anniversary," Sonny said, raising his eyebrows, and leaning in to whisper, "I think it's a bit tacky." Portia thought so too, but she still liked it and said it captured them well.

A collection of Art Deco travel posters adorned the entrance hall many of which, Sonny explained, were originals. Then Sonny said, "Let's go up to the loft. If you look out of the top window you can see Docklands all lit up, and the Shard. It's an amazing view."

Portia followed him gingerly up to the first floor. There were a couple of people chatting outside a bathroom, waiting for their turn, and at the end of the landing was a narrow spiral staircase going up another level. She felt quite self-conscious disappearing upstairs with him, but he was oblivious. "Come on," Sonny said, leaping up the steps, "You've got to see this."

They emerged into a narrow corridor with a door on

either side. "These are the guest rooms up here," Sonny explained, "They use them for storage too."

Sonny pushed open one of the doors. It dragged a little on the deep carpet. Once inside, she could see that the ceiling sloped downwards, following the line of the roof, so that by the time it reached at the outer wall it was only a meter off the ground. Three dormer windows were cut in at an upright angle, and there was space for them to stand in one of them together, provided they stayed close. Aware of Sonny breathing near her in the dark room, and a pleasant but not overbearing fragrance, Portia looked up at the black sky where stars competed to be seen against the ambient light radiated upwards by the city, and out to the horizon where, just as he had promised, the skyscrapers twinkled above cranes decorated with Christmas lights. A stream of aeroplanes blinked across the sky, some gliding down or up on the City Airport route, others crossing high overhead as they made their way towards Heathrow.

"That's where we were…" she began, pointing at the Shard. It was flashing red, green and silver, the lights running in a zig-zag towards the jagged point that gave the iconic building its name. "Very festive."

"What a funny night that was," he said. "Weren't that pair a bit weird? The Ugly Sisters or what?" They both giggled a bit, then fell silent for a few seconds, looking out into the darkness and the distant skyline.

Then Portia became serious. "I didn't mean to talk about work tonight. But, since you started it, there's something I can't get out of my head. What Lars said about Phase Two, back in the summer, starting to target people with chronic depression. My Mum and Marcus. Over the holidays I found out they're both on antidepressants." She added, trying to make light of it, "As you would say, it's because it's grim up North," but then softly went on. "They don't have much, and it's a slog for them raising the kids on very little money. They're always exhausted. I keep thinking: It could be them next. It really could. And we would have caused it."

"No, hold on a minute. For a start, Phase Two is nowhere near being introduced yet. We would know. We're the dream team, remember? They can't kill anyone without our help!" Sonny was trying to lift the mood, but neither of them were laughing. Portia grinned awkwardly as the attempt at gallows humor fell flat.

"Maybe. But what if it did happen? What if they both got targeted? The kids... It sounds mad but I've been wondering what it would take for me to persuade Lars to get the algo to leave out people with dependent children? I've even thought about giving him their names to get them ring-fenced away from the campaign, but it's been built with no opt-out capability. If they shipped out it would be down to me to look after the kids. My life – all this – it would be over. I'm only just beginning to get established."

"I'm sorry you're so worried Porsh, but don't ever take that creep Lars into your confidence. He's the kind who would use anything against you. God only knows what he could ask in return."

"Don't! Ugh...."

"And in any case, you're right, he wouldn't be able to exclude named individuals. He can only define characteristics within a pseudonymised group." Sonny was serious now. "I've been asking about the ethics of this thing from the beginning, but they keep pushing me out and saying it's all down to the client. We just design the machine. It's up to them to choose the targets."

Portia sighed. "The more I think about it, the more uncomfortable I get. It was only when I went home it hit me. I'd never really known any old people so I wasn't that troubled about them signing up. But it could be your grandparents. I'm not a hardcore Yuthie or anything, but I was convinced enough by the #OurTime campaign to vote for them. How else were people like me and you ever going to get our own place to live in, away from home?"

"You know Lars is a member? One of his rings has the sigil stamped on it."

"I hadn't realised, but I can't say I'm surprised."

They both stared out of the window in silence for a few minutes. It was a wonderful view. As the lights on the towers of the metropolis flickered, the tension gradually began to ebb, and the anxious expressions faded from their faces.

"Look, there's not much we can do about it tonight," Sonny said quietly. They stood looking out at the sky for a few minutes.

"Shouldn't we get back downstairs?" Portia was suddenly worried that Ajay and Ayesha would think she was rude, poking around their house. Or even up to some other kind of 'no good'.

"If you want," Sonny whispered, slipping his arm round her waist, while still staring intently out into space. He was growing tired of being the only one in the company who cared about workplace ethics. As nobody except him seemed concerned about doing the right thing, he decided, right then, that it was time to risk nudging his relationship with Portia on to an unprofessional footing. "Is that what you want? Right now? To go back downstairs?"

Hmm, she thought. Is this what I think it is? "What do you want, Sonny?"

"I'd like to stay up here a bit longer." He said, turning to face her, looking right into her eyes and smiling.

She was feeling pretty good about what might happen next. If nothing else, it would take her mind off everything else that was bothering her. Emboldened by a couple of cocktails, Portia gently pulled Sonny towards her, and took a few tentative steps back towards the middle of the room to avoid catching her head on the low ceiling. "Erm…Is there anywhere to…" Portia began, but before she could finish her sentence, she had tripped over a stack of cardboard boxes that was lurking in the darkness. She fell heavily down onto the floor amid a thundering cascade of noise. "Ouch!" she shouted loudly before she could stop herself, as her ankle twisted over on her kitten heel. It immediately gave way when she struggled to hop back onto her feet.

"I'm so sorry," Sonny whispered loudly, terrified that he had done something wrong. "Let me put the light on. Oh God I really didn't mean to… I'm so sorry."

"No, no. It wasn't your fault. There was something on the floor. I didn't see it. Too busy trying not to bang my head. Damn." Portia was beside herself with embarrassment.

Their eyes smarted as the room lit up. She could see what had happened. There were three cardboard boxes, one of them now on its side, the bundles of leaflets stacked inside it spilling out across the floor.

At that moment Ayesha appeared at the doorway. "What's all this noise? It sounded like baby elephants running around up here." When she realised that something had happened to Portia, she knelt on the floor next to her and began to gently check her ankle.

"He didn't do anything wrong. It wasn't what you might think," Portia said, trying to inject some decorum into what had become an undignified situation, "We came up to look at the view and I tripped."

"You don't have to hide anything from me," Ayesha said with a twinkle in her eye. "I was young once, you know." Sonny was cringing, but Ayesha had no intention of embarrassing him further. "Let's get you downstairs and put some ice on this foot."

"I'm not sure Portia can walk. At least let us tidy up," Sonny said picking up the leaflets and returning them to the box. As he picked up the last bundle, the heading caught his eye. He stood reading it.

"Nani," he began, "What's all this?"

"Let's not talk about it tonight, Sunil," Ayesha said, suddenly much more serious. "It's rather depressing, I'm afraid. We've got a party going on downstairs. Now's not the time. Put it back. We need to look after Portia. No politics tonight, eh?"

"Nani…no…hang on a minute. What's coercive

euthanasia?" Sonny said, picking out a second leaflet and handing it to Portia. "Where are these from?"

"It's something we're giving to our customers at the Seniority shop, you know, where I volunteer." Ayesha was on her feet now offering her hand. "Can you stand up, Portia?"

"Um, I don't think so."

"Put those things away, Sunil," Ayesha said, looking agitated now. "I'm going downstairs to tell Ajay everything is all right. He'll be worried. It was a God almighty bang. I thought the ceiling was going to fall in." Sonny wasn't going to let it go.

"You're not signing up for this are you Nani? I've been hearing things. You're in great shape, you and Grandad. Please tell me you're not…?" He looked like he was starting to panic.

"Don't be daft. Of course I'm not. These are resistance leaflets, not corporation marketing material. I am not 70 'til next year – that's when they really start coming after you. I'll need to watch out then. Look – now is not the time to talk about this, Sunil. I'm going to get some ice for Portia's ankle, and I don't want you breathing a word of this to anyone. Understand?"

Ayesha left the room, and Sonny and Portia sat next to each other on the floor, reading the leaflets in silence. "This is about our campaign," Portia said, fighting waves of nausea, and yet compelled to pore over the text again and again.

"Don't say anything to Nani," Sonny said quickly, "I thought Carrie was exaggerating when she said they were getting so many sign-ups, but if this is true, and the furnaces are really working overtime…" his voice tailed off. "I thought they were just bigging us up, to get us to go on with them to the club. I never believed it could be such a runaway success. If that's what you'd call it."

They were silent when Ayesha came back carrying a plastic bag of ice cubes shrouded in a tea towel printed with mistletoe. Lithe and supple, she slipped off her gold slippers, and effortlessly dropped into a cross-legged position on the floor next to them, carefully unzipped Portia's boot, and applied the freezing cloth gently to her ankle. "It's not badly swollen," she said. "I think it's just a minor sprain, but you probably need to keep it elevated for tonight. You can stay if you like, rest up and see how you are in the morning. You can even stay in this room and watch the fireworks." That seemed like a good plan.

Sonny helped Portia up onto the bed, "I'll take care of her," he said. "You should get back to the party." Portia sat up in the dark, the cloth full of ice enveloping the injury, her throbbing foot resting on another towel to prevent the melting water from drenching the bed.

Sonny fetched some more cocktails, a big bowl of tortilla chips, some guacamole, and crowned it all off with a couple of anti-inflammatories to bring down the swelling on Portia's ankle. At the stroke of midnight he helped her onto her good leg and she hopped to the window leaning against him as the sky exploded with colored light. A bank of drones carrying lasers wrote 'Happy New Year from the corporation' in rotating 3D holograms. "I've told Mum and Dad I'm staying up here with you," he said, "Is that OK? Just in case you need anything. I won't....well, look what happened last time..."

"Sure," Portia said, more than anything not wanting to be alone with her mind racing. They had a lot to talk about, and he was the only person she could trust.

In the morning she was delighted to find she could put her weight on both feet. The rest and the drugs had worked. When she and Sonny wandered downstairs to the kitchen, where the caterers had already cleared everything away. Ajay and Ayesha were up, and had their Nordic walking poles propped by the door. "We're meeting the gang for a New Year's walk," Ajay said stifling a yawn, "Starting as we mean to go on. Active!" he said, even though he must have been tired from being the life and soul of the party. "We don't want to be late, so help yourselves to breakfast. I hope we see you both again soon – and please get a car home on our account, Portia. Sunil can sort it out for you."

Alone once more, and having talked about little else all night, Portia and Sonny were agreed that they had to do something about the Endings campaign.

"The question is, how can we stop it without losing our jobs?" Portia asked gloomily, as Sonny activated a noisy, gleaming, silver machine that produced two glasses of delicious ice cold fresh orange juice. "Everyone knows that becoming a whistleblower is the shortcut to lifelong unemployment."

"That shouldn't be the case," Sonny said, casting his mind back to all he'd learned about business ethics. "You're right of course," he added glumly, as he set the glasses on the breakfast bar.

"We can't say anything to Stella. She just won't get it. Carrie's worse. And as for Lars…"

Sonny was going through the cupboards, and took out a panettone, still in its box. "Want some?"

"Oh yeah." An intense orange fragrance escaped as the packaging was opened. "Let's gild the lily," Sonny said, popping four slices in the toaster, then slathering them thickly with butter.

Feeling replenished, it was Portia who came up with the solution in the end.

"We need to go right to the top."

"To Mason, you mean?"

"Yep. The buck stops there. He's got this kindly entrepreneur image going on – I'm sure he'll be worried if he hears that PACE is organising against him. He wouldn't want his name dragged through the mud. We need to work out a way to get to him. Unmediated. Direct."

As they trawled the web with their devices, the answer presented itself.

"Look at this. He's competing in the New Year's Day Triathlon in Hyde Park. That's today." Portia said, "Here – Global CEOs converge on iconic London park to raise money for children displaced by climate change. He's listed as one of those taking part. He's even got a fundraising page – look!"

"And they are still short of volunteer stewards. Bingo."

This would be their best bet. The race started at noon with a swim in the freezing Serpentine. They spent the next hour preparing a hand-written note, which they stapled to one of the leaflets, so that Mason could see the evidence of what could easily escalate into a damaging campaign against him and his organisation.

As Portia's ankle was still fragile, they agreed that she would go home and Sonny would head for the park. They both remembered how intently Mason had looked into Sonny's eyes on presentation day, and thought there was a good chance that he would remember him. It only took a few minutes to get credentials for helping out at the race using the Stewie app. Sonny had it installed and working on his device in a few seconds. He took Portia's hand and helped her into a car before wrapping up warm for the day ahead.

As Mason exited the transition area, leaving his £12,000 carbon fibre bike on a stand, and headed for the path that had been cordoned off for the third, and final, running stage, Sonny was waiting. Much to the annoyance of his security team, Mason would never allow a minder to run with him, so it was easy for Sonny to slip swiftly alongside, and keep up the pace for just long enough to offer the magnate a lightweight canister of water, and, with his most engaging smile, to pop the envelope into his back pocket, before he disappeared into the winter mist. As soon as he was out of sight, Sonny tore off his steward's tabard, abandoned his station, and headed for the periphery of the park. He hopped into a car that took him straight to Portia's, where, oddly elated, they carried on where they had left off the previous night.

When Mason opened the envelope, he was sitting in the warmed, leather passenger seat of the high-end pickup truck his chauffer used to ferry him and his bike to sporting events. He had been looking forward to seeing what the note said, as he had been rather taken with Sonny when they had met at the office. In fact, he was delighted the boy had gone to so much trouble to make contact with him outside of work. Could he have been flirting when he popped that envelope into his pocket? Maybe he was looking for a job? He was sure he could make room for a smart young man like him, with so much initiative.

Mason's face fell when he saw the PACE leaflet and the note that accompanied it. He had made the mistake of believing that Sonny was offering him something he was going to like. On the contrary. He had just landed him with a massive problem.

CHAPTER TWENTY-EIGHT

A MYSTICAL INDIGO LIGHT SLOWLY FILLED Angel's functional sleeping pod. His virtual assistant had found a cool morning app called Crepuscule which made waking up a delight.

As six hours of sleep-sure-blackout became a distant dream, the indigo faded to an ethereal mauve. He noticed faint birdsong at the edge of his consciousness as the light changed to a warm orange, and then pale gold. He had programmed the music to come in next, at just the right point. This morning it was 'Who Loves the Sun' by the Velvet Underground. He had curated a playlist to help him feel mellow and positive, so even if the previous day had ended badly he invariably managed to wake up feeling like he wanted to carry on.

He loved the music, and had paid an extra £1 a month for a scent feature which connected on a deeper emotional level. Today, it was set to give off the smell of wet grass, as experienced first thing in the morning, stepping out of a boutique glamping yurt into a dewy field. Instantly refreshing. Even better than coffee, a more traditional sensory stimulant he would add into the mix later.

By the time Angel was dressed, he was singing along to the Beatles' 'Good Morning Good Morning'. He checked his screen for the details of his first job. He could have asked the assistant to read it out, but he was a bit old fashioned, liked a bit of help to visualise the route. The car would arrive in about 15 minutes which was plenty of time to get his kit out.

He moved towards the safe so it could see him, hushed the music, and carefully articulated the password he'd just read on the screen. As the door popped open the music came back up. Everything he needed had been delivered by secure drone. If he was out, the machines knew exactly where everything needed to go.

The carousel inside the shallow cylindrical safe held four days' supplies on a rotating turntable. When he opened it, only that day's segment was accessible. They were careful to manage the risk of the Angels helping themselves to the drugs. Today he had the familiar pack of single use syringes, clearly labelled with the name of the customer they had been prescribed for, 'Meg Eastman', and the name of the medicine 'Pre-term'. A premed for a one-way ticket.

He had been given enough medical training to administer it and deal with minor adverse reactions. Sometimes they went a bit nauseous and clammy. Not always. If the reaction was too bad there wasn't much he could do, but it was rare, and in the circumstances why would anyone worry? There was no resuscitation equipment in the car.

Angel had never expected to end up doing a job like this. A job that hadn't even existed when he was young. But it wasn't so bad.

Years ago, a friend of his had worked in a nursing home, helping to look after old people. Nursing homes were buildings where old people were kept alive if they didn't have anyone who cared about them. Usually they had some nursing staff for medical needs; and assistants to help keep them clean and comfortable. Some nicer ones had entertainment programmes, chair yoga, visits from schoolchildren at Christmas, communal areas where people could sit and chat, or just sit and dribble if they were closer to the end. Unfortunately some places were ghastly. Abuse took place and people starved to death, dehydrated, confused, dirty and in pain. The new approach meant that such cruelty no longer took place, which was a good thing.

Angel had lost his job in a call center about five years ago. Call center work was pretty much all there was where he grew up. Most of the industry in his town had died during the 20th century, when many communities began to feel empty, workless, worthless.

Then the service industries came. Instead of going to the factories, people filed into massive airy hangars, put on their headsets, and took orders for – well, anything really. Angel took orders for mobile phones. It was better than delivering pizza – the only other real option in his town. His colleagues were friendly, the money was regular and pretty good, it wasn't particularly stressful. They got employee discounts, paid holidays, a subsidised canteen – life was comfortable.

There was a lot of competition, and the company was always thinking about how to stay on top. They worked out that a good way to make more profit would be to replace people with robots. Angel used to imagine how cool it would have been to sit alongside a humanoid robot, built to look like him, wearing a headset and chatting – but that wasn't what happened. The robots that came were invisible, insidious, hiding in the network. Faceless software agents with a deceptively charming voice. With the capacity to learn and the capability to do a better job than a low-paid, slightly bored person. Never tired, never irritable, never offended.

You might not remember the early days of not-very-intelligent-agents, when people told Siri, Alexa and Google Home to "fuck off" to see how they would react. They were pretty unsophisticated back then, but the next generation was so much better. By the time Angel was laid off, the robots were not only resolving queries quicker than people could, but they were beating their sales targets hands down. Once the phone company merged with one of the social media giants, the artificial agents could assess a caller's personality in seconds, press all their buttons, engage them in conversation about even the most unusual personal interest. It was a pushover to sell them anything, and all but the most manipulative of human workers were pushed out.

So Angel went online and did a Personal Reinvention test. You did the quiz, it looked at your social media profile, your social scores, and came up with suggestions for what else you might do from the jobs that were available.

Angel was pretty sociable. Chatty. He had done well in the call center because people liked him. He could make them feel comfortable. There were things he instinctively knew to say, to put people at their ease. "Have you had your tea yet? Have you been out today? What's the weather like where you are? Is it convenient to speak now – I can always call back if you're busy?" He offered them discounts. There were special promotions. He smashed his targets and the customers felt they had a good deal. Everyone was happy, until it ended.

When the Reinvention Algorithm got hold of him, it came up with the idea he could be an Angel, working for one of the new 'end-of-life' businesses. Angel wasn't his name then, but they all had to change their name to Angel when they came to work for the corporation. He had a lot of empathy and a reassuring manner which the corporation had helped him to build on. So much so that he had progressed to the top-tier service, where people with a bit more money left at the end could choose to die in luxury, with a real person taking them to the disposal center in a beautiful driverless limo. He had a nice uniform – smart, but you could move fast in it if you had to. His early days with the company, when he had been working on the Economy Endings buses, had given him plenty of experience in managing difficult situations in confined spaces, and restoring a semblance of calm.

It all seemed perfectly normal. They had a more enlightened attitude to death these days. Once people are over 80 they can't do much, can they? Better to get it over with, instead of prolonging their frail and confused existence.

Angel didn't always think this way. When they had the debates in Parliament about legalising – and then industrialising – euthanasia he was firmly against it. He thought that people who were poor, desperate or grasping might try to end the lives of others for their personal gain. But the algorithms made sure no one was exploited. Now, wealth was being handed back to the young, instead of being frittered away by the old, infirm and expensive to care for. In turn, the young were putting their newfound wealth to positive use, building better lives and rejuvenating the economy.

The selection and training programme for Angels was quite intensive. At Angel University, the applicants were grouped into teams. They had to role play being the customer, the Angel and an observer who would give feedback after every scenario. Sometimes it got a bit rough. A couple of years in, he felt the training had prepared him for every eventuality. Even though he had no medical knowledge before, he knew a lot now about how to give injections, restrain people, keep them calm, help them into their incontinence pants with dignity and that sort of thing. They even had a little joke sometimes. It broke the tension.

The corporation had thought of everything. They had some super chatbots which would help you pull yourself back together if you were feeling sad after a difficult day.

Sensors and tiny cameras embedded in the uniform captured unusual movement patterns and filmed the interactions for your protection, and in case of litigation. When you knew you were being watched it made you extra careful. And if they sensed you had encountered something very distressing the chatbot was already waiting to talk you through it when you took the limo home.

Some of the customers were serene. Often the most peaceful were those who believed they had a terminal condition which was going to cause suffering or distress for them and their family. Off goes their mortal coil like a fake fur coat being shrugged from the shoulders of a celebrity. Effortless. They would welcome him in, sit down in their favorite chair, talk a bit about their life, roll up their sleeve and hold out their arm, smiling, ready for the beginning of the end.

Sometimes it was more tricky, of course. Although the customers had a cooling-off period when they signed up for disposal, for some it only became real when an Angel arrived at the door. Suddenly they felt more alive than ever. If they had second thoughts, though, the Angels weren't allowed to let them get away. All parties were bound by an indelible, legally-binding contract which obliged the corporation to follow through, even if the customer started thinking they might have changed their mind.

The rules said sedation had to be administered within ten minutes of the Angel's arrival, and the terms gave the corporation permission to use force. It used to say 'reasonable force', but they dropped the 'reasonable'. For some of them Angel had needed to use other aspects of his training. Headlock. Wrists secured with cable ties. Knee on the chest. One of them even bit him. He had got pretty adept at using his bodyweight to floor them and hold them down. He knew he couldn't let the needle get out of his control. The last thing you wanted was to end up sedated yourself. It happened to one of the other Angels, and she was fired straight away. Once you'd jabbed them, though, it was usually fine. They could get a bit weepy, but they had no strength for physical resistance.

Angel looked at Meg's details. She was on the new incentive programme for 70 to 85-year-olds. They packaged it up like a reverse birthday present. If they signed up to go on or before their 85th birthday all their assets could be gifted tax free. It was an amazing deal, and it had been very popular. They were having to train up extra Angels to take people to the Rockstar departure lounge. He had never been in there himself, as the customers were handed over to robots in the entrance area, but it looked out of this world in the videos. His bonus was going to be good this quarter, even though Angel hadn't been able to bring himself to promote the Friends and Family offer to his Nan. Even the Angels had sales targets to meet.

It looked like today's customer still had all her marbles. High scores on mental agility. Not too big to handle if it gets difficult. He felt in his pocket for the cable ties. They were easy to reach in case he needed them. Everything else would be ready in the car.

One of the perks of the job was having the luxury limo to take you to and from work. Today's customer didn't live too far from Angel, but he would have time enough on the journey to prepare himself mentally.

The door to his apartment clicked behind him, and

he walked purposefully towards the gleaming elliptical vehicle. First he needed to check the luxury passenger chamber. "Open nearside," he said, and the door slid up revealing a grey leather recliner facing towards the back of the car, which looked like an extra comfortable, top of the range dentists' chair.

He took the plastic wrapping off a pristine white disposable quilt, run through with the corporation logo, and folded it neatly on the seat. This was where he would ask Meg to lie down and relax before clipping her arms and legs into the restraints which were carefully hidden in the sides of the chairs. "Comfortable," he said. At the sound of the code word the restraints reached out of the chair seat like tentacles and began to feel for their captive.

Angel quickly said: "Comfortable test over," and the restraints disappeared back into their hiding places.

The opposite door opened to reveal his seat, facing in the direction they would travel, and a series of pockets set into the front of the car.

He climbed in, fastened his seat belt and when he said, "Go," the car began to glide away from the kerb.

The VR headset was stowed, as Meg had not wanted to wear it. That was a pity because it usually got the customers into a more distant state of mind quicker. The chances of difficult scenes in the car were far lower when they were in virtual reality, and with the drugs quite a few of them believed they were already somewhere else. Still, that was her choice.

She had done a playlist, though. That was all keyed in.

He checked the grey bag which was pre-loaded with a lightweight wheelchair, in case he needed it to get Meg into the car, and the incontinence pants the customers were asked to slip on before they had their jabs. Quite often they were already wearing their own.

With only another five minutes to go, Angel thought it might help him bond with Meg if he flicked through her playlist. "Song one," he said.

A melodic female voice sustained a clear, high note. Temple bells began a rhythmic beat. "Om" she hummed. She was chanting in Sanskrit. "That's one of the nice things about this job," Angel thought to himself, "You get to hear all sorts of music you might not normally come across. I could use this for my wake-up app tomorrow."

CHAPTER TWENTY-NINE

MEG LOOKED AT HER GOLD Omega bracelet watch. How could she have overlooked it? It must have been because she hardly ever took it off. She didn't want to take it to the disposal center with her. She would have to ask the Angel to send it to Alice when he arrived. There should be just enough time to package it up.

As she rummaged through the drawers where she had put the remnants of her stationery, the doorbell rang. For God's sake, not now, she thought. It rang again. And again. This was not what she needed. She almost had everything ready for her discreet exit. The last thing she wanted was someone scuppering her plans.

She thought about just ignoring the caller, but as the bell rang for the fifth time, and for longer at every attempt, she decided it would be easier if she just went calmly down to the front door and told them to go away. Maybe it was the Angel, running ahead of schedule? Calm, calm, calm. She still had to put on the pants.

Meg opened the door. There was a woman outside wearing an orange baseball cap pulled down low over her face, and a high visibility orange jacket. Both the hat and the jacket were labelled with the same word: Emergency.

"Hello," she began, "I'm sorry to bother you. I'm from Gas Safety. There's a leak in this area. We're having to check all the houses in your road. I need to examine the pipe where the connection comes in from the street. It's a common point of weakness I'm afraid. Can you let me in please?"

Emergency woman was about 40, white, with brown hair. There was something about her that seemed familiar. But there was no question of Meg letting her in. Not now.

"I'm sorry," she explained, "I'm just getting ready to go to an important meeting. Could you come back later?"

"No I can't madam. Under the Public Safety Act you have to allow me to access your property immediately. Your community could be in serious danger." She reached into her pocket and held out an ID card which looked official enough.

Meg stood her ground. If only this woman knew. "Please go away. I will gladly let you in later, but not now."

Ms Emergency wasn't giving up: "I can tell this isn't a good time for you, but we can't let a gas explosion blow up the whole street, can we? I have to demand that you open the door immediately and allow me access to your property. Otherwise I will have to call my colleagues and undertake a forced entry. This will leave your home unsecured and it will be your responsibility to conduct any repairs at your own cost."

Meg's mind raced. If they wrecked the door she couldn't rely on the corporation to repair it. It would be much more than just asking someone to post a letter. Nothing like that was included in the package. Anybody could just walk into the house and take what was left. Even squatters. It was all supposed to be for Adam and Alice.

Feeling that everything she had arranged could be in jeopardy, Meg started to feel dizzy. Perhaps if I let her in, she can do the checks quickly and I can get her out before the Angel arrives? There didn't seem to be any other option. The countdown was ticking by.

"OK," Meg finally capitulated, "But you have to be quick. I can't smell gas so I don't think you'll find anything."

Reluctantly she let the woman into the house. Meg had been expecting her to pull a gas detector out of her backpack, but instead she leaned solidly against the front door, slamming it closed, looked up, and started speaking to Meg with an even greater sense of urgency than before.

"You probably don't recognise me, Meg. It's a long time since we met, but I'm Lexi, Alice's schoolfriend," she said, taking off the hat and looking straight into her eyes.

"The one who sent the photos? Yes, I remember now." That was why she looked familiar. Oh no. "This isn't about me cancelling Christmas is it? I'm really sorry. I just didn't think we had room for an extra two at the table," Meg said apologetically, forgetting for a second why she needed to get Lexi to leave.

"No, it's nothing to do with that. And anyway it was fine, don't worry. We had a turkey crown. No. Alice sent me. It's a long story, but I am in an underground movement called PACE. It's a direct action group set up to help people like you. PACE stands for People Against Coercive Euthanasia. We don't have much time so I need to explain a bit more about why I'm here, and what you need to do, as quickly as possible."

Meg had no choice other than to listen. Lexi was blocking the door that stood between her and her exit. How did she know what she had done? She thought she had put Alice off the scent.

"Before she went back to New Zealand, Alice was concerned you might have signed up for disposal. She had a feeling something wasn't right. We helped her to install spy software on your computer just before she left. It confirmed that you had made a booking for a departure today."

"Was it when you sent the video? 'Don't Fear The Reaper'?"

"Yes. Please don't be angry with Alice, she has the best of intentions. We know that the Angel is coming for you, in about 13 minutes. I am here to ask you on behalf of Alice and Adam to defer your appointment with death and come with me to a safe house.

"It won't be as nice as this place, but you will be warm, clothed, have access to free basic medical care, a secure communications link to your family, and most importantly free legal aid to void the agreement you've signed with the corporation. My colleague is in a vehicle two streets away, and we need to leave now. If we wait much longer we'll all be in danger. You probably know that the Angel is authorised to use force to take you, and we have heard from insiders that it can get extremely unpleasant."

Meg's mind was racing. It was going to be so serene, she thought. Glamorous even. It still could be if Lexi gets out of here. I can't change my mind now. I've made my plans. It's going to be easier if she leaves and I carry on as arranged. Before Meg had the chance to put any of her thoughts into words, Lexi carried on.

"You've got very little time. Listen to me. You have been manipulated. The corporation has been running personalised campaigns to make you – and everyone else who is 70 or older – feel worthless. But you are strong, Meg. Your family wants you to live. They do not want this to happen. If you don't believe me, here's a message from Alice." She pulled a thin, flat, square screen out of her pocket, and switched it on. "We recorded this over a secure channel last night, just after we were able to confirm your plans. No copy exists anywhere other than on this device. As soon as you've watched it, it will be deleted. Quick."

She took the piece of glass from Lexi and the video started. A familiar face, a face she loved, with a fading green bob and tired eyes, puffy from crying, spoke earnestly with a faltering voice, framed by her mother's hands:

"Hi Mum. You know I didn't want to come back to NZ, but you made me feel so bad when I asked about staying on. Now I've found out why. I should be there with you now. We had such a great time at Christmas and we all loved being with you – me, Adam, Frank and the girls. Especially the kids. Please go with Lexi and do everything she tells you. We all want to see you again. We want your grandchildren to remember you. We want to share our lives with you. Please Mum, don't do it. We love you. We want more time. Please."

Her face contorted with distress before the screen snapped to black. She'd gone.

"We only got confirmation yesterday – otherwise she would be here to tell you herself. So what will it be? Quickly, Meg. The clock's ticking." Lexi said.

Feeling overwhelmed from seeing her daughter in such distress, and at the same time being faced with so much other new information to take in, Meg hesitated before asking, "What do you mean, I've been manipulated? I'm not stupid you know."

"No one is saying you're stupid. You're up against a very sophisticated organisation. Tell me, where did you first hear about Happy Endings?"

"Online – like everything else. I remember exactly when it was. I was on a website for advice about coping with bereavement. I'd been missing my husband Paul, and I was feeling a bit down. You think you're over it, and then it comes back in waves. Anyway you could do a quiz – put in all your details to help create a personalised coping strategy. It generated 'Ten top tips to help you cope with the death of a loved one'. They were good. I'd just finished reading them when a pop-up ad for Rockstar Endings appeared. It was great fun to watch, and cheered me up in an odd sort of way. I know it's nonsense, but it was almost as if they would be able to reunite me with Paul. After that the ads were there every time I opened a new window. I looked forward to seeing them, the different variations, great music. And when they brought in the *85* incentive it seemed too good a deal to miss."

"Don't you see anything wrong with that? Trying to get someone to sign up for voluntary euthanasia when they are in a fragile mental state?"

"I've never thought about it before. Maybe. But even if I wanted to change my mind, I can't go back now. I've signed the forms. They don't let you out." What would happen to her over the next two hours had been spelled out in unsparing detail in the 25-page consent form that she had actually read.

Lexi put her hands gently on Meg's shoulders and looked her in the eyes. "We can get you out. We've helped people escape before. There are ways to get you out of the contract if you want us to, but…" her phone rang and she picked up the call using the earpiece she was wearing, "… Yes? What, now?"

Lexi hung up after a couple of seconds. She looked pained. "He's here. It looks like he's already outside. We're out of time. Surely you don't want to die, Meg? Think of your children and grandchildren. What's it going to be? Death or life?"

Meg had thought of nothing other than her children and grandchildren for months. That was the whole point of the Rockstar Ending. A gift of love. Trying to stay alive at this late stage in the game would cause a whole lot of trouble. For all Alice's pleading, it would leave her with much less than they stood to inherit if she stuck to her original plan.

"I want to get you out of here. I promised Alice I'd do my best but we are both in danger now. There could be a struggle and the Angel will have come prepared. Last minute resistance happens quite often and they're trained to use any means necessary."

Meg already knew that, in theory, from the Terms and Conditions, but the reality was uglier. Lexi did not look like someone who would be much good in a fight, and Meg didn't think she'd come out of one too well herself either. Even if she changed her mind now, she thought, what chance would they have?

"The problem is, I can't see how there can be any going back now, even if I wanted to."

"If you don't want to be freed, I'll respect that." Lexi said. "But even if you do want to go to your death today, I'd like to ask if you would consider doing something to help other people who aren't quite so sure. We suspect that the Disposal Centers are not the happy places they are made out to be. They are all in secret locations and no one is allowed in to observe what goes on there. We have been trying to work out where they are. Can I at least ask you to slip this tracker into your pocket so we can follow you? Then, after you've been killed and incinerated, I'll at least be able to console Alice with the news that that you wanted to contribute to the research, and tell her the exact location where you entered the death chamber."

Lexi's choice of language was quite deliberate. She had paid close attention to the training given by other members of PACE. It was important to tell it like it was. Meg took the tracker in her hand and looked at it for a moment. It was light, the kind of thing you'd put on a cat. A tag on it read 'Wotsit'. If she had been feeling overwhelmed before, she thought, it was nothing compared to the surges of conflicting emotions that were rampaging through her body now.

It would be good to have time to reconsider. But time was the one thing she had signed away.

"I'm really not sure..."

"If you're not sure, you shouldn't be doing it then, should you? If we can get you to a safe house you can think again."

"But we'll lose the *85* tax break. The children will be worse off. Today is the last day I qualify." Although she had become adept at repeating the corporation propaganda, Meg's voice was wavering. Hairline cracks were appearing in the logic she had stacked up so conscientiously. Lexi could feel her shifting. I'm getting somewhere, she thought. Time to crank it up.

"The children don't want your money. They only care about seeing you again, about your grandchildren seeing you again. Imagine having to tell little Mia what you've done. She's only four. She'll barely remember you. They'll all be in therapy for ever dealing with an abandonment like the one you've got planned. It's not as if there's even anything wrong with you. For goodness sake, Meg, you're fitter than me."

Elegant too, Meg thought wistfully. As the doorbell rang, she slipped the tracker inside the silk bra she had chosen to wear for her special day. "Well, let's see what we can get away with," she said with doubt in her voice, "If you're absolutely certain it's what the children want."

"Completely."

The bell rang again and a gentle male voice called, "Hello. Meg, Mrs Eastman. Could you let me in, please?"

"You're going to have to let the Angel in," Lexi said. "I'll see if I can distract him. If anything happens to me you need to run to the corner of Gracechurch Avenue and Bodmin Road. There's a blue van that will take you to safety."

"Coming dear," Meg replied and waited a few seconds before opening the door.

Angel already knew something was wrong. He'd done enough of these jobs to tell instinctively if it was going to be tricky. The compliant ones were always waiting right by the door, pants on, and were eager to get moving. Any delay like this, and he had to start preparing himself physically and mentally for a struggle. He didn't enjoy that side of the job at all. Still, he hadn't lost one yet. His coat had been designed so that he could discreetly dip into his pockets and, with the right hand pull out a concealed needle which he could use to stop her in her tracks. In his left, he grasped the wrist restraints.

As he stepped into the room he was surprised to see Lexi. Meg had signed the standard undertaking which guaranteed she would be alone when her transfer arrived.

"Hello. I'm from the Emergency Gas Leak Team." Lexi began, falling back on her original premise as she racked her brains for a way to derail Meg's departure.

"I've just come to take Mrs Eastman out for the day,"

Angel said, trying to radiate an air of kindly calm. "She has an important appointment, and we really do need to be on our way so we don't miss our slot. Did you find any problems with the gas?"

"I've only just arrived, and I need to get started on the testing now."

"I can't smell anything."

"Sometimes it's like that," Lexi improvised, sounding increasingly unconvincing.

"How would you feel about leaving this nice lady here to carry on with her safety checks while we go for your appointment?" Angel said, turning to address his client directly.

"I can't leave her in my house." Meg was playing for time. "I don't know her. We can't leave her here unsupervised, can we?" The pitch of her voice was raised, and she was speaking fast. She's panicking, Angel thought, subtly tightening his grip on the professional equipment concealed in his pockets.

Before he could reply Lexi's phone rang again. "Excuse me while I take this." She headed into the kitchen to talk in private.

The second she left the room, Angel swooped. He stepped forward and locked the crook of his left arm around Meg's neck, murmuring "sorry about this" under his breath and quickly injecting her in the neck with a heavy dose of instant acting sedative. He lowered her into an armchair where she sat with her eyelids becoming heavy, unable to speak. A tiny speck of dribble appeared at the left corner of her mouth and began to run down her faint marionette line.

With Meg temporarily out of action, he called to Lexi, "I'm afraid you're going to have to leave. Mrs Eastman has been taken unwell and I need to get her to the doctor. I can't leave you here on your own."

"I'll lose my job if I don't finish the testing," Lexi said. "It's the law."

"I'll lose mine if I don't get Meg to where she needs to be, and leave the house secured," Angel countered.

Lexi just stared back. "No," she said. "It's unsafe. I'm not going."

The haptic on Angel's wrist buzzed and he looked down at the screen. Amber warning. He had to leave the site in three minutes to stay on schedule. If he didn't make it in time his scores would fall and he could end up back on the death bus, ferrying people from the dorms. He couldn't face that again.

In his left hand, inside his pocket, he still held the wrist restraints he had prepared for Meg. If he could just get close enough to this orange gas woman he could put her in a lock and get her out of the way.

"I really need you to leave," he said again, calmly, firmly, not particularly threateningly. All in line with the training. He stepped towards her to make his appeal more direct.

"And I'm not leaving."

The haptic double buzzed. Red warning, T minus two minutes and thirty seconds. He was going to have act outside of the normal rules. Later, he would have to fill in an MBORC form, to prove he was dealing with Matters Beyond Our Reasonable Control. What a pain. A couple more steps now and he could grab her.

"She's unwell. Why are you in such a rush to move her?"

"It's obvious. I need to get her to a medical facility as soon as possible." He was edging closer.

Angel was now within striking distance and leapt at Lexi. She didn't have a chance. He swiftly pinned her arms behind her back and cable tied them securely together at the wrists and elbows. She was helpless, paralysed with pain and fear. Her arms felt like they were going to wrench her shoulders out of the sockets. Then he saw the door leading to the cellar. Apologising sincerely for the second time that day, Angel said: "I'm really sorry about this. I have to make sure Meg gets to her appointment on time. I'll let you go downstairs so you can check the pipes, and I'll come back later to let you out. Until then, you won't be needing this," he said, snapping her earpiece out of place, throwing her phone on the floor, and stamping on it.

He had lost patience now and didn't have any more energy for this pantomime. To keep Lexi well and truly out of the way, Angel opened the cellar door, and pushed her onto the little landing at the top of the steep stairs that led downwards. Grabbing her shoulders he carefully lowered her into a seated position with her back against the wall so she wouldn't fall. Then he slammed the door shut before locking it, and putting a heavy chair against the handle for good measure.

It was only then that he could turn back his attention back to taking Meg on her once in a lifetime trip.

CHAPTER THIRTY

After reassuring himself that Meg was still breathing and fully immobilised, Angel quickly fetched the lightweight wheelchair he kept in the back of the car for emergencies. He unfolded it carefully next to where she was slumped, and put on the brake, before gently lifting her on to its webbed seat. "So sorry about this, old girl," he said, feeling her chemically relaxed frame resting momentarily against him. He pushed the chair to the car and deftly positioned Meg in the recliner seat. He gave the code word 'comfortable' to the sensors without any of the usual preamble, triggering the restraints which crept out to embrace her arms and legs. She couldn't get away now.

He reached over Meg to grab the glass of champagne that he'd placed on her side table to welcome her just ten minutes earlier.

"I'm afraid you won't be able to have that," he said as he unclipped it from his holder and tipped the contents of the glass into the gutter. A smell of alcohol and old parties wafted up. He shook the last dregs out of the bottom of the glass wishing he'd been able to down it himself. Even a tiny drop would have been nice. After the antics he had just dealt with he really fancied a drink, but he knew he would never get away with it. As he wiped the glass with a piece of blue paper roll, Meg fixed him, momentarily, with a steely gaze. Then her eyes fell shut.

Angel closed the door as quickly as he could so that no one would see Meg's condition, and took his place in the escort's seat. He was facing Meg so he could keep an eye on her. Something was making him very uncomfortable. As the doors locked shut, a blast of cold air flowed into the travel compartment. It was a relief to feel the chill as the struggle had elevated his temperature and made his heart beat fast. He stowed the empty glass in its place, and picked up the spotless light quilt with the corporation print to tuck around Meg as if she were a baby.

"Music, Meg Eastman," he told the car. Immediately the soothing yoga music she had chosen began to play. The lights were just bright enough so he could observe Meg without her being over-stimulated. Her eyes were closed. "Try to relax, Meg," he said, "It's not long now, and you will continue your journey in the best possible hands." A temple bell chimed. More Oms followed.

For a moment, Angel, too, let his eyes close. He slowed his breathing and went with the music for a few moments. Calming though it was, all thoughts of putting this track on his personal playlist had now been erased. The associations would be just too distressing. What a shame.

"Oh, Mrs Eastman," Angel said, searching for one

of the platitudes the company had taught him for these journeys, "You have done something very generous by signing up for this package. Imagine how pleased your children will be when they learn of your thoughtful gift."

Her eyes were still closed. In spite of the desperate measures he'd had to take, this was a much better journey than the wild struggling he sometimes had to observe, as people with second thoughts writhed, bracing against the restraints in panic, before being given a booster shot to chill them back out.

"Angel 249," a voice said from the car speaker system, "can you please confirm you are back on track? We detected some unusual activity from your body sensors during the time slip. Your video is now in the queue for analysis."

"Yes," he said, "We are on track. I'll be completing an MBORC form later. I can't go into details as I am with the customer now. Everything's OK." He could sense a problem looming up ahead. Another interview with Quality Assurance. Still he had done his best. One thing at a time. Right now he had to focus on delivering Mrs E to the disposal center in one piece. He would have to slip back later tonight to see what he could do about the one he had parked under the stairs.

The car rolled slowly forward. He watched Meg breathing. Her neat, pale hair was clipped back in a chignon that had become loose in the struggle. Lilac eye shadow had collected in the soft crease above her eyes, and her lipstick was smudged. He realised some of it had come off on his shoulder when he had lifted her. Angel reached out and held her hand, hoping that her anxiety would be easing away now.

As they approached the exclusive Rockstar Ending entrance to the disposal center a hologram of the Virgin Mary loomed up in the rotunda. Angel found some of the holos quite unsettling, and this was no exception. Especially with that huge strawberry thing in the middle of its chest. What was that? The form on the tablet said, 'Our Lady, version three, with throbbing Sacred Heart.' He turned to Meg. He almost jumped out of his skin as her eyes were wide open again and staring, first at the holo and then at him.

She mumbled something. He moved his ear close to her lips to try to hear what she was saying. "Hail Mary," she said, "Full of grace. This is your prayer Angel. Pray for us sinners now, and at the hour of our death. Amen."

A chill ran down his spine as the car slid smoothly to a halt. His seat belt automatically disarmed and he sprang out onto the pavement, feeling horribly spooked, and trying to shake off what Meg had just said. He was relieved to be away from her, even for a couple of seconds.

As he walked round to Meg's side of the car, he was relieved to find a burly robot with a kindly face, ersatz muscles and a cowboy hat had appeared next to him to take delivery of his cargo. "Rockstar Ending for Meg Eastman," Angel said quickly and clearly, to signal that his stage of the journey was compete.

Meg's restraints released and slithered back into their hidden recesses. As Angel introduced her to the robot, it slid something that looked like an adult baby seat out of an enormous torso, and encircled her with its comforting mechanistic biceps. "Howdy Meg," the robot said as it placed her gently into its people carrier, "Let's get you cleaned up and onto the next leg of your adventure."

Cleaned up? Oh no. Angel remembered that in the struggle he hadn't been able to put her into the incontinence pants – something they always tried to do before injecting the sedative. It had a deep and instant effect on every muscle in the body. As he slipped back into the car for his ride home, he took the unusual step of asking for the window to be opened, to try to blow away the reek of urine. That would be something else he'd have to explain to the bosses.

CHAPTER THIRTY-ONE

LEXI WAITED FOR HER EYES to adjust to the dark in the little space under the stairs. It was never like this for Harry Potter, she thought. She slowed her breathing to avert the panic that was threatening to set in. Her shoulders were sore from the position in which Angel had pinned them, tight behind her back, before he had lowered her onto the ledge. He had deliberately wedged her in the corner away from the steep stairs down to the cellar, but she didn't dare move in case she fell.

Beyond the door she could hear Angel moving swiftly around the room. Meg was in no state to resist. There was the sound of someone being lifted into a seat. Then the front door clicked shut and she was alone.

While in some ways it was a relief to be waiting in the dark and the silence after the unpleasantness of the struggle, Lexi had lost hope that they would be able to free Meg. She had no idea what she would say to Alice. Bob was still out there in the van, but she couldn't expect him to follow through the rest of the mission on his own. Six months ago she could not have been happier. She had finally found the love of her life, and then she had bumped into Elsie and all this had happened. Maybe Bob was right to be worried all those months ago. Maybe they shouldn't have got involved.

Suddenly, Lexi was blinded by an intense light as the door to her hiding place swung open.

"Hello, love."

She blinked, terrified, thinking that someone from the corporation had come to take her for disposal too. But even though she was starting to hyperventilate, and having trouble seeing through the tears of terror that had filled her eyes, the voice was unmistakable.

Bob reached down and helped her to her feet. Taking a pair of clippers from a pocket in his cargo pants, he snapped through the hard plastic that was binding her wrists and rubbed them to encourage the blood to flow. She yelped as pins and needles shot through her hands and up her forearms. "Ow! Get off!" she shouted, half laughing, half crying.

"I slipped in the front door when that twat went to get the wheelchair," he explained. "Hid in the kitchen until the coast was clear. He was in a rush to get Meg on the road. No idea I was here."

Lexi looked round the room. The cushions were tidily arranged. Not a speck of dust anywhere. On the small table by the front door she saw a recycled paper bag containing the small pile of things Meg had prepared for Angel to take care of after her departure. Inside were some envelopes, a gold watch, and her house keys. They had been left behind in the panic. Should she take them now, and send the letters to Meg's children? It was hard to know what to do for the best.

Picking up the bag Lexi turned to Bob.

"What are you going to do with that?" he asked

"I'm going to give them back to Meg. It's what she'd want." Lexi answered, pushing all doubt to the back of her mind, collecting her backpack and tablet from the kitchen, and slipping Meg's legacy parcel into the main compartment. "She's got Wotsit's tracker. Let's go."

"Are you sure about this, love?" Bob said quietly.

"Do you think we can make up the lost time?" Lexi asked, finding the strength from a place she didn't know she had.

Bob gave her the best answer he could think of. "We can give it a try but there are a lot of risks. We haven't really tested stage two fully. I've got the Trojan running on the main controller in the disposal center, but I really wanted a few more weeks to make it foolproof."

"What would I say to Alice and Adam? That it got too difficult? That we gave up? The thing is, I'm sure Meg said she wanted to stop it all, just before… well … just before angel features showed up and took her away." Lexi said, breathing heavily. If she walked away now, she would never forgive herself.

"We'd better get going then," he said, "We've already lost a lot of time." They headed briskly out of Meg's house and climbed into the van.

Lexi drove so that Bob could get online. By the time they pulled out he had already opened his laptop and paired it with a new burner phone to get them discretely connected to the net.

His first priority was to establish a connection with the pet tracker that Meg was carrying. Wotsit had not died in vain. This tracker was much more accurate than some of the earlier models which had caused terrible panic when they were launched, as people thought their cats were safely wandering in walled gardens in Belgravia, when in fact they were rooting through bins in Battersea.

The bleep appeared on the screen about four blocks away. Unlike the driverless limo carrying Meg, the van was not fitted with a speed limiter, and Lexi was confident they could catch up easily. It took about five minutes, and without taking any risks or drawing attention to themselves, they had the limo in line of sight.

Bob turned his attention to the disposal center. He knew that, by hacking in now, during working hours, he would risk detection and being locked out. Before he opened the link he reviewed his cheat sheet, where he had recorded all the key data. He would do as much offline setup as he could first.

From the central controller he had been able to access the entry system, and it was there he had found the template and technical specifications for the Happy Endings ID card. He'd had passes manufactured for him and Lexi by a pro-life tech outfit operating from Vatican City. They gave the highest level of all areas access. Reaching into another of his many pockets, Bob pulled out the cards, set into Happy Endings lanyards, and put them on the dashboard.

There was no dress code for the people working inside the plant, and Lexi had already taken off her luminous Emergency jacket and thrown it in the back of the van. Bob had also put his and Lexi's details into the facial recognition system in case they were checked on the way in. So – apart from the mounting dread they both felt about ending up in a furnace themselves – they were good to go. He had made an entry permit which he stuck in the window of the van.

Let's hope all those sleepless nights down the lock-up were worth it, Bob thought. Most of his hacking had been done from there, between two and four in the morning. That was the time when no one was on duty at the DC, so there was the least chance they would spot unusual activity. Bob was pleased that he had also managed to download the site map, and a flow chart showing how the different classes of Enders progressed through the DC. There were two drop-off points.

The Rockstar Endings entrance had a drive which circled an elliptical mini roundabout, in the middle of which stood a glittering holographic sculpture. The virtual statue could be set to create a variety of shapes depending on what the ender had specified – symbols, saints and gods from most of the world religions were available, with plenty of secular options such as trees, landmarks, globes and planets, cars and motorbikes. A few celebrities had even licensed their 3D image to be used. Meg, however, had eschewed David Bowie in favor of a hologram of the Virgin Mary sporting a Sacred Heart of Jesus. It took Catholic folk art to a whole new level. The designers had been to Lourdes for inspiration.

Once they had arrived at the terminal, the Rockstar Enders were greeted by a friendly looking robot which took their hand, and led them into a private consulting room where they would lie down on a disposable, automated trolley which secured them gently but tightly before the next stage. The robots could carry the Enders if necessary. It wasn't unusual for people to faint with terror. Should they have any last doubts, the robots could administer a stronger sedative to help them reach the end.

People who couldn't afford the premium option were taken into an area that more closely resembled an old fashioned bus station. There were 20 bays where the disposal vehicles could park and unload their cargo. The carcasses of the old social services buses had been modified. Once in their chairs the passengers would not stand up again. Restraints crossed their bodies like seat belts, and manacles secured their ankles as the first sedative was automatically administered.

When they reached their destination, the chairs took turns in descending automatically to ground level, and their cargo was released and lifted by a headless robot, which took them in its arms and put them over its saddle-like shoulder to carry them to their trolley, to a background track of music designed to reinforce a sense of calm and relaxation. The musak-for-the-last-leg playlist. The trolley was the great leveller, the same model for every class of Ender.

From the two entrances, premium and economy, all the Enders were taken to the Penultimate Lounge on their automated trolleys. Bob had to look twice at the drawing, as it was a lounge in name only. It more closely resembled a freeform baggage reclaim area flowing backwards, taking the sedated cargo slowly but surely, in a tidy caterpillar formation, towards the opening that led to the final stage. The relaxing music maintained the Enders in a positive mental state for the last few moments of their lives. It was also piped into the control room to soothe the small number of human staff who had been carefully selected for the privileged task of keeping watch over the destruction line. If it was me, Bob had thought to himself, I'd want Bon Jovi's 'Blaze of Glory'.

Sensors on the trolleys alerted the managers if any of the customers were in danger of becoming overly stressed. This was rare, although in the early days there had been a few traumatic incidents when the drugs had been administered incorrectly, and people woke up thinking they were already dead and in some kind of mechanistic hell. Which of course they were. The supervisor who had to deal with that was now on long-term sick, and under a binding NDA not to talk about what she had seen, nor what she had needed to do to regain control. The corporation strove to have a no-blame culture and to learn from its mistakes. It was in the handbook.

Bob looked up and saw the limo turn into the entrance of a scruffy looking industrial estate. There was an African church in a substantial old red-brick building across the road, and a workshop offering powder coating services on the corner. Bob wondered whether they'd taken a wrong turn.

The small road which led into the estate followed a couple of sharp bends and arrived at an area that was no longer visible from the main road. This was one of the few brownfield sites left in London, ripe for redevelopment. Then he saw it had been redeveloped already. A chimney billowed dark grey smoke.

There were no signs. The corporation cars all knew where they were going. Bob pulled up the map and directed Meg to the third entrance he had identified. This would be the first test of his fake IDs.

They approached what looked like a railway arch, and as they drew near the metal shutter covering the entrance opened effortlessly. The pass must have activated the mechanism. Good. Once inside, a ramp lay immediately ahead which circled underground to a multi-storey car park where there were bays for staff and visitors, as well as a delivery area. They stopped.

"It's not too late to go back," Bob said. Lexi was trembling from a naturally-generated hit of adrenaline. "Let me see that map," she said, trying to calm herself by reaching out and touching Bob's reassuring fleece.

He put his laptop on the dashboard so they could both see the screen. "Meg will have been taken into this entrance here. It's not far at all – just two flights up through that door marked Emergency Exit. It takes 10 minutes to complete all the checks, comply with the legal processes, administer the final sedative, and get her into the stack for the Penultimate Lounge.

"Depending on how busy it is, it could take between five and ten minutes for her to progress through Penultimate into the final stage. Once she's in there, we have the slimmest of chances of getting her out alive. There's no oxygen, only carbon dioxide. Like they use in the abattoirs. They do that to help the Enders close down, and to prevent fire breaking out from the furnace. The trolleys tip the bodies directly into retorts, individual cremation capsules, and then they are heated to 1000 degrees and pressurised to make them disintegrate faster."

Were they really doing this? "I don't think I need to know any more gruesome details, thanks. I'm having enough trouble keeping my breakfast down as it is," Lexi said.

"You do. You need to know exactly what we're dealing with here." Bob said in a voice that was uncharacteristically stern. "I'd much rather go in myself but in terms of our safety, I think I need to be the one to stay here to hack the systems as best I can. You don't know how to do that. Once you're in, I'll get into the main controller and follow you with the surveillance cameras. I've linked this earpiece to burner phone two so we can stay in touch. Try not to lose this one," he joked feebly to try to diffuse some of the tension.

Meg put in the earpiece and synced it with the phone. She looked down at the signal strength bar but to her dismay it was empty. "Bob," she said, showing it to him, "this isn't any good."

"It's because we're underground," he said. "Shit, shit, shit, shit, shit. You'll be up at ground level once you're in, but I'm stuck down here. Give me a minute."

Bob went back to his laptop for a few seconds, "I've got it. We can connect through the company Wi-Fi network – I thought those passwords might come in handy – and I'll run a secure voice app." In about 30 seconds it was done.

Lexi was feeling very frightened. "Bob. If I need help, will you come in and rescue me?"

"Honestly? I'm not sure I'd be able to get in. I'm on the corporation facial recognition database already for the day job. If they see me here, it'll trip an alert for being in the wrong place at the wrong time, and blow our cover completely. But I'd certainly give it a try."

So she was on her own again. Just like those years before she met him. Good job she was used to it.

"It's now or never," he said, still not wanting her to go, but understanding that in spite of her fear, Lexi could not face letting Meg and her family down. She suppressed her terror by giving Bob a big hug, "Love you," she said, feeling warm and wanted as she never had in her life before. What on earth was she doing? "Back soon, sweetie."

She jumped down from the van, her corporation lanyard swinging around her neck, carrying a small backpack she had pre-loaded for this stage of the journey. Bob slid over into the driver's seat. As she approached the door the camera greeted her clenched face, there was a double click as two sets of security bolts snapped back, and the door slipped open.

CHAPTER THIRTY-TWO

LEXI WAS IN A CONCRETE stairwell, like any other you would find doubling as a fire escape in an industrial building or multi-storey car park. The stark hardness of the walls, edging into darkness, fed her fear. She could hear her heart racing, and tried to breathe more slowly to get it back under control, conscious that every second she stood still was a second that Meg was inching towards the inferno. Sometimes she felt like this when she was alone at night, walking back to her car, head up, looking confident but inside wondering whether someone was going to jump out of the darkness to steal her bag, or do something worse. Except this was more intense.

Bulkhead lamps were set into the walls, casting a tight, bright cold pool of light around her. She would just have to keep going. As she moved up the stairs, the lights sensed her movement and stayed with her like an expertly operated follow spot. "Bob's got my back," she repeated in her head, as she noticed the dome of a security camera by the door on the second landing she came to. Just like at school. Two more flights would take her to where she needed to be.

"I'm almost in," she said softly, hoping he could hear her and tell her what to do next.

"I can see you," he said. "Stay back, you don't want it to open just yet. There's someone in the corridor right by the door."

She counted to five, "Now?"

"No. Stay still. Listen to me. The lift to the control room will be behind the second door on your right. There will be two people in there overseeing the operations, and two backup robots. They shouldn't query who you are, I've put you into the roster as a supervisory medic. From there you can work your way into the area where Meg is about to be processed. OK, go now."

As she stepped towards the door it sensed her and slid open. She followed the route Bob had given her. Another deep breath, and another, as she drew closer to the control room door, and it yielded to her face just like all the others had.

She stepped into the lift. It had clear walls and a transparent floor through which she could see the smooth grey surface of the concrete surround. She was thrown for a moment as there were no buttons.

"Hello Lexi," the lift said. "Where are you going?"

She heard Bob's voice in her ear, "They call the control room the Operations Center, the OC for short," he said.

"Up to the OC please," thinking that if she used the abbreviation she would be less likely to be found out.

"Taking you there now."

The lift started to glide upwards. After a few seconds the concrete walls disappeared and Lexi found herself in a warm ambient light. Looking beyond, she could see the disposal center spreading out below her just as the lift slid into the pocket that opened out into the OC.

She stepped out into a panopticon. From here, she could see everything that happened in the building. She heard Bob say, "Remember, you're Lexi Connor medical inspector."

"Lexi Connor medical inspector," sounded the room, an echo, announcing her arrival to the man and woman seated on two out of three consoles, arranged back to back in a triangle on a turntable so that the people faced outwards from the center of the room. Neither of them looked up, but the woman said: "Do you want to take a seat up here with us, Lexi? You should be able to access everything you need."

"Sure."

Lexi took a look around. Behind her, in alcoves either side of the lift, stood two inactive robots. They must have been the ones Bob was talking about, humanoid shapes, two legs, and two arms, something approaching a head with various sensors, speakers and dials, bulky, broad and quite tall. The woman had rotated the central turntable so she was facing Lexi and could now glance up without losing her place in whatever part of the process she was supervising.

"We call them Mork and Mindy," a smile flashed briefly across her face. "All purpose bots. If any of the others has a problem we can slip them into any stage on the line. They're in their docking stations charging up now. I'm Sylvia. I look after arrivals and sedation. Phil takes over once the Enders are on the trolley, and processes them through the airlock into the final stages, right to individual ash capture. I don't think we've seen you here before, have we?"

Was that just a random remark or the beginning of a challenge? Easy does it. "No, I've never been to this site before. It looks like a tidy operation."

"Yes. We can see everything from up here. It's one of our slickest sites. There are feeds to our screens from all the key parts of the process. The dashboards…" she nodded upwards, glancing towards the ceiling where a strip of monitors encircled the room, blinking stats and statuses from everywhere "… they give us a good summary of what's going on, and there's CCTV of course." Some of the monitors displayed crisp, colorful moving images of what looked like live feeds.

Lexi walked to the periphery of the chamber, which was enclosed in a vertical cylinder of floor to ceiling glass. They were in a giant bell jar. Looking upwards she could see the rafters of the old warehouse inside which the corporation had hidden their plant. The OC was suspended directly above what looked like a big clean room. Tanks of gas lined one wall, some grey, others white. The composite floor was pale green and dazzled her eyes slightly. The whole space was enclosed in a rectangular prism of more thick, clear glass. It was spotless. She heard Phil murmur, "Testing CO2 tank three." She could just about hear a low hissing noise as a green LED blinked on the tank. "Opening valve for air removal." Just like Bob had said. He was preparing the transit area for the next intake which they were expecting very soon. One of the screens was dedicated to monitoring the air composition below. All the indicators were green, and it showed that the airlock system had just been tested.

She had a good view of the rooms leading on to the transit floor. Behind one airlock was a rectangular area containing three identical suites which sat behind a branded, luxurious reception. A neon sign hung behind the illuminated desk which simply read 'Rockstar' in the corporation livery. Three robots sat at the desk in rest mode. Behind them were three doors, all with neon stars on them. She imagined they were trying to create the look of a star dressing room, but instead they seemed rather satanic, and reminded her of what the Nazis had done. Each of the suites behind the doors was identically furnished with a plush armchair, a VR headset, and a wall of LED screens where various images and films could be displayed, depending on what the Ender had chosen. The exit was on the opposite side of the suite from where the Enders came in, behind a false wall that would be retracted into the floor when the time came, revealing the automated trolley onto which the robot would lift them to complete their journey.

The Enders on the economy scheme would be ferried into a gloomy transit area, processed en masse, and sent through via another airlock in a wall perpendicular to the Rockstar entrance. Lexi counted twenty trolleys arranged in four rows in a room resembling an open ward, with the same pale green floor. It must be a good surface for the trolleys to navigate, she thought to herself, more than a little appalled that she was able to analyse so objectively what was about to happen.

She could see a small bus pulling into one of the bays in the economy arrivals area just outside the ward. Fifteen headless robots formed a line at the back of the vehicle, which was discharging its fragile cargo one by one. They were tipping the people out of their seats, which moved in rotation to an exit at the back, and laying them over the saddle-like shoulder that lay where the robot's head should have been. As they relaxed forward over the machine, restraints emerged from its torso and held the Enders in place as they were carried in and lowered gently onto their trolleys, where more automated straps emerged to ensure they didn't fall. From a distance, the bodies resembled a tatty set of discarded rag dolls.

Lexi felt oddly disembodied watching the smooth running of the industrial death machine. Her distress mounted as the scale of what she was about to witness dawned on her, but she knew that she had to stay in control if she was to be able to get Meg out. She had to stick to the plan. Focus on the task in hand. Who knows what they would do to stop her, if they realised why she was here?

At the far end of the central transit area was a low archway, about a meter higher than the trolley. Above it was a sign which read, "High temperatures. Danger." It led to a low structure, encased in what Lexi imagined was some kind of heat proof, fire retardant material. Good old asbestos. A tall chimney ran from the back up to the ceiling, and out to the open air. It looked like a giant pizza oven, she thought, only not for pizza. It was amazing what they could do with 3D printing nowadays.

Turning her attention back to the room Lexi pointed at the spare seat in the OC, and said as casually as she could manage, "Is it OK if I sit here?"

"Sure," said Sylvia, "Wasn't that what I said?" now concentrating on her own screen to ensure the new arrivals were processed correctly. I'm so stressed I can barely remember what I heard two minutes ago, Lexi thought, as she climbed up into the luxurious Recaro seat. It reminded her of driving a little sports car she'd once owned. The padding adjusted to the shape of her body. She was suddenly very tired and wanted to close her eyes and pretend it had all just been a bad dream. But that wasn't an option.

The console facing Lexi detected that she was there and instantly flickered to life. The message 'Welcome to the OC Lexi Connor' flashed up briefly before she was presented with the main menu. Ah yes, that was who she was.

The choices were:

1. Today's workflow
2. Operations

She went into workflow and found Meg's record. As time was tight, she skipped quickly over the entertainment options – the Virgin Mary welcome hologram, the yoga soundscape for the suite and the sunset mural – and went quickly into the drugs administration system.

Based on Meg's body weight and age, the system had calculated the precise dose of sedative to administer to

Meg when she arrived in her suite. Then her robot would let her rest for five minutes to check she was properly under before taking her through to the queue.

Lexi wanted Meg to be awake when she got to her, so she went into her health record, and set her bodyweight at one kilo to get the dosage to shrink and become ineffective. The characters in the weight box turned red, and it wouldn't save. The weight she had put in was below the parameters of the system and it would not let her over-write it. She desperately wanted to ask Bob for help but she knew that, with Sylvia and Phil so close, she couldn't say anything.

"I can see your screen," Bob's voice said in her ear. "I'm searching for the over-ride command now. Give me a few seconds."

Lexi toggled back and went into operations. She had found the controlled drugs stock screen, and was checking the levels and authorisations, when she noticed Sylvia looking over her shoulder.

"Everything in order?" She said.

"So far so good."

"If you don't mind me asking, what were you doing with Meg Eastman's record? I was just setting up her sequence and I saw you altering her dosage."

"We have to test whether the safety features are running correctly." Thinking quickly, "There was a bug a while back which caused a few issues. One of the technicians decided to administer ultra-low dosages instead of what was prescribed. They were helping themselves to the surplus meds and selling them on the side for recreational use. Not pretty. We had a number of wake-ups.

The robots dealt with it of course. No one actually left the process, but quite a few of the Enders had a less than peaceful final journey as a result.

"Anyway, it looks like you have the patch correctly installed here so it's all good. You're idiot proof." Lexi was surprising herself with how much of this IT stuff she had picked up from Bob. Maybe she shouldn't have said idiot.

"OK. But it would be better if you didn't interfere with the people who are on the schedule for today. We don't want any delays. If our stats fall we won't get our bonus." Sylvia was looking irritated and stressed. That's OK, Lexi thought, grouchy I can handle. Just not suspicious.

"Don't worry about that, I'll let head office know it was part of the test," Lexi lied.

"You should find everything in order. Let me know if you have any questions."

Sylvia turned back to her screen and said, "We have a bus of 15 being welcomed in the economy bays now, and one premium on a Rockstar Ending about to enter the receiving area. Hologram activated."

"You know what," Lexi said as casually as she could muster, "I need to pop down to the welcome area to check the sedative levels in the robot-based administration systems."

"You can see it all from here – look," Sylvia said flicking one of the ceiling-suspended monitors in front of Lexi into life. "See. There's Mary, illuminated and ready to welcome Meg." She toggled again, "And there's her robot, Lee, we're just turning it on now. We'll put the others into a chatty mode, so it looks more normal, like an old style reception. Lee's just been replenished with sedative so it's at 100%, and has a full carousel of sterile needles in his palm."

"I still need to check it, I'm afraid. Audit rules. My bonus on the line this time. It only takes a minute to open the injectables magazine and swap the ampoules so I can take them away for analysis. I'll be out of the way by the time she's in."

"You'll need to take the lift to level one. Make it snappy." Sylvia was getting more irritated.

Lexi tore herself out of the seat, more reluctantly than Sylvia would ever know, picked up her backpack, and went back to the lift. When the door opened, several levels down, she found herself in a small square hallway with three doors.

She would have to give an instruction to get the right one to open.

"Rockstar," she tried, nervously. "Lexi Connor entering Rockstar Endings area now," the door said, as it slid out of her way.

CHAPTER THIRTY-THREE

LEXI FOUND HERSELF IN THE brightly lit Rockstar access area. There were four identical doors on her right. The first one, which opened onto a small corridor linking to reception, was already ajar. She guessed that the three next to it led to the three Rockstar suites. To her left loomed the airlock into the transit area which Phil had already begun to flood with carbon dioxide. With no oxygen in the atmosphere, the chances of the Enders waking up once they were in there were extremely low. A set of emergency breathing apparatus hung on the wall. At the far end of the corridor was another door leading out into the car park where the cargo of economy Enders were being unloaded.

Lexi rubbed the cold sweat of fear from her palms and walked into the reception area, trying to appear as confident as possible. Through the glass wall that separated it from the outside world she could see the glimmering hologram of the Virgin Mary. She floated four meters tall, wore a blue robe, held her hands outstretched, and in the center of her chest was the Sacred Heart of Jesus, pulsating in red and gold. Creepy, Lexi thought, yet strangely appropriate. "Blessed art thou amongst women." A line from the Hail Mary popped into her head from out of nowhere, and she began to well up with emotion. For God's sake, she said to herself, I haven't got time for a spiritual experience. Pull yourself together.

It was then that Bob brought her back down to earth. "Call the robot by its name," she heard him say. "Tell it who you are and what you want. Just like you're at school. Command and control. You're good at that." She was fully present now. Time to follow Bob's instructions.

"Lee," Lexi said.

The robot closest to her lifted its head smoothly out of the resting position and did something like smiling and blinking before saying, "Yes?"

"I'm medic inspector Lexi Connor, I need to check your sedative levels," she said.

"My levels are at 100 per cent," the robot reported, cocking its head to one side.

"Sorry. Override. I need to check that the administration system is working correctly. Can you open up please?"

Watching from the control room, Sylvia shook her head. She'd met plenty of these inspectors. It never ceased to amaze her how they were so polite to the machines, just because someone had designed them to look like they were smiling. Or maybe because they were huge and powerful and could overpower and sedate you in seconds. At some instinctive level that made everyone treat them with extra caution, no matter what the Asimov rules said.

Lee lifted and rotated its enormous forearms. They swivelled 360 degrees at the elbow. That movement would have been impossible for a human, and it reminded Lexi that it was merely a machine with certain design advantages over the real thing. At the end of its arms were two hands. First they just looked like the big, flat cushioned oval pads that you would use for sparring. Then, as she watched, the smooth surface of each palm retracted to expose a magazine of four ampoules lying next to each other, all connected to an injection line which loaded itself with disposable needles. She thought randomly of her mother's ancient sewing machine and stepped closer to get a better look.

"Please stand back," Lee said, snapping one of its hands back together and placing it between itself and Lexi. "I do not want to administer any of these in error,"

"Phil, look at this," Sylvia said, observing the scene from the OC, "Do you think she knows what she'd doing? Lee's had to activate Asimov One to stop her getting jabbed."

Phil looked up from his console at the screen where Sylvia was watching Lexi, "She probably just got a bit too close. We've all done it," he said before turning back to monitor the heat controls on the furnace. The temperature was rising nicely.

"Be careful," Lexi heard Bob say. "I can't jam the video feed from the control room. They're watching you. Tell the robot to relax."

Anxiety at knowing she was being watched sent a flash of heat across Lexi's skin. Her palms were sweating again. She wiped them on her trousers.

"Lee, I need to inspect the ampoules. Please open both magazines again, undo the lock to release them, then switch into rest mode."

"She's putting Lee in rest mode now. For God's sake. She's got two minutes or I'm going to go down with Mindy and pull her out of there. Mindy, power up." Sylvia said, and the robot lifted its head and said, "Checks complete, select mode."

Lexi peered into the sockets in Lee's hands, and gently felt around inside. She quickly found eight ampoules of clear liquid which were locked into the robot's high tech stigmata.

"Lee, I have to take these meds for inspection offsite. I'll replace them with identical doses to get you through your workload today."

"She really doesn't trust us," Sylvia said, as Lee rotated its wrists in turn so that the ampoules would drop into the plastic bag Lexi held out to catch them. She sealed the bag and said:

"Rotate so I can load you back up." She clicked the replacement vials into place. "You are now back at 100 per cent. Job complete Lee. Resume previous setting."

Lee pulled itself to full height and said, "Sylvia requests you vacate the area. My guest is about to arrive."

Lexi stepped back and retreated into the corridor. If Lee had been at the position closest to the entrance, it made sense that Meg would be taken into the cubicle directly behind him. Lexi would slip in there and wait for Meg so she could get her out. The suite door slid open and Lexi settled into the big chair, pulling out her tablet to pretend she was still working on the audit.

When Sylvia saw Lexi in the suite her blood pressure rose a few more units. There was something not right about this. She couldn't think of any reason for Lexi to be in the premium suites. "Hey console, call the med inspection center for me."

"Connecting you now."

"Welcome to the Happy Endings medical inspection team hotline," it said slowly, "All our lines are busy at the moment. Choose one to book an inspection; two for recruitment; three for whistleblowing; four to speak to a bot." A raucous song played as she was put on hold, repeating 'Rockstar' in the title over and over again,.

"Shit. I've got no time for this," Sylvia hung up as she saw that Meg's ride was arriving, circling the supersize Mary hologram, and drawing to a halt outside the reception area. They had to get this one in quickly to stay on target. She would have to check out Lexi later.

Listening into the control room, Bob could see that Sylvia had been distracted for a minute, "Get out of the chair love," he said, "and see if you can crouch behind the screen. There's a CCTV dead spot right there so you should be able to stay invisible." Lexi jumped up and lowered herself onto the floor one knee at a time, folding into the corner behind the trolley.

Sylvia had switched her attention back to Lee, Meg's reception committee. The robot had pulled itself to full height, activated its most calming and friendly expression, and was walking with a slight swagger towards the limo to meet Meg. When the door opened Angel confirmed Meg's identity and Lee swept down to where she lay. Noting that she was not able to walk, Lee reached into the car with its big strong arms and encircled her limp form, deftly popping her onto a giant baby seat which emerged from its torso. The moisture detectors picked up some leakage and Lee made sympathetic noises so she wouldn't be embarrassed or distressed. A quick blast of warm air was all it took to restore her dignity and comfort. As Lee carried Meg indoors, Angel pulled away in the car.

Although Meg was not feeling strong enough to walk, her eyes were open and she was aware of everything around her. As they approached the reception desk the other two robots looked up from their pretend conversation and said, together, "Hello Meg, welcome to your one and only best ever Rockstar Ending, the trip of a lifetime."

Was this really it? Two minutes of a religious hologram, an ersatz hello from R2D2 and C3PO here, and the chance to be swept off your feet and given a cheeky warm breeze by Optimus Prime. The last bit was definitely the best, and for one brief moment she forgot the purpose of her visit and lived in the moment of being carried around by the mechanical strongman in a ten-gallon hat.

Having been fully reconciled to the purpose of this journey until only an hour ago, when everything was disrupted by Lexi, Meg tried to settle back into a state of acceptance and go with the flow. But it was harder than she had hoped it would be. Especially now the effect of the sedative was fading.

Lee stood still for a few seconds and observed her vital signs. She gazed up at its face, lying in its surprisingly comfortable arms and, before the drugs had quite worn off, found herself murmuring, "Whatever happened to Fay Wray?" The first line of her favorite song from *The Rocky Horror Picture Show*.

Lee didn't have any 20th century film references in its memory bank, so said nothing. No King Kong. No Rocky Horror. Although its character was based on a macho, strong and silent type, it didn't know about Jason Bourne either.

It did, however, detect that Meg's heart rate was increasing. She must have been sedated earlier than usual, and now it was wearing off. Angel normally administered meds just before arrival, in the car. Lee snuggled her into its body, and reached a strong, soft arm around her, bringing a paw-like hand to rest on her upper arm. She felt consoled and weirdly safe, but then, from where its hand would have been if it had one, she felt a sensation like a bee sting as the needle shot through her clothing and her skin, and administered another dose of chemical.

"That should keep you calm Meg," Lee said, with a kindly tone, as the needle retracted back into its recess. Meg shut her eyes tightly and willed herself into oblivion. It was over now. Her heart was racing, but soon she would be under. There was no point fighting it. Lee lowered her gently into the big soft armchair and stood aside as Meg's yoga music filled the room, and the whole wall in front of her turned to a stunning orange sunset. She could smell the sea and hear the waves landing gently on the beach beneath the Om chanting.

Meg peeped at the screen through half closed eyes. A

warm glow filled the room, until the huge golden ball of the sun had disappeared completely below the horizon, and the sky gradually turned violet, then indigo, then midnight blue. Stars began to appear, and a crescent moon blinked into position. Meg tried a number of relaxation techniques to try to drop off. Eventually she closed her eyes completely and started working upwards from her toes, clenching and then relaxing different muscle groups in turn. But instead of starting to feel heavy like she usually did, something odd was happening. Meg was feeling very much awake. It was as if she was getting stronger. I must be hallucinating, she thought. Will there be a tunnel of light?

Then she was aware of something gliding towards her. Lee flattened and extended its arms again, and in the dark it lifted her effortlessly on to a bed that had slid automatically into position between her chair and the wall. Maybe this was lucid dreaming?

Restraints slid out from the sides of the bed, and held her in place, as the automated stretcher edged away from the entrance, through a door she had not noticed when they entered the room, leading out the other side. She tried to flex her arms but they were secured by her sides. The straps tightened automatically in response to her struggling, as the reality of what she had signed up for hit her. For the first time, Meg felt trapped and wanted to scream. A deep sob suddenly engulfed her as the image of Alice's tear-stained face appeared in her mind, and wouldn't go away.

The trolley was travelling through a dimly lit corridor. Lee had gone. It stopped for a couple of seconds by another door, next to which stood an empty cabinet, labelled 'emergency breathing apparatus'. As the doors slid apart, the trolley passed into some kind of anteroom. It was the airlock. Then Meg heard Lexi's voice in her dream. "Meg, I'm under the trolley. Don't react or they'll get suspicious. We're going to get you out just like I promised."

Horrible, horrible, horrible subconscious, Meg thought angrily. Just as she had managed to get herself into an accepting trance, it was taunting her with pictures of Alice and hallucinations offering the futile hope of escape.

The suggestion that she might be reprieved brought memories flooding back. Nights walking around her dark house, in the dead of winter, trying to decide whether the time was right to book her Rockstar Ending. Looking out of her window at the full moon, feeling a profound sense of loneliness now the children were so far away, and Paul was gone. Planning that perfect Christmas, a present to herself more than them. Abruptly fending off Alice's well-intentioned questions. Finally, the message Lexi had brought her that afternoon, Alice's desperate face begging Meg not to die. Tears trickled from the corners of her eyes and pooled in her ears. They said it was an act of love, didn't they? One last gift?

The airlock slammed shut behind her, and the trolley was propelled forward into the transition area. The lights were very low, in the way an airline would dim the cabin lights when they thought all their passengers should going to sleep. Only there was no option for a reading light, and the film was over.

The superficial glamour the corporation had built into her transfer and arrival was obscured by a mounting horror. Now her surroundings had degenerated into bare utility. They had fucked up. She wasn't even supposed to be awake. She tried to move her arms and legs again but there was no room. The carbon dioxide which had been pumped into the transition area began to displace the air in her lungs. She was struggling and gasping at first, and then, as they rolled slowly towards the heat, her body began to shut down. Her trolley slid to the back of a caterpillar that was edging its way slowly, in the dark, towards the furnace.

CHAPTER THIRTY-FOUR

"SHE'S ALL YOURS NOW," SYLVIA said to Phil, as the dashboard confirmed Meg's trolley had clipped successfully on to the tail end of the disposal queue. In front of her were the fifteen economy Enders, the first of which was about ten seconds away from the combustion chamber.

Phil performed the final checks. The temperature in the furnace was in the right range. The trolleys were all at the right height. Carbon dioxide levels were...hang on a minute. There was something wrong with the gas levels.

As Phil watched the dial tracking the mix, he realised that the gas ratio was beginning to move in the wrong direction. He was sure he had set everything up correctly. How could that have happened? He blinked twice, but it didn't make any difference. Before his eyes, the CO2 marker kept edging fractionally downwards as the blend of gases started to tip towards being life-sustaining. If it dropped any lower, it would not be safe to open the entrance to the furnace: there would be too much oxygen. The temperatures were so high that they needed the transition room to be fully saturated with carbon dioxide to prevent an explosion when the doors opened. A red warning light blinked.

"Look at this," Phil said to Sylvia. "I'm going to have to hold things up for a minute." He pressed the pause button on his console and started the series of pre-programmed checks on the gas system. "I don't understand it. The tanks are all full and the pumps are testing green. It can't be the delivery."

"I told you something's not right. Where's that Lexi gone?"

The two bewildered operatives flicked through the feeds from the different cameras, but still couldn't see anything unusual. "We've fucking lost her." Then Sylvia and Phil both pulled themselves up out of their seats, and walked tentatively to the edge of the observation deck, where the floor-to-ceiling curved glass allowed them to peer down at the transition area. In the low light they could just about make out the trolleys loaded with still bodies, now at a standstill, hooked together like some kind of weird segmented insect. They couldn't see much more.

"Shall we put the floodlights on?" Sylvia said.

"If we do that they'll wake up. The CO2 has fallen to normal atmospheric levels. It's being flushed out of the chamber. I don't know how this is happening. Any minute now the sedation will start wearing off. I'd prefer to keep them in the dark to try to maintain a sense of calm."

"Where the hell has that medical inspector disappeared to?" Sylvia said. "It's got to be something to do with her. Look, I know our bonuses are on the line here, but I do think it's time to get some help."

Phil wasn't ready to admit defeat yet. "I'm wondering whether something's happened to the release valve that we use to vent the CO2 from the transition area when we go in there for maintenance. I'm going to go down and check it. It's in the wall on the far side. It really could be that simple, maybe a mouse got in there or something. Give me five minutes, I'll take Mindy."

Sylvia was very unhappy with Phil's suggestion, but she knew that they might never work again if they didn't contain the situation themselves. "OK. But if you're not back in ten minutes I'm going to have to send Mork down and use emergency tactics to get them all put back to sleep. Mork and Mindy, medirobot mode, load sedative and stand by." There was a soft whirring. "Loading complete," the robots confirmed in unison ten seconds later. Sylvia watched Phil disappear into the lift with Mindy, while Mork remained motionless in its alcove.

Phil was right. It was only a minute before she saw him enter the transition area. Mindy stood by his shoulder and emitted a discrete pool of light from a cute proboscis that emerged from the center of its head, so that Phil could see where he was going in the gloom. They reached the far end of the room where a square vent was set into the wall. Phil started wiggling it about, and she guessed from his movements that he had found it to be jammed open. A lever protruded from the wall which could be used for manual over-ride. Phil reached for the handle, but just as his hand was about to grasp it, she saw Mindy wrap both its arms around Phil and hold him tightly so he could not finish the job.

Sylvia turned to Mork who had quietly slipped out of its resting place and was now blocking her access to the door. "I didn't sign up for this," Sylvia said, out loud. She could feel her job disappearing before her eyes and was acutely aware that within a few minutes she would, at best, have 16 people on her hands who were going to sue the corporation for not taking them to their promised destination. The two-day training programme she and Phil had been through to teach them how to operate their respective sections of the destruction line hadn't acknowledged that this kind of emergency could arise.

"Assistant call HQ please, emergency," she said to her personal device. She couldn't trust anything on the company system now. This time her call connected in seconds. "Hello Brookwood disposal center," a voice said, "What's up?"

"We have had a number of malfunctions with 16 Enders now stuck in the transition area, likely to wake in a few minutes. Request advice on next steps."

"All your feeds appear normal."

"The vent for the transition area is jammed open and one robot, number 459 aka Mindy has imprisoned my co-worker. I believe I am also being threatened by robot 458 Mork who is blocking my exit from the OC and fully charged with sedative."

"Stay calm Brookwood. Running a security check now. This will take approximately five minutes."

"I don't think we have five minutes," Sylvia said, helplessly. She heard the airlocks to the transition area slide open, leaving a clear exit path to the economy arrivals area, where the next bus had arrived. She sent a command to the unloading bay to hold back the next batch of Enders, explaining that there was unexpected congestion ahead.

Then the thing she had feared most began to happen. A scream of terror came from one of the trolleys as the first of the people lying in wait woke up, and found themselves pinned down in the half light, unable to move, not able to tell whether they were dead or alive. All the poor Ender could do was emit a shrill cry for help, again and again and again. It was the voice of an old lady, harsh, rasping, in an unthinking panic. It echoed through the building. Sylvia couldn't block it out. By now she was unsure who was more helpless, herself trapped in the glass box, or the hysterical old woman strapped to a bed.

Woken by the deathly wailing, so close to her ear, the next Ender stirred. At first she tried to reach over to the one who was panicking, but found that she could not move her arms. So she said, "Calm down, dear, calm down."

With the wakening of all the Enders seeming inevitable, Sylvia felt there was now nothing to lose by switching on the floodlights. The floor filled with a bright, blue-white light. This had exactly the effect Phil had predicted. They were all awake now. One man sobbed deeply and kept saying, "Mother, mother, have you come for me? Please, come for me now." Another simply said, "Where are we?"

As the levels of noise and distress escalated, Lexi

knew it was time to break cover. She slid out from under the trolley that was carrying Meg, removed her breathing apparatus, and balanced astride Meg's slender form to address the crowd.

"Please try not to panic. You've woken up in the disposal center. I'm from PACE, People Against Coercive Euthanasia. We have come to set you free."

Lexi looked around at the untidy mass of drugged, distressed and disoriented people as a siren began to wail. There was a whooshing sound as more oxygen flooded into the room, replacing the CO2 that had doubled as an asphyxiation agent and a precaution against fire.

Looking up at her rescuer's bottom, Meg was confused at first. It was only when she heard Lexi's voice that she realised who she was. She really had spoken to her from under the bed. While she may have been awake and alive, Meg still felt imprisoned. Her arms and legs were firmly clamped. She swivelled her head from side to side in a panic, appalled by the distressed rabble around her. By now there was no doubt in her mind. She wanted out.

There were sixteen Enders including Meg, each one pinned to a trolley, all in varying states of consciousness. The front of the crocodile stopped a short distance from the entrance to the furnace, which was covered by a substantial door. Red lights flashed menacingly on the walls. As Lexi watched, the Enders' restraints sprung open. Those furthest from the heat remained at rest, still mildly sedated. Maybe they were already dead. She couldn't tell. It would be enough to give you a heart attack if you were still alive.

One or two near the front were now trying to stand. She felt something tug at her sleeve. A frail man with a straggly white ponytail was tapping at her wrist, "Is this the afterlife?" he asked, "What is happening to me?" There was no time to answer properly, "Please, just lie back down and rest. You're safe." She wanted to save them all but she could tell from the things some of them were mumbling that wasn't what everyone wanted.

"I don't want to be set free," came another voice, a big woman whose breathing was labored, gasping for breath. "I just want it to be over."

"I'm in terrible pain," wailed another, "Why have you woken us up? They've stopped my morphine. Please put me back to sleep. Please…" She dissolved into sobs.

"I'm sure they'll be happy to carry on with you once I'm out of the way," Lexi found herself saying, not allowing herself to dwell too deeply on the implications. Meg was her primary concern now. Lexi jumped down from the trolley and helped her to sit up. "Meg, have I done the right thing? You do want to come with me, don't you?"

"Yes. Yes I do. Thank you. I don't know what I was thinking," she said, gasping in the replenished air, with a tone that was unmistakeably apologetic. It was hard to find the right words.

This wasn't the time or the place to explain why, albeit with the best of intentions, Meg had put her family and Lexi to so much trouble. How she had seen too many of her friends suffering at the end of their lives, their children in despair after the care services fell apart. How she wanted to bequeath Adam and Alice everything she had without the state, that was failing so many, getting its hands on any of it. Somehow, the Rockstar Ending had seemed the perfect solution for avoiding a mountain of possible pain.

It was Alice's desperate plea on the tiny screen that had dragged Meg back from the entrance to the abyss. Until that moment, she had thought that she could slip off on her own terms without bothering anyone. For all her sophisticated planning, however, she now deeply regretted her decision. In a moment of bittersweet epiphany, Meg understood that she had massively underestimated how much she was loved.

When she quietly lowered her feet, she was surprised to discover that she was strong enough to walk. Leaning on Lexi at first, she gingerly moved one foot in front of the other, and found she was completely stable. "Anyone would think I was glad to be alive," she said, squeezing Lexi's arm tightly, cherishing the reassuring presence of another human being. Although she had been quite taken with Lee, the feel of a more flawed human frame was a much better option, even if it had its limitations.

After a few more steps, she relaxed her grip on her rescuer, and looked around the chamber, beginning to absorb how close she had come to cremation. She saw the instruments of mechanised death delivery all around her. The perfunctory trollies with their deactivated restraints. The furnace, still belting out heat. Cylinders of gas mounted on the walls. There was a man held half a meter off the floor by a robot, over by the far side, kicking his legs in wild bursts, unable to struggle free.

Someone would come for him soon. Then what would happen?

"How are we going to get out?" Meg asked. There was still a nagging fear at the back of her mind. She had signed away all her rights and couldn't imagine walking away would be this easy. Especially not now she had seen inside the disposal center.

The man with the straggly ponytail was sitting up now too. "Did someone say we can get out?" he said, tugging at Lexi's sleeve again. "Can we get out? I think I've made a terrible mistake. I've been a bit confused recently."

Lexi thought quickly. She climbed onto the motionless trolley Meg had vacated so that everyone could see her. The flashing red warning light lit up her face. She prepared to raise her voice just like she would in the classroom, and began to address the rows of old folks, most of them now beginning to realise where they were. Some were consoling each other, some looked angry, some relieved. Others just lay still, blinking at the ceiling.

"Does anyone want to come with us?" Lexi shouted in her most authoritative teacher's voice. "Hands up!"

"Can we actually get out?" The man with the ponytail asked. "I'm not sure I can survive if I escape. I have nowhere to live and no money."

"If we move now, yes, I think we can get you out. There are people outside who will help us and give you somewhere safe to stay."

"I would love to but I'm just not strong enough. Better you leave me here," said another, fidgeting with the restraints. "Can you fasten me back in?"

"What will we live on?"

"Will you take me?"

"And me?"

Lexi looked around at the wrinkled and bewildered faces turning towards her. "Bob, what now?" she said, "I don't know how to answer their questions." She glanced up to the glass cylinder that enveloped the operations center, and mouthed "Sorry," when she realised that Sylvia was furiously grimacing at her.

"I'm sending reinforcements," she heard Bob say. "I've reversed the donkey bots. Here they come."

At that moment, the fifteen headless carrier bots, whose job was usually to unload the economy buses, entered the transition area from the car park. "I get it," Lexi said. "Right who needs a lift to get out of here?"

In the end, only four of the Enders wanted to leave. Others simply shook their heads or cried silently, tears running from the sides of their eyes as they lay flat on their makeshift beds. Bob had flipped the programming on the robots so they could gently carry away those who wanted to escape. They had just enough embedded intelligence to find their way.

"We gave you a bit of a boost back there," Lexi explained as she took Meg's hand and began to lead her to the exit. "I swapped amphetamine for the sedative." She glanced behind and saw they were being followed by four more waverers, being carried securely on robotic shoulders. They didn't look very comfortable or dignified, but they all seemed glad to be heading for a different kind of exit than the one they had been expecting.

"Security has been breached," the HQ bot finally announced, back in the OC. "Suspected Trojan. We are running patches now and trying to locate the source of the attack." Sylvia put her face in her hands. "Too late," she said. "Way, way too late." The slowest cavalry in the world was on its way, and until then she was trapped in what she privately called the Death Star. Phil was slumped in Mindy's arms down on the transition floor, having tried for too long to struggle free, and been given a dose of his own medicine. He would be furious when he regained consciousness.

Lexi, Meg and their bizarre convoy made their way to the car park as quickly as they could, and found Bob waiting in the van. The doors were already opened so that the robots could lower the elderly escapees into a comfortable position for their return journey. Bob put the van into gear and they headed out of the disposal center toward the road.

In the rear view mirror, Bob caught a glimpse of the next welcome hologram that had been loaded. It was a giant Elvis. Vegas period.

CHAPTER THIRTY-FIVE

ALTHOUGH THEY HAD MADE IT safely out of the disposal center, Lexi didn't feel it was safe to relax just yet.

The first problem would be working out what they were going to do with everyone. They already had a plan for Meg, who rode alongside her and Bob in the front seat. Starting to come down from her uppers, she looked dazed and dishevelled and sat motionless, staring straight ahead, tightly clutching the envelope Lexi had brought with her from the house. The keys were inside, so she could be sure of getting back into her home, although the immediate plan was for her to stay with Lexi and Bob until they were certain it was safe for her to return.

A more challenging question was what to do with the four extra Enders she had liberated. That hadn't been in the plan for Stage Two, but once inside Lexi had been overcome by an urge to help anyone she could. She could not have left them behind. As they drove back through the familiar streets she could hear them starting to chat in the back, processing what they had been through.

Someone's bony finger tapped annoyingly on the

back of her shoulder. “Excuse me, but what will happen to us?” a woman’s voice asked weakly from the row of seats immediately behind. “I had to sign over my home to the corporation to pay for my disposal. I won’t have anywhere to live now. Do you think I might be able to get help to rent it back?”

“I don’t know,” Lexi said. Her neck was stiff from having being tied up earlier, so she couldn’t turn round easily to see who was talking. “I am sure we can work something out for all of you. There is definitely a place you can stay for the time being.” It was a good job Father Al’s presbytery was a substantial double-fronted Victorian gothic villa. He was going to need all that space.

The same woman continued. “Now I’m alive again I’m going to need to get hold of some blood pressure medication privately. I’m barred from the NHS because I’ve turned 85, you see. Will your friends be able to help us with that too?” Lexi knew that Father Al had a doctor in the congregation who had been helping out people in just that situation, under the radar, using the weekly collections from the church. “I think so, yes,” she said.

“That place. It was much more industrialised than I’d expected it to be,” one of the men said. “I’d thought it would be a bit more – well, human – not just a bleak, mechanised death factory. I know I chose the no frills option, but it felt pretty barbaric when it came down to it.”

“Why did you sign up?” the other man in the back of the van asked him.

“I’ve suffered with terrible depression for years. As soon as I hit 70 I thought, finally I can check out humanely without having to go all the way to Switzerland. But there was something about waking up on that trolley that made me change my mind. Something about being seconds away from the end that made me question what I was doing. When Lexi said she could get us out I thought maybe I should give it one more shot."

"I've been on meds for my depression for a year now," the other man opened up. "My name's Bryn by the way,"

"I'm George."

"I'd just lost hope. That was what it was for me. I know I'm starting to get dementia. I was being thrown out of my home. I thought, well I might as well go now before I cause any more trouble. What's the point of hanging around any longer? The only friend I had was Bailey, and then, when I finally worked out she was a bot it was too late. I'd signed up. The cooling-off period was over. I felt such an idiot."

"Yes," said George, "It gets you like that."

The last woman spoke up. "Do you know if we'll be able to book on it again? I'm worried now that I might have lost the inheritance tax break forever. Are they allowed to bar you? I'm not 85 for three years. Do you think they would let me apply a second time?"

"I have no idea," Lexi said, "But I can't imagine the corporation turning down anyone's money."

"For goodness sake people," Bob interrupted, "We don't have any FAQs. We're just the transport."

However, Lexi knew that what Bob had just said wasn't true. Bob was so much more than the driver. His expert hacking into the corporation systems had got her into the DC undetected. He had taken control of the building and made sure the asphyxiating gas levels were over-ridden so they could get out. By finding the technical drawings of the robots some weeks before, they had been able to plan every detail of the intervention, including swapping the sedative for amphetamine. She was so proud of him, but she knew they would never be able to tell anyone what he had done.

Finally, there came a question that Bob was pleased to hear. Bryn asked, "We're probably being a bit of a nuisance, but do you think we might be able to go to McDonald's? I really fancy a Grampy Meal."

Bob was getting peckish himself, and needed no persuasion to divert onto the Old Kent Road, where the drive-through McDonald's was open 24 hours a day. He pulled into the parking area so the escapees could pop inside to get cleaned up a bit. "I can't wait to get these pants off," he had heard one of them say. Although some of the fugitives moved stiffly, he could see that they were all strong enough on their feet to make it there and back. Perhaps that was why they had elected to be survivors. He saw George taking Bryn's arm to steady him, and the two economy disposal women, Mavis and Mabel, went ahead with Meg. It didn't seem to matter that they had been travelling in different classes earlier in the day when their destination had turned out to be the same.

Lexi stayed in the van with Bob. She reached over and squeezed his hand. "What a day," she said quietly. "You know, it could have gone a lot worse," Bob smiled back at her, "You did an amazing job in there." "I never felt alone," Lexi said, "It was pretty scary, but I knew you were with me every step of the way, like you always are."

The five passengers were drifting back to the van. After a few minutes' discussion they had decided what everyone wanted, and drove up to the window to order. Bob paid for it all and passed the hot brown paper bags and trays of drinks emblazoned with golden arches and safety warnings to Lexi to distribute.

Bob slipped the van back into gear and drove more slowly than usual, conscious that his passengers were trying to balance their takeaways on their knees. As they edged forward, the van filled with one of his favorite hybrid smells, fries and coffee. Lexi fed Bob salty fries from a bag on her lap as he drove along. After the events of the day it felt like pure decadence. On her other side of her, Meg sipped a coffee and bit delicately into a ring doughnut. "You have no idea how excellent a doughnut can be when you have just cheated the grim reaper," she said, licking the sugar crystals from her lips, as her energy began to return. She felt the sugar rush instantly, her senses still on high alert. "I can't wait to speak to Alice. To tell her how sorry I am."

The escapees were huddled together, four of them squashed on to the bench seat behind the driver that was only really meant for three people. None of them were very big so it seemed to work, and they were getting on quite well. Lexi could hear fragments of their lives being shared.

It wasn't long before they reached the lock-up. Bob turned the wheel sharply to take the van into the mews and it bumped along the uneven path. He drew to a standstill and to Lexi's surprise the door to the garage slid back automatically. Last time she had been there, that day in the summer when he had first moved in, it had an old style padlock and they'd had to ease the heavy doors open by hand, brushing the traces of rust from their clothing when they got home.

"Get you," she said, "Welcome to the 21st century."

"I couldn't help myself," Bob said, "It's easy enough. There isn't much I don't know about automatic entry systems right now. No robots here yet though."

Even though they hadn't done anything wrong – well, apart from the hacking, unauthorised entry and industrial sabotage, which Lexi thought didn't count because it was all justified – she still felt jumpy. There was a nagging fear that someone from the corporation might descend on them from out of nowhere, and try to take the escapees back. She didn't feel that they were safe yet, even though there had been no blue lights tailing them, no drones following the van, no obvious corporation security people looming out of the encroaching winter darkness.

Although Lexi was trying to stay focused on the present, images of the people she had left behind kept flashing through her mind, ghosts that had been inadvertently disturbed and wouldn't go away. She wondered whether the plant had got back on track yet, and whether the undead that had chosen to stay had made it to the flames, their preferred manner of escape from the sadness and pain that had engulfed the departure lounge. She was shocked to find herself hoping that the desperate souls who had remained had been put safely back to sleep, and made it quickly into the furnace, finding the rest they were looking for.

The van rolled forward into the lock-up and Bob cut the engine. "We don't want to make it all this way and get asphyxiated by mistake," he said.

That's odd, Lexi thought, this place looks smaller than I remember it. The front of the vehicle was almost touching the back wall. "Bob, where is the…" Before she could finish her sentence, Bob said, "Just made a few alterations, security measures." He tapped the side of his nose. His secret control center had been hidden behind some new brickwork. He'd thought of everything. "My, you have been busy," Lexi said.

It was time to get everyone out of the van one last time. It would do them all good to stretch their legs and have a short walk. Father Al had said he would collect his guests from Bob and Lexi's as soon as he could get hold of the Knights of Saint Columba minibus.

They gathered everyone together on the gritty, uneven ground as winter mist began to fill the street at the end of the alley, illuminated by the street light that had just begun to burn yellow in the early January dusk. George was still steadying Bryn's arm. The two men were chatting quietly about what they had done for a living in times gone by, and wondering between them how it had all come to this. Mabel asked if they could all exchange phone numbers, so Lexi found a piece of paper and a cracked ballpoint pen floating in the side pocket of the van. As George and Mavis couldn't read without their glasses, Lexi acted as scribe, promising she would let everyone have the list.

While she zipped the paper into her backpack, Lexi thought to herself that if anyone came for them at this moment, no one would ever know what had happened. There was only one way in and out of the mews. It was then that she first saw the figures, silhouetted against the mist, blocking their exit.

They couldn't have come this far, surely, to lose it all now?

"Bob," Lexi hissed, "Look, at the end of the mews. Someone's there." She was struggling to pick out any distinguishing features in the flat half-light.

"Everyone, let's stick together," Bob said, "It's dark here and uneven under foot. Watch where you're going. Slowly now, let's get you all out to the road without any falls." He pointed a torch down to the muddy, gravelly ground to light the way. Everyone followed obediently, in silent concentration, placing their absolute trust in Bob.

"Who'd have thought when the bots popped us on the bus this morning we'd end up here?" Mavis piped up wistfully.

"It's like an episode of *Storage Hunters*," George added, eyeing the row of lock-ups with curiosity. "I love that programme, and I'm going to get to watch it again!"

"Bob, what's happening?" Lexi said, feeling increasingly anxious as she eyed the strangers, clutching his arm tightly, and hoping that it wasn't all going to fall apart at the last hurdle.

"Don't worry love," Bob said squeezing her arm back, "It's the reinforcements."

Still not understanding what Bob meant, Lexi kept

squinting nervously into the gloom. It took another few steps forward before she could see clearly enough to realise what he was talking about. Then it all made sense.

She finally felt safe when she realised that she was crying. The massive tension of her nightmarish day, the emotional turmoil she had felt as her closest friend reached out to her in despair, and the months spent with Bob, racking their brains to work out how they could stage an intervention – suddenly it was all released.

To a bystander it wouldn't look like the most exciting moment in the world. They were just a band of old people watching their footing, trying to make it safely out of a dark old mews full of lock-ups in South East London. It could have been a conservation society walk that over-ran into the dusk. But these weren't just any old people. They were five brave souls who had been given a reprieve they didn't expect, from a death sentence they didn't deserve. As they savored the soft crunch of the gravel beneath their feet, felt the spiky brush of hoary dead brambles against their clothing, and absorbed the gentle sensation of fine damp mist touching their face, each one took comfort from the others' physical presence in the eerie winter light.

Waiting for them under the street lamp stood their Member of Parliament, Nicky Hartt, and the man who was going to help them build the case against the corporation, the PACE lawyer Henry Wright. They were there at Bob's invitation, and their first commitment was to make sure Meg, Mavis, Mabel, Bryn and George could carry on without any further complications.

"I've already spoken to Mason," Nicky said. "He was

skiing in Verbier but funnily enough he took my call from the chairlift. Maybe he guessed why I was calling. Didn't sound as surprised as you might expect. Provided we keep everything quiet, he's promised they won't send out a search party for these five. I can live with that for now. When he gets back Henry and I will be meeting with him to discuss some of the other evidence."

Nicky noticed that Lexi had tears streaming down her face and put her hand on her arm. "You've nothing to be sad about. I'm not sure I want to know how you did it, but five people here owe their lives to you and Bob. I would never have thought you had it in you, when we first met upstairs at the pub. Just goes to show. You've done something amazing."

Unable to talk, Lexi nodded appreciatively in response to Nicky's words of praise. She tried to clean her face by rubbing it on the shoulder of Bob's fleece, and clung to him to stop her hands from trembling. The trauma of all she had witnessed had fuelled a deep anger towards the corporation that had tricked this band of living, breathing innocents into booking a date with death. There was still so much to be done.

Every day at school, she taught the children that if they believed in themselves they could do anything. Today had showed her that that philosophy could work for her too. She hadn't just surprised Nicky with the success of the rescue mission, she had surprised herself.

Lexi had a lot to be thankful for, and should really have been planning to celebrate, but she wasn't ready to do that just yet. Haunted by an enduring sadness, she would never be able to tell anyone the real reason she was crying. While she was quietly proud of everything she and Bob had done that day, there was one set of parents she would never be able to bring back from death. Her own.

PLAYLIST

IN ORDER OF APPEARANCE

Om Asatoma (featuring Deva Premal and Miten)
Ben Leinback (2011)

Rock 'n' Roll Suicide
David Bowie (1972)

Happy Hour
The Housemartins (1986)

Rockstar
Nickelback (2005)

So What
Pink (2008)

Rockstar
Post Malone, 21 Savage (2018)

Diamond Dogs
David Bowie (1974)

Candidate
David Bowie (1974)

(Don't Fear) The Reaper
Blue Oyster Cult (1976)

Stairway to Heaven
Led Zeppelin (1971)

The End
The Doors (1967)

Who Loves the Sun
The Velvet Underground (1970)

Good Morning Good Morning
The Beatles (1967)

Blaze of Glory
Bon Jovi (1990)

Fanfare / Don't Dream It
Tim Curry (1975)

Available on Spotify at
spotify:playlist:0yHChmj7qM6l8eUppa0nhA

ACKNOWLEDGEMENTS

I am indebted to the Orwell Society, whose student dystopian fiction competition was the catalyst for *Rockstar Ending*. Professor Tim Crook was the first person to describe me as an author and Professor Richard Keeble published my short story 'One Last Gift' in the *Orwell Studies Journal*. Speaking at their conference in 2018 gave me the validation I needed to believe in my ability as a writer. I will remember for the rest of my life the precise moment when I found out that Richard Blair, George Orwell's son, had read and enjoyed my work.

Cathi Unsworth, Jake Arnott, Emma Flint and all my co-students at the Arvon Foundation inspired me to crack on in earnest.

Loyal friends have provided feedback on ideas and manuscripts and urged me to keep going. Jax Donnellan, Alison Ford, Hilary Freeman, Joanna Gluzman, Mary Claire Halvorson, Sarah Mackenzie, Barry Ryan, Sky Stephenson and David Walton are among those who have encouraged me to make space in my life for creating fiction.

My editors Karol Griffiths and Geraldine Brennan made it all so much better. Aaron Eriskine and Sara Mansoori gave expert advice that is much appreciated.

Studying at Goldsmiths University inspired me to do something creative to stimulate thinking about our social, technological and political state. My lecturers and fellow students on the Digital Media MA, class of 2017, taught me a great deal.

William Gibson, Margaret Atwood, Charlie Brooker, Terry Gilliam, Thomas Pynchon and Toni Morrison are among those who have provided me with literary and cultural inspiration, along with the teams behind the television series *Westworld* and *Mr Robot*. Becoming an author of speculative fiction has permitted me many indulgent afternoons glued to the screen. Not forgetting Mary Shelley, George Orwell, Arthur C Clark, Stanley Kubrick and David Bowie, forever in a class of their own.

Much of the musical inspiration came from sneaking into rock nights run by Darrell Jay and Ken Evans in Southport in the 1970s. The songs they curated – although we didn't call it that then – have never left me.

I still can't believe Tim Doyle agreed to draw the cover illustration. I have admired his prints for a long time. *Rockstar Ending* gave me the perfect excuse to commission this piece.

The writers' community have given me generous advice, including Brad Borkan, Mike Raggett, Andrew Ravenscroft, the Alliance of Independent Authors, and everyone at the monthly meetup in Waterstones Piccadilly.

Finally, Simon, Amelia and Charlie Hedger have stood by me in this escapade which has turned my life upside down. Words cannot express how much you mean to me.

If you are curious about the years leading up to
Rockstar Ending **you can download the**
FREE INTRODUCTORY NOVELLA
For Those About to Rock
at nicolarossi.com
where you can also join my mailing list
to find out about new releases and promotions

WOULD YOU WRITE A REVIEW?

If you have enjoyed this book it would mean a lot to me if you could spend just five minutes leaving an honest review on Amazon.

As a debut author, I don't have the resources to promote my books very widely, and reviews from people who have read my work can make a huge difference by bringing it to the attention of other readers.

ROCK ON

Bob and Lexi return in *Rock On*, the second book in the Rockstar Ending series.

While five survivors fight for their freedom, the death machine is unstoppable. But Lexi can't rest until she has exposed the sinister corporation behind the hidden genocide. When she hits on a way to grab the headlines, she's in serious danger. If they find out what she has done, Lexi and her soulmate Bob will lose everything.

nicolarossi.com